TWISTED SECRETS

BOOK 3 OF THE TWISTED MINDS SERIES

KETA KENDRIC

D1521377

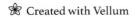 Created with Vellum

ACKNOWLEDGMENTS

Readers, from my heart, thank you. Without you, I am invisible, nothing more than a big imagination without the pulse that brings it to life.

Jessica Watkins, JWP Publishing, thank you for seeing something special enough in my writing to give me the opportunity to reach and entertain readers. My gratitude is endless.

Honey Berewa, your editing skills are exquisite. You let me know when to pull it back, upgrade the words, or toss it out completely. Your knowledge and keen eye for the written word is priceless.

SYNOPSIS

Megan: Have you ever fallen so deeply for someone that you'd be willing to do anything for them? I was willing to do anything for Aaron including leaving him if it meant keeping him from getting tangled up in my past. Aaron wasn't going to let me run, even if there was an army after me, he'd gather arms and prepare for a war.

Aaron: Letting Megan go wasn't an option. She'd become a part of me that I couldn't live without. Some of the horrifying secrets from her past had been revealed, but I believed Megan's final secret had the power to rain down hell-fire on my MC, and I'd been right. When my father went behind my back and called my cousin Ansel for back-up, I knew that all hell was about to break loose, and I ended up preparing to fight an adversary so dangerous, my life teetered on the brink of extinction.

WARNING

This book is an interracial romance that contains strong violence and sexual content and is intended for adults. If you are easily offended or squeamish about harsh or demeaning language, murder, and violence, this is not the book for you.

1

PART I

AARON

It had only been two weeks since I'd tracked Megan down and brought her back to my house. I was supposed to find her and kill her for infiltrating my MC, but my dick had stopped me. For as strong as I thought my mind was, for once in my life, my dick had been right.

Not killing Megan had led me to finding out how she'd ended up the way she had. The story behind her actions was so gut-wrenching that it justified her twisted behavior.

Yesterday, we killed seven men together after they'd chased us and followed us into a patch of Copper County's thick woods.

Once we fled the scene and settled, she tried to run from me again. I didn't think I was going to have another problem with her running from me again. As her punishment, I gave her a fucking she won't soon forget. I had her ass praying on her hands and knees for me to stop.

In all honesty, I didn't know it was possible for someone like me, with a heart as black as coal, to love someone so deeply. I'd do anything for Megan—rob, cheat, commit murder—anything. She likely assumed I'd been talking out of my ass when I told her as much, but I'd meant every word I'd said to her. If someone harmed a hair on her head, they'd feel my wrath.

I glanced at her in the dim light of the early morning, lying against the passenger's door panel of my truck. She'd passed out on the drive back to my house since I'd kept her up all night.

As I drove, my mind fell on the men who were hunting us. There was no way of confirming who the mercenaries were after yesterday —her or me. Logic stated they were a group that could have been after Megan because my usual suspects were bikers, gang members, or the occasional wanna-be gangsters making a name for themselves.

The guys I led into the woods yesterday had come out of nowhere and struck with military precision. They didn't care about killing innocent victims if it meant taking out their target. Unfortunately, I was not altogether sure who their target had been.

My MC had hundreds of members spread around five states, and we had many enemies. Megan was only one woman. Who the hell could have been after her that could not only afford hired guns but who could also afford to track her? If I hadn't known about her books and D hadn't followed the money trail to her friends, I would probably still be looking for her.

The Russians had come at my MC years ago with the same level of aggression as the assassins that attacked us yesterday. It's one of the reasons why I kept military-grade weaponry in my possession.

The men yesterday spoke Spanish—that much I was sure of. I couldn't recall our MC having any type of beef with any Hispanic groups, but I had to consider that there were a few in our MC known for stirring up trouble; the kind of trouble that led to dead bodies.

A flicker of light flashing across my cracked driver's side mirror drew my attention. I glanced at Megan who was still out before I leaned up and squinted into the mirror to get a better view of the squad car behind us. Most of the Copper County cops left my MC alone as long as we kept our drama out of the public's eyes and laced their pockets.

"Shit," I mumbled as I took in two unfamiliar cops. My truck looked like it had taken a slow stroll through hell, and what looked like two unfamiliar Copper County Police officers were pulling me over. When they saw Megan, they were going to take whatever they had planned to the next level.

To make matters worse, we were on a stretch of backwoods roads surrounded by trees, so these asshole cops could do whatever the hell they wanted and get away with it.

Maintaining careful movements, I reached over and took the gun Megan had wedged between her hip and the console and placed it under my seat. I did the same to the one I had tucked in my waist.

"Megan," I called out after I shook her shoulder. She jumped up, frantically searching her surroundings, likely thinking we were being attacked. In a way, we were about to get attacked if the mean scowls on the officers' faces as they exited the black and white squad car was any indication. I hadn't spotted them on the highway, so they had likely been parked off the roadway, painting their lips with powdered sugar when they spotted me.

My eyes remained on the officers in the mirror as I spoke to Megan.

"We are being pulled over by the cops. I don't know these assholes, so I'm going to need you to stay quiet and answer only what they ask you."

"Okay," she said, stretching her neck to look back. She reached for the gun that I'd already hidden.

"I put it under my seat. Stay still," I told her, my voice starting to project my agitation although nothing had happened yet.

The officers approached my truck from both sides, taking careful sideways steps. The sight of my damaged vehicle riddled with bullet holes caused them to grip their pistols as they drew and aimed them at the ground. They stopped at the back edge of the sides of my truck. One had his eyes on me in my mirror, the other I presumed kept an eye on Megan's door as her side mirror had been shot off the truck.

When they stepped out and away from the tail end of my truck and turned towards me and Megan with their weapons aimed at our heads, I closed my eyes and prayed. I prayed that I wasn't going to have to take the life of two Copper County police officers.

"Roll the windows all the way down and both of you stick your hands through the open windows!" The one on my side shouted the words as he edged closer to my position. My gaze was locked on him in the mirror.

"Any sudden movements and we will kill you. I will blow your fucking head off your shoulders!" he shouted. My irritation was heightened by the cocky arrogance in his voice.

As I slowly eased my hands through my window, I glanced at Megan doing the same. We just couldn't catch a break. Was three or four days without drama too much to ask for?

The closer the officer came to me, the more I was convinced that this situation was only going to get uglier. The unmistakable sound of his approaching steps as they grew closer matched his cracked reflection in the mirror as it grew larger.

My eyes focused on a specific location in the mirror and didn't miss the deep frown on his face. The steady aim of his gun at my head kept me quiet, but nothing was going to take away my hostile nature, my own grimaced face, or the liquid fire coursing through my veins.

"I'm going to open this door and you're going to be a good dog and move out of that seat slowly."

An angry growl escaped my throat when he called me a dog. Now, able to see him standing outside my door, he took the gun in one hand and ensured it stayed level with my head as he used his other hand to open my door.

Just as my door started to creak open, I heard the other officer yell, "What the fuck? Joe, do you see this shit. Look who he has in the truck with him."

Upon hearing his friend's discovery of Megan, Joe's fucking finger flexed on the trigger and damn near sent my brains all over the back of my seat.

Joe pushed his gun even closer to my head as he leaned forward and peeked around me. His eyes remained on Megan a long time before they landed back on me. Disgust was written all over his face. Every frown line he had stretched tighter and deepened.

"So, you're one of them confused motherfuckers, huh? You like that black poontang?" he spat his questions at me. "Step out of this truck, son, I'm about to teach you what your fucking father should have taught you when you were younger," he barked his angry words, his voice laced with pure hate.

I rolled my shoulder and eased out of my truck, taking a deep and steadying breath. The partner hadn't asked Megan to get out yet, and I hope he had sense enough to leave her alone.

As soon as the first pebble crunched under my boot when my feet touched the ground, I was snatched by the shoulder and pushed towards the hood of my truck.

"Get out of the truck, nigger girl," the partner said to Megan as my face was being pressed into the dented hood of my truck. The jagged metal nudged angrily at my skin, anxious to slice a hole in my face.

Movement on the other side of my truck captured my attention, but I couldn't see anything with my face turned in the opposite direction. My head was trapped between the twisted metal of my hood and the barrel of Officer Joe's gun as he shoved it into my cheek.

"You are going to learn today," he whispered harshly, placing his mouth close to my ear as he leaned into me. His hot breath rained over my face as a few sprinkles of spittle dotted my cheek.

The sound of Megan's whimper caused me to resist as I struggled to get up. "You better be still before I blow yours and that black bitch's brains all over this highway. I'll leave your asses in those woods as dinner for the maggots and worms."

Patience. Patience. Patience. I repeated inside my head. If I made the wrong move, it could lead to Megan getting hurt.

"Can you believe this shit, Cass? I believe this motherfucker is willing to die for that black bitch."

I could hear Megan taking deep breaths and wasn't sure if the officer had her pressed over the hood or not. My body was coiled so tightly that there was no way the asshole standing over me wasn't being poisoned by my anger.

The officer who'd been addressed as Cass spoke. His deep voice projected over my hood, "I'd never do some backwards shit like this, but I could certainly understand the appeal, especially with this one."

"Cass, shut your dumb ass up. If your father heard you say some dumb shit like that, he'd punch you in the fucking mouth."

The butt of the officer's service gun sank deeper into my jaw and the tight bitterness in his voice intensified. "What's your name, son? I need to know who I'm about to give lessons to."

I didn't answer because my mind was consumed with the best way of taking these motherfuckers out without getting Megan killed in the process. My fists tightened, sounding as if I were cracking walnuts.

"I said, what's your motherfucking name, asshole!" The words oozed slowly between the officer's clenched teeth. His hatred at seeing me with Megan had him about to lose his life because I was at the end of my rope.

The low tone of Megan's voice sounded and snapped me out of the hot zone, but I couldn't understand her words.

"Shut the fuck up, bitch. I didn't tell you to talk!" Officer Cass yelled.

"Look at his cut!" Megan yelled, disobeying a direct order from the racist cop.

Patience had vacated my body entirely and I shook from the effort it took to contain my rage. The treaty we had with the Copper County Police Department was about to be ripped to shreds along with this bastard's body.

"Joe!" his partner Cass called in a low tone laced with concern. Joe didn't answer his partner because he was too busy glaring down at me, taunting with more of his vicious words.

"Joe!" Cass yelled his partner's name this time, his voice dripping with nervous tension.

"What? Don't you see I'm busy over here?"

"Joe, look at his vest."

Joe's grip on my neck eased as did the gun he had pushed damn near through the side of my cheek.

"August Knights," he read out my MC's name in a low tone. Then dead silence fell over the scene for what seemed like an eternity. A slow wind swept through the leaves of the surrounding trees, making it sound like they were applauding the officer's ability to read and determine that he was flirting with death.

Joe's tight grip left my neck and so did the butt of his gun from my cheek. His shoes scraping the concrete sounded as he backed away from me. I eased up, lifting my body to an upright position.

The first place my eyes went to was Megan standing on the other side of my hood. The officer was standing behind her. Brows pinched and eyes begging for mercy, the sorry sack of shit knew he'd fucked up.

"Are you okay?" I asked Megan, not giving a damn about the dicks standing behind us.

She nodded her head, keeping her gaze locked with mine.

"Did he put his fucking hand on you?" I spit my words over the hood at the stone-faced officer standing behind Megan.

"No," she said in a shaky tone as her gaze landed on the officer standing silently behind me. He hadn't said a word since he'd read the words on my cut. Megan had no idea our MC had a long history with the police in Copper County, which had me wondering how she knew to tell the cop to look at my cut.

"Hey, man, I didn't know you were an August Knight." The officer shuddered.

"Me either. I just transferred down here four months ago," Joe, the one behind me said in a humbled tone.

His partner standing behind Megan had his weapon holstered and had both his hands raised in surrender. "Look, man," he said, shaking his head. "I don't want any trouble with your group. I didn't know who you were until I got a good enough look at your vest."

"Let's go, Megan," I said as I dusted my hands over my clothes. Then, I reared back and socked the motherfucker behind me in the face so hard that I felt his nose crunch under my fist. He fell to the ground, landing on his ass as he clenched his nose, blood oozing between his fingers. He scrambled backwards when I moved, thinking I was going to hit him again.

Instead, I moved toward my open truck door. I didn't glance back at the officer. I was afraid to look at him because of the twisted shit my mind kept yelling for me to do. I needed to be away from this situation because I wasn't sure I had the strength to contain the obscene amount of rage coursing through me.

Once we were back in the truck I sat, gripping the stirring wheel. Hunched, the bloody-faced officer walked briskly back to his squad car. His partner had already retreated to the vehicle and had climbed in.

"Are you okay?" Megan asked, her soft tone easing some of my tension. The haze of rage that surrounded me started to fade away and the world started to sound and feel normal again.

"I'm good," I told her, my loud and angry tone, indicating I was anything but good. She reached across and placed a hand on my arm, which shook with tension under her soft touch.

"It's okay. We're okay," she reassured, and I didn't know if she was asking a question or making a statement.

My gaze landed on the hand she had placed on my arm before I glanced over at her. "You and me, we are always going to be okay. I just need a moment."

With that, she dropped her hand and allowed me to take my moment. Mentally, I soothed my nerves as close to calmness as I was going to get them. I started my truck and drove off, leaving those asshole cops sitting in their car. The sight of them grew smaller in my cracked mirror as I proceeded to my destination.

Those police officers had no idea the person they'd been taught to hate had just saved their lives. Even now, I wanted to turn around and release my rage by pounding on their bodies, but I had more important things to worry about. I had to figure out who was hunting Megan and me and more importantly, how to stop them.

2

AARON

We'd just been in a situation that could have turned deadly and Megan sat next to me as cool as a cucumber. My tension had eased as well.

"How did you know to tell that cop to look at my cut?"

She smiled before glancing in my direction. "I didn't know if it would work, but after hearing some of what you and your father were talking about on the phone and after your father had started allowing me to enter the board room during some of the meetings, I concluded that you all had ties with law enforcement."

"That was smart," I complimented her, making her smile deepen. I hadn't even considered explaining who I was to the cops. Knowing that Megan was in danger, all I saw was red. She was my weakness, and I needed to find a way to balance caring for her and handling my business as usual.

I avoided the normal route to my house, although it was off the beaten path. I'd taken the scenic drive that was nothing more than an overgrown path through the woods that would take me to within a stone's throw away from my house. It was the same path I'd taken when I discovered that Chuck and his crew had landed on my doorstep.

Knowing that Megan had been in my house alone with them had driven me past the point of madness. It was the first time that I realized I would do anything to protect her, even if it meant giving myself up.

I'd ditched my truck in the woods that day. After snooping around and discovering the men hadn't harmed Megan, I sneaked into the house. If I hadn't feared for Megan being hurt in a gun battle, I would have handled Chuck, Clint, and Dutch in an entirely different manner.

My actions that day marked the first time I'd acknowledged my weakness. At my attempt to be careful, I'd nearly gotten both of us killed. Megan saved my life that day. Although my intent was to avoid a gun battle, she'd initiated one that had lured us away from the grips of death.

The idea that a group like Chuck's had lurked long enough to find my house made me aware that this new group may have the means to find a way to my doorstep as well. How long had this group been in town? How long had they been watching me and Megan?

Last night, I'd warned my MC about the dangerous group lingering, but I wasn't worried. For as dumb as my MC sometimes acted, when it came to life or death, they would choose life and survival by any means necessary.

I found a good spot plush with thick trees and vines to park in the woods behind my house. I made a move and started to climb out of my truck to go and check the house, but Megan stopped me, gripping my arm. "I want to come," she insisted.

I said the magic word, "Please," again and she stayed put in the truck. She was afraid to let me out of her sight now that I'd confirmed my loyalty to her.

My boot-clad feet trounced across the roots of trees and broken twigs as I crept closer to my house. My instincts told me that after that shootout yesterday, this group already knew who we were. If they were after Megan, they may have tracked her to my MC.

When the back of my house came into view, everything appeared normal, but I approached with caution.

Using the key I'd left tucked into the overhead paneling, I opened the back door. A flick of the knob sent my back door creaking open. A tap of the metal tip of my gun sent the door swinging over the area where Clint's dead body had lain over a month prior.

My gun remained aimed and ready to fire as the cold steel of my back-up pistol rested against my lower back. Although the house was in order, careful steps led me through my kitchen as I kept my ears peeled for lurkers.

When I stepped into my bedroom, my gaze landed on the area where my safe room was hidden. The thick boxed headboard of my bed kept the entrance of the space hidden. The room sat snug between the walk-in closet and bathroom. I was the only one who knew about the secret space since I'd reduced the size of my closet to build it.

Attached to the wall of the hidden room, I'd strategically constructed my headboard that contained a latch to release it from the wall. The half door hidden behind my headboard opened into the closet-size safe-room.

After reaching into the thick wooden front of the headboard, I unlatched it from the wall. Two forceful heaves sent the bed out of my way. I stooped before the half door and entered the combination that would spring the door open.

Within minutes, I'd entered the room, retrieved money, extra guns, ammunition, and re-concealed the location. I packed myself a bag, packed Megan's backpack with the items of hers that I could find and headed out in case there was a lookout watching the house.

Megan and I needed to regroup so we could plan our next move. We needed to figure out who the hell was hunting us. Even if they weren't initially hunting me, my actions in those woods had put my MC and me on their radar. However, when they'd attempted to take my life and Megan's, they'd place themselves on my radar as well.

I walked away from the house that I'd lived in for three years not knowing when I'd return. The last few drops of dew glistened off leaves as the sun started to rise higher in the sky. The hike back to my truck went by in a blur.

My mind worked overtime, processing the group of mercenaries we'd encountered yesterday. I was hesitant to say the word mercenaries in front of Megan, not that she couldn't handle it, but she'd been through enough. I didn't want her to stress any more than she already had or worse, have her take off on me again.

Of all the things she should have been worried about, she was worried about me getting hurt. *Me.* When my own mother was alive, she didn't care that much about me. Knowing that someone cared if I lived or died put a spark of color in my heart and brought a smile to my face.

3

AARON

I'd lived surrounded by danger for so long that my body sensed it. My internal sensor for picking up threats sent my eyes jetting around the area that led to our MC's clubhouse. The dead, empty air swept into my rolled-down windows and filled the cab space of my truck. The air alone told a story I was not ready to hear yet.

The bullet holes in the wood siding of the clubhouse were visible through my dusty windshield as I drove closer. The busted front window and the front door hanging lopsided told me all I needed to know. I turned my truck into the woods to ensure it remained hidden. Once I found a good enough spot, I glanced over at Megan.

"Stay in the truck and put one of those guns in your hands."

No questions, no back talk, only actions. This was one of the reasons why I loved Megan. She reached down next to her sexy-ass hip and made the Beretta appear. The familiar slide and clap of the weapon being charged made my mouth inch into a smile, despite what I might face inside our clubhouse.

My roving eyes scanned my surroundings once more as I exited my truck with my weapon aimed and ready to put a hole in someone.

At 08:45 a.m., it was too early for anyone but my father to be at the clubhouse.

The front end of his truck peeked from the far side of the house when my gaze went in the direction of where I knew it would be parked. My father slept at the clubhouse more than he stayed in his house. I reckon he preferred the clubhouse more because it had been his and my mother's home. He claimed they'd been happy there once. How anyone, even my father, could have been happy with my hateful mother was beyond me.

There were no visible dead bodies at my first glance of the area. There was no spilled blood. But, the broken glass on the ground indicated that my father had at least shot back at someone. Therefore, he was either dead, dying, or inside killing someone. Entertaining the idea of my father being dead sent rage blazing through my veins.

As much as my father got on my nerves, I loved the old crow. However, there was one thing I knew well about him. He was a fighter. He would go up against the devil if it came to it.

The faint scent of vehicle exhaust lingered in the air mixed with the unmistakable scent of freshly-fired guns. Whoever had been there, hadn't been gone long and could double back. Several bullet casings dotted the ground, and the deep imprint left by tires scratching on the lightly graveled parking area in front of the clubhouse was visible.

After glancing back to ensure no one was creeping up behind me, I eased the lopsided screen door open and used the toe of my boot to kick the wooden door further open. Shards of glass fell from the square panes that once framed the heavy door, alerting anyone inside to my entrance. Once the door was open, I swept my body around and let the barrel of my pistol lead the way.

"Dad!" I called out. "You alive?"

Out stumbled my father with a gun jammed down the front of his pants. He had another gun aimed, and it was leading him out of the double doors of the kitchen.

"Motherfucking bastards shot me in the shoulder. I called Karla to come and pluck this bullet out and sew me up." I smiled at the lovely words my father acknowledged me with.

Karla was a nurse my father had dated off and on for years. Although she was married and about twenty years his junior, whenever my father called her to patch up an injured member of our MC, she came without question.

My father stepped into plain view. His faded black T-shirt was wet with blood as it clung to his shoulder and chest area. I should have been more worried, considering how bloody my father was, but he was a tough old bird that didn't like to be coddled.

"Fucking mercenaries, like you said. I think they came here as a warning. If they'd wanted me dead, I probably would be. They were in a black SUV with tinted windows. When one stepped out of the vehicle, and I saw a gun in his hand with a silencer attached, I didn't wait around to see what the fuck they wanted. I started shooting, and they sure as shit didn't mind shooting back."

The people we were dealing with weren't bikers, and I was starting to seriously doubt they were an enemy of the MC. Megan may have been right that these assholes were after her.

"Who the fuck are these people, Aaron?" my father asked. He knew that I should've had an answer to that question by now. Just because I was willing to go to war over Megan didn't mean my father was and it damn sure didn't mean the rest of my MC would.

"I don't know who the fuck they are," I replied. "We deal in guns and drugs, so it could be a faction trying to take over our gun business."

My father shook his head, his mind obviously running wild over who was targeting us. My flimsy excuse would work on the rest of the club, but my father knew better.

I didn't like the quiet amusement in his eyes as he stared me down.

"I called your cousin, Ansel," he revealed as a wicked smirk creased his face. His revelation left me speechless for a few moments.

"Why the fuck did you do that? Why the fuck didn't you at least

wait until I figured out who the hell these people are?" I rolled my
eyes at my father before pinching the bridge of my nose.

"Dad, you know as well as I do, Cousin Ansel's ass is as crazy as
fuck and he's as out of control as these damn mercenaries. He likes to
kill for the fun of it and he and his band of killers don't give two fucks
about who dies as long as somebody goes to hell."

I attempted but failed to shake off thoughts of my crazy-ass
cousin. Two years ago, I'd left the MC for two months to help our gun
supplier with a little problem they had that could've demolished our
gun deal entirely. While I was away, my father ran into a little trouble
with a rival MC. Long story short, the MC was no longer heard from
after my father called my cousin, Ansel, for his brand of help.

Ansel and his crew ate through a third of the motorcycle club and
killed over twenty-five men in less than a week. The rest of the MC
had scattered or had gone into hiding for all we knew. We'd never
heard anything else from them after Ansel got a hold of them. The
Feds and every agency in the country was still sniffing around for
some of the bodies.

Cousin Ansel was who you called whenever you'd run out of
options, not when you hadn't even figured out the problem yet. I
cupped my forehead and rubbed my tired eyes. "How long before he
arrives?" I asked my father.

Ansel lived and worked illegally out of California. He was a
member of our MC and often joined us whenever we gathered and
went on group bike rides.

"He said he'd be here sometime tomorrow," my father answered
with that smirk still on his face.

I leveled him with a hard stare and prayed that his shot shoulder
was hurting like hell. He threw up his palm on his good side in reaction to my angry glare.

"What did you expect me to do, Aaron? You called me last night
telling me you and that black wife of yours had dropped seven bodies
in the woods. Next thing I knew, the damn television was lit up with
dead bodies and a blown-up car like a fucking war had taken place in

those woods. Before day hardly breaks, motherfuckers are blowing holes in the clubhouse with silenced weapons."

When my father put it that way, it did sound bad. I'd been too busy searching for and fucking Megan, my, *black wife*, as my father had so elegantly put it, to care about checking out the news.

My dad leaned in and lowered his voice like someone was listening to us. "Is *she* with you now?" The fact that my father was referring to Megan as my wife meant he'd managed to swallow his pride and accept that I was not going to get rid of her.

"Yeah. You got a problem with it?" I asked, daring him with my gaze to say something stupid.

He shook his long, crooked finger at me. "You know fucking well I got a problem with it, but we got bigger problems to worry about than you claiming a woman who's forbidden to us."

My dad's loud laughter irked my fucking nerves as he shook his head. That damn smirk had returned to his smug face.

"You know how Ansel is. What do you think he's going to do when he sees your new woman?"

The ache in my head grew sharper, and my left eye started to twitch. The idea of what Ansel might do once he found me with Megan sent my blood pressure shooting through the roof.

"Dad, stop flapping your damn gums and make yourself useful. Warn everybody about what's going on so they can be ready if more shit goes down. To be on the safe side, send them to the safe houses. I'm going to do some sniffing around. If they found the clubhouse, someone who knows us was likely bought and has sold us out or was tortured and forced to talk. But that doesn't matter. The mother-fuckers came at us, so either—"

"They die or we die," my father and I spoke the statement simultaneously. Whenever we went into survival mode, that specific statement was tossed around a lot. Crazy thing was, we meant it.

4

AARON

After questioning my informants spread around the area, I staked out known areas for trouble. The only useful information I found was that a new group had landed in town asking questions and sniffing around for someone. They wore the same tactical style clothing as the ones we'd left dead in the woods wore.

The group was lurking, but they weren't giving up a lot of information. In Copper County, something as simple as what you wore or what you drove could give you away. Whispers were saying that there were two groups, one in town and a second leg lingering outside of town. What their mission was, no one seemed to know for sure. The information I truly wanted was where these people were staying.

Megan didn't leave my side as I went around investigating and talking to every contact I had. We ended up staying at another motel after I'd agreed to meet the rest of my family at the safe house the next day.

~

I PULLED up outside my MC's safe house and parked. It was a place

I'd purchased a few years ago for members who'd gotten themselves into trouble and needed to lay low or hide from criminal charges.

The house, like my house, wasn't under my name and only our chairmen knew the location and had the right to give a member in trouble sanctuary at the house. For some members, this was going to be their first time seeing and knowing the location or even knowing that there was a safe house.

The house was a two-story, brick, four-bedroom home in an upper middle-class, quiet neighborhood. I'd added a six-foot privacy fence around the property—more for security than privacy.

My Aunt Mona lived in and took care of the house until we needed it. She claimed to be afraid of the lives we led, so when any of us came around, which wasn't that often, she went back to her estranged husband until we left the house.

The house had a large basement that we used for our meetings from time to time. Any one of the club members could be down in the basement within the hour, planning and strategizing.

I placed my hand atop Megan's to keep her inside the truck with me. I needed to have a serious talk with her. She glanced up at me as her small hand turned and cupped mine.

"No matter what, you don't know who these people are. If this is a group truly after you and the MC finds out, some of them will not hesitate to turn you over to them as long as they can get something out of the deal."

Her mouth worked up and down before she spat her words out. "I don't want anyone getting hurt because of me. You should tell them that I might have brought this trouble to your doorstep."

I pursed my lips and shook my head, turning it slowly. "No. I'm not a hundred percent certain that these guys are after you. Until I am, you say nothing."

The space between us grew silent and tight. Ever since Megan had told me about her past of how she'd been brutally raped and forced to watch her foster father murder and rape young girls that he'd gotten her to lure to him, I couldn't shake the story. After she'd uttered her foster father's name, I couldn't shake the idea that I knew that name.

"Carlos Dominquez. I hate to bring it up right now but, who the fuck was your foster father?"

Her throat bobbed before her neck sunk into her shoulders and her head dropped. "Have you ever heard of DG6?" she asked in a shaky voice.

This time, my mouth worked back and forth without words. The confirmation of who her foster father was slammed into my brain with the force of a bullet. This was the big secret she'd been keeping from me. This was the reason she used an alias. This was why she'd felt the need to protect me by leaving me. This was why she'd been running for years.

A deep calming breath of air that I desperately needed filled my lungs before I spoke. "The famous DG6 gang. There isn't a criminal around that doesn't know what DG6 is."

The air started to seep out of the truck, growing thinner by the second, causing me to struggle for breaths.

"So, your foster father was a member of the gang?"

Megan unclamped her clammy hand from mine. Her leg started to bounce as she clenched her hands together and wrung them so hard that it looked painful. I didn't like that far-off look in her eyes.

"I killed Carlos when I was fourteen. That was ten years ago, Aaron. My foster father wasn't just a member of DG6—he was one of the original six."

Her confirmation caused a cold chill to race through my body.

"He and his five brothers started the gang. I didn't find out that Carlos was a part of the gang until after I'd landed in his care. He was using his status as a foster father as a part of his cover—hiding in plain sight from some of the murders he and his brothers had committed."

Megan's words stunned me, and I was virtually speechless for the first time in my life. DG6 had started out as a small gang that had spawn into a cartel that had the meth market locked so tight that only the suicidal were brave enough to challenge them.

Megan remained silent, letting the words she'd spoken claw their way into my head.

"You killed an original member of DG6?"

I couldn't believe I was sitting next to someone who'd survived DG6's wrath. "And what about your foster brother and mother? Were they a part of the gang too?"

She nodded her head, moving robotically.

"David was Carlos' blood nephew. Carlos' wife had been with him since high school and was as much a part of DG6 as he and the nephew were."

Since there was very little oxygen in the cab of my truck, I found it difficult to form words and talk. My grip on the stirring wheel loosened, and my hands fell to my sides. I stared straight ahead, not seeing anything in front of me because a million thoughts sparked inside my brain at the same time.

Megan's confirmation explained why the foster mother hadn't lifted a finger to help her and why her foster brother was as ruthless as his uncle. Megan had been placed in a house with a bunch of fucking poisonous vipers. It was a wonder she'd made it out of there with her life.

"Fuck," I uttered, more to myself than to her. "This explains some shit. That's why they never released the family name to the public. That's likely why they were able to put you away without going through the courts. It was to protect you. The law couldn't allow your location to get out."

My body turned in the seat. I wanted to see Megan's face when she answered my next question. "Your time in that asylum—you hadn't actually lost your mind, had you?"

"No, I don't think so. I'd been daydreaming about killing my foster family for a long time. I didn't have a choice. I had to kill Carlos."

She sounded as if she were still convincing herself that she'd done the right thing.

"I couldn't let him keep killing young girls. I also knew that if I killed him, being who he was—an original member of one of the most dangerous and deadly gangs in the country—I would have to stay hidden by any means necessary. I knew, even at fourteen, that his family was never going to stop hunting me. I knew they would kill me no matter what Carlos had done to me. When I killed him and his family, I purposefully pushed my brutality to the extreme. I had to look as crazy as possible in the hopes of getting into one of the most secure prisons or mental asylums in the country."

My gaze bore into the side of Megan's head as she cleared her throat. She continued to glare into the windshield as she prepared to tell me the rest of the most unbelievable shit I'd ever heard.

"I even went as far as making a list of the top five most secure mental asylums in the country. Even if I had gone to prison, I had planned to do everything in my power to get committed. While I was killing my foster family, I must have at some point really snapped because I went even further than I had planned. In the mist of stabbing Carlos, I figured why not stab him for each time he'd raped me. I did the same to David. Marina, I stabbed her ten times for each girl Carlos had killed and ten times for sitting by and allowing him to rape me. My actions ended up getting me thrown in number one —Ravencrest."

I knew from the media that Ravencrest was still known for being one of the most secure mental asylums in the country. The place rivaled some of the most secure super-max prisons.

"Ravencrest was one of the places I knew DG6 would have a hard time getting to me."

My forehead creased. "So, what was your plan for when you got out?" I tried to shake off the idea that a fourteen-year-old could or had to think like this. This shit was unbelievable.

"I honestly never thought I'd get out. I didn't know the authorities had found a video of what was being done to me until I was up for release. The video is what helped to free me. It justified my actions, I suppose. Once I was released, I didn't know how to work or co-exist around normal people anymore. The one thing I did have was my harsh upbringing that had taught me how to survive."

She took in a deep calming breath. I'm sure she had to prepare her mind to reveal the rest of the story she had buried in her head.

"I lived on the streets for months and traveled across several states following other homeless teens. I was hiding in every crack and corner until my husband found me. I was eighteen, and he was twenty-one when we married. I was mindful that DG6 would always hunt for me, so I stayed indoors as much as I could. My husband's military status kept us moving around, which was perfect for someone with my past. If my husband hadn't been killed in the war, I would have left him. I believed DG6 would have eventually tracked me down and killed us both. After my husband's death, I received an inheritance, and I've been running ever since."

So, that was how she'd been able to live and move around without an income. I turned my attention back over to Megan.

"The longer I was on my own, the better I became at hiding and staying a step ahead of DG6. I tried to never let myself get comfortable in one place. I knew that DG6 wouldn't stop until I was dead or worse, their prisoner. I've never been afraid to die. It's why I do some of the crazy shit I do. However, I'm terrified of suffering. Seeing what DG6 does to their enemies and witnessing what Carlos had done to those girls is what's kept me running all these years. I know it sounds crazy, but I'd rather die a quick death at the hands of a stranger than a slow agonizing demise at the hands of DG6."

"Fuck," I said. Complete sentences escaped me. DG6 had been killing, raping, and taking the country by murderous storm for over a decade. They'd killed more cops and federal agents than any other gang in the country by blowing up three police stations.

Once was to keep a police informant from presenting information in court. A second time was to kill three rival gang members. Finally, they'd blown up a part of a police station because one of the cops inside had been having an affair with one of the DG6 member's wife.

DG6 didn't care about killing innocent people or large groups of innocent bystanders to get what they wanted. Their merciless appetite for violence and destruction was what raised their danger meter well above groups like ours. They intimidated law officials to the point that most were afraid to even pursue them.

Now, I understood why their hired guns were willing to stop at nothing to get their target—*Megan*.

My eyes fell closed on a deep inhale that I released it slowly before placing my hand on Megan's shoulder.

"Okay, Megan, we can't ever tell my MC that these motherfuckers are after you. My MC is ready to fight because those motherfuckers came into our hometown and started some shit. So, if this is DG6, let my MC think they are after *me*. Besides, I was the one who dragged you back into town in the first place. So, I'm the reason they're here. It's my responsibility to protect you, but I can't protect you and keep my MC from doing something stupid at the same time."

She stared, unmoving with her mouth agape.

"Megan!"

She jumped.

"Do you understand what I'm telling you?"

"Yes. Play dumb and don't let anyone know I have a bunch of homicidal lunatics after me."

When I turned to climb out of my truck, Megan's low passive voice stopped me.

"Why are you doing this, Aaron? Let me disappear and lead these guys away from here."

For as smart as this woman was, she still didn't get it. I reached across the seat, gripped her shoulder, and pulled her clean over the console until she was straddled across my lap. One hand gripped her waist as I clenched her jaw in the other.

"You made me a promise, Megan. What was that promise?"

"That I wouldn't leave you again," she answered.

"I don't care if the fucking entire Mexican cartel is after you." *Which was what DG6 may as well have been.* "There is no way in the fucking world I'm letting you go, especially not off to someplace on your own while a bunch of fucking contract killers are chasing after you."

My face went cold as my eyes bore into hers, a hint of the killer in me peeking out.

"If this is DG6, a lot of people are about to die, Megan. Either they die or *we* die. If our time comes, we are going to die like we lived—fighting. If I die before you, you fucking keep fighting. Promise me!"

"I promise," she choked out. She shook her head before leaning in to give me the most passionate kiss she'd ever laid on me. My dick jumped up the moment her lips covered mine. My dick obviously didn't understand the difference between a compassionate kiss and a lusty one.

When Megan sucked on my bottom lip and pressed it between hers, before slicing her tongue across it, I started to think that maybe my dick was smarter than I had given it credit for.

I eagerly accepted her hot, moist tongue as the heat started in my face and rained down my body.

"You keep that up, and I'm taking out my dick right here, parked in this damn yard."

She giggled at me but kept teasing me with her mouth.

The cab of my truck became filled with our sighs. Anxious lips smacked and lustful moans sounded as our hands roamed and groped hard at soft parts that heaved and bobbed under our erotic movements.

Bump! Bump! Bump! Went a loud pounding outside the window.

5

MEGAN

The sight of Aaron's gun rising to the glass presented itself before my brain told my body to panic. Someone stood outside the truck knocking on Aaron's window, and I wasn't sure that they were aware that Aaron had a gun aimed at their head. We were parked in the front yard of Aaron's safe house. Had the assassins tracked us down already?

My first thought was that someone was about to shoot at us until I glanced up into the handsome face of a man who could've easily been Aaron's brother. He didn't have a beard, but the resemblance was undeniable. The dimming sun didn't hide his intense and mysterious hazel eyes and his short, dark hair—features that seem to be the only difference between him and Aaron.

Aaron didn't turn me loose as he flipped the key in the ignition and flicked the button that rolled his screeching window down.

"Cousin Ansel," he said with no enthusiasm whatsoever.

Cousin Ansel hadn't taken his eyes off me since I'd glanced into his face.

"What's your name, sweetness?" he asked me, still not acknowledging his cousin. I swallowed and raised an eyebrow, unsure of what to make of him staring at me so intensely. I couldn't tell if his intentions were good or bad.

Ansel leaned in the window, and I backed off as his gaze strolled over the parts of my body he could see.

"Put your fucking eyes back in your head, Ansel. She's not on the MC's menu."

Ansel held a hand up to his cousin, but the smirk on his face said he had no intention of stopping his flirty ways, especially not with me. His eyes still hadn't met Aaron's. He opened the truck door from the outside and it creaked and groaned from some of the damage it had endured during the attack.

I climbed out of Aaron's lap and let him get out first. I was mindful to grab my gun before I made a move to follow Aaron out of his side of the truck. Ansel stood there, reaching up to help me down after he'd shoved Aaron out of the way.

Aaron stood next to his cousin, grinning and shaking his head. They were almost the exact same towering height and build. Their facial features were similar enough for them to be brothers instead of cousins.

The smile on Aaron's face let me know that it was okay to move. I inched closer to the edge of the driver's seat, one hand gripping the back of the headrest and the other with a firm grip on the pistol.

Ansel wiggled his fingers, extending his reach closer to me. I glanced at Aaron once more before I made my next move. His head nodded once in my direction, indicating that it was okay to allow his cousin to help me down.

My mouth flew wide open when Ansel gripped my waist and lifted me from the truck like I didn't weigh an ounce. The gun I had in my hand struck his shoulder from his quick body-grabbing movement and because I suddenly needed to find something to hang on to.

Cousin Ansel didn't seem to notice the heavy pistol lying atop his shoulder as I tried to steady my hovering body and keep a grip on the gun simultaneously. He was slow to set me on my feet, but when he did, his gaze roved over my body as he turned me around. I gasped at the sudden intrusion of his strong hands on my waist, spinning me. I felt like a rotisserie selection of meat being prepared to be devoured.

"Cousin, you've been holding out on me," Ansel spoke to Aaron, but his curious eyes remained on me. His lips didn't turn up, but the smile shining in his eyes deepened.

"You have finally stepped out of the old-time regime your father rules and started dating *real* women. And she has a fucking gun in her hand. My dick's getting hard."

Ansel's statements were dramatic and animated like an actor auditioning for a part he knew he wouldn't get. His eyes darted back and forth between the gun in my hand and my face. It was as if the idea of me having a gun in my hand was too much for his mind to comprehend.

My teeth sank into the inside of my lip to keep from laughing because Cousin Ansel was clearly crazy, but not in a bad sort of way. I had assumed Aaron's family was strictly against the whole mixing of races as far as dating or even socializing was concerned, but Cousin Ansel didn't seem to care one bit.

Aaron snickered at his cousin but glowered at him with a stern eye in the same breath.

"Ansel, I know your crazy ass is into that Dom and sub shit, but this ain't that. So, like I said before, put your fucking eyes back in your head. We aren't in high school anymore."

I didn't know what Aaron's last statement meant, but he took my hand from his cousin's and urged me forward with his other hand planted in the small of my back. This was about as formal as Aaron had ever been with me. Ansel trailed us, and I could sense those big, intense, green eyes locked on my body.

Once we entered the living room, I found myself surrounded, treading water in an ocean of tall and well-built Caucasian men. At least five stood around the living room, talking so loudly that the sound echoed off the walls and rattled my insides. The moment they saw me with Aaron, you could have heard a mouse pissing on a cotton ball.

Aaron bid the men a quick greeting, gripped my hand, and urged me to follow him. He led me across the living room where eyes, no doubt followed me into a small hall that separated the kitchen from a door that went down and into the basement. Each hard step I took downward represented a strike against the nails I was likely putting in my own coffin.

Aaron didn't seem all that worried, but if his MC found out that *I* was the reason they were in this safe house in the first place, they were going to kill me.

I knew most of the men from the time I'd spent working for the August Knights. As I glanced around the dimly-lit, dreary basement, stumbling over my own feet, I questioned why Aaron had brought me down here. I wasn't a member, would never be a member, and I most certainly didn't feel welcomed.

Shark watched me with a deadly gleam shining in his blue-eyed gaze. He stared at me from across the large table he sat behind as he rubbed his shoulder. Aaron had told me he'd been shot. Shark knew I'd infiltrated his MC by feeding him a false story. The fact that I had somehow managed to make his only living son fall in love with me probably ticked him off even more.

After Aaron directed me to a seat, I sat with my body glued against the arm of a weathered, brown couch that sat behind Aaron's chair at the table.

While working for the MC, I learned that they didn't allow women into their inner circle, especially not while they discussed business. I was likely the only woman in the entire house and I was sure I'd be the only one in this basement.

After I shot someone the second day I worked for them, they started allowing me to see and hear things that most other women never would. Even now, I found it difficult to believe that they'd allowed me into the boardroom at their clubhouse while they conducted meetings.

Although I'd earned a touch of respect from the MC, I knew enough not to push it. I knew the best thing I could do was stay in my place, remain silent, and play dumb.

I sat on the couch unmoving, glad the big, high-sitting, heavy, dark-wood table and Aaron's body kept me mostly out of their views.

The basement was huge. The walls were a dusty blue. There were no windows, and from what I could tell, there were only a few small, vent-like square holes that acted as ventilation.

The only way in or out of the area was up the steps. The wide area contained three large couches lining two walls and a large table surrounded by ten chairs in a setup like the one at the MC's clubhouse. There were no pictures on the wall and no other furniture. The scent of leather and stale cigarettes permeated throughout the space.

Although the area was open, the air around me tightened and grew more suffocating with each new member that entered the space. I watched member after member as they clumped down the steep, unpainted wooden steps.

Some members sat at the table and others took seats on the couches. No one sat on the couch next to me, although there was room for three. Instead, they squeezed four each on the other two couches or stood against the wall.

Cousin Ansel sat at the table next to Aaron with his back to me. With Aaron and Ansel's two big bodies in front of me, it helped stifle a little of my anxiety and made me a little less visible.

Occasionally, Ansel would glance back at me with an inquisitive look on his face.

I didn't know what to make of him, but there was one thing I was certain of, he was a killer.

There was a trait etched in a person's eyes that I'd learned to read or sense. The vibe I'd sensed in Aaron was the same as I sensed in Ansel. He'd killed men, and from what I could tell, *lots* of them. Ansel presented a playful personality, but behind those pretty hazel eyes was the heart of a killer.

Since most of the guys had gotten used to seeing me, I received a few odd looks, but no one had said anything about my presence in the basement yet. Those who didn't know me glanced around Aaron and Ansel to sneak peeks at me. Did they know Aaron and I were together?

The last member that entered the basement slammed and locked the door from the inside. The *clink* of that lock echoed inside my brain. The *clunk* of the man's heavy footsteps made the steep steps groan and reminded me that I was locked in with a group that could kill me as easily as DG6 intended to.

Nine instead of the usual eight sat around the chairman's table. Ansel made up the extra member.

As I observed the room more closely, confusion sent my eyes darting about like marbles inside my head. Each time I was brave enough to glance up and catch one of the men staring at me, they'd skirt their eyes away from mine. What was going on with these bikers?

Shark slammed his big fist on the heavy wood of the table, and all voices and movements ceased.

"If you don't know by now, we have a new adversary. Those motherfuckers shot me, shot up the clubhouse, and tried to take Aaron out at the damn grocery store."

No one said anything in response to Shark's words. They stared intently, letting the information sink in. Shark's strident voice pulled me out of my thoughts and continued to emanate throughout the basement. "So far, we don't know who these motherfuckers are, but either—"

"They die, or we die." They'd all spoken the statement at the same time, loud and sure. Even the people sitting on the couches and standing against the walls had recited the words. I scanned the room with curious, roving eyes. Each person in this room seemed ready to go out in a blaze of glory if that was what it came to. The realization that I'd grossly underestimated this MC, hit me.

"Fucking right," Shark continued. "They came at me, and my son, so they must die. I don't give a fuck how many of them show up, you better put dick in the fucking dirt or die trying."

Agreeing words sounded around the table and heads nodded with enthusiastic faces. It was like a bunch of switches had been flipped to kill mode. I swallowed the large lump in my throat as I struggled to breathe past the suffocating testosterone that was being released into the air. They were willing to die and they didn't know that these men were after me.

"Informants couldn't tell us who the fuck these people are. So, all we know is there was a group of about ten that came into town some days ago sniffing around for information. They may also have a secondary team hidden some place outside of town. Aaron took out seven of those motherfuckers the day before yesterday. The shit made the news, so the area is not only going to be full of motherfuckers we need to kill, but it's going to be congested with pigs, Feds, and all kind of law enforcement."

I sat and listened to the men speculate on who this new adversary could be. They discussed strategy on how to best handle the group. It surprised me to find out that most, if not, all the members had already sent their families away. The club's bar and strip club would remain open, mainly as traps to catch their adversaries. A five-man crew, armed and prepared to kill, would be deployed to stake out each location.

The only place any of the men were to lay their heads was here at this safe house or the second safe house the MC owned on the other side of town.

Once the group had planned their first line of defense, fifteen of the twenty-three men in the basement departed like soldiers with their assignments.

Aaron swung his chair around to me. "We're staying here tonight."

I nodded my head, stunned. I'd never seen anything like this. They were seriously considering going to war.

Just as Aaron started to say something else, Cousin Ansel swung his chair around. His eyes drifted away from me and landed on the side of his cousin's head. Aaron knew he was being ogled by his cousin, but he kept his gaze on me.

"We got a lot to talk about, cousin." Ansel's words were low. He leaned closer to Aaron and dropped his voice even lower. He seemed not to want the remaining men to hear what he was telling Aaron. "We need to have a serious discussion about how your *girlfriend*, who happens to be strapped, was allowed to sit through a club meeting without anyone saying shit about it."

Ansel didn't have to say the rest of what he was thinking. The fact that I was African-American should have been the number one reason why I shouldn't have been allowed inside their meeting. The fact that I was the only female and may well have been one of the only females allowed inside their sacred meeting also had Cousin Ansel's antennae up.

Ansel glanced at me. He managed to make a devious smile look charming. "No offense to you, sweetie, but I'm a couple of puzzle pieces away from a clear picture here."

I half nodded and half shrugged. "None taken."

Truth of the matter was, I still had trouble figuring out what was happening. No one had ever explained anything to me. Other than the pieces I'd put together while working for the MC, I didn't know why my presence hadn't incited an internal MC war.

Ansel's eyes landed right back on the side of Aaron's head. "Aaron, what the fuck is going on? And tell me *everything*."

Shark added his two cents after hearing his nephew's question to his son. "That's right, Aaron. Tell your cousin every fucking thing. Don't leave out a single fucking detail."

Aaron placed his hand up to his forehead, clearly not wanting to get into explaining me to his cousin. He definitely wasn't in the mood for his father's comments.

Aaron finally glanced over at his cousin. "It's a long fucking story, Ansel. Let me get Megan settled, and then we'll talk."

6

AARON

"So, let me get this straight. She shot Scud at the clubhouse, killed Chuck inside your house, and helped you clean up and bury the bodies? Plus, she killed two of the seven you led into the woods a few days ago? Get the fuck out of here."

This was the first time in a long time I'd seen my cousin dumbstruck. I had proceeded in telling him Megan's backstory, including the details about her foster family, who they truly were, and of her being forced to lure innocent girls to their deaths.

Ansel gripped his chin with his thumb and index finger, more than likely, his mind envisioning some of what I'd divulged to him about Megan. "You're telling me that little innocent-faced woman I pulled out of your truck did all that shit? Plus, not only survived, but killed an original member of DG6?"

Ansel didn't give me a chance to answer his questions, his mind was probably working at warp speed. "How the fuck did she get Uncle Shark to agree to her crazy-ass proposal in the first place?" The loud snap of Ansel's fingers echoed off the walls when he realized something. "That's why Unc didn't challenge that crazy shit you pulled tonight, having her in the club meeting. She'd already been in and out of the MC's meetings before she even knew who the hell you were."

Ansel was having difficulties grasping the story I'd told him. We'd grown up together and had become as close as brothers. His mother, my aunt, had taken her own life when Ansel was only eight, and federal agents had shot his father when Ansel was twelve. Shark took him under his evil black wings and raised him along with Ryan and me.

Most people assumed Ansel and I were brothers. Our mothers had been twins, which was the explanation behind the close resemblance he and I shared, I supposed.

All throughout high school, Ansel and I traded girls like baseball cards. I didn't think there was one girl that I'd slept with that he hadn't also slept with and vice versa. We made a sport out of it, most times rating them on his scale versus mine. I usually graded much easier than Ansel's crazy ass, though.

However, I think he picked up on the fact that I had no intention of sharing Megan with him. In case he didn't understand my first few warnings, I reminded him again.

"Megan is off-limits, Ansel. I mean that shit."

"Okay. You don't have to keep telling me that shit. I get it. She's special, the one, the one you'd be willing to go to war for."

Those specific words got my attention, especially the way Ansel had placed emphasis on them.

"What makes you say that?" I asked, trying but failing to keep my brows from pinching as worry crept into my brain. Ansel acted a fool, but I knew he was a lot smarter than he let on.

"This group of mercenaries...I don't think they're after you or us at all. If they were after anyone in this MC, you'd know who they were by now. Those motherfuckers want *her*, and you don't care if you have to go to war to keep her safe. This could be DG6 after her for taking out a fucking original." Ansel glanced at me, his gaze locked on mine. "And you call me the crazy one?"

"I—"

Ansel threw up his hand, cutting me off. "I get it, but not everyone in this MC is as open-minded as me. If they knew you were willing to lay their lives on the line over a woman, they would probably kill her or turn her over to those mercenaries. If they knew it might be DG6, they'd kill you and her."

Ansel twisted his neck left and right, popping it. He heaved a deep sigh and his forehead creased as deeply as mine. He was still digesting what I'd revealed to him about Megan's past and a possible DG6 crisis. However, the fact that he was still sitting with me eased my tension.

If Ansel had any intention of telling the MC the real reason why we were going to war, he'd have walked out of the room and shouted the shit to the house—after he'd put a bullet in Megan's head. *Yes, my cousin is that deadly.*

However, after we gave each other our stare of understanding, I knew he'd stand by my side and help me fight if it came to it. If I cared about something or believed in it enough, even if he still held doubts, Ansel would always take my side.

"Does she mean enough to you that you can't live without her?" he asked. The seriousness in his tone and gaze crashed into mine. "If you let me kill her, this can be over before it even starts."

In a normal family conversation, one might have been upset over a question like this, but I guess you had to know the person to understand them.

"I can't let you kill her, Ansel. She means that much to me."

He shrugged it off as if we weren't just talking about him killing the woman he knew I would protect with my life.

He asked, "Does she even know that she's somehow managed to earn respect from this MC? Do you know how fucking shocked I was to not only see you with an African-American woman, but to see her sitting inside a club meeting? That shit still has me tripping the fuck out."

Ansel kept talking. However, his questions weren't the kind he wanted answered, but they were more to express his surprise at what he'd witnessed. His brows remained pinched as astonishment surfaced in his gaze.

"Do you know how much effort it took for me to sit at that table and keep my mouth shut? The only other woman I've ever seen in an August Knights meeting was your mother, and that's because she was as vicious as any of the guys."

The idea of Megan's progression within the MC was as big a shocker to me as it was to Ansel. However, Megan was nothing like my mother. My mother was an alcoholic, an abusive troublemaker, and an evil, vindictive woman. I believed until this day that she wouldn't have hesitated to put a bullet in my brother's head or mine if it served the MC.

My father had his faults, but he'd never laid a hand on my brother or me. The only time I could remember my father raising a voice to my mother was when he'd catch her mistreating either of us. She'd killed herself in a head-on collision, driving drunk. Thankfully, she hadn't taken anyone to hell with her after going head to head with an eighteen-wheeler.

Ansel's heavy sigh pulled my attention. He closed one eye and stared at me through the other. "So, Megan's been killing since she was fourteen? And she's killed at least six people that you know about?"

I nodded, but his question had me wondering how many others Megan may have killed that she hadn't told me about. She'd confirmed that she had infiltrated other organizations. Had she killed people within those groups?

Ansel's lips turned up into a tight smile. His mind was likely doing somersaults around the idea of Megan being a killer.

"I can fucking see why you want her, that's for sure. She's sexy as fuck and she ain't afraid to murder a motherfucker. She's a sexy, little, sociopathic, serial killer. And she must have the best pussy in the world to send you this fucking far across the line."

My mind couldn't formulate a response to Ansel's comments because in a way, he was right. I was sure I wouldn't have been interested in Megan if she was normal.

Ansel continued with a slow teasing shake of his head. "I'm telling you now, cousin. I won't sleep with her, but if you get yourself killed over her, all bets are off."

The pointed glint in Ansel's hazel eyes made me aware that he was dead-ass serious. All I could do was laugh at my crazy cousin.

7

AARON

By the time I made it back to our room, which was thankfully, the only bedroom on the first floor, Megan was laid on top of the covers. She'd fallen asleep waiting for me. I crept into the bathroom and didn't bother pulling clothes from the duffle I'd packed at my house. I wasn't going to need clothes after I woke Megan up.

Fresh out of the shower, I quickly toweled myself off, slapped on some deodorant and slunk my hot body in the bed next to her. She had on the only outfit I liked seeing her in, one of my shirts. My dick was already hard and poking into her side when she stirred.

She let out a low, lazy moan, and as soon as her eyes met mine, she smiled. I'd turned the lamp off but left the bathroom light on to give us some illumination.

When Megan turned towards me, I lifted my shirt over her butt, and a pleasing smile brightened my face. Smooth-brown and plump, the sight of her bare ass filled me with a desire that only she could elicit. A low groan escaped as eager fingers slipped around her waist before I pulled her closer.

My lips skimmed the soft skin of her neck as I palmed one of her supple ass cheeks. My mouth roamed over the tender flesh of her neck and dragged over her collarbone until my lips clamped on to her nipple through my soft cotton T-shirt. A nasally moan escaped her as she squirmed under my play.

My hand slid over a shapely hip before gripping and pulling her hot middle into my hard dick. Her breathy whine heightened my arousal and urged me to move faster. It was shameful how hot this woman could get me. When I lifted the tail end of my shirt and slipped it up her silky body, she assisted in slipping it over her head.

We feasted on each other's bodies before I spread her legs and dove, dick-first into her tight, welcoming pussy. We were hissing before I could get a good rhythm going. My palm pushed against the inside of her thigh, opening her wider while sending her leg up higher. The slight repositioning sent my dick in deeper and made her pussy clench tighter around me.

"Aaron, you're hitting my spot, baby. Don't stop."

An exhausting, "Oh shit!" escaped me before a loud mixture of a moan and groan rattled my throat. Nothing could have made me stop but a damn bullet in my brain. The mattress groaned, the box-spring knocked, and the damn headboard smacked against the wall. A damn marching band may as well have been passing through the room as much noise as we were making.

"Someone is going to hear us," Megan pointed out before she bit into my neck to quiet her loud moaning.

"I don't care. They're grown. They know what women and men do behind closed doors," I managed to say before my mind was over-powered by the intoxication of our sex.

I didn't know if Megan had heard my statement, not while my dick was stroking that tight buddle of nerves that she said was her spot. I kept hitting it hard...hard enough for her to forget all about who was going to hear us.

When she started gasping, scratching my lower back and shoulders up, and yelling my name repeatedly, I knew I had her. She often left marks on my back, neck, and arms. Maybe I was a bit twisted, but I liked seeing the marks she left on me. They were beautiful reminders of the love, passion, and lust we shared.

"You're about to make me cum, baby. Shit!"

I'll be damned if I wasn't about to cum too. At this point, that fucking headboard was about to knock a damn hole clean through the wall, but I couldn't stop. My ass was possessed by the power of this woman's pussy.

With every hard thrust, our yells grew louder, and my fucking mind sank deeper into that zone that only *she* could take me to. I'm sure it was the same place that hard drugs took addicts to. There was no denying shit at this point. I was addicted to Megan and death was likely the only thing powerful enough to take me away from her.

With our height difference, I still hadn't figured out how she managed to get her legs wrapped around me the way she did but having her wrapped around me made our session that much more intoxicating. The way she gripped and tugged and pulled me into her, made me love her harder and deeper.

Her responses urged me to give it to her however she wanted it. Her reactions were the best motivators and gave me the strength I needed to force my body to last for as long as I could go, even when my mind screamed for me to explode inside her.

"Oh, my fucking God!" I roared. Vocalizing how good our sex felt was the only way to keep from going insane. My dick was so slick with her wetness that the wet-hot slippery warmth enticed me to thrust harder, faster.

Our moans competed with the noise of my thighs slapping against the inside of hers. A deep tingling sensation shot up my spine before my dick kicked and bucked inside her. It literally felt like her pussy was pulling at my entire body.

My vision blurred for a few seconds before my world exploded and left me in murmuring pieces as her tight walls clenched around my dick and kept the intoxication zooming through my body.

Megan must have pulled the covers over us because I passed out after I'd exploded inside her. I couldn't even recall pulling my dick out of her. I'd slipped clean out of this world, and my mind must have shut down before it returned from the pleasure zone. My eyes fluttered under my lids as I struggled to move my relaxed body. I found the strength and raised my head to see Megan was sitting over me handing me a glass of water.

A satisfied smile filled my face and met hers as I reached for the glass. She ran her hand lovingly over my damp back, and I didn't miss the love she had for me shining in her gaze. How the fuck did she always seem to know what I needed whenever the hell I needed it? And she'd had the nerve to question why I couldn't let her ass go. She could wipe that shit out of her head. She was never leaving me again if I had anything to say about it.

8

MEGAN

The least I could do was cook for these men. They were about to take on a group that was aiming to kill them and had no idea *I* was the reason for it. A hint of embarrassment and a twinge of guilt lingered within me for what they might have heard last night between Aaron and me.

It was only when the sun shone through the window that I'd seen the damage the headboard had done to the wall. Beige paint had been scratched away, and a series of dents were left along the area where the headboard had repeatedly slammed into the wall.

Aaron refused to change a thing about how we fucked. He said the crew were all grown and knew what women and men did behind closed doors. But, I didn't think Aaron and I did what normal people did. We could take an hour nap and be at it again and each time was a new adventure.

Our sex was addictive, something I assumed would have burned out by now, but it hadn't. We weren't even close to slowing down and we were as crazy for each other as we'd been that first two weeks I'd spent with him.

I reined in my thoughts and inserted the second load of blueberry muffins into the oven before reaching up to turn the bacon. I hissed and tried to shake off the sting as grease popped from the sizzling bacon. I wasn't sure if the men ate grits, but since they were in the cabinet, I cooked a pot of those as well. The pan of fluffy scrambled eggs sat off to the side as steam rose from them.

Cooking was like therapy for me. Like running and writing, cooking helped take my mind off the dark cloud that constantly hung over my life. A deep smile took over my lips. Although running, writing, and cooking helped to set my mind at ease, they were nothing compared to what Aaron could do for me. His brand of therapy could literally make me forget that the rest of the world existed. He knew how to make me forget my own name.

"You cook too?" I jumped at the sound of a voice that had quickly become familiar to me. "No wonder my cousin has lost his mind over you."

Ansel's teasing voice sailed into my ear. The fact that he'd snuck up on me and was close enough for his minty breath to brush my neck proved how deeply I'd sunk into my mind.

"Good morning. Have a seat, and I'll fix you a plate."

I'd expected that Ansel wouldn't listen to my suggestion, but he took a seat across the table, facing me. Undoubtedly, so he could watch me. The way he watched me made me nervous. It reminded me of the way I watched Aaron sometimes.

The way I studied Aaron was probably not healthy. I studied him with an obsessive curiosity because I wanted to hang on to every memory of him just in case. As I spooned some grits next to Ansel's eggs, I peeped at him over my shoulder. As I expected, his eyes were laser-locked on me.

The tension in my shoulders coiled at the idea that I was being studied. When I glanced back once more, I forced a smile although my vexing thoughts never stopped. "Is there anything you don't eat or like?"

"No, there's nothing I won't eat," he answered, and I could tell he wasn't talking about food.

I added two muffins and some bacon to the plate I'd started. When I placed the food in front of Ansel, it wasn't hard to discern that my actions had stirred his curiosity about me. I think I confused him.

"Orange juice or water?" I asked.

"Juice, baby. Get me some juice," he answered in a seductive tone that made me smile at his antics. Maybe I didn't confuse him. After I placed the glass of juice in front of him, he caught my wrist before I could move it away from him.

There was no use hiding the fact that his touch had my hand shaking. It wasn't fright that Ansel set off in me. He set my nerves on edge—made them frantic and charged like exposed wires. I was good at taking myself out of the spotlight, but with this group, especially with Ansel, I felt like I was center stage.

"You do this kind of thing for my cousin?" he asked. I could tell by the curiosity in his gaze that his intention wasn't to scare me. It seemed he was fighting to understand me.

"Yes. All the time," I answered, trying but failing to keep my voice steady. "He said he likes my cooking, and I like to cook, so..."

After I eased my wrist out of Ansel's strong hold, I returned to the stove to remove the bacon. I needed the grease to pop on me now to ease the tension still rolling through my body.

The sound of approaching male voices alerted me that more men were coming. I recognized Shark's voice, and I was willing to bet that Wade was with him. Shark and Wade seemed the closest of all the men. As far as I had figured out, Wade was Shark's half-brother. They had different mothers but shared a father. This made Wade, Aaron's uncle although he was only four years older than Aaron.

Their plates were fixed and ready by the time they took their seats at the table. Neither of the men greeted me good morning, and I hadn't expected them too. Shark sat at the head of the table next to Ansel, and Wade sat behind me with his back to me.

Ansel watched me with intense curiosity as I placed Shark's plate in front of him. I reached back for Wade's plate and placed his as well. After I set the men's juice in front of them, I went back to the stove to remove the second pan of muffins.

A low chatter among the men started behind me. This situation

---

was new to Ansel, so I understood some aspects of his curiosity. The men and I had never had a verbal relationship, but I think we respected each other enough that our non-verbal communication was enough.

As the thump of the next set of boots grew closer, I realized it was none other than Aaron. It was shameful that I knew the man's footsteps.

Thankfully, I was turned away from Aaron as he made his approach because my smile spread about as wide as the table was long. I'd finally accepted that I loved that man with everything I had, so it was difficult to keep my emotions in check when I was around him.

When strong hands slid around my waist and warm lips caressed my neck, my body damn near melted as fast as the butter melted across the muffins. Apparently, I wasn't the only one who had a problem keeping their emotions in check.

I never suspected that Aaron would engage in public displays of affection. But, when it came to his relationship with me, there were no clear-cut explanations.

"Good morning," he whispered in my ear before he nipped my earlobe.

"Good morning," I replied in a low tone as embarrassment warmed my brown cheeks, likely lighting them with a pinkish glow. The silence in the kitchen let me know that we had an audience. I swallowed the awkward state I was left in when Aaron stepped away from me.

He sat across the table next to Ansel. When I turned to bring Aaron his plate, Shark and Ansel's unreadable glares were fixed on me. Their unwavering stares filled me with a hint of unease as both seemed ready to spill whatever comment teetered on their tongues.

My tension didn't let up until I was standing next to Aaron, placing his plate in front of him. My hand brushed across his back lovingly. The action was almost automatic, and I didn't realize I'd done it until after it had occurred. Now, I was the one making public displays of affection.

It was becoming apparently clear that we didn't have any control over how we reacted to each other. I couldn't be close to Aaron and not want to touch him. When I returned to the table with his glass of juice, Shark had dropped his gaze, but Ansel's hard stare remained on me. He obviously was still having trouble figuring it all out, although I knew Aaron had told him my story.

Wade cleared his throat, and without looking in my direction, he asked, "Hey, Megan, can I get another one of those muffins?"

"Sure," I replied, surprised but glad when someone other than Aaron talked to me. I lifted the fattest muffin with a set of plastic tongs and placed it on Wade's plate.

"Thanks," he said in a low tone.

"You're welcome."

Ansel's eyes widened as he glanced back and forth between me and everyone at the table. I could literally see his eyes volleying between us all. I couldn't imagine what was going through his head. Hell, I was still figuring it out.

Returning to my station at the stove, I turned the last of the bacon as the men engaged in an animated conversation about sports. Thankfully, the lively discussion took the focus off me. Two more men joined the group: Shane and someone whose name I didn't know, but I had seen before. The noise level increased with the additional men.

Ansel participated in the boisterous conversation, but his eyes never strayed too far away from me and my non-verbal interactions with the MC. Aaron's face was likely unreadable to the rest of the table, but I was sure his positive facial expressions each time we made eye contact were reminders that I didn't have anything to worry about where the MC was concerned.

Although the table was full, I'd counted eight men left in the house last night. For the final two men, I fixed and wrapped them a plate and left it on the stove. Even if the men never came for their plates, I didn't have to worry about the food going to waste. I knew from experience that this was a group that wasn't going to let a cooked meal go uneaten.

As the table started to thin, I began the process of washing the dishes and cleaning the kitchen. Aaron sent me a slight head nod when he walked out with his father and his uncle.

By the time I had everything cleaned, the only body left sitting behind me was none other than *Ansel*. His eyes were literally burning a hole in my back. I could sense him staring across the table at me. Although I wasn't as nervous as before, his presence still had me a bit uneasy.

For reasons I had yet to understand, I sensed that I could talk to Ansel, despite his alarming stare. I turned and faced him. Now, if only I could get him to stop staring at me.

My arms folded over my chest before I took a step closer, grateful that the table was between us. "What is it?" I asked. "Why do you keep staring at me like that?"

"I think I'm starting to get it now," Ansel stated. "At first, I thought my cousin had lost his damn mind, but the pieces are starting to fall into place."

My forehead creased. I wasn't sure what he was talking about, but he didn't say anything else. He got up from the table and left me standing there confused.

9

AARON

Three days later, I was comfortable enough to leave Megan at the safe house. My dad and the other chairmen handled ongoing business, and they'd grabbed a few of the prospects to help clean and board up the clubhouse. I hadn't asked and didn't have any doubt that Megan could handle herself if she had to, but there was always someone at the safe house with her without me having to ask someone to stay.

Ansel and I had searched every corner of Copper County, attempting to track down the group that had shot my father, shot up our clubhouse, and fired at Megan and me. Ansel rode shotgun with me in my truck, speaking on the phone with one of his contacts to see if members of DG6 had made their way into Copper County.

"Okay, thanks," he concluded. He swiped the screen and gripped his phone in his clenched hand as his chin pulled tight.

"What is it?" I asked.

"Nothing. As far as my FBI contact knows, DG6 hasn't made a move from any of the spots they have eyes on. Trust me, the FBI, ATF, and probably, the damn CIA are watching them. They can hardly take a good shit without eyes on them. But, those motherfuckers have paid so many people off that they still manage to conduct their illegal business without resistance."

"So, your contact...how do you know you can trust him?"

Ansel's devious smile spread wide before he tucked his lip and sucked his teeth.

"My contact is a *she*, and I can trust her because she is one of my subs."

My gaze left the road as my neck snapped in my cousin's direction.

"No shit! The FBI is into that *life* too?"

Ansel laughed, shaking his head at me like I was the one missing out.

"Fucking right. You'd be surprised at how many pantsuit-wearing motherfuckers like to be tied and whipped and even tortured. You'd be surprised at what gets some of those tricky motherfuckers off."

I didn't think I wanted to know. Ansel had fallen headfirst into that life after he'd met a widow who convinced him that he would make the perfect Dom. Ansel attempted to convince me to embrace the life after introducing me to two of his subs. Of course, I slept with them, had even tied them up and made them beg for my dick, but that life required too much planning and thinking for me.

The role playing, the sex toys, the safe words. I preferred to get straight to the point when it came to sex, and I didn't want a mother-fucker beating on me or teasing me before we fucked each other. However, I don't think I'd have a problem with letting Megan do whatever her little heart desired.

Ansel continued. "If DG6 hasn't made a move, that doesn't mean they haven't contracted a group to do the job. You did say the ones you encountered acted like mercenaries, possibly a paramilitary group, right?"

As the scene replayed in my head, I nodded absently. My cousin was a better puzzle solver than I was, but Ansel's problem was his patience. I had a short supply of patience myself, but Ansel wanted what he wanted when he wanted it and rarely made compromises.

"DG6 could be testing us with their first line of defense. So, they can adjust and up the ante on us to try to weed out our weaknesses," I added.

"Now, you're catching on, grasshopper," Ansel replied, like he was teaching me something.

He liked talking to me like I was the younger one, but I was older than him by a year. Fortunately, we'd both spent some time in the military. Not only did we have a desire to prove ourselves as men, but we'd siphoned the rigorous training we knew we'd need, being who we were in a family like ours.

I'd spent four years in the marines from age twenty to twenty-four, and Ansel followed suit three months after I'd joined. He'd spent four years in the army. We both aimed for the toughest training and hardest assignments. He'd made it onto a ranger team, and I'd made my way onto an off-the-books black-ops unit.

After surviving dangerous deployments and missions that didn't exist as far as the government was concerned, we both fell right back into the illegal shit our family had always participated in upon our return home.

If we were going to find any viable leads on this group hunting Megan, I had to call on my secret weapon. After the first ring, D answered my call.

"D, we need to talk, but I need you to make my phone so nobody can hear us talking."

Ansel glared at me but didn't comment. He wasn't the only one who had contacts. I didn't trust this group that was hunting us. They'd tracked Megan to Copper County and had found our club-house, so there was no reason to think they hadn't found ways to spy on us.

Ansel knew about as much as I knew. Therefore, he knew I'd finally accepted that DG6 was behind the attack and were hunting for Megan. It only took D a minute to call me back. I placed the call on speaker.

"We're clear, Knox. What you got?" D asked.

"There is a group after my MC to kill us, which is nothing new, but I think it might be DG6 or maybe—"

"Wait! Pump the fucking brakes, Knox. Did you just say *DG6*? What the fuck are you doing fucking around with that fucking den of fucking rattlers?"

Four fucks in one sentence. I'd gotten D's full attention. Ansel sat listening with a smile plastered across his face.

"Them motherfuckers train their babies how to shoot before they're even old enough to take their first steps," D continued, giving us his interpretation of DG6.

"D, concentrate on what I'm telling you. I said, I think it might be DG6. It could also be a group that they've hired to fuck with us, but my cousin's contact in the FBI hasn't been able to track movement on any members of DG6. Will you pull something out of your nerdy hat and see if you can make a connection? Or see if DG6 could have hired somebody to take us out. Fuck, make sure it is DG6 first."

An exhausted sigh escaped me, and out of the corner of my eye, I could see Ansel eyeballing the hell out of me. The sound of D's fingers already setting fire to a keyboard could be heard over the line. I was about to add more fuel to the fire I'd set in D.

"D, if it is DG6, they might be after Lacey Daniels." I had revealed almost everything to Ansel, so he knew that Megan was also Lacey Daniels.

D huffed into the phone. "Knox, wait the fuck up. I thought you put a bullet in her head weeks ago?"

"D, you have a way of finding out shit that nobody else can. If you dug into Lacey Daniel's past like I know you did, then you'd know what was done to her and why I couldn't kill her. And trust me, the shit they released to the public was the watered-down version."

The long, quiet pause let me know that D was connecting the dots. For a while, all I heard was my tires eating up the highway and D's fingers striking keys.

"So, let me guess. That foster family she killed all those years ago was DG6?"

"Yeah," I answered, not surprised at how fast D had pieced the shit together.

"Knox, man, what the fuck have you gotten yourself into? Those motherfuckers aren't goanna stop until she's dead, no matter how much time has passed. They don't care about what their people did to her. I know you, Knox. Your crazy ass will try to kill their whole fucking clan if it comes to it."

D took another long pause. I already knew what he was thinking. D rarely passed up a chance to step away from the computer and participate in what he called field missions.

"If you need me there, Knox, just let me know. Also, that suit-and-tie-wearing motherfucker, Dax, is back on the prowl too. He's getting hired for half-million-dollar hits. You know how he is. Mention the word *danger*, and he'll come running."

Ansel's eyes grew big at those words. As much as my cousin enjoyed killing people, he was likely getting ideas from some of the shit D was saying. D, on the other hand, was just as bad as my cousin. Both D and my friend, Dax, would come running if danger called.

D's legal name was Derrick Michaels, but *Danger* Michaels would have been more fitting. However, I wasn't going to point this out to my friend. Like my cousin, D apparently saw himself differently than the way I saw him.

"D, I'll say no for now, but if I tell you to come, you know shit is blown all to hell."

"I know, Knox. I also know I've lost count of how many times you've saved my fucking life, so I got your back, no matter what the fuck is going down."

"Thanks, man," I said and hung up before Ansel could get the words out that I knew were brimming on the edge of this twitchy tongue.

"Hey, can you link me up with Dax?"

Just as I'd thought. I knew my cousin well. "Don't you think you're into enough shit? Now, you want to add contract killing to your resume?"

Ansel shrugged. "Fuck it. I'm young. The world needs people like me to rid it of evil. I want to enjoy the things I enjoy doing while I can. If we survive this DG6 shit, it will guarantee me six-figure hits."

The way my cousin's mind worked made me wonder if he'd been

wired right. He'd just admitted that he wanted to enjoy killing while he was young enough to.

I shook my head, attempting to shake out the idea. Despite how twisted my mind was, my cousin made me seem like I was the normal one. Ansel was smart and business minded. He dressed in suits and hung around with the wealthy, but it was his dark side that he managed so well, unsuspecting victims didn't see it until the monster came out.

He owned two successful clubs that catered to the rich and twisted and several other small businesses that he'd acquired over the years. He and I shared the same gun supplier, and being in California where the market was bigger, Ansel was able to push twice the shipment of guns as I could.

After a long silent moment, a chuckle from Ansel sounded.

"What's so fucking funny?" I questioned him.

"I was thinking about the kind of unit you were deployed with. Was it a unit full of fucking killers?"

I laughed then. It did appear that most of my old unit had gotten out of the military and turned to a life of crime. Aside from D and Dax, there was also Luke and Gavin who'd linked up and started their own security firm down in Georgia. Knowing the men the way that I did, I was sure they did a lot more than security.

I was distracted, but my eyes didn't miss the two unfamiliar men climbing out of a black SUV that was like the one that had followed Megan and me into the woods. Ansel's gaze followed what my eyes had locked onto. Finally, after days of searching, this unfamiliar group that I now stared at, could be our first lead.

One of the men pumped gas as the other two exited the vehicle and walked into the Quit Mart. I pulled my truck around the side of the bowling alley where we could observe and not be spotted.

10

AARON

Ansel and I sat low in the front seat of my truck, eyeing the unfamiliar men. From the angle we were parked, I couldn't see what their license plate said, but I was willing to bet it was out of state.

DG6 mainly operated out of Texas, New Mexico, and Arizona. As far as I knew, the gang had originated in Texas, which was likely their main base of operations. Texas was also the place where Megan had been placed in a house with a bunch of killers, raped, and tortured to within an inch of her sanity.

"We need to follow these motherfuckers," Ansel stated the obvious. "I wish we were on our bikes or that I'd driven my truck."

"Me too," I voiced absently as I watched the one pumping the gas swirl a toothpick around in his mouth. He wore a pair of those tactical khakis that contractors and law enforcement officials wore and a police-blue Under Armor polo shirt. His attire was a dead giveaway that he wasn't from our neck of the woods. I was willing to bet these were three from the group of motherfuckers that had attacked Megan and me and shot my father.

I started my truck and pursued the black SUV once the men reloaded and took off. When the license plate came into view, I texted it into D. Nothing on the license plate identified what state the vehicle was from, but I was confident in D's ability to find out what others didn't want you to know.

Since my truck was missing a passenger's side mirror, had visible bullet holes, and a cracked back window, I stayed as far behind the group as possible. When they drove into the parking lot of the most luxurious hotel Copper County had to offer, The Copper Grand, I drove into the lot of a hotel two buildings down the road and across the street from them. Using the binoculars that I kept in the center console, Ansel and I took turns using them and sat and watched the men exit their vehicle and enter the hotel.

The hotel was fancy enough that you had to walk through the lobby before taking the stairs or an elevator to your room. We sat for about thirty minutes to see if any of the men would return to the vehicle and leave. I wanted to get one of the men alone so I could question him.

Ansel and I agreed that he should return to the safe house to pick up his truck. My truck with its damaged body was way too suspicious and easy for people to describe and spot. I didn't expect Ansel back for at least thirty minutes, so I climbed out of my truck and found a comfortable spot to wait.

The thick branches of a tree on the far side of the hotel lot kept me hidden from view. I sat on a thick patch of grass, peeking through binoculars at the hotel the targets had gone into and the vehicle that they had driven.

If they decided to take off before Ansel returned, I had no idea what I would do. However, I was compelled to keep watch. What I wanted to do was walk over to the hotel to see if I could gather some information on the men, like their room numbers perhaps.

Just as I started to get antsy and rose to walk towards the hotel, Ansel wheeled his big black dually truck into the parking lot. The good thing about having a truck in this town was that you blended in. Around here, trucks were all that mattered as far as vehicles went. Even the women had adopted the habit of driving trucks. Ansel pulled up near me, bringing his truck to a scratchy stop. I ran to the passenger's side and climbed in.

"What you wanna do, cousin?" Ansel asked with one eyebrow stuck in the air as he glared at me sideways. I hadn't even closed the door before Ansel asked his question.

I knew my cousin. The prospect of killing someone not only had his trigger finger itching—his entire body likely needed a scratch. Despite what others may think of me, I didn't like killing people. Killing had become a part of my life that I had to learn to deal with, like paying taxes. You didn't want to do it, but you knew you had to.

As for Ansel, he embraced killing like one would embrace a hobby. He wanted time with it. He wanted to shape it and improve his techniques. My gaze left him and landed back on the vehicle of the three men who likely had no idea that death lurked outside their windows.

"Calm down, kill boy," I teased Ansel. "We need to figure out if they are with the group Megan and I left in the woods. Once that's confirmed, either they die or we die."

The far-off glint in Ansel's eyes and the devious smirk that danced across his face caused a chill to run up my spine. He was likely sitting there dreaming up ways to torture the unsuspecting group.

I loved my cousin, honest I did, but I seriously wished my father hadn't called him. He was about to drag me into some shit that I likely wasn't prepared for. Ansel was like that extra drink you knew you didn't need but drank anyway. Then, later, you found yourself in a situation that you didn't remember getting yourself into.

"I think we should sit on this group," I suggested. As badly as I wanted to confront the group, patience and planning had always given me an advantage over my enemy. I eyed Ansel, knowing my words likely had no effect on him. "They could lead us to the rest—if there are more of them."

Ansel's head whipped around so fast that it appeared he'd forgotten he was steering his big-ass truck into a parking spot across the lot from the suspects' black SUV.

"I'm not good at playing the waiting game, Aaron."

My fingers spread over my forehead, and I squeezed. "I don't like waiting either, Ansel, but what good will it do for us to bust in there, find these guys, and kill—"

He cut me off with a wave of his hand. "Who said anything about *killing*? We need to torture them for information first," he said this with a straight face as if we were talking about meeting a bunch of guys to play a casual game of basketball.

"Why the hell should we wait until they lead us when we can get them to tell us what we need to know right now?"

He did have a point, no matter how twisted it was inside his head. Although I'd thought about doing exactly what Ansel had suggested, I would have avoided the unnecessary bloodshed and waited and let the guys lead me to their group. Ansel preferred to beat the information out of the men so he could know faster. Lack of patience was definitely my cousin's weakness.

My head tilted as I thought about what I wanted to do. I could sense my cousin's eyes on the side of my head, eyeballing me like a dog whose bone I was holding back. His anxious hand tapped against his leg. He didn't smoke, but if I had a cigarette, I'd give him one to calm his damn nerves. After making him suffer for a moment longer, I decided to put him out of his anxious misery.

"You've got a point, cousin, but these men are mercenaries. After that encounter in the woods, I know that at least some of them have dished out or have been on the receiving end of torture before."

He laughed at me, his chuckle filling the cab of the truck. "Trust me. Being in the life and having to kill when the moment arises, I've picked up some techniques that could make the manliest man sing like a fucking bird."

Shit! I thought to myself. I didn't doubt what Ansel was saying. The first time I'd accidentally walked in on my cousin with one of his subs, I stood in the doorway with my mouth gaped open. The woman was locked inside one of those dog cages on all fours, licking or drinking something out of a metal dog bowl. She seemed way too damn happy to follow whatever twisted and cruel commands he was dishing out. The shit he did gave me pause, so I couldn't imagine what Ansel would do to someone he planned to really hurt and torture.

"There's a chick at the front desk." His voice pulled my attention. "You can use that pretty-boy long hair of yours to get the room numbers we need."

"So, what? You're my fucking low-budget pimp now?" I asked as a smirk filled my face.

Another chuckle left his throat. "These fucking women around here look at you like you're a fucking god. And you can pull off that whole bad-boy, pretty-boy routine. You used to do that shit in high school. You had chicks thinking you were such a good guy when really, they were sleeping with the damn devil. Look at you. Even now your eyes look all innocent and shit. Me, I'd scare that fucking woman into submission or to death—whichever happens first."

Ansel took a long pause before speaking again, and that devious smile had inched back across his lips.

"But that damn Megan—she ain't scared of my ass. I'm not used to people not being afraid of me, especially not a woman. She has that whole innocent thing down to a science like you, but she has darkness in her. She hides it, but her darkness is as bad as what we carry around. She—"

The seat squeaked as I leaned forward in the truck with a loud huff. "Ansel, can we get back to the fucking subject at hand. We need to concentrate on how we're going to make these motherfuckers tell us where the rest of their crew is located. *If* these are the right motherfuckers."

"Yeah, yeah, yeah... You don't want me thinking about your woman. How fucking hot, she is. Nice tits. Plump ass. Sexy. I heard you two last night too. I bet she—"

"Ansel! Fucking concentrate, man. Get Megan off your fucking mind."

Ansel was getting me agitated on purpose. He thought he was slick. He knew that talking about Megan would get me riled up enough for me to give in to his plan to go into that hotel and torture those men.

He'd done this kind of shit since we were kids. He'd drive me crazy until I gave him what he wanted. In this case, part of what he wanted was Megan, but that shit wasn't happening unless it was over my dead body. Ansel understood as much, but he wouldn't be him if he didn't try to break me anyway.

Crazy thing was, if anything happened to me, Ansel was the only one I'd want Megan with. He knew her background, what she was capable of, and I could already tell that he'd started to care about her enough that he'd keep her safe.

11

AARON

After I'd stuffed my face with Megan's good cooking, we'd retired to our room and showered. As soon as she stepped out of the bathroom, I stopped her as floral scented steam followed her out of the door. My hands roamed her body and the lust in my gaze made words unnecessary.

Megan had heard bits and pieces about what Ansel and I had done with the targets at the hotel. She'd been eyeing me with an inquisitive stare most of the evening.

"What did you do with Ansel today?" she asked, even as her mouth parted and her breathing increased from my hand sliding under her shirt and over one of her warm soft tits.

"We tortured three of DG6's hired guns for information on the whereabouts of the rest of their crew. We need to know where the heads of DG6 are located so we can find and kill them. It's the only way to put an end to this hit they have out on you."

Her face was pinched with enough tension that it appeared she wanted to cry. She had questions to ask me, so many, she didn't know which to ask first.

My lips covered the warm softness of hers before she could spit out a word. She accepted my kiss as I massaged her tongue with mine, making her moan into my mouth. As soon as I removed my lips from hers those tense lines returned to her face.

"Aaron, you can't do this. These people have armies of soldiers who are willing to kill for them. I can't let you go off on some mission that could start a war. I won't!" Megan exclaimed, raising her voice to ensure I understood her stance.

It took everything in me not to laugh at Megan's attempt to raise her voice at me. She was such a quiet woman that it baffled me that she could pull the trigger or stab a man in the heart if she had to. It was her eyes that told her complete story. If Megan actually vocalized half the shit she was thinking, it would probably scare the shit out of people...even *me*.

"Megan, Ansel and I tortured and killed three men for information and left them inside a hotel. Shit has gone too far for us to stop now."

She shook her head, begging me with those sad innocent eyes, not to go any further with our plans. "I don't want anything to happen to you. Please, don't go after these people."

I'd just told her we'd tortured and killed three men, yet she was worried about me getting hurt.

"We were able to confirm the whereabouts of the rest of their crew." I told her as she continued to shake her head at me. A ten-man crew was housed in a two-story, eight-bedroom house in Marshville, a larger town, three counties over.

The house was in the wealthy area of Redwood Pines, so no one would expect it was the safe house of a bunch of hired mercenaries, deployed to take out and kill a woman. The large house posed as the group's hive or temporary operations center according to the information we'd gathered from the men we'd tortured. We were also able to confirm that their orders came directly from DG6 and *Lacey Daniels* was their primary target.

Their information confirmed just about every speculation I'd had about this situation. DG6 had deployed a small army of men because their intel had informed them that Megan was possibly being protected by a large group of armed men—*us*.

The men didn't confirm the exact location of DG6's headquarters or home base. We'd been unable to extract an address from them, which led me to believe they didn't know it. These men were hired guns, that DG6 wasn't going to share their secrets with.

All we could get out any of them was one of the DG6's key locations of an old dude ranch in Texas. The men had spilled their guts before they realized Ansel and I were going to kill them anyway.

Megan stared at me and widened her eyes when I took too long to respond.

"The plan is already in effect. Ansel and I will leave in about six hours, around 2:00 a.m., to recon the place. We can't wait too long. When the guys we murdered today don't check in with their people, they are going to deploy more people here. Keeping them out of Copper County is best for your safety and the MC's. It may take us a day or two to complete this mission, so I'm going to need you to be patient."

Megan's firm stance softened after I placed a tender hand on her hip and relaxed my facial expression. She begged with sad eyes. "Please, Aaron, don't do this. Let me keep running. I know how to hide myself. No one else has to die because of me."

"Do you think I'm going to stand by and let you spend the rest of your life running from these people? That, I will not do. If we don't take a stand against these people, they are going to keep coming at you until they kill you. The fact that DG6 has others doing their dirty work says a lot about them. They have weaknesses and vulnerabilities that we can take advantage of. It's time to make a stand, Megan."

She moved in closer to me and rested her face in my chest before her small arms encircled my waist. My chin rested on the top of her soft hair after I pulled her into a tight embrace. Neither one of us said a word. We relished the feeling of each other's warmth for a minute.

MEGAN

A minute of quiet reflection was all that was going to be had between Aaron and me. All it took was for his hands to slide past my lower back and drop over the globes of my ass. I was up with my legs wrapped around the man's body at the slightest gesture from him.

My lips slid over and between the firm and urgent movements of his. As much as I struggled to drown out my nagging thoughts, they kept tugging at my mind. This could well be the last moment Aaron and I had together, so I had to make it special. I had to find a way to let him know, besides words, that I appreciated him, loved him, and would go to hell for him if I had to.

When he sat us on the bed, I climbed off him before he could get at me. Tonight, I was going to get at him. I tugged his hand after me as I moved us closer to the headboard.

"Just sit back and relax please," I said with a lusty smirk on my face.

Aaron listened to my command and relaxed against the pillows that I'd propped against the headboard behind him. As I undressed him, taking off his T-shirt with slow ease, my fingers brushed his warm skin as his muscles rolled and tensed, responding to my touch.

He had no problem lifting his lower body to allow me to pull down his boxers. His dick was already hard and standing to attention, which made my pussy ache with anticipation.

I smiled; it pleased me to see and know how much he wanted me. I ran my fingers up his muscular thigh while eyeing him, eager to see his reaction to my touch. His gaze rushed up to mine when I bypassed his dick and concentrated higher. My lips massaged his neck first, tasting, teasing and enjoying his warm, smooth flesh.

"Mmm," I exhaled as I let my tongue slide down until my lips wrapped around his tight pink nipple. I bit it, tugging the puckered skin between my teeth. My action pulled a low hiss out of him as he stared.

The desperation in his gaze urged me to keep exploring. By the time my mouth made the slow journey over his tightly pulled abs, I had him in such desperate need, his eyes seemed as though they were screaming the word *please!*

His breath hitched, and his body eased back onto the pillows when I wrapped one of my hands around his dick. I'd finally touched him where he'd needed it most, and it had relaxed him and eased some of the tension I'd been building in him. But I wasn't ready to release him fully. My teeth sank into his muscular thigh, making him jump before I kissed his taut flesh. His nerve endings were likely on fire by now.

My hands massaged up and down his dick with soft strokes, teasing him on purpose as I let my warm breath wash over the head. Precum leaked over my nimble fingers as I massaged upwards then back down with slow wanton ease. The sight of his dick so hard from my deft strokes made my mouth water and had me swallowing rapidly.

"Megan, please," he begged.

I kept my grin hidden but was more than willing to give him what he wanted. It wasn't my intention to take as long as I had, but it couldn't be helped. He had a lot to offer, and I didn't take advantage of his full package as often as I should.

My eager mouth slipped over the swollen head of his dick. My tongue slipped out over the hard softness, anxious to taste the pearl of precum that had leaked out. My eyes slid closed, and a pleasing sigh escaped my throat at the taste of him and the feeling of his hardness filling the space of my mouth.

A throaty moan escaped as his warm juices spread over my tongue. I loved the way he tasted. Cum that I'd tasted before was salty or bitter. Aaron's was sweet and tasty like a special drink that only he possessed.

It took some concentration and slick tongue moves to get his massive dick wet, but I'd accomplished the task. My mouth could only accommodate half of it no matter how far I stuffed it down my throat.

I used my hands to take care of the bottom half. Aaron didn't seem to mind the job I was doing. His chest heaved, and his body stayed in a constant state of tensing and relaxing. His encouraging, lust-filled voice was sweet music to my ears.

"Megan...so good," he heaved out between harsh breaths and gritted teeth. The tone and sound of his voice told me he was on the verge of cumming. Knowing so, I maintained the slow, intense bobbing and sucking that was driving him crazy.

"Fuck. Megan!" he yelled, right before his dick expanded and grew impossibly hard, and the sweet flow of his semen rained over my tongue. I swallowed it without a second thought.

"Fuck, you're swallowing." I vaguely made out his first few strangled words as an avalanche of curse words was released from his mouth. He'd said the same thing the first time I gave him head. Had other women he'd been with let such a sweet substance go to waste? The sight of me swallowing his juices seemed to make more flow from him.

The first time I'd enjoyed the taste of him was during my first two-week stay with him. He'd told me on numerous occasions that he'd enjoyed my blowjob, but I'd not had many other opportunities to go down on him after he'd tracked me down and found me.

We were always so hot for each other that we usually went straight to the point with minimal foreplay. However, I'd garnered some strength tonight and changed up whatever plan he'd had in store. I didn't relinquish his dick until I was sure I'd sucked every drop of his orgasm out of him.

His exceptionally tall body lay spiraled out over the mattress with his eyes closed. He was so relaxed that it appeared he'd fallen asleep until he raised his head and smiled at me. When he rose, his hand went straight to my thigh.

If the way he licked his lips was any indication, he was going to eat my pussy, but I had plans to make this night about him. I shook my head no, and he cocked an eyebrow at me, daring me to stop him.

I hadn't given him much head over our short affair, but I'd lost count of the number of times he'd had his mouth and tongue buried in my pussy. The man could eat pussy as good as he could fuck, so I ensured I pulled a pillow next to me, because he was going to have me screaming the roof off this safe house.

It was bad enough the house had likely overheard his name yelled repeatedly hundreds of times over. If the damn headboard knocking against the wall wasn't enough, they'd likely overheard him telling me that I had the best pussy in the world and me telling him I was addicted to his dick.

Aaron didn't give a damn about what anyone overheard, but the notion that others could hear us was embarrassing to me. It's funny, but I didn't seem to think about being embarrassed until after our sexual acts were over.

It likely hadn't been five minutes since he'd buried his face between my thighs, and I was already screaming and coming undone as my body shot off to another galaxy. My fingers tightened, gripping his hair as I rode a high so damn addictive, I'd do anything for it.

His tongue lapped up my juices as I lost my mind. He'd injected me with a drug that only he knew how to produce. A drug that literally melted my bones. My blood sparked with pure satisfaction as it coursed through my veins and relaxed my body.

Once I regained the ability to breathe normally, my eyes followed

Aaron's movement as he scooted back to the head of the bed with his back against the headboard. A wide grin filled my lips as I forced my body to roll to the side and follow him.

His hand sat at his side as his gaze worked its way over my body while I was making my approach. Our eyes locked, and the lust in his heavy gaze made my insides quiver with the anticipation of what was to come. The look alone was enough to speed up my recovery of him turning me into a puddle atop the mattress.

Aaron kept his legs splayed wide, which meant even wider for me. His massive dick welcomed me with a few stiff and waving bobs. My hand glided into his palm as he assisted me in climbing aboard, taking my hand as if he were seating me at an elegantly-set table. I didn't go straight for the prize, but it made its presence known by falling against my stomach with a fleshy smack.

I devoured Aaron's mouth, licking, sucking, and nibbling his lips. The man tasted better than drinking water on a hot and humid day, and he made me thirsty enough to drink an ocean. His fresh soapy scent and masculine aroma invigorated my senses and made me want to linger in his presence that much more.

If something happened to Aaron on this crazy mission he and his cousin were intent on going on, I honestly didn't know what would become of me. I'd proven that I wasn't brave enough to kill myself, so my only other option would be to turn myself over to DG6 and let them do whatever they had plans to do to me. I'd never been this obsessed with anyone or anything. I couldn't explain us any more than I was sure Aaron could.

Even now, I considered turning myself in if it would help to keep Aaron out of harm's way. He had no idea the dumb shit I was willing to do if it would keep him safe. The idea of something bad happening turned my firm kiss into a soft, emotion-laced one. Aaron noticed.

Carefully placed palms cupped my face as his gaze bore into mine, the depth of his love shining through. I vocalized what I saw mirrored in his gaze.

"I love you, Aaron. Please don't go on this mission in the morning," I begged, the pleading in my tone was apparent as I fought to hold back the stinging tears that started to pool in my eyes.

Aaron didn't hide the way our connection affected him. He stared intently into my eyes, his face pinched with a mixture of confusion and understanding. "I love you too," he replied softly. The unrestrained emotion behind his declaration reached into my chest and swallowed my heart before it caressed my soul.

When our feelings grew beyond anything we could control, he covered my lips with his and eased his tongue into my mouth. All it took was his hot tongue and his hands palming my ass for my juices to unfreeze and start flowing again. The sensual exploration of his tongue mingling with mine made me forget how to inhale.

My emotions married my lust and our kiss deepened as Aaron assisted in raising me up higher on my knees. I unclamped my right hand from around his neck and let it slip between us.

Hard rippling abs brushed the back of my hand as it slid down and around his glorious hard and throbbing dick. The anticipation had my hand trembling when I aligned his dick with my dripping wet folds.

The moment I started to slide down on it, all concerns of him chasing down assassins and DG6 disappeared. The only thing that filled my mind was Aaron and how well he ignited my senses. The slow and steady rhythm kept my body humming with lust-fulfilling excitement.

We broke the kiss, only to catch our breaths. I rested my forehead against his. This session between us was great, it was wonderful, but it was also different. Our emotions were involved this time—the weight of them mixing with our desire. How we'd managed to keep such strong passion at bay was a mystery to me. Now, it flowed over us, through us, all around us like a new sense that we'd created together.

The few times before when love had made its presence known, we'd managed to pretend that it wasn't there. Now, that we'd professed those three sacred words to each other, and accepted that they'd been spoken in sincere truth, our connection had grown even stronger.

My mind and body overflowed with different emotions, making me fight for every breath I took. I didn't know if I was coming or going. My body was on autopilot as I continued to ride Aaron, sheathing him deep inside me. The pressure of the deep penetration was too much but not enough at the same time, verging on pain, but brimming with overpowering pleasure, emotionally driven, but physically intense.

When tears started to leak from my eyes, I knew we'd surpassed our norm. Aaron must have spotted those wet telling drops because his thumb brushed under my eyelid and over my cheek before he took my lips and made me swallow my quivering breaths.

When I was certain my body and mind couldn't take anymore, the tension in my belly tightened, and my body started to tingle. Forced to break the kiss, I had to scream or yell out to expel some of the emotion and pleasure that had engulfed me and filled my body to near bursting. My pace increased, and Aaron's big hands palmed my ass, spreading my cheeks as he urged me to ride him faster.

"Oh my God. Aaron!" I yelled, breathless. Repeatedly, those same words tumbled past my lips. They were the only words my mind had latched on to that I was able to squeeze past my constricting throat. If the men in the house hadn't known it before, they knew it now. Aaron was the deity I prayed to repeatedly.

He thrust his hips upwards, sending his dick impossibly deep inside me. This was usually the point where I sped up my rotating hips. This time, however, I slowed my pace and let the magic consume me right before I was yanked down into the next world.

My eyebrows tightened over my squeezed-shut eyes that had rolled to the back of my head. My lips fell apart, but my words got lodged in my throat. I had a death grip around Aaron's neck as I continued to rock my body against his, chasing the sensations that pounded hard inside me and grew in their thundering intensity. My eager body matched the urgency of his hips as he drove faster and harder.

I wasn't the one who bit into Aaron when the pleasure was too much for me to handle. This time, he bit into my shoulder, the pressure of his bite unexplainably adding to my satisfaction. He groaned in pleasured delight with every powerful thrust that met my grinding rotations.

"Megan." My name fell from his mouth. "Sorry," he said, before he kissed the area he'd bitten, unaware that I enjoyed the sweet ache.

12

MEGAN

The dewy grass kissed the bottom of my bare feet as I stood outside Ansel's truck, clinging to Aaron. Thick and heavy clouds hid the moon and added a deeper layer of darkness to the early-morning sky.

I could see neighboring porch lights on in the distance, but the numbing silence around us let us know the rest of the world was at rest. I had a bad feeling that I couldn't shake, even as Aaron whispered encouraging words into my ear. Although I was confident in his ability to take care of himself, the nagging darkness that loomed over me wouldn't leave.

"Don't worry. I'll be fine," he whispered into my hair as his lips sought my neck. "Besides, I've got my crazy cousin watching my back."

As if on cue, Ansel walked up. "Break this shit up. Megan, you have nothing to worry about. I'm here."

Ansel's arrogant words put a smile on my face and gave me the courage I needed to ease up the tight hold I had on Aaron. I was acting as if I was never going to see him again. He squeezed me and kissed my forehead before he stepped back.

My heart sank as I took one last look at him and turned away.

Once I made it back inside the house, I knew what was going to happen. I'd do nothing but bite my nails, worry, and attempt to shake the agonizing chill of doom that had crept right back onto my shoulders.

"So, I can't get a hug or a "thank you." I mean I'm about to face whatever the hell this chump over here is about to face too." Ansel's words were aimed at my back.

I turned around to face him, unable to hide the smile that had crept onto my lips. Ansel stood next to Aaron, looking like his brother. He lifted an eyebrow, waiting for me to answer his question.

"Well?" he said to me before he glanced at the side of Aaron's head. I glanced at Aaron too. I'd already hurt him by sleeping with his father and not telling him. Therefore, I didn't even want to look at another man, especially now that we'd established such a strong mutual connection.

A playful eye roll and a sigh left Aaron as he nodded his head in my direction. Ansel must have noticed Aaron's gesture because his smile spread wider before he threw out both his muscular arms, inviting me into his hold.

I stepped forward, anxious—almost afraid. I went up on my toes and reached my arms up to capture Ansel's neck. Next thing I knew, I went flying into his hard chest—full body-against-body contact. A sharp gasp left my mouth as he squeezed me to him and held me in place. His arms were wrapped around me so tightly that I couldn't release the sharp breath he'd made me inhale.

Although I was a bit disoriented, my arms still managed to tighten around his neck and shoulders. I tried to back away, when the hug lasted longer than it should have, but I wasn't strong enough to get away from the tornado named Ansel. When his face drew closer to mine, I dropped my head to avoid his lips.

When I was released, it took only a second for me to realize it was Aaron who had torn me out of Ansel's tight grip.

The teasing smirk on Ansel's face as I stood staring at him in wide-eyed shock said he'd had every intention of kissing me. The smile on Aaron's face as he shook his head at his cousin eased some of my tension. Although Aaron had a smile on his face, his eyes told another story. I believed he'd do his cousin harm if he tried to take things too far with me.

"Please be careful," I forced out. The words rushed out of my mouth as my gaze volleyed between them both. Before I took the final steps, I needed to take towards the house, my gaze landed on Aaron's and locked. The lump that formed in my throat wasn't one I could swallow. I forced my legs to turn my body and carry me away before he saw the tears that had started to sting my eyes. Not even Ansel's shocking hug had subdued the ache that squeezed my heart at Aaron's departure.

When I turned the knob and pushed the front door open, I heard Aaron tell Ansel, "I'm going to kick your ass. Keep your hands off my woman."

Hearing them laugh was a good sign, considering what they were likely about to face. Their laughter was the last pleasant sound I heard before I closed the door behind me. I stood against the inside of the front door, listening as the roar of Ansel's truck faded with each passing second.

Just when I thought things couldn't get any worse, Shark walked into the living room. He stood in the doorway that led into the kitchen and stared at me as tears streamed down my cheeks. The flow had started, so there was no stopping them now, so I didn't bother wiping them away.

"He's going to be all right. All you need to do is believe in him. Believe that no matter what happens, he'll find a way to come back." Shark nodded his head once to ensure I understood his words.

I bit into my quivering bottom lip, trying but failing to stop the flow of my tears and the tremble that had started in my body. As soon as I nodded my head towards Shark, he turned and left me there. I assumed Shark hated me, but I was starting to find that when it came to these men and this MC, I'd grossly underestimated them at every turn.

My head leaned back and against the front door before I pushed my body forward and headed towards the bedroom that Aaron and I shared. Aaron hadn't left me without company. I bunked with a PK380 pistol to the right side of the bed and a Beretta to the left. Aaron was sure that the safe house was safe, but the unease that plagued my body had me sitting in the middle of the bed staring up at the shadows that waved along the dark ceiling.

13

AARON

The hardest thing I'd ever seen or done was witnessing my younger brother Ryan's death and standing by helplessly as he was being lowered into the ground at his funeral. Now, I had another to add to my list of hardest things.

Leaving Megan took it out of me. I understood why she was worried. I was more worried about her if something happened to me than I was worried about death. Although I was a tad confident, I wasn't as arrogant about facing deadly situations as my cousin was. Any number of circumstances could occur that would send death in our direction.

Although I was willing to do what was necessary to stay alive, I accepted the fact that I had no control over it. My only concern at this point was leaving Megan to face this harsh life alone. This was a new experience for me. I never used to think about dying or how it would affect anyone until I met Megan. Now that I had someone to live for, it appeared death lurked at every corner of my life.

Ansel must have noticed my solemn mood because he didn't tease or taunt me during the hour-long drive to James County. Instead, we talked strategy and how best to handle the situation without getting ourselves killed. That we were both ex-military was a plus. It meant we knew how these guys thought and how they would react to an attack.

It took us hours of searching the spotted patches of thick woods behind the targeted house to find a good spot to park Ansel's truck.

Thankfully, the house was situated in an area where the nearest neighbor sat about a mile down the partially-wooded road. I'd assumed the place was in some type of subdivision, but the large homes clearly belonged to owners that could afford to buy hundreds of acres of land. The space was congested with fat pine trees, their barks bore a reddish tint, giving the area its name: Redwood Pines.

Between Ansel's duffle bag and mine, we had enough weaponry and firepower to take out a small military installation. I'd brought my grenade launcher, and Ansel had brought a damn 50 Cal machine gun.

Who did he think we were fighting, Al Qaeda? I didn't have much room to judge my cousin's choice in weaponry, though. Since I'd essentially started a war in those woods with DG6 and their operatives, I suppose we had unconsciously planned for one.

It had taken some swift maneuvering, but we'd gotten the truck through the congestion of the dense woods. There were a few areas where we'd had to exit the truck and cut a path through the woods.

We'd even re-mapped the path to mark our way and ensure we had a good understanding of how to get out of the woods swiftly if things went sideways. Ansel maneuvered his truck over large ruts and dips until we made it to within a quarter mile of the target location.

The house stood large and stately enough to be classified as a mansion. Its dark bricks stood strong, covering two levels that reared over a pool in the backyard and supported a three-car garage. If DG6 could afford to put their hired guns up in a place this nice, I'd like to see how they treated their bosses.

The gangbangers that had DG6 tatted all over their bodies were nothing more than a bunch of untrained foot soldiers and were likely why the leaders of the gang had opted to use mercenaries to take care of what they'd deemed serious business.

I found it difficult to believe that they had sent an army of men after a five-foot-five, barely over a hundred-pound woman. Well, I take that back. I could understand them upping their efforts to capture or kill Megan. She had killed an original member of their gang as well as the gang member's nephew and wife, so they weren't going to stop until she was dead.

She'd also managed to elude the group on her own for nearly a decade, which proved she was fully capable of taking care of herself and worthy of their efforts. But, Megan had me on her side now, and I was determined to put an end to the threat that constantly loomed over her life.

"D, what you got for me?" I asked after my phone rang only once. I put the phone on speaker and sat it on the tailgate of the truck so Ansel and I could listen.

"Knox, you have your laptop up?" I had no idea why D had insisted upon me bringing a laptop, but I was curious to find out. "I sent you the blueprints of the house," he explained.

"I've also tapped into a satellite near your location, and it'll get us a peek inside the house by allowing me to tap into other digital devices."

"No shit!" Ansel said before I could respond to D's statement. I'd introduced Ansel to D over the phone so they'd know each other's voices and so that Ansel could listen in on whatever updates D discussed.

"No shit," D answered Ansel back with a chuckle. "Watch this."

My laptop sat on the tailgate next to the phone. D took control of it remotely, and with a few clicks, he had an aerial map of the area we were in on the screen. He zoomed in tight enough that roofs of houses started to come into view. Since it was after six in the morning, the sun had chased away the darkness, allowing us to clearly see what D was showing us.

As soon as the house we targeted came into view, D zoomed in close enough for us to see the guard standing inside a small guard shack near the front gate. D spied so close in fact that we could see the guard place a cigarette up to his lips and take a drag from it.

When D hijacked the camera on the guard's smartphone that was sitting someplace behind him, we were that much closer. We actually saw the ingrown hairs on the back of the man's neck.

The shit was something straight out of a damn spy film. I'd known D for over seven years, had deployed with him, had slept in a foxhole with him, and had killed enemy forces with him. However, I'd never gotten used to the amazing shit he could do with a computer.

More spying showed us guards on either side of the house and one in the backyard. Ansel and I stood in wide-eyed shock at what we were seeing. D had been able to do this type of surveillance in the military because we had top-secret clearances that gave us access to technology and devices we weren't supposed to be able to touch as regular civilians.

The crunch of nearby twigs breaking caused Ansel and I to draw our weapons and aim in the direction of the noise almost immediately. The clicks of our weapons caused the surrounding woods to grow eerily quiet. The moment Ansel and I holstered our weapons, D asked, "Everything all right in your neck of the woods?"

"Yeah. It's a fucking rabbit hopping his happy, little ass around. He was about a second from getting his ass blown off."

D laughed at Ansel's comment before he returned to giving us live views and angles of the property we were planning to infiltrate. Just like he'd said he would do, D adjusted the zoom close enough to one of the unobstructed windows to allow us a view of the inside of the house. He tapped into a few devices, a smart television, a few smartphones, and a laptop that gave us close-up snapshots of our enemies' faces.

We counted three contractors sitting around a large table eating breakfast and talking, likely discussing their assignment. We didn't have audio, so we were left attempting to decode their words. Another guy sat on a couch, flipping through the channels on a large-screen television mounted on the wall.

We couldn't see anything through any of the top windows, and D had been unable to connect to any devices that could sneak us a peek. However, we got a peek at the top of the stairs and a small piece of the hall on one of the two upstairs wings.

We'd also taken a trip down the hall on the first floor. One of the first-floor bedrooms was being used as a possible surveillance room, but there was nothing in the room that D was able to connect to that allowed us a look inside.

"How long do we have this feed?" I asked D. "I want to study these motherfuckers and the blueprints."

"You'll have this feed for as long as you need it. Believe it or not, it was easier hijacking this satellite than it is to get into the lowest level NSA encryptions."

I didn't want to know the kind of national security violations D was breaking or was involved in.

"I appreciate this, man," I said, my words edging out quickly because I hated any type of sentimentality. Megan was the only person who could somehow drag any emotional shit out of me.

"Yeah, man. We appreciate this shit," Ansel repeated. "My cousin didn't tell me he had high-level contacts like you on speed dial."

"No problem. Happy to help." D chuckled. "Knox, remember if you need me, just give me a call. I counted at least twelve in that house the first time I scanned it. There could be more."

Although I knew D couldn't see me do it, I nodded my head.

"If shit gets bad. You know what to do, D."

I'd filled D in on every aspect of Megan's story and my feelings for her. Well, except for the personal shit like our explosive sex life, but D knew about as much as Ansel did. If shit went bad, D would link up with Ansel to keep Megan safe. If both Ansel and I perished, D knew where the safe house was.

"Yep. Later, Knox."

"Later, D."

I didn't have to glance up from my monitor to know that Ansel's glare was upside my head.

"What?" I asked, not bothering to lift my gaze to his.

"Motherfucker, I knew the military put you into some black-ops shit, but you didn't tell me you were connected like this. Your man highjacked a fucking satellite and was talking about NSA encryptions and shit."

I waved Ansel's comments away. He used to be a damn ranger, so I knew with a great degree of certainty he had as many, if not *more* connections than I did.

Also, two of the men who had traveled from California with him were his ranger buddies, Scott and Marcus. I hadn't missed the matching tattoos on their arms, which told me they all used to be in the same squad. Ansel had introduced them to me the day he'd arrived, but I hadn't seen them since.

After D had shown us what was inside the house we targeted, Ansel contacted Scott and Marcus, and they had agreed to join us. They were likely already on the road heading in our direction. With them on the way, we would be four trained killers versus two, which meant this party was likely going to be a bloody one.

14

AARON

Scott and Marcus arrived a little after nine o'clock that morning. The tailgate of Ansel's truck had become our operation's center.

We'd laid low most of the day, studying our targets. We'd lost the satellite feed a few times, but D had gotten it back for us. Shit, he may as well have been our fifth man. When we were studying the targets and figuring out a way into the house, he entertained our concerns and made suggestions.

I, as well as Ansel, had packed a bedroll and his men didn't have to be told to do the same. However, I did recall Ansel telling one of the men on the phone to make sure he brought Tina. I assumed Tina was an object, but when I asked Ansel about Tina, he remained tight-lipped and kept a huge smile on his face.

We'd studied the people in the house and the blueprints for hours. We took advantage of the satellite feed to spy on and get real-time accounts of the activities taking place inside the house. The all-male crew mostly lounged around, but there was one thing—the most important thing—we noticed. None of them were too far out of arm's reach of a weapon. The men who surrounded and guarded the perimeter of the house were a part of the crew. They took turns guarding the place, rotating every six hours like they expected to be attacked.

The nearest neighbors were about a mile or more away, which was good news because we didn't have to worry about collateral damage. If the nearest neighbor heard the distant sound of gunfire, hopefully, we'd have completed our mission and disappeared before the authorities arrived.

Speaking of the mission, our aim for this one was to obtain the grid coordinates or some type of a geographic location for DG6 other than a dude ranch in Texas. The man Ansel had tortured at The Copper Grand Hotel revealed that the last two original members of the gang frequented the ranch and that some of their family lived there. Two out of three of the men we'd tortured informed us that there was another DG6 heavy hitter that hung out at the location in Texas as well.

The concept of taking out the leaders in this gang and making it crumble from the top was a far better plan than picking off the little guys. However, we had to find these infamous leaders first, preferably, the one sending groups of men to hunt Megan.

As the sun started to retreat, Scott offered to run a recon on the house of mercenaries to find out if there was anything we could have missed using the blueprints and our spying eye in the sky. I didn't understand the extent of what Scott was offering until Ansel explained it.

"When he says recon, he means all the way in, up the stairs, down the stairs, and throughout the house."

I glanced at Scott with a questioning gaze. He was over six-feet with a medium build—a big ass target, so how he planned to do what Ansel had suggested was beyond me. Like D, Scott looked harmless, but if he could do what Ansel was saying, he was as dangerous as my cousin.

Often, I found myself in situations where I had to be stealthy, but to get into a house filled with contract killers and snoop around was on another level. To do it with cameras and motion detectors surrounding the place was going to make the man a magician.

"I know what you're thinking, Aaron, and the answer is yes. He's *that* good," Ansel assured as a sneaky smile crept across Scott's face.

"I've seen this fool slink in and out of so many enemy camps that I've lost count. Then, he'd come back with a map and detailed descriptions of anything or anyone that might have been a threat to us."

I glanced at Scott again.

"Do you guys even know why we're doing this? Do you even know why we are about to engage a group of mercenaries that we're probably going to torture and kill?"

Scott and Marcus said the same thing—that they were there to help Ansel. I didn't have to be a psychologist to see that these men craved violence, maybe even lived for it. They were also loyal to my cousin and were possibly the same caliber of crazy as him. I guess it was the same thing D was willing to do for me. If I called D, Dax, Gavin, or Luke, they'd be willing to jump into the fray, and I'd do the same for either of them in return.

Scott agreed to go on his recon mission a little after 7:00 p.m. When he returned an hour later with details on the location of guns, where everyone slept, and confirmation that D had been right about twelve members, I was floored. And it took a lot to floor me.

Scott had been able to locate and cut the feed that triggered the motion lights. He'd been able to get into the surveillance room and had gotten a few glimpses at what the cameras saw around the house, finding us a few extra blind spots. He'd been reluctant to manipulate the devices because he was a reconnaissance expert, not a tech guru like D. Earlier, D had attempted to manipulate the cameras and motion detectors, but the technology of the security equipment had been too much for the satellite technology to overcome.

We studied the information Scott had provided along with the live feed. By ten o'clock, we'd all pulled out our bedrolls or whatever we intended to sleep on and were resting. We decided the best time, like we'd been trained, was to strike around 2 a.m. while the crew was relaxed and most of them would be asleep.

With my sleeping bag spread out on the hood of Ansel's truck, I stared up at the stars glistening beyond the fluttering leaves of the trees surrounding us. Megan was the last thing on my mind before I started to drift.

15

AARON

When my eyes popped open at Ansel attempting to pull my sleeping bag from under me, I had my gun aimed at his head before he got his sneaky fingers around the edge of it. He threw up both hands with a devilish grin on his face when he caught sight of my weapon. The darkness lurking in the woods around us was alive. Its lingering silence pressed down on me, making me more aware of my surroundings.

"Just seeing if married life has softened you up, that's all," Ansel added. I couldn't see him clearly, but I could tell there was amusement all over his face. I didn't think either of us had ever been in a committed relationship before. My affair with Megan was the longest relationship I'd ever had. Ansel didn't have relationships. He had subs that he either broke or dismissed when they couldn't keep up with his demanding lifestyle.

Shoving my gun down the back of my pants, I rose. "I have never been nor will I ever be *soft*."

Ansel stood watching as I slid from his hood. The dim lighting didn't hide the fact that a grin was still on his face. "You know, cousin, I was wondering what's going to happen to you when Megan leaves you for me."

I shot a deadly glare over at him, but I was sure he caught my shadowy smile. "That will happen over my dead body," I said with certainty.

"You sound sure of yourself, cousin. I mean, I'll be torn up over your death, but what I'll be gaining..." Ansel threw his hands behind his head and stared upwards, being his usual crazy self.

Ansel was joking now, but in a few minutes, he was about to turn into a fucking monster—a rabid-ass dog with razor-sharp teeth that was a motherfucker to control. I walked past my cousin and headed to the back of his truck.

Scott and Marcus were back there strapping themselves into equipment. We mostly used the moonlight to prepare ourselves so there was minimal light from our flashlights. The scene reminded me of the way we had prepped for the deadly missions we went on when I was in the military.

The small tin of black camo I'd taken from my cargo pocket made its way around the group as I proceeded to strap my holster around my waist and leg. One of my pistols went into the belt around my waist, and the other went into the holster around my leg. I even had a backup piece strapped to my lower leg at the rim of my boots.

Ansel walked up as I was putting on my Kevlar vest. He watched me with a knowing smile on his face as I inspected my combat knife and sheathed it.

"You brought Tina?" he asked Marcus. The big smile on Marcus' face insinuated that he had.

Marcus strategically lowered his head where I noticed the tip of a big metal box sticking out from the bottom of the back of Ansel's truck. Ansel lifted the box and sat it on the tailgate. The box landed with a heavy thud. Dust flew up from the area he sat the box in, causing me to fan flying particles away from my face.

When Ansel opened the box, I smiled. Tina was a damn sniper rifle. The rifle he'd used while he was in the military was named Tammy, which was the same exact model as Tina who was the obvious replacement for Tammy after Ansel had returned to the life of a civilian.

Ansel stood there under the light of the moon putting the weapon together. The distinct sound of metal slipping and sliding into metal grooves and slats was the only sound that coursed through the air. When Ansel slid the receiver back and attached the drum of bullets, I knew he meant business. He'd told me that he and each member of his ranger team were qualified as expert marksmen.

My rifle sat dismantled in my duffle on the back of Ansel's truck. I hadn't given it a name, and I'd had it for three years. I was good enough to own a sniper rifle, but I hadn't immersed myself enough as a rifleman to consider myself a true sniper. I was more of an in-your-face kind of killer.

Ansel placed his mouth to the side of Tina's pistol grip. "I'm handing you over to Marcus, but don't worry, baby, Daddy's coming back." He kissed the treasured weapon.

Each of us slid our listening devices into our ears so we could communicate with each other. We went through a series of mic checks to ensure everyone had a functioning device. After we went over the plan once more, we were finally ready.

Ansel glanced over at Marcus and Tina. "Take care of my baby, Marcus, because I know she's going to take care of us."

Marcus nodded his head before lifting Tina and walking away, allowing the darkness to swallow them.

After D confirmed he'd found a way to somehow blind the cameras, the rest of us prepared to go in. In all black tactical gear, our faces smeared in black camo, and hidden by the darkness of night, we were virtually invisible.

Geared up, we were ready for just about anything. We gave each other a once over, not moving anything except our eyes. We'd said all that needed to be said with a glance. We each flipped the night gear over our eyes and the low whirr blended with the sound of chirping insects and animals calling in the distance.

Ansel gladly took point as Scott and I followed. He'd glared at me when I'd suggested he take point. If there was one thing I'd learned over the years was that any effective leader had to know how to follow. *Who was I kidding with that canned bullshit?* The only reason Ansel was leading me anywhere was because I knew he could.

A flood of memories hit my brain, making a smile inch across my lips because this mission felt eerily familiar to my days in the military. At the edge of the fence-line in the backyard of the property, Ansel's upward fist stopped us in our tracks. It was funny because we'd been in two different branches of the military, but an upward fist was all it took to not only jerk me out of my memories but to also stop me in my tracks and put me in attack mode.

Ansel called Scott forward. Scott had rigged the fence so that three of the standing wooden boards swung up enough that it would allow us entry and not look tampered with. Scott easily found the boards and lifted them so we could pass through and enter the backyard.

Once inside, we low crawled closer to the back of the house and pool area. There was a large light attached to the back of the house that illuminated a portion of the backyard, but not enough to keep us out.

Viewing the yard area on my computer had been misleading. The area was massive. It felt like we'd been crawling towards that house for hours. The low-cut grass cushioned our knees and elbows and gave off a low crinkle that mingled with our accelerated breathing.

By the time we reached the area near the pool where the motion lights should have come on, I swiped at a sheen of sweat that had pooled on my forehead. It was a sign that I wasn't in as good a shape as I'd once been.

Ansel directed our eyes to the guard as he made his approach from the opposite side of the house from us. He walked uncaringly through the light, unknowingly blinding himself to us. He must have left his area to use the restroom or switch out duty with another guard because we should have encountered him much sooner than now.

We'd hidden in a patch of darkness outside the light shining from the back of the house. The man passed only feet away from our boots, as we lay flat on the grass near the pool.

Ansel signed to us that he was going to take out the guard. Scott hadn't initiated any type of aggression on his earlier recon because any slip up on his part could have started a premature war without us there to back him up. However, this time, we were ready to do whatever was necessary to take out our adversaries and to obtain the information we sought that could eventually help us find our true enemy—DG6.

Ansel moved with the stealth of a black panther creeping up behind the man like a moving shadow. Scott and I remained in place, prone on the ground. First, we heard a muffled groan of agony, then, the distinct *thump* of a body hitting the ground.

Within seconds, Ansel was back in front of us, gesturing for us to follow him with the guard's weapon shoved down the back of his pants. Once we made it around the pool, he directed both Scott and me to the east.

Taking out the man on the east side of the house had been quick work for me. He never saw me coming and was permanently asleep before his body hit the ground.

"Target two out. East clear," I spoke quietly but knew that I was being heard in the tiny mics that were linked with Ansel, Scott, and Marcus.

"Target one down. West clear," Ansel informed the group.

I hadn't heard Scott traveling behind me nor had I heard him pass me, but less than ten seconds later I heard, "Target three out. Front clear," Scott confirmed. He'd taken out the man inside the small brick guard shack so he could take control of it.

"Outside perimeter clear," Marcus added. His voice was broadcasted with a scratchy quality to it since he was the furthest away from the rest of us.

"Enter at will," Ansel commanded.

I was set to enter through a side window, Ansel was going straight through the front door, and Scott was our eyes out front. He'd taken up a position inside the guard shack near the northwest front of the house. Marcus and Tina were out laying in the darkness watching from the front northeast.

After I used a glasscutter to make two fist-size holes in the window, I stuck my hand through the first hole to cut the alarm feed before reaching into the second hole to unlock the window.

Ansel must have taken the keys from the downed guard because I watched him from my dark corner inside the house as he unlocked the door and walked in like he owned the place. He'd taken out the light over the front door, but the larger light, like the one in the backyard, kept watch over most of the front yard. D and Scott hadn't been unable to cut those specific front and back lights. They must have been wired and controlled from within the house somewhere. The alarm hadn't sounded. Apparently, Ansel had deactivated that as well.

The sleeping mercenary on the couch had no idea that we'd gained access and the house was no longer safe. The rest of the crew must have been asleep as well. Ansel glanced in my direction, knowing from our plan where I should have been. The guard on the couch started to stir, turning his body towards Ansel who stood right above him.

Ansel lifted his arm up high and stiffened his hand into a knife-hand, which came crashing down on the back of the man's neck. A loud fleshy *crack* sounded and was followed up by a deflated *huff* from the man. From my angle, it appeared Ansel had chopped through the man's neck with his hand, but I knew he'd hit the switch on his neck that would knock him out.

With the temporary threat taken out, we split up and swept the house, seeking out mercenaries and looking for information that would lead us to DG6. The clap of weapons firing echoed in my ear, alerting me that one or more of our team members was engaged in a gunfight. With the earpiece in my ear, it was hard to tell if the sound came from the inside or outside of the house.

I tiptoed up the stairs, a mixture of moonlight and the outside front light illuminating my path. There was a dim light in the hallway I crept closer to, but I didn't hear any sounds. Just as most of my body cleared the stairs and I leaned forward to peek down the hall, a bullet sailed past my head and lodged into the wall on the side of me. The bastard or bastards on that wing had been waiting for me. We'd been careful up until this point and had followed our plan emphatically. What had alerted them that we were even in the house?

After running up the last few steps, I dived across the hall, landing in a small nook that kept more incoming bullets from piercing my body. My scuffling to dodge bullets had left me without control of my body as I came out of my rolling dive and collided into the wall. In my ears, my crashing body sounded like thunder had boomed inside the house.

I pushed myself up to a standing position, making my body hug and kiss the wall as bullets tunneled their way through wood and plaster next to me. The nook I'd heaved my body into contained a door that I found locked.

From studying the feed and blueprints that D had gotten us access to, this should have been the maintenance closet. D and Scott's information meant I knew the areas of this hall like the back of my hand. The indentured entryway I stood in was the only thing keeping a bullet out of my body.

The mercenary actively shooting at me was using a silencer on his weapon. His actions and my body slamming into the wall had likely awakened the others in the remaining two bedrooms on the corridor.

My ear was alive with the sounds of constant weapons' blasts. Each location had a distinct echo, indicating that more than one from our team was engaged in a shootout.

A quick peek around the edge of the wood showed me a glimpse of the shooter standing behind the cracked bedroom door with his gun sticking out of it. I also caught a glimpse of the dim hallway light that I needed to kill.

It hadn't even taken a minute before one set of bullets had turned into two sets. The angry slugs ate at the edge of the wood protecting me. When the bullets stop flying for a second, I chanced a quick peek, reached my hand around the corner and released a few shots from my own silenced pistol.

My first shot took out the hallway light and left the hall in shadows of bouncing light. I dropped my night vision goggles over my eyes and flipped them on. The only sound at this point was harsh breathing and bullets thumping and pounding into wood. As soon as I was rewarded with a second paused moment, I peeked around the splintered wood and fired off three quick shots.

A loud cry and the unmistakable sound of a body colliding into a wall let me know I'd hit one of the mercenaries. I waited until the barrage of retaliating bullets that came at me slowed. When the bullets paused again, and I heard the familiar clinks that indicated that at least one was reloading his weapon. I took the opportunity to sneak another peek around the corner.

After taking a good aim at one of the cracked doors, I fired. The kick of the pistol in my hand was followed by a loud yell. "Fuck! I'm hit." It was another of the assassins yelling from one of the rooms further down the hall.

"Yes, at least three maybe four. Hurry!" The man spoke urgently into a device. I couldn't see that bastard, but I heard him. I flipped the night gear to thermal imaging and caught a glimpse of two heat signatures. Incoming bullets sent me back and kept me pinned against the wall I was hiding behind. I tried to look around the bend of the wall again and nearly got my head blown off as the whirl of hot lead flew past me.

I spoke in as clear a voice as I could and alerted the team. "They are calling for backup. Grab a hostage and abort mission."

The punch of un-silenced shots going off in another part of the house alerted me that Ansel had his hands as full as mine were.

"Scott, get in here," Ansel demanded in a strained voice. It sounded like he'd been injured.

When I felt the coldness of a chill inching up my spine, I instinctively turned and fired at one of the men creeping up the stairs. The bullet landed in his skull and slung him over the side railing of the staircase. His body smacked into the ceramic tiled floor below.

I needed to get out of this damn nook because this mission was blown. These motherfuckers hadn't all been asleep like we'd assumed or they may have had some other form of alerts or monitors that we'd missed. We'd taken down four upon entry. There were two down on my wing and the one I'd shot on the stairs. Ansel was handling some on his end, and we had no idea how close their backup was.

Since bullets had stopped flying in my direction, I took three deep breaths and walked out of the nook I'd been pinned in. Relying solely on my body armor for protection, I prayed the enemy wouldn't get off a headshot on me.

My first three shots went flying towards the first cracked door my eyes landed on. I didn't have to wait around to know that I'd put a bullet into the person waiting there. A portion of his body prone on the floor behind the half-open door was visible. I dropped my empty clip and fed my pistol a new one before I fired rapid shots at both doors further down the hall.

Since the doors were across the hall from each other, I swiveled my body, shooting back and forth between them. The fact that no bullets were flying back at me meant that any occupants were either dead or had fled further into the room.

I sent two shots into the door behind me and kicked in the door in front of me. The room appeared empty, which meant that the occupant of the room had fled out the window or had been some-place else inside the house.

The splayed body behind the last door on the hall belonged to the one who had called for backup. After a quick check, I saw that he'd been speaking into his cell phone. I didn't know if the backup group was five or thirty minutes out. I left the hall and ran back down the stairs.

16

AARON

A limping mercenary captured my attention as soon as I'd cleared the bottom of the stairs. I aimed, prepared to blow the man's head off his shoulders, but he held his hands up high.

"I'm unarmed," he grumbled. His annoyance at being captured was evident in his angry tone. Good. This meant he could be the hostage we needed to get information out of. Our main goal was to find out the location or locations of DG6's bosses. We needed to find the person or persons in charge of running the organization. They were who had the authority to take the hit off Megan's head.

These guys were just the bastards who'd agreed to work for DG6. I landed a quick strike to the back of the unarmed man's head and propped his limp body up against the wall. I tugged the plastic tails of each of the set of zip ties I'd applied around his hands and feet to bound them. Anyone from our team who saw him sitting against the wall in this manner would know he was not to be killed.

A popping noise called my attention towards the dark hallway of the first-floor wing. Pulling my night goggles down over my eyes, I crept into the darkness with my gun ready. Our four-man team should have been heading back to our base of operation by now, but the silence in my ear lurked there like a spying person.

There was no way in hell I was leaving without my cousin. I'd called into my mic twice for Ansel with no return answer. He was either dead or actively engaged. A quick sweep showed me that my cousin had taken out the two on the first-floor wing already.

The popping noise I'd heard was the electric currents that still flowed through the plugged-in flat-screen television my cousin had used as a weapon to take out one of the mercenaries. So, where the hell was he? Where was Ansel?

Like he'd heard my thoughts, his voice buzzed into my ear. "We've got company. Retreat!"

Immediately afterwards, he announced, "Two SUV's with a team of about ten. Heavily armed and wearing Kevlar." Ansel's words were followed by a steady and violently loud flow of gunfire.

The approaching team of mercenaries had likely been warned about how heavily equipped we were, so they had arrived better prepared to handle us. As I heard the screech of tires out front, a blast erupted, rocking the place on its foundation. Dust and debris rained down on me as I ran back towards the living room. Were they shooting grenades at us?

I snatched up my hostage, slung him over my shoulder, and headed towards the back of the house. When my boots cleared the last few steps to take me out of the large living room area, a mercenary armed with a raised assault rifle aimed at my head, entered the front door.

When his head suddenly exploded from a gunshot behind him, Marcus and Tina came to mind, but Scott was the one who came stumbling into the doorway, jumping over the man's body.

"They've got Ansel pinned down," he yelled as he dropped a clip and reloaded his weapon. Harsh breaths left his body as he slid up beside the large window that provided a view of the front yard. "Crazy bastard sent me in to take a hostage while he holds them off."

"Here you go," I told Scott. I heaved the hostage off my shoulder and tossed him at Scott. There was no way I was leaving my cousin out there to face a fresh group of armed mercenaries alone.

"Marcus, I'm coming out the front. You still out there?"

Static sounded before Marcus' voice entered my ear. "I got your back, but hurry. They're dismounting the vehicles."

I inched up to the front door and prayed that Marcus and Tina would cover my ass with sniper fire. I ran out of the front door, blasting anything and anyone who didn't look like Ansel.

I'd dropped and fed my pistol two more clips by the time I made it to the guard shack that I found Ansel ducking behind. Marcus had saved my hide two or three times over, shooting or pinning down the bastards that aimed to kill me.

"Why the fuck didn't you retreat so we can torture the mother-fucker we have?" I yelled at Ansel over the constant blast of gunfire. A vapory cloud of gun smoke lingered around us as the familiar scent filled my flaring nostrils.

Ansel had a damn smile on his face as he ducked back behind the shack, bullets whizzing past his damn skull. The light from the front of the house gave off enough brightness that we and the mercenaries saw each other clearly enough to know where to aim, despite it being after two in the morning.

"You know me, cousin. I couldn't leave my man out here. Plus, I plan on killing as many of these motherfuckers as I can."

The bullets struck the building protecting us with such powerful force that the chips flying from the bricks peppered against me with enough power to break the top layer of skin on my arm. I wanted to scream and yell at Ansel for being so damn crazy and cocky.

He and Scott had had a window of opportunity to escape. Was he trying to get himself killed or was he so addicted to killing that he didn't mind dying while doing it?

The top portion of my body zipped around the bend of the shack as I let off three shots. I counted two black SUV's parked V-shaped in the road outside the fence. If I had to guess, their men were going to flank Ansel and me on both sides and pin us down. Marcus and Tina were our only hope now for making it out of this shit alive.

Just as I'd predicted, two men came from the east and two from the west of the yard—two from Ansel's side and two on my side of the shack. Marcus' sniper rounds kept them down, but there was only so much he could do to keep four men coming at us from different directions when our front was occupied by gunfire also.

"Fuck!" I yelled. I dropped the empty clip from my .45 and drew my nine. I was down to my last two reserve clips of ammo.

"We might have to make a run for it," Ansel expressed as he leaned around the crumbling bricks at the side of the small building and fired off a three-round burst. A few seconds after him, I let off more shots.

Pow! Pow! Pow!

As if disciplining a child, I continued to yell at Ansel. "Are you out of your fucking mind? Those are real bullets coming at us in case you haven't noticed."

"And this is real body armor we have on. If we can keep a bullet out of our head, we have nothing to worry about. Besides, Marcus is still out there."

It was official. My cousin was crazier than I was. The worst part about the situation was he was right. If we managed not to get shot in the head, there was a chance for us to make it into the house and into the backyard.

"You got my back, cousin? Marcus? I'll go first, test the waters," Ansel said, shooting the entire time he spoke his insane ass words.

This crazy bastard was about to step from behind the shack and into the incoming fire, counting on his unlikely ability to keep a bullet out of his head, and my mind was twisted enough to let him try it.

"I've always got your back," I answered him right after I pushed my back up to the wall, dodging more bullets.

"Got you," Marcus assured through static in my ear, but I could still understand his words.

Without so much as a three count, Ansel ran his mentally unstable ass into the line of fire. With Marcus and me covering his ass, he'd made it about fifty feet away from the front door before a bullet struck him in the back, knocking him off balance. He hit the ground hard, and I could tell from the lighting at the front of the house that the impact had knocked the wind out of him.

"Fuck! Fuck! Fuuuuuuk!" I yelled as I watched him writhing in pain on the ground. His mouth gaped open as he gripped at his chest, attempting to get air into his lungs. The body armor had luckily stopped the shot from being a fatal one. The shooters knew Ansel was down and not fatally wounded, so why hadn't they taken the shot that would kill him?

Then it hit me. They wanted to take one of us alive. They wanted to do exactly what we intended to do with the hostage we had. I held my hand out and away from the back of the shack. I let my .45 hang loose in my hand as I tossed it. Then, I followed up that action by doing the same to my nine.

"I'm coming out!" I yelled, hoping they realized I'd surrendered my weapons. I took slow steps from behind the shack with my hands raised. I had one eye on the guys slowly rising from their positions on the east and west side of the yard to get a better look at me. Since it was dark, they likely assumed I didn't see them, but I saw them, every one of those bastards.

The ones behind the SUV's remained in place. They had to know by now that we had another man out there covering our asses. With one hand held high, I pointed at Ansel who was still down, so that they'd know I intended to check on him. I sidestepped slowly over to my cousin.

About twenty paces behind us was the front door of the house. Ansel was sitting up by the time I was standing over him.

"You good?" I asked.

"Yeah...no headshots," he replied breathlessly.

I glanced at the scene in front of and to the left and right side of us. Ansel limped up, with my assistance, to a standing position. We stood back to back. I faced the front gate with Ansel behind me, facing the wide-open front door. Thankfully, his weapon had been knocked out of his hand and was laying a good distance away from him. He was insane enough to pick it up and tempt fate *again*. I hoped he wasn't fool enough to pull out one of the backup weapons I knew he had.

"Quite a fucking pickle we are in, isn't it?" Ansel asked, still struggling to catch his breath.

"They want us alive, Ansel. For once in your hardheaded-ass life, I need you to listen to me."

I could feel Ansel shaking his stubborn head behind me.

"I know what you're about to do, Aaron. Let them take us both."

Although I knew Ansel couldn't see it, I shook my head. "I need you to take care of Megan. Besides, I know you're going to come for me if I don't get myself away from these bastards first."

"Don't fucking do this, Aaron," Ansel insisted. "Don't you dare try to be a fucking hero." With guns aimed at us from just about every direction, this was not the time for us to be having an argument.

"When I say go, I need you to fucking listen, and go, like I fucking tell you to!" I yelled with finality as my back stiffened against Ansel's. Scott and Marcus could also hear me, so they knew as well as Ansel what was about to go down.

Ansel didn't answer, a sign that he might listen.

"Marcus!" I called.

"I got you," Marcus confirmed in a scratchy voice in my earpiece.

"Me too," Scott announced from some place in the darkness.

"Ansel, go!" I yelled.

I didn't know if I was about to die or not, but I couldn't allow these men to take both of us.

At the sound of Ansel's boots beating up the ground behind me, I started shooting. I'd tucked my spare pistol down the front of my pants and was hopefully using it to save my cousin. The first shot that connected with my body knocked the wind out of me. It hit against my chest so hard that I lost control over of the top half of my body and was snapped backwards.

The second shot had me breathing fire as it knocked me off my feet—another chest shot. I didn't have the strength to lift my hand to shoot back. Although I struggled against my impaired body to suck in some air, I still had enough awareness to look over my shoulder in time to see Ansel cross the threshold of the front door of the house.

By the time I found enough strength in my arm to lift my pistol again, it was kicked out of my hands by one of the mercenaries. Three stood over me, which meant the rest were likely laying down fire towards Marcus' area to keep him at bay. When I stared up from my downed position with a mean scowl on my face, one of the mercenaries standing over me reared back and punched me square in the jaw.

They hadn't put a bullet in my head because they wanted me alive. I knew better than anyone that I'd likely end up dead within forty-eight hours whether I talked or not. One of the men scratched roughly at my ear. He extracted my earpiece and stomped on it, severing my connection with Ansel, Scott, and Marcus.

I fought the ache in my chest as air started to flow into my burning lungs. The Kevlar had stopped the bullets from getting through, but the painful burn in my chest and my inability to breathe properly indicated that I likely had a cracked rib...possibly two.

A loud groan came from deep in my throat as I was yanked up from the ground by two of the men. They moved swiftly with me between them as their third man remained at our backs, protecting them. They half dragged my crumpled body forward, and I hobbled along on weak legs. They marched me past the guard shack, through the gate they'd opened and towards the SUV's.

The rest of their crew protected the two who had me, but Marcus and Tina, Scott, and even Ansel were out there in the darkness, still making their lives a living hell. Our crew had killed one of the three who had taken on the task of getting me to the vehicle. And I was sure I'd glimpsed another in the bushes, falling face first in the dirt.

One of the two who had me raised the back of the black SUV. They both took a firm hold on me to bend me over and into the vehicle headfirst. My fucking body failed me, and I was unable to gather the strength I needed to fight the assholes forcing me down.

The side of my face kissed the rough carpet of the vehicle, and the cold steel of the gun pressed into the back of my neck registered. A loud fleshy *thump* sounded before my head exploded in pain, then blackness...

17

ANSEL

Peering out the living room window, I could see them dragging my cousin towards one of the two SUV's they'd left on the street.

"Marcus, you got a shot?"

"No!" Marcus yelled in a strained voice.

Two of the motherfuckers in the bushes I was shooting at were firing at Marcus, keeping him from doing his job. I needed Tina in my hands so I could wipe those bastards off the face of the earth.

Scott was behind me on the other side of the living room, giving them hell as well. None of us had retreated to my truck in the woods.

I aligned the sight of my .45 a hair above where I'd seen the flash of a gun's muzzle. It was where I estimated one of their heads would be.

I fired, and out he fell, stumbling from the bushes, disoriented. A second thought never crossed my mind as I aimed for his head and pulled the trigger.

I fired on the ones who remained in the yard—who were smart enough to lay down cover fire at Scott, Marcus, and me—keeping us from interfering with the fuckers that were getting away with my cousin. One had even been smart enough to shoot out that big-ass light that was attached to the front of the house, making it difficult for us to find our targets even with the use of night goggles.

The darkness and my distance kept me from firing on the two leading Aaron to the back of that SUV. I couldn't take the chance of accidentally killing my cousin. "Marcus?" I yelled.

"No shot! No shot!" he yelled back, and I could hear him letting off shot after shot on his end, making Tina sing.

I vaguely made out what I assumed was one of them running back to the passenger's side of the vehicle. Before I could get a shot off at the vehicle, the tires screeched, its engine roaring into the darkness.

The distant scream of sirens alerted me to the fact that the cops were coming. Within minutes, this place was going to be swarming with local cops who'd likely been called by the very mercenaries that were getting away with my cousin.

"Marcus! Scott! Let's go!" I yelled. Each answered consecutively. They knew me well enough to figure out what we were going to have to do if I was ever going to see my cousin again.

My boots ate at the once shiny floor of the living room and hammered onto the stairs as I rushed up them. I sprang the closet door open and dragged my hostage out. He was going to tell me where they were taking my cousin or he was going to know what it was like in hell.

WHEN THE THREE of us stumbled into the safe house with not one, but two hostages, Shark's eyes grew wide. His eyes remained on the front door, undoubtedly looking for his son.

After we'd secured the hostages in the basement and stepped back into the hall that led to the living room, we were met by my uncle's deadly gaze. He stood there with his beefy arms folded over his chest. His unblinking cold, blue eyes met mine and may as well have been blow torches.

"They took him. Aaron gave himself up so I could get away."

Angry rage-filled flesh crinkled on Shark's face. "You let a bunch of fucking mercenaries take the only fucking son I got left? You better make those motherfuckers you dragged in here tell you where they're taking my son."

Aaron and I were admittedly crazy. Our minds were a bit twisted. We had a streak of danger in us that verged on insane, but on the rare occasion my uncle Shark got angry, I knew enough to keep my mouth shut and to do what he said.

The only other time I'd seen a look on my uncle's face that menacing was when his younger son, my cousin, Ryan, had been killed. My uncle Shark and Aaron had gone on a killing spree so vicious over Ryan that no one knew the exact body count. We had our faults. We had our weaknesses. We were even a bit damaged. But, if someone touched our family, we unleashed a part of ourselves that rained down hell on earth.

I nodded my head towards my uncle. "I promise you I will find Aaron or die trying."

~

I STOOD outside Aaron and Megan's bedroom door for a still and quiet moment before my knuckles connected with the wood. The tap of tiny feet running towards the door registered before Megan sprang it open.

The smile on her beautiful face disappeared the moment she saw my long face. I scratched the side of my chin, not sure how to tell her that Aaron had been taken. Tears had already started to pool in the corner of her eyes.

"Aaron?"

"He's alive. But..."

The poor girl's entire body started to shake as she stood there in what must have been one of Aaron's T-shirts.

"They took him," I forced out before I had to catch a hold of one of Megan's arms as she stumbled over to the bed. I sat on the bed next to her.

"I promise you, I'm going to get him back."

She glanced over at me with tears rolling down her cheeks. She pointed her shaky fingers at her chest. "Give me to them. I'm who they want," she volunteered in a weak voice.

"Nope, that's not an option. Aaron made me promise to take care of you and even if he hadn't, allowing you to turn yourself over to them would never be an option."

She stared straight ahead for a moment, just sniffling, her small body making the bed bounce. She stood and walked over to the dresser, slid into some pants first, then took out a bra and shirt. She started the process of pulling up the long T-shirt she had on, and something must have reminded her that I was still there. She stopped, walked into the bathroom and closed the door.

My forehead crinkled when she stepped out of the bathroom fully clothed and with her tennis shoes on. I scanned her from head to toe. Her shirt was askew, and the strings of her shoes were left untied. When she started stuffing clothes into her purple backpack, I stood.

"Megan, what are you doing?"

"Packing," she answered in a low nonchalant tone without elaborating.

"Packing for what?" I asked as I took a step closer to her.

"If they are out there looking for me, then all I have to do is stop hiding, and they will find me."

My arms went across my chest.

"I'm not letting you leave this house. We have hostages. One or both are going to tell me where they are keeping Aaron."

Her big eyes held a determined glint. "Once they tell you where they're keeping Aaron, you're going to kill them, right?"

Aaron told me she knew the rules of this life better than she let on, so I gave her a straight answer. "Yes. Those motherfuckers tried to kill us, and their buddies took my cousin."

"Aaron will be in the same kind of situation. I know that he isn't going to tell them what they want to know, but it doesn't matter. They are going to kill him anyway."

She was right. They were going to kill Aaron no matter what. The only thing we had in our favor was who they were attempting to get the information out of. Aaron wasn't going to tell them shit no matter how long they tortured him. This would buy us some time to track and find him.

"Will you at least have enough faith in me and let me get him back before you go sacrificing yourself. Even if you traded yourself, it doesn't mean they'll release him."

She plopped down on the bed and released a deep sigh. "This is my fault. I begged Aaron not to do this. I told him to let me go. I ran away from him twice because I didn't want him to end up hurt or killed because of me."

"Megan, this is not your fault, and I understand why my cousin couldn't let you go. I understand why he's fighting. And if you want someone to blame, blame me. He was taken because of me."

She raised her gaze to mine, clearly not understanding my words.

"If I hadn't been trying to take everyone out instead of retreating when the right time came, he wouldn't have been taken. So, I'm going to do what I have to do to get him back."

She didn't look convinced and based on the defiant look on her face, I didn't think she was going to listen to me.

Am I going to have to tie this woman up to keep her here? I had serious work to do and people to torture. When I stood and walked towards the door to exit, Megan followed me.

"Where are you going?" I asked her.

"With you."

"I'm about to go and torture a motherfucker to try to find out where they're keeping my cousin."

She glanced up at me, looking innocent with those big-ass sad eyes and said, "I know."

After she spoke those two words, those big, brown, innocent eyes held mine, and a touch of madness peeked through. Aaron was right about one thing. Megan presented a picture of innocence to the world that could fool anyone. She had fooled me until I'd looked deeper and saw what was staring back at me.

At this moment, I realized she could be as dark as any member of the August Knights. I also realized her darkness was how she'd won over the members of our MC. The sight of that gun shoved down the front of her pants was further proof that Megan was not your typical female.

She kept her cold gaze locked on mine, almost daring me to stop her from following. I shrugged, turned, and headed to the basement with Megan hot on my trail.

18

AARON

The light wave and sway of my body and the vibration of the engine let me know that we were moving. My eyes jittered under my closed lids, and I struggled to open them. The pain in my chest—hell, the pain in the back of my head registered and made me stifle a groan.

There was too much pain for me to be dead, so it was safe to assume they hadn't shot me in the back of the head. My senses were all creeping back into my body one by one. They'd stuffed me into the back of their SUV after striking me in the back of the head. The seat in front of my area was raised with someone sitting there. The other seat was flattened so they had a view of the top half of my body.

I didn't want them to know that I was awake, so I kept my body still. Since a portion of me was under the edge of the folded seat, it kept some of my movement hidden. They'd taken my gun and large combat knife, but had they found the small hunting knife I kept hidden in the secret pocket I had on the inseam of the waistband at the back of my pants?

Struggling to angle my body without moving the top half while attempting not to accidentally kick the seat of the person in front of me was a fucking task. With my hands zip-tied behind my back, I was forced to lift my shoulders without them noticing.

It took some doing, but I reached the area I'd been aiming for, and just as I'd hoped, the knife was still there. Apparently, these men weren't as well-trained as I'd thought they were.

I worked my fingers between my belted waist and wiggled the knife free. Once I had it free, it took more nimble finger movements to work the knife open and cut the thick zip ties they had around my hands.

Now, I had to figure out how I wanted to go about this. Number one and two sat in the front seat, number three was in the second seat on the passenger's side, and number four was in the third row in front of me. Number four sat turned in the seat so that he could watch me. He had his hand on his weapon, but sadly for him, the weapon was holstered, and he was dozing off.

If I could take out number four, who was sleeping on duty, and get his gun, I could possibly take the others. The odds were stacked against me, but what other options did I have? They were driving me someplace so they could kill me either way. The way I saw it, if I was going to die, I was going to die the way I wanted to—fighting.

I sprung up from my position and plunged the knife into the chest of the man in the seat in front of me. As his body jerked and blood started to wet his shirt, his hand slipped from his pistol to clutch at his chest. He attempted to yell out, but his voice was lost as he choked and gagged on the blood that was filling his throat and drizzling down his chin.

At the sight of what was going on, the driver swerved, jerking the stirring wheel so hard that the tires squealed. The move tossed me sideways and pulled me away from the pistol that had been inches from my grasp. I struck the passenger's side paneling. I didn't know if it was dumb luck or if the driver saw me grabbing for that gun, but his swift maneuvering had likely saved their lives.

The driver recovered the vehicle quickly. Still in my position against the paneling, my eyes fell on the gun that I needed, but I couldn't make a move to take it, because number two and number three's guns were aimed at my face.

When I heard the click of number three's weapon in the second seat and saw the deadly gleam in his eyes, I closed my eyes, and Megan filled my mind.

"Don't kill him!" the driver shouted.

"Why the fuck not?" number three snapped. "He just killed Randy."

"Because Sorio wants him alive. His little girlfriend killed Sorio's father, so we have to find the bitch or Sorio is going to start killing us," the driver answered.

Number three glared at me, his finger flexing on the trigger. He wanted to put a bullet in me badly. "Sorio thought that bitch was already dead. Then three years ago, he got a tip that the little bitch was still alive. What if the tip was wrong and we're chasing a fucking ghost? It's one fucking woman. It shouldn't be this hard to kill a fucking woman. We've damn near lost our whole fucking team."

The driver glanced back at me before putting his eyes back on the highway. "She is very much alive. Sorio got a hold of the bitch's medical records. She uses a different name, but it's the same fucking DNA that was left on his dead father all those years ago. As much as I want to kill that motherfucker back there, we can't kill him, yet. This is the closest we've gotten to getting Daniels, and he can tell us where the hell she's at."

Number three relaxed his arm but kept his weapon aimed at me. "Everyone that gets close to this fucking Daniels woman ends up losing their lives. I mean, what is she, a fucking sorcerer?"

No one answered number three's question, but it was becoming clear that they had been hunting Megan for a long time.

"Tell me we're not transporting this animal to Texas?" Number two, the one riding shotgun in the front seat asked.

Texas?

The driver must have been this group's leader because he seemed to have more knowledge than the others. I should have killed him first because he'd just sentenced me to any number of days of torture.

There was no way in hell I was telling them where Megan was, so they were wasting their time. If Ansel didn't find me before they killed me, he knew to get Megan out of Florida.

"Yes, we're taking him to Texas. The boss has a plane waiting for us about fifteen miles down the highway, and he specifically told me to transport a live lead if we got one."

"And you think Sorio is going to be able to break him? He's a fucking August Knight. They come out of the womb getting tortured."

Hearing how they were talking about our MC caused my eyebrows to shoot up. They thought we were a bunch of savages. I guess they could have been right. We were vicious when we had to be. I relaxed against the back hatch of the vehicle and smiled.

"Sorio also told us not to engage these hicks and to take the bitch when she was alone," number two stated.

"Rednecks, not hicks," number one corrected.

"Same fucking difference," number two whined.

"Sorio didn't want us stirring up more trouble than we had to because these fucking rednecks are more connected than anyone would think they are. But, George had to show his balls and led his team to a fucking shootout in a public place, and you saw what happened to them in those woods," number one warned.

"Well, I'm not afraid of these August hicks," number three stated as he cut his eyes at me and shook his gun in my direction.

With the zip-ties gone, I reached behind me and lifted the handle that would make the door rise, but the driver had been smart enough to lock it. *Fuck.*

Minutes later, we arrived at a private airfield where a small private jet running on the tarmac awaited us. The plane hummed to life before a loud burst of air shot from someplace behind it and made the plane roar with an ear-splitting noise.

With a gun to my head and one to my back and my hands re-tied, I had no choice but to march towards the plane. A glance back showed a crew already cleaning out the SUV, pulling the man I'd killed out. The pushing and shoving I received had me clumping up the steps and stumbling across the doorway to enter the plane.

The crew didn't take any chances with me this time. Once they had me seated in the back seat in front of the restroom, they roped my ass to the seat of the plane like I was cattle. Then, I watched one stroll up to me with a needle in his hand. With a mind full of rage and trussed up like a damned animal, I was unable to defend myself from whatever they were about to inject me with.

My eyes followed the needle as it inched closer to my twitching arm. The tiny prick registered, and seconds later, my eyelids became too heavy for me to hold open. I faded slowly, fighting and urging my mind to stay awake. The last thing I saw before my lids closed for good was the face of the man who'd been driving the vehicle. He stood before me with the needle, preparing to pump me with more drugs if he needed to.

19

ANSEL

When piss came spilling from the seat of the rickety wooden chair I had the mercenary strapped to, I took a step back. I'd been torturing the man for an hour, failing to find out where his people had taken my cousin.

We'd divided the basement in half. On one side of the ratty beige blanket I'd hung, I was torturing the mercenary I'd hidden in the closet. On the other side of the blanket, Shark was torturing the one Aaron had handed over to Scott.

Megan stood at the edge of the divide, watching us beat, kick, stab, fry, poke and prod these men to within an inch of their sanity. She observed and seemed to be studying what we were doing to the men. Not once did she look away. It didn't matter what we did or how barbaric our cruelty became, she stayed.

After nearly two hours, Shark and I both took breaks. When we made it into the kitchen, Megan waited there for us with two ice-cold glasses of water. "I know that you guys know what you're doing, and I'm sure you'll get more information out of these guys, but may I suggest something?"

Shark spit his words at Megan. "What? You know how to torture men? Watching and actually doing it are two different things." Shark looked over at me. "I'm going back down. You can take suggestions if you want to. If it weren't for her, my son wouldn't have been captured by mercenaries."

"Unc, Aaron was captured because of *me*," I corrected, my words bouncing off his back as he walked away.

Shark didn't say so, but his shoulder was bothering him. He kept adjusting the sling and rubbing the arm of his injured shoulder. He turned before crossing into the basement. An authoritative finger pointed in my direction. "I wasn't born yesterday. An unknown group that Aaron, of all people, didn't know about. Who else could they be after if not her?"

Shark shoved his thumb towards Megan who'd dropped her head. He glared at her for a long moment before he took the steps down into the basement. His angry steps traveled out of the open basement door into the kitchen with us.

It was safe to say my uncle knew that we were fighting adversaries that were chasing Megan. But, as far as Shark was concerned, with them having Aaron, the fight had officially become ours. I took a few steps closer to Megan, and she stepped back. "What was the suggestion you had?" I asked her.

She glanced up, surprised. "You want to hear what I have to say after all the trouble I've caused?"

"Yeah. Let me hear it."

THIRTY MINUTES after Megan made her suggestion, she, my cousin, Mark, Shark, and I drove out to the clubhouse. We were taking our mission for information, *out back*. After having Mark help me dig, of all things, a fucking grave, we lowered the mercenary into the hole, kicking and screaming his head off. Wade had shown up with the pine box he'd gotten from his wife's sister who worked at the funeral home.

Megan's suggestion was that we bury the man alive and use the communication devices we use on our mission so that we could communicate our questions and hear his response from inside the coffin. Her knowledge of some of the things we did had me wondering if there wasn't anything my cousin didn't share with this woman.

She was certain the man's own mind would scare him far worse than the physical abuse that we were inflicting on him.

I didn't know if the stunt would work, but even I had to admit it was one hell of a plan. She may have been right in her assessment because this guy screamed more inside the box than when I was beating the piss and shit out of him. I didn't know his name and didn't care to know it. My only mission was to find out the location of where his friends had taken my fucking cousin.

"If you can hear me, say yes, and knock twice on the ceiling of your box."

The man spoke a shaky "yes" and followed it up with two loud thumps that came from the pine box sitting four feet in the ground below. His terrified voice sounded loud and clear in my ear. I'd fitted Shark, Megan, Mark, and Wade with an earpiece each so they could hear the man speaking as well.

"Where are your people taking my fucking cousin? And don't tell me you don't know." I spoke loud precise words, ensuring the man heard every syllable. "If you're not ready to talk, the next thing you will hear is dirt covering this coffin."

For the first few minutes, the man would not budge. Each time he didn't answer my question I'd let him hear me throw more dirt on top of him. His labored breathing indicated that his air supply was thinning, which from what I could hear, terrified him even more than he already was.

"Are you ready to tell me where your people are taking my cousin?"

"Yes, fucking yes!" the man spat out through ragged breaths. His sharp intakes of air and his constant thrashing about inside the box let us know he'd started to panic.

"Where are they taking him?"

"Texas! They are taking him to Texas," he huffed out through harsh breaths.

"Texas is a big fucking state. Where in Texas are they taking him?"

"Chantil, Texas. Small town. The ranch is about ten miles outside the town."

"Do you know the address?" I asked, noticing the desperation in his voice.

"There is no address. No one is supposed to know who the place belongs to. There are only a few properties outside the town."

"We are in Florida. Are they driving all the way to Texas?"

"No. Our boss will fly them there."

"Who's your boss?"

"Sorio. Sorio Dominquez."

I didn't know a fucking Sorio Dominquez. He couldn't have been one of the original gang members. D and my contact with the FBI had provided us with all sorts of information on the Dominquez gang, but nothing about a Sorio.

"Is Sorio one of the original six?" I asked the man.

"No, he's the son of Carlos and he wants the girl more than anyone."

Fuck!

Mark and Wade gave me and Shark funny looks, but none of us said a thing. They were likely wondering who Carlos was and what girl the man was talking about. They never looked in Megan's direction, so they likely hadn't pieced the puzzle together yet.

Frankly, I couldn't believe how well this stunt with the coffin was working. The man was spilling his guts, giving me way more information than I'd expected to get out of him. I glanced back at Megan whose eyes were glued to that coffin. She wanted to know where Aaron was as badly as everyone else in the MC...probably even more.

My cold stare fell back on the wood of the coffin. Not an ounce of emotion stirred within me as I drew and emptied a clip of hot slugs into where the man's head and chest were. Wade and Mark jumped back and looked at me as if I'd lost my fucking mind. Megan and Shark hadn't even flinched. The way I saw it, I'd done the man a favor by putting him out of his misery. I picked up one of the shovels and started covering the coffin. Mark joined me as Megan, Shark, and Wade waited.

"We should keep the other hostage alive. If that motherfucker down there was lying, we'll have the other one to get information out of," I explained, not looking at anyone as I continued to shovel dirt into the hole.

"I don't think he was lying. He sounded like he was shitting bricks inside that box," Mark stated.

"How did you come up with some shit like this anyway?" Wade asked.

My eyes traveled in Megan's direction before I pointed at her. Wade, Mark, and Shark's glares all shifted in her direction. She stood staring out at the stars with no idea that all eyes were on her. I was starting to notice that she had a one-track mind when it came to my cousin, and like me, she didn't seem to care what she had to do to get him back.

None of the men said a word, but I understood the elongated glares they had aimed at Megan. If they already hadn't realized, they were beginning to understand why Aaron had chosen her. She was becoming one of us no matter what our rules were and no matter what was supposed to divide us.

"Megan," I called, getting her attention. "Let's go."

"No, you are not going to Texas," I said to Megan in the calmest voice I could muster. We had made it back to the safe house, and she was packing that damn backpack again, stuffing her clothes inside despite my protests. She wasn't listening to a goddamn word I was saying to her. She was preparing to go with my team to rescue Aaron from that damn ranch they were likely torturing him on.

"I'm going. If it weren't for me, he wouldn't be there," she said.

Damn, she was hardheaded as hell. I got that she was tough.

Given the shit she'd been though, she had to be. But she wasn't trained for combat and would only get in the way.

"I can wait in the car. I'll stay out of the way," she said, using that low, innocent-sounding voice.

It was like she knew what I'd been thinking. However, I had the impression she only wanted to go so she could find a way to trade herself for Aaron. When it came to this woman, I was at a loss, trying to figure her out. But, if there was one thing I was beginning to understand, the bond between her and my cousin was endless.

"No. Stay here where it's safe. I promised Aaron that I'd keep you safe. Staying your ass here in Florida is the safest place you can be."

"I'm going," she said with finality. She slung that damn purple backpack over her small shoulder after throwing her cute little chin up in defiance.

I closed my eyes and prayed for the patience I knew I didn't have. How did Aaron do it? I wasn't the least bit equipped with enough patience to deal with a woman right now. Not when I had important shit to do like kill people and find my cousin. I turned to walk away, and she followed.

"Fuck, Megan, *stay*. Heel. Sit. Fucking listen. What did my cousin do to get you to listen to him?"

My boots thumped loud against the floor, and that little, hard-headed-ass woman was still following me. She was going to follow me straight out the front door if I didn't stop her.

I turned and shoved her until she fell back onto the living room couch. "You can't go. You are not going." I stared firmly like a father disciplining his child.

She looked at me like I was the small one. Like I wasn't the big mean man standing over her. I easily outweighed her by a good hundred pounds, but she didn't seem to give a damn.

She leaned forward, glaring up at me. Those big brown eyes held mine. "You're going to have to tie me up or kill me to keep me from going. If you don't take me with you, I'll find another way there."

She spoke in such a quiet easy tone it was difficult to believe she was volunteering to be a part of a group that was preparing to travel halfway across the country on a mission to likely kill a large number of people. And worse, she could be one of the ones who ended up dead.

Shark entered the living room with an unreadable expression on his face. "Take her," he ordered. "She's survived among us for months. Guns, blood, and bodies don't scare her. She's like a fucking cancer that can't be killed, one you just learn to live with."

Megan didn't take offense to Shark's statement. Shit, she looked as though she wanted to thank him for saying it. I waved my arm for her to stand. "Come on. Stay in the fucking truck when we get there and don't get in the damn way."

She nodded her head and followed so close behind me, the lip of her tennis shoes scraped the back of my boots a few times, ensuring I didn't leave her. When I glanced back at my uncle, he was shaking his head, and I couldn't tell if he was frowning or smiling.

20

ANSEL

"D, I hope you don't mind me calling you." I spoke into Aaron's phone.

"No, man. But, if you're calling me from Aaron's phone, that means he's dead or they got him."

"They took him. We think we may have the place, but on the off chance that the motherfucker we tortured was lying, we would like to make sure they took him to the place he specified in Texas."

"*Texas*? They took him to Texas?"

"Long fucking story, D. You know as well as I do they're going to try to torture information out of him. I'm sure you know Aaron is not going to give them what they want. We are going to attempt to extract him before they kill him."

"Fuck! Are you anywhere near there yet?" D asked.

"No. We just hit the highway. It'll take us about seven or maybe eight hours to get there. As far as we could gather, he's on a ranch outside of Chantil, Texas. It's a small town that's not supposed to have too many outlying properties. Is there any way you can find and pinpoint the location for us?"

"I'm already on it," D answered. "I'll call you back."

Click.

I rode shotgun as Scott drove. Megan and Marcus sat in the back. I had two dirt bikes strapped to a trailer we were hauling behind one of the two vehicles we'd stolen.

We'd stolen two SUV's from the last place anyone would expect them to be missing from; the police impound yard. We didn't want to take the chance of using our own vehicles just in case something went wrong and the enemy got a hold of them. One trace of our VIN numbers would give them more information on us.

Wade followed us in the second stolen vehicle. He'd brought along my twin cousins, Jake and Jackson. The twins stayed as high as the clouds in the sky, but when it came to anything combat related, they were all in, no matter how dangerous or deadly the threat.

About halfway through the drive and as soon as we crossed the line from Mississippi to Louisiana, D called me back. "I found the place. They have Aaron in some type of barn out behind the main house. Did you bring the laptop?" D asked.

"Yes. I'm turning it on now."

"I'm sending you the satellite feed," D said.

Scott took his eyes off the highway to glance at me as D talked on speaker. I scanned the feed that started to cover the laptop with keen eyes.

D's voice came back over the line. "This damn place is guarded like a fucking fortress. It's about fifteen miles out from the town, far enough that they likely don't get visitors unless they are invited. The property sits on acres of wide-open land. There are four buildings: the main house, a barn, and two other smaller shacks. The closest woods are nearly three miles out, so it's going to be hard to sneak up on them."

Fuck, kept repeating through my mind. They had strategically placed themselves in an area that they knew would be hard for their enemy to infiltrate. They would see us coming for miles around, even at night. How were we supposed to sneak into a place that had been stealth-proofed?

"To make matters worse," D said. "They have the watchful eyes of about ten guards and cameras all around the place."

"Fuck! Fuck! Fuck!" I shouted, filling the cab of the vehicle with my heated words.

The five men with me were tough, but if this place was protected like D was saying and if they saw us coming from miles away, there was no damn way we were getting in there.

"Let me see if I can come up with something," D suggested. "I'll call you back."

"Okay. Thanks, man."

How in the fuck were we supposed to get my cousin out of that place?

I STUDIED the feed on the laptop so hard that my eyes started to burn. But, the information I'd gained from watching the activities that went on at this place said a lot. There were ten guards, the hired mercenary types, strategically placed at certain locations, with automatic weapons in their hands or strapped to their backs. I'd watched them switch shifts, which meant there were at least twenty of them.

They operated like the crew we'd dealt with in Florida. The one named Sorio was who they were likely protecting, along with a few other civilians.

This place appeared to be some type of DG6 safe house. I made out the one I assumed was Sorio. He didn't look any older than me, so the assumption that he was Carlos Dominquez's son was likely the truth.

If that were the case, I somewhat understood his desire to want Megan dead for killing his father. He wanted to avenge his father's death if for no other reason than to say he'd done it.

I'd watched who I assumed was Sorio along with his wife or girl-friend sitting on the porch while a maid served them food and drinks. The woman had her back to me, so I couldn't see her face. The grainy feed didn't give me a clear picture, but I watched them intensely.

They paid no attention to the armed guards that swarmed about the place, likely used to them.

The most shocking revelation was the sight of a kid. A boy, no older than ten, played in the front yard near the fence where the guards were located. He tossed a football around with no one to toss it back to him.

The house was two levels high, but there was a separate guard tower that sat a level higher than the house. It was one large square-shaped room that stood on thick metal support beams and constructed of mostly wood—a lookout tower that allowed them to see for miles around. There were large viewing binoculars affixed to tall tripods pointing north, south, east, and west.

D had been right, they guarded this place like a fucking fortress. But, they had no idea the amount of determination I poured into a situation when I needed to succeed. I was going to get my cousin back if it killed me. The one thing the Texas bunch didn't count on was that none of us gave a damn about dying.

Scott, Marcus, Wade, and the twins knew or at least understood and accepted as much. I was sure that Megan knew and accepted it too. The low hum of the vehicle idling down alerted me to the fact that we were close to the ranch. The woods D had identified surrounded the back and east sides of the house.

The trees were wider spread here. Some of the leaves had browned and started to thin. These woods weren't as thick and plush as the areas we were used to in Florida. Nearly three miles of wide-open space was what we'd have to travel to reach the property.

D informed he'd caught a glimpse of Aaron when he'd managed to take over one of the guard's smart watch. Although D had confirmed that he was inside the barn, I hadn't spotted Aaron yet on the laptop feed, but there were hints that led me to believe he was exactly where D had said he was.

The maid I'd seen had taken food inside and exited the barn quickly. The guards posted at the front and back entrance of the building also confirmed that they were likely holding a prisoner inside.

I hadn't seen Sorio enter the barn yet, and we had no idea what they'd been doing to Aaron for the sixteen hours it had taken us to verify the location information, prepare, and travel to Texas.

Since it was after seven o'clock in the evening, we were going to lay low, strategize, and plan. We all gathered around the laptop, attempting to come up with a plan that would get us over a three-mile hike to the ranch without being spotted.

We couldn't come up with anything that didn't result in us being picked off until we were all dead. Even my idea of using the 50 Cal to take out the tower and using snipers to cover us wouldn't work. There were too many holes in each plan. There were too many areas not covered and too many ways for us to all die. A fucking suicide mission.

We'd been going nonstop since the day before, so we took turns resting and keeping an eye out on the group we hadn't figured out how to overtake yet. Just as I was about to doze off in the front seat of the stolen SUV with the laptop sitting in my lap, Aaron's phone buzzed.

"Hello?"

"Hey, I think your plan to use the 50 Cal and snipers might be the way in. But you're going to need at least three more snipers."

What the hell was D talking about? He knew we didn't have but two sniper rifles—mine and Aaron's.

"Dax, Gavin, and I will be there in about six hours. You remember the four areas we identified where they have static automatic weapons posted? Four snipers to hold those positions and the 50 Cal to take down or keep that damn tower busy could work. Use the dirt bikes to get across the three open miles while the rest of us keep the soldiers busy."

Closing my eyes, I let D's plan run through my brain. He remained silent on the other end, allowing me to think. I gripped my chin, my gaze pinned on the phone I spoke into. "How are we going to get snipers and the 50 Cal close enough without being seen to affect the areas we need to hold?"

D chuckled. "We are going to blind them. Well, at least half blind them. I can take out their surveillance equipment easily. They will be left with the same long-range sight equipment and night gear that we will be using. It will even up the fight. Plus, we are bringing ghillie suits."

"Did my cousin ever tell you that you're a fucking genius?"

D laughed at my comment. "You know how your cousin is. He doesn't issue compliments. But, that fucker will send you a box or a bag of money out of the blue in a heartbeat."

I laughed, thinking about my cousin's ways.

"I'll call you when we're close," D said.

"Appreciate it, man. See you later."

My mind fell back to my cousin. Aaron didn't spend money like me. I bought houses, cars, clothes, and jewelry, took exotic trips, and rented yachts and private planes. Aaron didn't do shit but ride and work on his motorcycles in his spare time, make money for the MC, and stir up trouble occasionally.

I was sure Aaron's ass was sitting on a ton of money because he rarely spent any. It was nothing for him to stuff a brick or two of cash in one of those big-ass indestructible security envelopes and send that shit. He'd done it to me three times. His way of saying thanks, I guess.

You either liked Aaron or you didn't. If you didn't like him, you wanted to kill him, but if you liked him, you'd be willing to kill for him. If you loved that bastard like me, his father, the MC, or Megan, you'd go to hell for him.

His relationship with Megan had shocked the shit out of me because he'd never shown care or concern for anyone except family and the MC. Even now, as I glanced over the torn black upholstery at Megan lying across the back seat of the vehicle, I had a hard time believing she'd made such an impact on him. After being around her and finding out about her past, it still stumped me that he would fall for her to the point that he was willing to go to war over her. It meant that he considered her just as much family to him as I was.

And Megan was about as bad as Aaron. Hard to figure out, but so far in love with my cousin that she was willing to hand herself over to one of the most dangerous gangs in the country. After having been through the hell she'd suffered as a teen, after having been hiding from the group for nearly a decade and knowing the types of shit they could do to her, none of it had deterred her from her quest to save Aaron.

21

MEGAN

The whirr of an engine and the snap of twigs breaking under tires assisted in pulling me from a sleep that I was sure wasn't doing me a bit of good. My elbows dug into the hard upholstery of the leather seat when I forced myself up. My blurry vision focused on the shadowy face of Ansel glancing back at me from the front seat.

He tilted his head, eyeing me like I was some creature he needed to study.

"That sound you hear, it's Aaron's friend, D, and two others he served in the military with. They are coming to help us rescue Aaron."

I sat all the way up and dropped my feet to the floor. After pulling my gaze away from Ansel's, I craned my neck around, interested to see these friends of Aaron's. No headlights meant they were using night gear to trek the tree-lined path.

It wasn't lost on me that most of them seemed to have figured out that their newest adversaries, DG6, were chasing me. Now, that they'd captured Aaron, I was sure that DG6 had officially become the number one enemies of the August Knights. I was quickly learning that this MC was much more capable, smarter, and willing to lay down their lives for each other than I would have given them credit for.

"Stay here," Ansel said as he threw his door open and exited the vehicle. Ansel didn't have to tell me to stay inside the vehicle. I was reluctant to show my face because I didn't want the men looking at the reason that Aaron was in this mess in the first place.

After rising to my knees, I squinted to get a better look at the three guys that had exited a dark-color SUV that had pulled up close to the vehicle Ansel and his men stood next to. I could tell, even in our dim setting that they'd exited the vehicle with cautious movements.

Their shadowy figures indicated that they all appeared to be as tall and fit as Aaron. Ansel and his men remained in place at the open hatch of the SUV behind the one I was in. They'd unhooked the trailer carrying the dirt bikes from the back of the vehicle and parked the vehicles back to back. They stood statue-still as the men inched closer to them.

"Nice to meet you, man," I heard Ansel say as he reached out and shook hands with who I assumed was D. From my view inside the truck, they were all tall, dark shadows. At certain angles, I could make out a few features, but nothing that gave me a clear picture of these guys.

"This is Dax and Gavin," D introduced the other men.

After brief greetings were exchanged among the men, they gathered at the back of the SUV behind me and conducted a strategy session. I stayed put inside the vehicle, but it didn't stop me from cracking the window further so I could listen to their plans for retrieving Aaron from a ranch full of hired killers. Discussions about 50 Cal machine guns, sniper rifles, guard towers, and most importantly, Aaron being in the barn, came up.

"There is a woman and a kid here too, so beware. I'm a motherfucking nightmare when I need to be, but I don't harm small children. I don't hurt women either...well, unless they want me to." The group laughed at Ansel's comment about women. It even made me crack a smile. I remember Aaron had commented that Ansel led an unusual sexual lifestyle.

After the men spent hours planning their operation, a significant amount of time was spent gathering, snapping, and clicking together all sorts of equipment. Amid all the snapping and clicking, the man I was certain was D said, "I'd like to meet Megan if you don't mind."

His words set my heart to a hammering beat, making me slide down from my spying position on my knees. I sat stiffly in the back seat, biting into my bottom lip. After I took a few deep breaths, I braced myself as the sound of approaching footsteps grew closer.

When the door nearest me creaked open, three sets of inquisitive eyes landed on me, and not even the darkness outside hid their interested roving gazes. They wanted to see the reason why the man they respected so well had been captured. The interior light inside the truck shined on me like a big spotlight, and there wasn't a thing I could do but sit there and be watched.

The first big hand reached towards me, and I took it. "I'm D. It's nice to meet you, Megan."

"You as well, D. Thank you for coming here," I stated in my normal low tone.

D nodded his head, and a puzzled look crossed his face before another big hand shoved him aside and reached towards me. This time, however, the man leaned into the light, and I saw his face more clearly than I'd seen D's. I took his hand that was nearly in my lap because his eyes were busy soaking me in.

"I'm Gavin," he said before his eyebrows shot up and a deep smile creased his handsome face. "Damn, you're pretty. I can see why—"

Before he could finish his sentence, the third man of the group yanked Gavin back by his shoulder and reached out his hand towards me. "I'm Dax. Nice to meet you, Megan."

The three men looked like they were auditioning for a photo shoot. Did everyone Aaron know look like models? Maybe it was that they were ex-military and knew how to keep themselves and their bodies neat and fit. My roving gaze worked its way around the group that stood gazing at me. I was literally surrounded by a bunch of well-built, well-trained, strikingly good-looking killers.

D reached for my hand to help me out of the truck. He seemed to be taking me in as much as I was taking him and his crew in. Ansel stood off to the side, watching the exchange. The one called Gavin didn't hide the fact that he was thoroughly checking me out.

"Aaron has always had good taste," Gavin volunteered while looking back at me with a devilish grin. "However, I didn't know he was into brown—" D popped Gavin playfully in the back of the head, cutting off his words before shaking his head at his friend.

They sat me on one of their armless little camouflaged folding chairs as I watched them prepare for war. The time was nearing three o'clock in the morning and the men wanted to act before they lost the cover of darkness.

They decided to proceed with their plan at 3:45 a.m. due to a few last-minute preparations they needed to make. The five men, consisting of D, Dax, Gavin, Scott, and Marcus dressed in what they explained were ghillie suits. The suits would make it difficult for them to be detected as they approached the ranch, especially in the dark.

It was only after I saw one of the men fully suited that I understood the significance of the suits. It appeared that they were wearing a part of the landscape, which would hide them during their three-mile hike towards the ranch. To me, they looked like they were all dressed as Chewbacca from Star Wars.

Four of the men in the suits were armed with sniper rifles, and two of them had sniper rifles with grenade-launchers attached. Marcus had the 50 Cal machine gun. Ansel and Wade were set to use the dirt bikes to get to the barn after the Chewbacca lookalikes took out the specified targeted areas.

The twins, Jake and Jackson, would stay back and proceed if they were called forward. My instructions were to stay in the truck and stay down. I asked for an earpiece so I could hear what the men heard. Surprisingly, Ansel and the men fitted me with a listening device without resistance.

I was playing my part as the helpless woman, but if they thought I was going to sit by and let DG6 kill Aaron, they had tragically misjudged me. If shit went bad, I was going into that barn even if I had to run through hell to get there.

D, even while in Chewbacca gear, was on a laptop. I was quickly finding out that there wasn't much the man couldn't do when he had a digital device under his fingers.

"They're blind," D announced. "I temporarily took out their cameras. They are now looking at a recording I made of their surveillance feed over the last fifty minutes." He glanced around at the men. "We're about to run out of darkness, so I had to stop recording. That means we are going to have to hustle."

I didn't have to be ex-military to know they had to pull off their mission before they lost the darkness and within fifty minutes if they didn't want to be seen on camera. It meant the ghillie suit wearing snipers had to trek the 2.7 miles they'd specified to the ranch and back, and in between, Wade and Ansel had to ride in on the dirt bikes to rescue Aaron from the barn.

I was doing the math in my head. I could run about a seven and a-half-minute mile. Even if it took these men eighteen to twenty minutes each three-mile way on foot, that only left Wade and Ansel roughly ten minutes to get Aaron out of that barn. They were cutting it close...*real* close. Maybe I'd missed something while I was eaves-dropping on their plans. They had stood back there and planned for hours.

One last time, they went over the plan of what each person needed to do and where they all needed to be. I only understood half of their short-hand method of verbally communicating. They had gear strapped to nearly every vital part of their bodies. When everyone bowed their head for a quiet moment of prayer, I bowed mine too. I prayed for the safe return of Aaron and all the men.

Ansel stepped over to me. "Here, take this. I know you won't hesitate to use it if you have to."

"I already have a gun," I reminded Ansel.

"I know, take this one too. It will give me a little peace of mind."

I took the extra pistol from him and climbed into the back of the truck when he pulled the door open. Once he closed me in, he stood outside the window and stared at me for a brief moment before rejoining the rest of the men.

My face sat inches from the glass of the window as I took in the dark view outside the truck. Each man conducted a vocal mic check to ensure their communication devices worked. Hearing their voices so clear in my ear made me smile despite our harrowing situation.

The synchronized beeps of watches went off. I didn't have a watch, but I could hear them beeping in my ear as if I was standing near the men. I remembered them saying the next time those watches went off, it meant they needed to be back at the trucks and heading out.

First, the Chewbaccas stepped into the darkness and disappeared. So, this was where they must have been making up some time, sending them out to march part of the three miles before their official start time. I waited, watching the remaining men watch the darkness. Anxiousness weighted my body and consumed my mind enough that I hadn't paid attention to how much time had passed. The next thing I heard was D's heavy breathing in my ear.

"Striker one in place." About thirty seconds later another voiced announced that striker two was in place until all the Chewbaccas had made it to their points. It was safe to say they hadn't been spotted by our adversaries, which meant they were out there ready to start a war. A scratch sounded in my ear, alerting me that someone was about to speak.

"Ansel and Wade, get ready," D ordered sharply.

The next thing I heard were the engines of the dirt bikes coming to life. Then...

Chah! Chah! Chah!

Boom! Boom!

Tap! Tap! Tap! Tap!

The listening device amplified the sound as if I was right in the thick of the action. From my position, nearly three miles away in the truck I could see fire light up the sky. It appeared as if lightning flashes were going off.

"Tower down! Tower down! Ansel. Wade. Go! Go! Go!"

When Ansel and Wade heard their cue, they took off like bats out of hell, scratching up dirt and debris that pelted the side of the truck.

I could hear the roar of the bikes through the earpiece and imagined the rush they must have felt speeding into the heart of a firestorm.

Jackson and Jake took their positions, aiming into the darkness towards the property. They laid prone on the ground with machine guns at the ready. Night goggles were attached to their faces and back up weapons attached to their legs. I didn't miss the hot red tip of the joint ignite with each puff as the twins passed it back and forth between each other. Functioning while high had likely become their norm.

My instructions were to stay put inside the vehicle that I'd overheard was armored. How they'd managed to steel armored vehicles was beyond me, but a brilliant idea, considering the situation we were in. All-out war was taking place in front of me as the sky continued to light up and the booms of the powerful weapons seemed to vibrate the ground even at my distance away.

After I slid across the seat to the opposite door away from the twins, I creaked it open and moved quickly away from the truck. I needed to get to the next vehicle where they'd left some of the spare equipment.

22

ANSEL

Even with the tower gone, the cameras out, our snipers, and a fucking 50 Cal, these guards were still prepared enough to make our mission hard. They couldn't see Wade and me well, so they aimed at what they heard.

Wade and I were targets because of the noise the dirt bikes made. However, each time they fired at us, our snipers would know where to shoot. With the noise of the bikes clouding our hearing, we could barely make out what else was going on out there with our men.

When Wade veered in the opposite direction from me, I knew we had nearly reached our targeted areas. Wade was to post up behind the shack on the west and be my backup if I needed him. I pushed on and sped towards the wide dark shadow that cast at the back of the barn.

Once I was close enough to the barn, I stopped the bike and laid it against a cluster of bushes. After dropping into a horizontal position, I scanned and low crawled to the barn's back door. The crackle and pop of gun blast never ceased in my ear. The unmistakable blast of the 50 Cal lit up my earpiece.

Our sniper team had thankfully taken out the barn's rear guard. I peered down at his crumpled body as I stepped across the man and made my way closer to the back door. With a continuous flow of gunfire erupting, I had no problem shooting the padlock before I repeatedly kicked the huge back door of the barn to get it open.

Once I entered the barn, all manner of rusted and cobwebbed equipment filled my dark view. I brushed stringy webs from my face as I inched towards the only light that shined in a stall near the front of the building.

An angry boom shook the ground under my feet, and the listening device reacted with a loud, elongated scratch. I kept my eye on the lighted room in my front view.

A set of muffled voices sounded as I peeked around the last corner that gave me a view of the stall. Two guards stood near Aaron, who was hanging from the ceiling by thick braided ropes. His head hung low as his chin sat against his chest. His arms were pulled taut, carrying his body weight as the ropes dug into his raw wrists. His black T-shirt was so badly ripped, it barely clung to his limp body.

Near enough to make out their accented words, I listened as I crept closer.

"What kind of people does this he know? It sounds like World War III out there."

"I don't know, but it will be over when the backup gets here."

Backup? These motherfuckers believed in backup. At some point, they must have radioed for more guns. I had to get Aaron the fuck out of there and now. I also had to warn everyone that backup was on the way, but I couldn't risk speaking and giving up my position.

My brain switched to kill mode, and my body followed. A slug to each head took out the two talkers. I stepped over their jittering bodies to see if Aaron was still breathing. He was out, but that tough bastard was still drawing breath. From the looks of him, they had worked him over really good. The right leg of his jeans had been ripped up to his thigh. If the bone sticking out of his leg above his calf was any indication, I'd say we were going to have a hard time getting back to the dirt bike.

It took great effort and precious time to cut Aaron down without injuring him further. He moved and groaned and attempted to throw a punch at me.

I dodged his whirling blow in the nick of time. "It's me, goddammit. I'm trying to save your ass."

"Ansel?" he murmured. Both his eyes were bloodshot, and one was nearly swollen shut. There was no way he was walking on that damn leg. Blood gushed out around the protruding bone every time I moved him. *Fuck!*

"Bite down on this," I instructed while shoving an old piece of leather between his teeth. Then, I gripped and tore off the tail end of his bloody shirt and found two broken pieces of discarded piping as stabilizers.

Aaron knew what I was about to do. He pushed the bit of leather deeper between his teeth and took a couple of deep breaths.

I talked loud so that the crew would hear me. "They have backup on the way. We may have to split up to get out of here."

"Roger that."

"Tracking," and more acknowledgments sounded into the earpiece.

With a quick yank, I straightened out Aaron's leg, causing him to whimper and take in harsh, desperate breaths. After I placed the piping on both sides of the gaping laceration, I tied the top and bottom tight enough that it would at least relieve some of the pressure of Aaron's movements. Once I got him standing, he hobbled along as I dragged him out of the stall. We were moving too damn slowly.

"I'm going to have to carry you," I said, unsure if my half-conscious cousin heard me. I shoved my pistol down the front of my pants and handed Aaron my spare handgun before I bent to sling him over my shoulder in a fireman's carry. The bastard was heavier than he looked. Were his fucking bones made of iron?

Winded, harsh breaths burned my lungs by the time we made it to my bike. Our snipers were doing their jobs keeping the ranch guards busy. Thankfully, Aaron and I hadn't been met with gunfire.

The wail of a revving engine sounded and a large crash somewhere along the front side of the property sounded and urged me to move faster. If that noise was what I pictured it might be, a vehicle had just driven through the fence and was likely preparing to run any one of us down.

Like the scene from a fucking horror film, the bike refused to start. With every kick and turn of the throttle that it didn't start, I cursed.

As if spurred by the sudden emergence of a bullet zooming by my ear, the engine of the dirt bike rattled to a growling start, and Aaron and I shot off like a rocket, kicking up dirt and grass. Aaron had me around the waist with one hand and had his gun aimed into the last remnants of nightfall with the other.

I sped through the dim light without the aid of night vision. I couldn't see the sun, but that bastard was lurking somewhere, eating up the darkness we needed. However, the dim light gave us enough illumination to keep us from crashing into anything.

"Everyone, head back. Jake, Jackson, take Megan and go now in one of the trucks."

The twin's voices didn't carry well over the roar of the bike's screaming engine, but it sounded like one had said they couldn't find her. Megan had gotten the very last earpiece and it was damaged. She was only linked in to listen, so she couldn't tell me where the hell she was if the twins had lost her. Were they high? I was going to kick their asses if they'd let someone sneak in behind them and take her.

23

ANSEL

The fucking blinding light of a vehicle running behind mine and Aaron's asses had me pushing the engine on the bike past its breaking point. With the erratic and evasive movements of the bike, I didn't know how the fuck Aaron was hanging on to me with one hand as he fired off rounds at the bastards chasing us with the other. The vehicle behind us was so close that I could feel the heat from the engine breathing down my neck.

I didn't have to see it to know that Aaron had shot out one of the headlights. The blinding light behind us had dimmed considerably, and the truck had backed off for a few seconds.

Our brief reprieve didn't last long. When the bike went jetting forward and flew out of my control, I expected to feel the bone-breaking crash. The vehicle had bumped us from behind, but I'd yanked the wheel just in the nick of time to keep us from meeting the ground at a break-neck speed.

When the engine of the vehicle chasing us revved up to rear end us again, I gave the bike all it had and braced for the impact. One of Aaron's shots must have hit the driver of the vehicle behind us because the impact I expected never came.

The sound of the vehicle dwindled until only the squealing rattle of our bike could be heard. My eyes remained on the shadowy tree-lined woods that grew closer with every passing second dead ahead of us. We were going to make it.

I didn't slow the momentum of the bike until we were only feet away from the tree line. I cut the engine before the bike stopped moving. The roaring sound of another bike close behind made me realize that Wade had been right on our tail. It occurred to me that Wade had likely helped to keep that damn vehicle from running Aaron and me down. After his bike came to an abrupt stop, he dropped it and ran over to me to assist me with Aaron.

"Megan!" I yelled as I kept an arm under one of Aaron's shoulders.

"You brought her here?" Aaron questioned through gritted teeth. I didn't answer as I spotted another vehicle approaching, its headlights resembled angry eyes as they grew closer, eating up the three miles of distance from the ranch.

"Striker team, where the fuck are you guys? It's about to get hot in these woods." I knew they had to hike by feet, so they were at least five maybe even seven minutes behind us. If backup from the ranch had arrived, five to seven minutes could mean our lives.

"Twelve. Fanning out, flanking area," D growled in the earpiece, but it was broken. "Leave bikes and go." D must have been getting closer to us because his voice started to become clearer the more he talked. "We'll hold these bastards back. Go! Go! Go!"

If D thought I was leaving them out there to take on whatever backup DG6 had called in, he could think again.

Aaron's pained voice sounded in my ear. "If D says go, fucking go! He knows what to do."

"Nine remaining. They're in the tree line now. Get down! Get down!" D barked into the earpiece again.

There were fucking mercenaries in the tree line, and the twins had lost Megan.

"Striker four near ground zero," Marcus informed through the earpiece in a hushed voice. With Marcus someplace near the tree line with us, it meant that half of Aaron's hardheaded-ass team and Scott were still out there. So was Megan. DG6 had been serious about keeping my cousin and about protecting their property. There had to be more to this damn ranch than DG6 was letting on.

"Megan!" I yelled as Aaron's crumpled body clung to mine. Wade let Aaron go so he could watch our back as I made my way towards the vehicle. I propped Aaron against a tree and aimed to the right of us when the hairs on the back of my neck stood. I fired off three shots, aiming for the head. The bastard went down, but him being that close to us let me know that they likely had us surrounded.

"Megan, where in the fuck are you?" I called out, but not too loud because we had company now. Her little ass didn't answer me, but I swore I spotted her creeping towards me, tiptoeing over the grassy plan of the woods. It was dimmer inside the tree line than it had been in that open stretch of land, so my eyes were still adjusting. It was a strange mix of light and darkness that made night goggles fifty-fifty for usefulness.

It was Megan that I was watching, and her fucking gun was aimed at my fucking head. Something was wrong. When she waved for Aaron and me to get the fuck out of the way, I knew one or both of us were dead.

Bam! Bam! Bam!

I didn't know where Megan learned to shoot, but the bullets from her gun passed so close to the side of my fucking face that they warmed my cheek. When I glanced back, she'd taken out a mercenary that had managed to sneak up on Aaron and me. The damn sun was starting to crest, so we didn't have the cover of nightfall to hide us anymore.

"There are more of them around here, and another truck just pulled up," Megan informed us as she yanked a set of night goggles over her head and tossed them aside.

I handed Aaron over to her. "Get him inside the truck," I instructed.

When I turned, my body went flying back against the side of a tree. Megan and Aaron stumbled to the ground or maybe she'd pulled him down. I couldn't tell. My vest caught the bullet that struck me, and I gasped, choking on the last remnants of wind that had been knocked out of my lungs.

Two days in a row I'd been shot in the chest. This shot, compounded with the one from yesterday put me down, although I was sure the bullet hadn't gotten through.

Wade lit the bastard up that shot me and ended up taking two shots to his chest and shoulder area that sent him flying back to the ground. His agonizing cry signified that he'd also been shot.

"Everyone down!" My anguished voiced cried out, hoping the men understood me as I was just now accepting that this mission was getting more out of hand by the second.

DG6 must have sent one hell of a backup crew. Jake and Jackson were engaged in their own gun battle. Blasts from both their guns went off to the left of me. Megan struggled with Aaron in front of me. Marcus had the damn 50 Cal talking. Our snipers were out there shooting anyone who wasn't us. Wade writhed in pain on the ground to my right. All I wanted was a breath of air.

On all fours, I struggled to get air into my crumpled body, and my fucking hand refused to work. It wasn't until the peppery sparks of pain awakened in my arm that I felt the warm liquid drizzling down the inside of my arm. They had clipped me in the arm, and I hadn't even realized it.

When I looked up, Megan had propped Aaron against the next tree. She had her little body in front of his, facing him. She peeked around the tree that protected them and was aiming her gun out into the trees on the opposite side. Neither she nor Aaron had a fucking vest on, so they were in the most danger.

A cold chill hit me, making me turn in time to see a shadowy figure approach Megan, as two were approaching Aaron's front. They had motherfuckers coming at them both ways. I was sure I was yelling my fucking head off, but I couldn't hear the words coming out of my own mouth.

Aaron spotted the ones in his view first. He raised his weapon, and as Megan turned to help him, he pushed her to the ground and started firing. I could see bullets shredding the tree trunk next to him as pieces of bark flew into the air. Without a Kevlar vest on, any shot could kill him.

Although Aaron had pushed Megan to the ground, she was still shooting at the man approaching them from the opposite side of that tree. Aaron's bullets were hitting the men in front of him, but the handgun I'd given him was no match for the automatic weapons aimed at him. I shot round after round at the men. Relief swept through me when one fell. They were definitely wearing body armor. Aaron shot the second man, but the bastard wouldn't fall.

One of my bullets dropped the man continuing to fire at my cousin, but a final shot escaped the man's weapon before his body hit the ground. It was as if I could see the moment with crystal clear, high definition vision. The shot struck Aaron in the head, jerking him back so hard that it sent his body slamming into the tree trunk behind him. He tumbled, headfirst to the ground, his lifeless body falling in what appeared to be slow motion. Dead or not, I unloaded the rest of my clip in the man that had shot my cousin.

24

ANSEL

I stood there, frozen, not believing what I was seeing. Reality smacked me in the face, and I snapped out of my trance.

"No!" I yelled so loud that it likely alerted every enemy to my position. I didn't even realize I was running until I was standing over Aaron. Megan's scream lit up the woods as she scrambled over to him on her hands and knees.

"Aaron! Aaron! Get up please!" she begged through heart-wrenching wails that raised goose bumps on my arms. She pushed with all her might to turn Aaron onto his back. Once he faced us, I could tell at a glance that my cousin was almost gone—the tremble in his limbs, the involuntary jerking of his muscles, the haunting, hollowed, glazed-over look in his eyes.

When a bullet struck the back of my Kevlar and yanked my body forcefully in the opposite direction, I didn't feel the pain of the powerful impact. I simply turned and started firing. The sight of my cousin so limp and lifeless had numbed me.

As I continued to fight off the fucking roaches that kept creeping through the cracks, Megan's cries continued to seep into my mind, reminding me that the bastards I was killing had shot my cousin. All I saw was red at this point, so angry that my nostrils flared as bullet after bullet left my gun. Two new clips had been fed into the weapon by the time I stopped firing.

"Ground Zero, go now. There are three more trucks heading for the tree line," D announced into the earpiece. The eagerness in his voice hinted at the amount of danger headed our way.

I dragged my body over to Aaron and Megan who was kneeling over him rubbing his cheek. She clutched his limp hand against her chest. When I saw his eyes fluttering open and closed, I leaned down further to make sure I wasn't imagining what I'd seen in the dim lighting. Only minutes had passed but they had brought with them more of the sun's rays that allowed me to see Aaron clearer than before.

Had he been shot in the head? I squinted. Was that blood pooling under his shoulders? The pool of dark liquid expanded before my eyes as the rusted scent made its way up my nostrils. Life was seeping from Aaron's body. I froze, no longer able to recall my motor functions.

When I forced my body to move, I leaned close enough to make out the small entrance wound near the hairline of his left temple. The bullet must have exited somewhere out of the back of his head or neck. His skin had already started to pale as his lips shivered from the coldness of approaching death.

I placed my ear over his mouth when he tried to speak. "Take her. Take care..."

He was telling me to take care of Megan, who looked about as crazy as an escaped insane patient. Aaron turned his gaze away from me, looked up at Megan and smiled before his eyes closed, and his hand went slack inside hers.

Aaron's body sat frozen in time. My face relaxed. Every emotion within me raced to the surface when I reached towards my cousin. When I shook his shoulder, my hand on his lifeless body sent chills racing through me. My heart stopped pumping blood, and my brain ceased to send messages to the rest of my body. My eyes forgot how to blink.

"Aaron," I called, aware that my voice was too low for anyone to hear. All my senses went away, and I was only left with sight and the numbing silence that my cousin was no longer there with me.

The moment Megan realized he was gone she started screaming. Her loud, wailing cries snapped me out of my daze and made me realize we were still in danger. The pain in her anguished voice took the last pinch of strength I had left. The way she clutched Aaron's lifeless hand and the pleading in her eyes and voice took whatever little piece of my heart that wasn't already shattered.

She'd completely lost control of her own body, unsure of which way to turn or move. I had never seen someone love one of us as much as I knew she loved Aaron. She would do anything to bring Aaron back, to see him open his eyes or to hear him speak again, but he was gone.

"No, Aaron, please. I love you, Aaron, please. Don't leave me. Please, Aaron, please don't leave me," she begged desperately, her cries mingling into one long continuous word.

Her hand shook so badly that she appeared to be in the middle of a nervous breakdown. Her unblinking eyes were deadlocked on Aaron's face as tears spilled from them in fast-moving currents. Aaron was gone, but Megan continued to hold on to his limp hand, shaking it to try to wake him up.

"No. No. No. Aaron, please, Aaron, don't leave me," she begged and pleaded so hard that I was sure she'd forgotten about us being hunted by the same assholes who had shot my cousin.

With hair all over her head, tears streaming down her cheeks, and what must have been Aaron's blood smeared all over her disheveled clothes, she looked deranged. Megan had lost her shit right in front of me, and I didn't know how to help her because I'd lost my shit equally as bad.

"We've gotta go!" Jackson yelled and stopped dead in his tracks when he saw Aaron laid out on the ground in a pool of blood.

Megan continued pleading. I remained kneeling next to my cousin in shock, my eyes darting back in forth between him, silent and still, and Megan, frantic and crying. For the first time since I was a kid, I didn't know what to do. I felt helpless, useless, and worthless. This was a situation I couldn't fix, a problem I couldn't solve.

Jackson looked from me to Aaron and back behind him. When he reached back, aimed, and started shooting, I knew we were out of time.

"We've gotta go, Ansel. There is about ten more of them coming."

I heard Jackson, but at the same time, I didn't. I knew we had to move, but my body wouldn't. Jackson clutched my shoulder, shaking me out of my daze.

"We've gotta fucking go, or we are going to die too. We go, regroup, come back, and avenge our cousin," he urged.

Jackson was right. I couldn't die. Not today. I couldn't die because I had to avenge my cousin's death. I had to take down DG6 if it was the last fucking thing I did with my life. Jackson ran over and started the truck. He left the back passenger's side door open for Megan and me.

When I could think straight enough to get Megan to safety, I saw that the girl was just standing there in front of Aaron with her eyes closed. She'd turned towards the area that Jackson had fired into moments ago, where the bullets were flying from. It took me a moment to realize what she was doing. She was standing there waiting for a bullet to hit her. She was facing a fucking firing squad with not an ounce of regard for her life.

I could clearly see in the dim lighting that she wasn't in her right frame of mind. I tried to shake her out of it. "Megan! Megan! We've gotta fucking go." But she was too far gone for me to shake some sense into her.

Jake came running towards me from the direction of the truck behind the one we were supposed to be climbing into. "I've got Wade in the second truck. We've gotta go! Get in the fucking truck..."

Jake's words slammed to a stop when he noticed what was holding us up. Flying bullets made him duck and shoot in the direction the bullets traveled from. Megan yelled at the top of her lungs, continuing to face the fire. "No! Aaron! No!" She'd become nothing more than a screaming target. I tried to force her to follow me, but that crazy-woman strength was powering her.

"I'm not leaving him! I'm not leaving him!"

When a bullet struck the tree near her body, the damn girl didn't even acknowledge that death was seconds away from her. She was ready to die. The will to live was supposed to be an overpowering force that made you fight for your life. Megan's will had been extinguished when Aaron died. She was ready to die. I picked her up and tossed her over my shoulder, kicking and screaming. Jake had my back, firing off round after round as I ran towards the truck.

Once we were safely at the vehicle, I tossed Megan in before I entered after her. Jake ran around to the vehicle behind us and took off. A bullet struck the window next to me with a hard thump right next to my face, but the bullet-proof glass stopped it. Jackson threw the truck in reverse and proceeded to get us the hell out of there.

Our teams were specially trained for this type of battle, but with the number of mercenaries swarming around the place, I didn't even know if they were going to make it. I was the one who had called D, so if they died here on this Texas ranch, their deaths would be on my hands.

"We can't leave him. We can't leave him." This crazy woman had gotten most of her body across my lap and had sprung the door open. I had to keep her from hopping the rest of the way over me and out of the damn fast-moving vehicle as bullets continued to pelt the body of our SUV.

"Strikers, the package is down. Please pick up the package on the way out!" I yelled into the earpiece as I slung an arm over Megan's chest, pinning her against the back of the seat. I didn't have the heart to tell the men that the package, Aaron, was not only down, but he was dead. I'm sure they already knew what I was telling them to do. If they escaped the ranch, I wanted them to pick up Aaron's body. I'd fully intended to bring my cousin with me, but I'd had to pick up Megan to keep a bullet out of her.

"Roger that."

"Tracking."

A few other acknowledgments came across the static-filled earpiece as I sat in the back of the SUV feeling like a lump of worthless shit.

25

ANSEL

Scott and Marcus and the three from Aaron's crew, D, Dax, and Gavin were still at war. Marcus and Scott weren't going to stop fighting until they or the enemy was dead. I was confident that Aaron's crew would do the same.

The scratching in the earpiece wiped out the constant sound of gunfire. I'd lost my connection with the rest of the team as Jackson drove us further away from the ranch. He was driving the vehicle like a mad man, giving the engine a run for its money.

We followed the dust of Jake and Wade in the vehicle in front of us. This was the first time I'd fled from a gunfight. Seeing Aaron dead had fucked me up so badly that even I knew to call it quits.

This mission was fucked. If only we'd had Aaron to do the planning. He was one of those people who would plan for weeks or months if he had to. The bastard would study every angle, escape route, and every other damn aspect of a mission down to the shit schedule of the guards before he would proceed and carry out a mission.

Unfortunately, we didn't have the luxury of time on our side and had gone in half-cocked. Now, Aaron was dead, and his team and mine were still back there fighting.

Aaron's dead. The words burned through my mind, eating at my brain like acid through flesh. The image of Aaron, lifeless and devoid of anything that made him the Aaron I knew, fucked my head up. *I'm never going to see my cousin again.*

"Fuck!" I yelled as the idea of him being dead drilled its way deeper into my tortured brain.

My curse had erupted through the cab of the vehicle and caused Jackson to glance back over the seat at me. Tears started to fall from my eyes. The foreign droplets slid down my cheeks, leaked from my eyes, and scared the shit out of me, but I couldn't stop them. Aaron was more than just my cousin. He was my *brother.* He was my fucking big brother.

WE DROVE until we came to the small town of Engles, Texas, about sixty-five miles away from the ranch. I'd managed to get my wounded arm to stop bleeding and was thankful I'd only been grazed by a bullet.

The fact that I could see Wade's head moving in the vehicle in front of us was a good sign that he was still alive. As long as he was breathing, we would find him help.

I hadn't figured out how to tell Uncle Shark that Aaron was gone. He was going to kill me or Megan or both of us. But, knowing my uncle the way that I did, he would wage full-fledged war on DG6, and I would be right there with him.

We couldn't take Wade inside the hospital in the condition we were in, so I had Jake and Jackson set him near the emergency entrance. I instructed him to hobble into the emergency room and lie his ass off about how he'd gotten shot. We'd stripped him of the gear and equipment and cleaned him up as best we could. We'd ditched the second vehicle in the hospital parking structure like it belonged there. We sat across the street and watched the hospital staff run out to help Wade.

"We'll come back and check on him later tonight," I informed Jackson. "For now, find a motel where we can hold up."

Jackson's red-eye glare met mine in the rearview mirror before he nodded his head. Jake sat in the front passenger's seat with his head laid back on the headrest. I didn't have to look in his face to know that he was crying. His shaking shoulders and repeated sniffing told me so.

Aaron had been tough on the twins over the years, but he was more of a father figure to them than their own father was. When they would get into trouble, even if the shit was their fault, Aaron was right there to back them up. He'd gotten them out of more money problems than I could count, and they both would have been dead three times over if they hadn't had Aaron watching their backs.

My gaze landed on Megan. I didn't have the slightest clue as to how I was supposed to help her. Her head was laid across my lap, and the rest of her body was tucked into a tight knot on the seat. A riotous mass if thick curls was all over the place. Her anguished cries had gone on and on until she'd either passed out or run out of sound. Occasionally, her body would jump with a start. I was as helpless with her as I had been seeing my cousin lose his life. So, I simply rubbed her head and let her suffer in peace.

My mind fell on my team and Aaron's. It'd been over an hour since we'd left them in the heat of battle. I placed Aaron's phone to my ear and dialed D.

"Yeah," he answered. His voice breathed a touch of life back into my deflated body.

"You don't know how fucking happy I am to hear your voice. Did you all make it?"

"Yeah. Marcus took one in the back, but it didn't hit anything vital. Gavin took a leg shot. It missed his dick by an inch, but he's good. We had to flee on foot. So, we couldn't pick up the package."

Fuck!

"I'm about sixty miles out, but I'm going back to get my cousin."

"Let me know what time," D said.

"No, D. You guys have put yourselves through enough shit. I got this."

"Let me know what time," D repeated. His adamant voice let me know that he was about as hardheaded as Aaron was.

"I'll text you later tonight," I replied before I ended the call.

26

ANSEL

fter D hung up, the idea of avenging Aaron took over my mind. Like Megan, I was going through the motions. All I could think about was the fact that I was never going to see my cousin again, and the assholes who had taken him from me.

As badly as I wanted to kill someone, I had to take a page from Aaron's book and calm the fuck down. Patience wasn't my forte, but if I was going to avenge my cousin and do it right, patience was going to be a necessity. I couldn't allow what had happened to Aaron to happen again.

We checked into a flea-bag motel that was nestled on a desolate back road, hidden from the main flow of traffic. I shared a room with Megan because I was afraid to leave her alone. She was like a zombie, eyes dead, mind on autopilot, and not talking.

I couldn't get her to eat, drink, or utter a word. I could tell it in the helpless lean of her body and the haunted glint in her eyes that she just wanted to die. My cousin's death was ripping my heart apart, but Megan had sunk to a whole other level.

I couldn't even enjoy the fucking fact that I'd had her naked in the shower with me. The poor girl was so out of it, I'd had to strip her out of her bloody clothes and help her to shower. Once I got her cleaned up, I dug through her backpack and helped her into the pajama set she'd packed.

After tucking her into one of the beds in our room, I stood over her and observed. Aaron told me to take care of her, but I feared that there wasn't enough of her left for me to take care of. My finger stroked her damp curls before I brushed a few away from her face. "Don't worry, Megan. I'm going to get those motherfuckers. All of them. I'm going to dismantle DG6. Either they die or I die."

Seeing Megan like this pushed my mind further into revenge mode because I wasn't sure if she was going to recover. Hell, I didn't know if I would recover. All I kept seeing was Aaron's lifeless body on that ground and that bullet when it struck his head and sent his body flying back against that tree.

I dialed the number I'd been dreading for hours. When I placed Aaron's phone to my ear, Uncle Shark answered on the first ring. "Aaron?"

Fuck! How was I going to tell him that his last son was dead? "Unc, it's me, Ansel." I swallowed the fucking mountain-size lump in my throat.

"Where the fuck is Aaron, Ansel?"

"Unc, Aaron's gone," I choked out. My voice didn't sound like my own having to speak those words.

"Mother Fuck!" my uncle yelled into the phone as some object in the background struck with the force and sound of thunder.

Someone in the background must have asked him what was wrong. I heard him say, "They killed Aaron. They killed the only son I had left." His growling voice returned loud in my ear. "They're going to fucking die or we die."

My robotic reply was automatic. "I agree, Uncle Shark. They are going to die."

The line went dead.

～

MOMENTS LATER, I rolled to the edge of my wobbly mattress and fought gravity to keep from tumbling to the floor. Swiping at a few droplets that edged down the side of my head, cold sweat clung to my skin. The last twenty-four hours had my brain quaking and about ready to explode as my mind conjured the events that had led to the greatest lost I'd ever suffered.

Aaron had visited me in my dreams and in my unconscious state, I didn't have any other choice but to listen to his wise words. His last words hadn't been those he'd spoken to me in those woods, telling me to take care of Megan. Instead, his last words had just seared their way into my brain, presenting a lesson I should have learned long ago. Aaron's words had been so loud in my head that they had downloaded themselves into my memory banks.

"Don't do anything until your head is clear. Don't go after anyone. Don't fucking plot any revenge scenes. Take Megan and go the fuck home. It's over. Don't engage. Don't do shit. Go the fuck home and work on your patience."

Patience had always been my greatest weakness. It had also been the one thing Aaron had been harping on me to embrace and practice for years. The way I felt right now with a heart full of vengeance, I didn't know if I could abide my cousin's words even when I knew the best thing to do was to adhere to them.

I glanced over at Megan. Her body was pulled in a tight ball, nothing more than a lump under the covers. She was hurting just a bad as I was, but the difference was she had released her grief. Her problem was that she had so much inside that it had consumed her.

Only a part of my heart was left inside my chest, but the part I had left had to be strong, sure, and careful. "I can no longer be who I was," I mumbled in a low tone. I couldn't be the hot head, hot-tempered, arrogant ass that I'd always been.

I had to find the patience I'd never had and embrace it like it was my last breath. At twenty-six, I'd finally learned a life lesson in the harshest way possible. I had to lose the one person who meant the most to me to learn how to embrace my own life.

Aaron had left me the one thing that meant the most to him in his life—Megan. Now that my mind wasn't as clouded with thoughts of revenge, I could think more clearly. I could no longer walk carelessly into danger as I once had before. Patience was going to be my new guide.

Megan had survived for a decade without endangering anyone's life except her own as far as I knew. She'd been siphoning her strength wherever she could get it. She knew how to be quiet, humble, and patient. Her methods weren't the most practical or even sane, but she'd done one hell of a better job at keeping herself safe than we had.

This was all my fault. Aaron was dead because of me. If only I'd let Aaron plan this out and not rushed him into this madness. Megan blamed herself for Aaron's death, but he'd decided to enter the fight. As well as I knew my cousin, once he'd decided on something, there was no changing his mind.

If I'd been in Aaron's shoes, knowing what I knew now, I would have done the same damn thing. Aaron had decided on Megan and the devil himself couldn't have ripped that woman away from my cousin.

My uncle wanted retribution for Aaron's death and he was likely going to get it or die trying. I was going to help him, but I wasn't going to make any moves unless provoked. Nope, I was going to sit my ass down for once in my life, grieve my cousin's death, and take care of Megan like he'd asked me to. For once, I had to accept that I'd been beaten.

Bruised, battered, and bloody, I had to heal, and I had to ensure the woman lying in that bed would heal as well. I was going to listen to my cousin and find the one thing I'd never had—patience.

27

MEGAN

bout six months later...

It had taken me months to find some semblance of normalcy again. Aaron's death had nearly killed me. As a matter of fact, I think I'd died and had been revived several times as large chunks of time had gone missing from my head.

If it hadn't been for Ansel and the promise I'd made Aaron that I would go on and fight, I wouldn't have survived. I'd been held up in Ansel's California home the entire time, and DG6 either couldn't find me or thought I was too much trouble to be bothered with.

Ansel had been patient with me and caring, but I knew he still grieved for his cousin as much as I did. He'd made every attempt to get me out of the house over the months, but I wasn't ready and I didn't know if I would ever be.

Ansel had never told me about where he went when he left for days at a time, but I knew it had something to do with DG6 and avenging Aaron. Just like I'd begged Aaron, I begged Ansel to leave it alone and let me run. However, Ansel was just as hardheaded as Aaron and wouldn't hear of it. I was afraid he'd end up getting himself killed too.

As I sat on Ansel's large leather couch in the living room, flipping absently through the TV channels, the doorbell rang. Normally, it wasn't a big deal to hear a doorbell ring, but in the six months I'd lived with Ansel, his doorbell had never rung. I didn't even know that there was a doorbell.

Ansel's maid slash house manager, had taken some leave, and Ansel had left, dressed in one of his suits, informing me that he had a business meeting to attend to.

Therefore, I was alone in the huge seven-bedroom, five-bathroom, immaculately decorated home. Like Aaron, Ansel had standards that were surprisingly refreshing and somewhat sophisticated. Ansel's standards were pricier than Aaron's were, and considering who he led you to believe he was, you'd never know he lived like a king. Other than guns, I still wasn't sure how Ansel made his living, but he lived well.

At a glance, I didn't see a shadow on the other side of the designs in the thick glass of the door. The only other people on the property with me were the four around-the-clock guards that Ansel insisted on at all times. I'd caught enough of one of their conversations to know that the guards were some of Ansel's friends from when he was in the military. I'd already met Scott and Marcus, who'd visited for about a month but had left a few weeks ago.

The guards never rang the doorbell because they all had keys and ensured they announced themselves before entering. Maybe, one had accidentally hit the doorbell or forgotten his key inside.

Ding Dong. The bell rang once more. Its alarming sound danced against my eardrums and filled my body with tension. My wide-eyed gaze shot back to the door as I stood on wobbly legs.

I crept closer to the thick glass door. The shadow on the other side appeared out of nowhere, making me slide to a quick stop, my bare feet squeaking against the floor. Although my body was no longer in motion, my heart was beating double time.

The asymmetric designs of the etched glass in the door made the shadow appear tall, dark, and menacing. Had DG6 finally tracked me to Ansel's house? All I knew of my location was that we were somewhere in the state of California. Ansel never told me where I was, and I didn't ask.

Up until now, I'd felt safe in the huge house. The place was more secure than a damn fortress. A palm print, retinal scan, voice acknowledgment as well as a six-digit code got you as far as the front door. Whoever was at the door, had blown through at least five security measures. If this was DG6, it meant they'd killed the guards and they were finally about to kill me.

Tired of running, being afraid, and worrying about when they'd finally find me, I crept closer to the door. My gaze locked on the dark figure on the other side. A part of my brain was telling me to run like hell and hide for as long as I could, but another part was telling me to open the damn door already.

My glance went back to my phone sitting on the coffee table, and I jumped with a heaving sigh when the doorbell chimed once more. *Ding Dong.*

"Open the damn door, Megan," I whispered nervously to myself. There didn't appear to be a weapon in the dark figure's hand.

"It's one of the guards, Megan. Stop being paranoid," I scolded myself, mumbling under my breath.

Reaching up to the keypad, I punched in the code to disarm the alarm with shaky fingers. My gaze was locked on my unsteady hand as I reached up to flip the first deadbolt, my legs trembling under my body.

My stomach was rolling in knots, my heavy breaths blowing harshly past my lips. I forced myself to reach for the last deadbolt, the only thing keeping me from seeing if it was death waiting on the other side of that door or if my paranoid brain needed to relax.

The sound of the final lock flipping open may as well have been a gun blast to my eardrum. My trembling fingers twisted the doorknob, but I paused before springing it all the way open.

I inhaled deeply, closing my eyes as I pulled the door towards me, waiting for the bullet to strike or the knife to slice into a major artery. The heat from the bright sun enveloped my body, the low chirp of a bird's voice found its way to my ears, but I remained in place standing with my eyes glued shut.

After about five seconds of standing there, I'm sure looking like an idiot, I opened my eyes, and the vision standing before me made my heart freeze in my chest before it exploded.

"*Aaron?*"

28

PART II

REGINA

The night of the farm rescue...

A vibrating rumble shook me from my dreams, and I jerked awake fighting my sheets and comforter to get out of bed. A skin-grating noise like the sky was being unzipped found its way to my ears before it started to rain bricks.

Instead of climbing from my bed gracefully, my left foot lost its fight with the covers, and I fell to the floor with a hard thud that shook my insides and emptied my lungs of oxygen.

The constant booms of what I assumed was weapon fire caused trembles to shake the ground above. I was probably in the safest place on my family's farm—the cellar they'd converted into my home and office. I remained in place, lying on my floor as I contemplated sliding under my bed.

The men who guarded the farm often practiced shooting at targets, so I was familiar with the muffled sound of gunfire. However, this was much closer than usual. It sounded as if guns were blasting off right above me.

The flashing blue numbers, the only light that waved through the darkness in my room, told me it was 3:52 a.m. and it would still be as dark outside as it was in my room.

Although I lived on the basement level, it didn't hide the fact that it sounded like a war was raging outside. Confined to the cellar, I was rarely introduced to what went on outside.

It hadn't always been so, but thanks to my family, my life had been converted to a lonely, dreary shell of what it used to be. Before I was uprooted and transplanted here, I'd lived a normal and somewhat pampered life. The daughter of the infamous Emilio Dominquez, I'd breezed through medical school with ease at Cornell University in New York before entering their residency program.

After my father's death, I became enslaved by my own family. I was yanked from my residency at the Presbyterian Brooklyn Methodist Hospital after I'd invested a promising eight months in my career. Here at the farm and without my father's intervention, I was forced to do the jobs my family assigned me or risk being eaten alive by the den of slithering poisonous reptiles that they were.

Another loud boom rattled the surface above me to the point that vibrations danced over my skin. On my belly, I slid under the bed as my gaze searched pointlessly through the darkness. The only explanation was that one of my family's enemies was outside, retaliating for a crime we'd committed against them.

However, this was the first time I was aware of that our enemy had located and attacked the farm. After being here for nearly three years, I was sure that no one would find this desolate plot of land that sat in the middle of the flat plains in Texas.

The hate I held for my family knew no bounds. I knew I should be grateful for the few rays of light they shined on me, but I was filled with too much scorn to be grateful to my family for anything. They allowed me two weeks of freedom. One week every six months. During my weeks, I leaped to freedom like a dog who had been chained to a tree in the backyard.

My family hated me. A friendly conversation—not ever. A warm hello was never going to happen. Not even a half-eaten chicken bone was going to be thrown my way as far as my family was concerned. My family was run by a horde of men who hated women. It was as if their blood was tainted and their minds were programmed to disburse blatant disrespect and hatred among the female population.

During my last break, I'd had so much pent-up loneliness inside me from being caged up at this farm that I'd called all my friends, rented the best hotel room and spent my time relishing the company of people who treated me like a person.

My family had made my friends believe that I was practicing medicine in Mexico as an explanation as to why they didn't see me often. Because of who my father was, it wasn't a big stretch. The idea sounded like a good one, and they'd bought it. However, I had accepted the fact that if they were truly my friends, they'd have known that I'd never taken an interest in practicing medicine outside the United States because I'd never intended to leave New York.

My mother was a beautiful African-American woman that my Mexican father had met in New York. I had one picture of my mother that I'd stared at so much that I'd memorized every line of her face. She'd died when I was seven, so I hadn't gotten much of a chance to get to know her. I'd chosen to live in New York because it was the only connection I had left to my mother. But, my family had even taken that from me.

Another rapid round of shots sounded, causing me to cringe and grit my teeth. I hated guns, and if I was hearing shots underground, it meant the world as I knew it was crumbling.

A rare smile crept across my face at the idea of the farm being destroyed. If my family's enemy happened to find their way into the cellar and found me, my only wish was that they killed me fast.

However, if they wanted to take me as a hostage, it could possibly lead to my freedom, since I was essentially already a hostage. How horrible a thought that my capture could well lead me to my escape from the tight grip my family had on me.

The top of my head struck the wooden underside of my bed when an alarming, earth-shaking blast erupted, shaking my surroundings. The faint sound of particles sprinkling from the ceiling and hitting the linoleum floor sounded, making me inch myself further under the bed, sliding on my stomach. My skin grazed the floor making a squeaky noise.

As I waited with bated breath, a line of sweat inched down my forehead, making my eyes twitch. The tight space under my bed didn't leave me room to swipe at the irritating drizzle, and the sound of my harsh breaths would have alerted anyone sweeping the area for captives, so I fought to quiet myself.

Was that the sound of footsteps growing closer or was my mind messing with me? I tilted my head, searching for the sound and waiting for the unknown.

My dilemma grew more intense as the dust I'd disturbed when sliding under my bed started to settle at the back of my throat. My body lurched in preparation for a sneeze, but I slammed my eyes shut and covered my nose and mouth, stifling what demanded to be let out.

A muffled groan-sneeze escaped as the sound of footsteps grew louder and stopped. They were standing right outside my door, and I didn't know if it was the enemy I knew or the unknown enemy attacking the enemy I knew.

"Regina! You okay?" came a loud whisper through the cracks of my door.

It was Bradley, one of my family's guards. He checked on me from time to time, taking it upon himself to stick around and chat with me. His presence made me uncomfortable, and I was sure the only reason he cared enough to keep me company was because he wanted to sleep with me. It was hard to miss the way his gaze stalked my body or the way his tongue slithered around his mouth and lips when he was near me.

Although he made me uncomfortable, I'd never pushed him away. When you were stuck in the cellar on your family's farm, burning dead bodies for a living, you tended to appreciate any company you could get, no matter their intentions.

"I'm okay, Bradley," I called out to him. My head slid from my hiding spot when he shoved my bedroom door open. The dim shadow of his head came into focus before he leaned inside and shined a flashlight around my dark room. He aimed the light on my face, as I remained prone under my bed, squinting my eyes against the brightness.

"What's going on out there? It sounds like a war," I asked, my voice rushing out, anxious to satisfy my need to know.

"It was a damn war," he confirmed.

Was that all he was going to say? The guards rarely talked to me, so I was sure they had been ordered not to interact with me unless it was necessary. Therefore, Bradley was breaking one of the warped rules my family had set in place where I was concerned.

My face drew into a tight frown at the sight of him, standing there holding my door open. What the heck was he searching for inside my room if there was a war raging outside?

"We managed to get things under control after backup arrived. We hunted those assholes down like dogs and ran them into the woods."

The smugness of Bradley's voice wasn't lost on me as he talked about my family bringing in backup criminals. My chipped nails clawed at the floor as I struggled to pull my body from under the bed.

"I thought no one knew about this place?" I asked, hoping Bradley would give me more information. "Were they trying to take the meth supply?"

He hadn't turned the damn flashlight off, and I didn't miss the way he moved the light up and down, taking my room and me in fully. He'd never been past my bedroom door, so his interested gaze studied the dark interior.

"They weren't here for the meth," he finally answered. "They came here to rescue their friend, a biker that your cousin was trying to get information from."

Based on the sound of things, I was going to be swimming in dead bodies. After eight years of school and graduating in the top ten from medical school, I'd been forced to ditch my dream of becoming a heart surgeon to become an undertaker of sorts for my family.

"You may want to get prepared," Bradley suggested, stating the obvious. "A lot of bodies are coming your way."

A deep sigh didn't help the tension that started to coil in my neck and shoulders. I nodded towards Bradley to acknowledge his warning. He stood, eyeballing me in that creepy way he always did, making the hairs on my exposed arms stand before he spun out of my doorway and eased the door closed behind him. The light thump of his steps faded, and I released another agonizing sigh.

With my face raised to the ceiling, I took in several deep breaths, preparing myself to spend my morning with a group of fresh dead bodies my family had created.

29

REGINA

T he blasts of weapon fire had finally ceased. Although I couldn't see a trace of daylight at my level, I sensed that the sun had started to light the sky. To keep my mind occupied, I cleaned, spraying and wiping everything with industrial strength disinfectant.

My workspace was a dreary room that was the perfect motivator for depression, a morgue and on occasion, a hospital if my family needed it to be. The vast room was equipped with a large metal autopsy table that sat in its center.

There were four body freezers built into the wall and varying types of medical equipment and supplies spread throughout the room. There was also an incinerator, its smoke and debris fed into thick pipes that led to the surface.

Over my sturdy, dark jeans and long-sleeve cotton pullover, I wore my thick plastic coveralls. My instrument table was lined with a bone saw, bread knife, skull chisel, hammer, rib cutter, scalpel, and three types of scissors, just to name a few. I rarely used all the tools since I wasn't performing full autopsies, but I had them at my disposal anyway.

The large shiny metal table that sat in the center of the room waited patiently for the bodies that I would undress, clean, and pluck bullets and metal from.

The guards who worked for my family usually thumped down the steps to enter the cellar, but they also had the option of an elevator that was installed for easier access and body deliveries. The hum of the elevator was followed by the sound of the squeaky wheels of the large cart they carried bodies on.

"Oh joy," I mumbled sarcastically as I rolled my eyes to the ceiling.

My job was to prepare the bodies of my family's victims or casualties so that I could burn, bag, and tag the ashes. What a job. I'd gone from promising heart surgeon to the spooky bag-them-and-tag-them lady. And my family ensured I stayed busy, dragging bodies at various stages of decomposition in from unknown locations at any given time.

The clunk of the cart hitting the double doors that led into the room sounded before a tall, beefy guard with a deadly gleam entered. The bars of the cart were gripped tight in his hands as three dead men lay in a heap in front of him.

The guard didn't bother greeting me as he wheeled the stack of dead men to within a few feet of the autopsy table. The disgusted frown on his tightly pinched face indicated he had no intention of unloading the men with dignity.

He proved my point when he grunted and bared his teeth before shoving the handles of the cart up and dumping the men into a pile at the foot of the table. The clattering of their bodies hitting the floor sounded as he jiggled the cart to ensure he'd gotten them out.

He glanced up at me and smirked after he'd completed his task. Without a word, he turned and headed through the metal double doors, bumping them open loudly with the mouth of the cart on his way out.

The sound of the squeaky wheels called back and may as well have been curse words as I stared at the stack of dead men in front of me. All three appeared to have died as the result of gunshot wounds to the head, although the rest of their bodies were littered with bullet holes as well.

The sight of one's brains smeared all over the face of another who was missing a part of his jawbone would have given most people nightmares for weeks. However, I'd seen so many horrific scenes of death that I was afraid I'd eventually become immune to what was supposed to be horrific.

Two black circular gunshot wounds marred the face of the third man. He'd lived long enough with his wounds that his face had swollen to twice its normal size and was painted in hues of purple and blue. Beautiful colors that sat painting the surface of death.

Their bodies lay in a bundle that I eyed at different angles, attempting to figure out which to yank from the pile first. I'd gotten used to dealing with the dead, but there was one thing that still creeped me out: their eyes. There was something ominous about the ones who died with their eyes open. There was also a lingering sadness surrounding them that squeezed my chest and made it difficult for air to get into my lungs.

I was convinced that remnants of the dead lurked in this space, spying on me. My bedroom was only steps away on the other side of these walls, and some nights the haunting feeling of being watched would feed my insomnia.

One of the men's head was thrown back so it hung upside down. Thankfully, his eyes were closed, but his chest poked out like he was fighting to take a breath.

"You don't hear him breathing, Regina. You always do this." I reminded, talking to myself in a low tone.

Restricted mostly to the cellar at my family's farm by order of my cousin, Sorio, I was only allowed to leave my subterranean home on a few occasions. I could leave to gather food from the main house and sometimes my cousin would make me sit with him and have lunch or dinner. The endeavor was often emotionally painful as Sorio always found ways to belittle me or call me names.

My family was the infamous DG6, which meant they were as close to being above the law as any family could get. Some people called them a gang and others labeled them a cartel. For me, being in the position I was currently in, I feared the only way I'd get away from them was likely in death.

They had the meth industry in the palm of their hands. They killed anyone who challenged them and crushed any competition in the meth market because of the secret ingredient they added to the drug. As a result, my family had the most loyal addicts and a reputation for being the most vicious killers out there.

Two of the main chemists who cooked the batches of meth were my cousins. However, unlike me, my cousins were proud of the work they did for my family.

Casting aside thoughts of my evil bloodline, I prepared for the job at hand. I swiped the face of my phone to fill the lifeless space with music. Kendrick Lamar and all the best hip-hop and pop were about to keep me company. I gloved up and tied my mask tightly around my face.

"Girl, bend your knees and do a proper lift. These dead men are heavy and don't care about your back," I told myself out loud.

I laughed, amusing myself easily. The longer my family kept me at this farm, processing their dead, the more it seemed I was losing my grip on reality and my ability to interact with normal society.

The rusted scent of blood and the rotten aroma of exposed brain matter climbed up my nose like a living creature, tightening my throat as saliva flowed over my tongue. The odor opened my tear ducks, flooding them with water, but I swallowed my reaction and proceeded with my job.

My hand slid under the stiff shoulders of the man who hung slightly off the top of the pile. His legs were entangled and covered by the lower body of the brain matter leaker.

"Work smarter, Regina," I reminded myself.

Putting a halt to the heavy lifting I was about to do, I wheeled over the smaller metal collapsible table that was perfect for moving and lifting the dead onto the autopsy table. A grunt escaped me, scratching my throat as I yanked the heavy man free of the pile and dragged him onto the smaller table. His body was bulky from all the gear he wore that obviously hadn't protected him from death.

When I finally had his crumpled body aligned with the large autopsy table, I repeatedly shoved until he rolled into place. His head slid across the metal of the larger table, making a wet swiping sound as I continued to shove, finally getting all of him onto the table.

I made quick work of cutting away the man's clothes and spraying him with the cleaning solution my cousins had formulated and insisted I use on each body before I burned them. I attempted to but failed to ignore the hissing and gurgling sound that invaded my ears. It was the man's bowels releasing. The mask on my face could only do so much to protect me from the bodily gases that were as toxic as the most potent chemicals.

I wasn't sure of what my cousin's cleaning solution contained, but it worked wonders on cutting into the vile odors that I'd never gotten used to. I sprayed the man liberally with the solution, glazing him like a cook would prepare a turkey for the oven.

Once I'd cleaned the man and his blood and bowel movements were mixed and sucked down the drainage at the foot of the table, I prepared to extract the bullet from his head. Another of my unpleasant tasks would involve checking the rest of him for other metals.

When I reached towards his head with the scalpel, his eyes popped open with a low flick. "Whooh!" I shouted before I jumped back. *Jesus!* I should have been used to this by now, but the eyes got me every freaking time. And this man's eyes seemed to be following me. He couldn't get any deader than what he was, so why was I letting this freak me out?

I closed my eyes and took a deep breath, filling my lungs with the rotting aroma of the dead before I reached out again. I placed my gloved fingers over the man's eyes, holding them down for a few seconds before I let go. Maybe his soul was just leaving his body because the hairs on my arms started to move, springing up in patches as a chill crept down my back and made me shiver.

Surrounded by the presence of death, I glanced around every

corner of the room, knowing that something outside the spectrum of my vision was lurking. I had the sense that the evil deeds of these dead men had seeped out into every crevice and surface of this room.

My stomach rolled, making me breathe harder as my hair prickled up on my neck, and it felt as if icy fingers were walking down my spine. The scalpel between my fingers shook across my view, as the tremble in my hand grew more intense.

I couldn't shake the presence of evil surrounding me, suffocating me. I sat my scalpel on the instrument table and marched out of the room. Inside the dark hall, I breathed a little easier as I filled my lungs with fresher air.

"Come on, Regina. How many freaking times have you done this? Get it together," I urged, attempting to motivate myself. It wasn't like I could quit, so I turned back, shoved the doors open, and prepared to continue my task.

After checking the man for metals, I prepared to roll him back onto the smaller metal table, so I could get him into the incinerator. Thankfully, his eyes hadn't popped back open.

This was my life. I was nothing more than the undertaker for one of the biggest crime families in the country. There were occasions when I was called upon to performs blood transfusions, treat gunshot wounds, and perform other medical procedures, but since I'd been transferred to the farm, those occasions had become few and far in between. Besides, we had other family members who gladly provided their medical expertise.

I cared nothing about earning my family's loyalty. All I wanted was to be set free. I wanted a normal life. I wanted the boot my family had on my neck taken off.

At twenty-eight, I had a lot more living to do, but living under my family's rules had condemned me to an inmate's life. My quest to escape my family wasn't ever going to be over. I was going to find a way to escape them even if it killed me.

30

REGINA

If I weren't so damned lonely, I'd be rude and insist that Bradley leave. Instead, I had a dead man's genitals staring up at me as Bradley stood watching. The man I was preparing was one of my family's guards. I'd never known his name, and here he was, bared in front of me in the most intimate and vulnerable way possible.

"I'll go and get the last of them," Bradley stated as if he were doing me a favor.

"Mmmm," I mumbled without glancing up at him. Bradley's stalker-like ways were starting to make me consider the loneliness of my situation. Eventually, I was going to have to tell him to stop hanging around and talking to me.

After the chill that Bradley left clinging to my skin wore off, I maneuvered the guard onto my rolling table and prepared to turn his two hundred pounds of flesh, blood, and bones into a few pounds of ashes.

I wheeled the man over to the incinerator that had already eaten five of his buddies or enemies. My fingers slipped into my thick flame-retardant mittens. I opened the incinerator, and the intense flames inside the small glass door danced and called my attention.

Squinting, I reared back and away from the heat as I shoved the tip of the table over the lip of the entrance and proceeded to push the man by his shoulders. Once I'd gotten him most of the way in, I hit the red button, and the flaming hot metal conveyer inside the fire pit easily sucked him the rest of the way into the flames.

Once I secured the door and aligned my rolling table back in its proper place, I prepared to work on the next poor soul who was fool enough to work for my family or fight against them.

As I walked towards the next two, one caught my full attention. Blood, at some point, had poured from his head and crusted against his face and neck. His torn black shirt and likely most of his back appeared to have been covered in blood as well. His skin was pale white, but he didn't...

"Regina, here are the last two."

I jumped. I'd been focused on the dead man and hadn't heard Bradley's approach. He was preparing to dump the last two from the cart on top of the man I couldn't stop staring at.

"No, put them over there!" I yelled louder than I'd intended and pointed at the area I wanted Bradley to place the men. My head tilted, taking in the man I stood in front of. He was sitting, slumped against the wall like he was exhausted and had fallen asleep. I was so distracted that Bradley had to wheel the cart around me.

He proceeded to dump the last two bodies, and I could hear them hit the floor before he wheeled the cart back around me and towards the exit. I didn't have to glance up to know that he'd stopped and was staring at me again.

"Are you okay, Regina?"

"I'm fine," I replied absently, not giving him a bit of my attention.

Dead men don't sweat.

"Regina, are you sure you're okay?" Bradley asked, staring from me to the man I'd finally pulled my gaze from.

"I'm fine, Bradley," I said, forcing a smile.

Bradley ushered his head towards the man I'd been staring at. "He was the one that all this mess started over. His high-powered friends came to break him out of here after your cousin took him from some place in Florida. As you can see, he didn't make it."

I didn't need or want Bradley figuring out what I was so intently studying.

"Thanks for all the help, Bradley, and you have a good day," I stated dryly, hoping he caught the hint that I wanted to be left alone. I had no idea what part of the day it was anymore and didn't care. It was always dark and dingy in my world.

Bradley continued to stare as the muffled creek of the fire burning the man inside the incinerator reminded me of wood burning inside a fireplace. Only this wasn't wood—it was the crackle of human bones burning. When Bradley finally caught on to my cold shoulder, the sound of the wheels on the cart signaled his departure.

"See you later, Regina," he hollered back at me over his shoulder.

"Yeah. Later, Bradley," I muttered, not bothering to glance in his direction.

As soon as the hum of the elevator registered, I locked myself into the windowless autopsy room with three corpses, a burning body, and a possible zombie.

"Dead men don't sweat," I mumbled the words aloud as I dashed over to the pale man who'd captured my attention.

Checking his neck for a pulse, nothing registered, but it didn't mean I was misreading a sign of life. A bead of sweat had drizzled down the man's clammy skin. Laying him flat on the floor, I checked several areas for a pulse and found the tiniest spark of life pulsing within him as I pinched his neck.

My medical training rose to the surface of my brain as I applied life-saving techniques. Although he'd lost a significant amount of blood, he no longer appeared to be bleeding, which was a good sign.

After checking for swelling and discoloration, I didn't find any other gunshot wounds other than the obvious entrance wound near his left temple and a smaller exit wound under his left ear. Since the exit wound was significantly smaller, it was safe to say he likely had bullet fragments lodged in his head.

I didn't have to be a traumatic brain injury specialist to know that if he had any of that bullet left in his head, it would cause enough swelling that it would require that I drill a hole in his head to relieve the pressure. Otherwise, the sliver of a pulse running through him would vanish for good.

Bradley had tossed the man onto the floor like yesterday's garbage, but I moved him with careful ease now, collapsing my smaller table so that I could lift him onto the larger table to examine him and figure out if he could be saved.

Cleaning the wounded areas quickly, I surveyed the damage. I was going to have to drill into this man's head if he was going to see the light of day again.

"Then what, Regina?" I asked myself out loud. "He's your family's enemy. What are you going to do with him if you save him? Live happily ever after with him in your basement home?"

The part of my brain that made the logical decisions was right. Even if I saved this man, there was only one way off the farm for us and it was more than likely: death.

"You know what? Damn it," I huffed out as the other more irrational part of my brain took control.

Once I was a hundred percent sure I'd talked myself into saving this man, I rummaged through the walk-in closet full of medical equipment until I found everything I needed and hooked him up to a ventilator.

I prepared an intravenous drip to send liquids into his body. I took care in cleaning him of all the blood and dirt that was stuck to his skin. I was such a pervert for admiring his body, especially with the knowledge that he was alive—barely alive, but alive enough that it felt strange.

The amount of art on his body also called my attention, causing me to study his tattoos as I cleaned him. "August," I uttered out loud. August was a part of a large tattoo on his back in thick black font. The rest of the words were unreadable due to deep scratches and bruising in the area. "August, that's what I'll call you," I informed the man like he could hear me.

Even in his damaged condition, August was strikingly good-looking with his shadowed chin. He had a nice head of hair that I'd had to wash three times to get the blood out. I'd peeled his eyes back a couple of times, to peek at them. The state of his condition left his eyes a dingy dark blue although I guessed they were usually a more vibrant, shiny blue.

"The enemy of my enemy is my friend," I sang the statement repeatedly into the musty death-filled air. The remaining three men sat there, forgotten as I attempted to do what a part of my brain kept telling me not to. In this case, any enemy of my family was my friend. Therefore, this man was worth saving. Since Bradley had a sneaking habit of walking up on me without warning, I was going to have to find a way to keep my new patient hidden.

A thousand questions fired off inside my brain as I worked to save the man. Had he lost too much blood to be saved? Was his brain injury too severe for him to recover? Was he going to be a vegetable if he woke up? I'd had a few second thoughts about attempting to save him, but something in me wouldn't let me give up on this man. My problem would come with trying to hide him if he did survive.

31

AUGUST

My mind was set adrift, teetering someplace between this world and the next. Sounds and vibrations echoed through me as if I were a sheet flapping in the wind. Adrift in an unfamiliar world, I wasn't cold or in pain. I was just...lost.

"This is the motherfucker who brought death here today," a voice said, catching my attention, but I couldn't move or see, so I couldn't react to what was being said.

"I'd like to shake the hand of the man who shot this bastard," the voice continued.

Were those words echoes in my head or had they come from another person? They sounded so crisp and clear. If I could move, I could alert someone that I needed help. But, what did I need help from? I had no real sense of what was wrong with me. Forcing myself to speak was as useless as trying to move or see. Was I dreaming?

A hard jolt awakened my awareness as an alarming amount of noise flooded my ears. But just as fast, I was evaporated in nothingness before an overwhelming sense of gloom encircled me. What was happening? Where was I? Where were the voices coming from? Why couldn't I feel or see anything? The only senses that seemed to be working were my sense of smell and hearing.

My mind was filled with black fog and useless musings, no distinct memories. It hovered in the murkiness, frozen in regret and despair. One moment my mind teased, giving me a sense that a memory would spark, but the next moment, recalling my own name or age or anything that hinted as to who I was, became a frustrating task.

I was lost inside my own head, not knowing up from down, left from right, or ass from dick. Maybe I was trapped in a dream and as soon as I was awakened, the world as I knew it would return.

Death. Death is what I smelled. The rancid odor floated up my nose, in my case, it must have floated into my mind because I couldn't feel anything to know for certain that I had a nose. I could do nothing but endure this state I was stuck in as I was unable to move or feel. I had to be asleep, trapped in a nightmare.

I struggled to think beyond the darkness, but my efforts pushed me further from what little awareness I had. The voices dwindled, and the only other sense I had, dissipated and not even the scent of death existed anymore.

My mind delved deeper, finding the deepest blackest closet to lock me into. The silence entombed me, shattering my remaining senses. It snuffed out everything, introducing me to the deafening sound of nothing before it left me in an endless black dream.

A JOLT of thundering sounds coursed through my consciousness, but like before, not all my senses had returned. I had no awareness of time or space. My sense of smell and sound was all that I'd been granted. I didn't know if I'd appreciated either sense before I was cast into this darkness, but I appreciated them now.

The sound of what I guessed was metal scraping against metal floated into my ears and continued in a repeating pattern that went on for what seemed like hours. Sight and touch remained out of my reach, my brain trying but failing to regain the use of them.

"Hey, Regina, here's three more. I think there's at least two more. When I bring the rest, you want me to stay and help you?"

"No, Bradley. My family won't take too kindly to you helping me with what is supposed to be my job. I appreciate you asking, though."

So crisp and clear were the words. An empty pause in words left me wondering if I'd faded back into my dream. Another harsh jolt opened the floodgates on my pain and an intense amount shot through my head but lasted only a few seconds before it disappeared again. The pain sparked awareness within me. I wasn't dreaming. I was alive. I was clinging to reality, but I didn't know how to stay on the correct plane. I didn't know how to stay on the right side of life.

32

REGINA

I t took time and work, but I turned the walk-in closet that was filled with supplies into my patient room. I'd found random places throughout the large autopsy room to stash most of the equipment I'd taken from the closet. Most of it, I placed in the empty drawers and body lockers that I rarely used.

August's breathing had gotten stronger in the hours he'd been on the ventilator, but he was a far cry from being well enough to survive. He'd had several broken ribs, his fibula bone in his right leg was broken severely enough that it had cracked through the side of his lower leg. Someone had attempted to stabilize the wound with pipes and rags.

It appeared he'd attempted to sew up a knife wound in his side that had started to heal, but the gunshot to his head had nearly ended him. Thankfully, he had enough blood left in him that he didn't require a transfusion.

He'd been shot, beaten, left with broken bones, and laying out someplace on my family's farm for hours barely clinging to life. God was not through with this man. Based on some of his tattoos, he belonged to a motorcycle club, and a dear friend named Ryan had been killed.

August had been shot in the back once, appeared to have been stabbed in the back twice, and now, there were bullet fragments in his head. The fragments were deeply embedded, and it was too risky a surgery for me to try to extract them.

I'd studied cardiology, hoping to someday become a heart surgeon. Although I wasn't a neurosurgeon and had only briefly studied neuroscience, I believed this man stood a better chance of survival if I left the bullet fragments in place without trying to probe around in his head to remove them.

I'd prepared my instruments with nervous hands. Drilling into his head had been easier than facing the anticipation of the task. I'd drilled the small hole and allowed the blood build-up to flow from his brain into a stack of towels I'd piled under his head. The time I'd invested in medical school was proving to be time well spent.

I'd worked an all-nighter. Actually, in my case, it had been all day, ensuring my patient was well hidden and medically stable. I also had to complete the task of taking care of the rest of the bodies before they started to decay.

Although I was allowed, I rarely left my underground prison because I didn't like being watched. Each time I surfaced, all eyes landed on me. From the guards posted on the grounds to those in the lookout tower, I was always ogled like an alien who'd parked my UFO and threatened to probe their bodies.

Except for food, an occasional outing for fresh outside air, and to travel to and from the few buildings that were in our community, I stayed out of sight and out of their minds. Since I had August to take care of now, the last thing I wanted was to call attention to myself.

IT TOOK me three days to build up the courage to leave the cellar and August's side. I'd bagged and tagged the ashes of eight dead men and stuffed them into a rucksack so I could deliver them to my cousin, Luis.

In case Bradley and the other guard had given Luis a head count of the nine bodies they'd brought to me, I filled a ninth bag with ashes, using equal parts from the eight dead I'd cremated.

I eased up the splintered steps of the cellar, using my back to push the slanted wooden door open. The bright sunlight assaulted my eyes, and it took a moment for me to adjust. Once I was on solid ground, I kept my head down and forced my legs to get me to my destination as quickly as possible.

Usually, I took a moment to enjoy the sight of the clouds or a stray insect flying, anything that served as a reminder that there were still beautiful things left in the world. Today, my mission was to do everything I needed to do outside the cellar in a fast and unsuspicious manner.

My cousin, Luis, met me at the door of his workspace. His head went up once in greeting before he took the bag from my hand. Luis and I were the same age, only a month apart. He was one of those guys who was smart enough to be dangerous. He was short and stocky and perfectly content with making drugs that destroyed people's lives.

Since I was out, I decided to walk over to the main house and stock up on food. I retrieved a shopping bag from under the kitchen counter and searched for nonperishable and microwavable food items.

"Looks like you're stocking up, cousin."

I cringed at the sound of my cousin, Sorio's voice, wishing I could disappear into a cloud of smoke to avoid interacting with him. If there ever was a man I hated, it was my cousin, Sorio. He was a big part of the reason that I was a prisoner. He was the epitome of his father, Carlos, a misogynistic lunatic who saw women as disposable objects.

"Yeah, I've been putting in a lot of extra work lately. I guess it's given me more of an appetite."

Sorio laughed, snorting as he pointed at me. What could be inside someone's head to make them so vengeful and hateful?

"An appetite. Girl, as fat as you are, you don't have one appetite, you have *four* of them."

He continued to point and laugh as I hurriedly closed the cabinets and refrigerator and made my escape. If I'd had a gun, I would've unloaded it in his face. He loved to call me fat. *Arrogant prick.* I was a size ten, possibly a twelve, but in his mutated brain, I may as well have been five-hundred pounds.

It took less than a minute for me to go around the main house to the shabby wooden door that was the entrance to my home. I'd never been happier to see my basement home than I was at this moment. After stocking my food in the small refrigerator, and pantry area I had in my bedroom, I smiled at the thought that I had someone to come home to. Someone my mean cousin didn't know about. Someone who I prayed would one day wake up and kill Sorio for me.

After I unlocked and stepped into the closet I'd transformed into August's hospital room, I crept in with a ready smile. The hiss of the ventilator blended with the low whisper of the infusion pump that pushed fluids into his body.

I checked his vitals and ensured he had enough liquids and vitamins going into his system. My palm brushed across his forehead before I cupped his stubbly chin.

"Hey, August, you're looking better today," I greeted him with a hint of excitement in my voice.

Although he wasn't out of the woods, the fact he was alive after what could have been a fatal gunshot wound had pride springing up within me. He was the most interesting thing in this dreary place. He was also a good listener as I sat with him and spilled my family secrets, and my vow to someday escape them.

August was the first long-term patient I'd had to myself. As a new doctor, we shared patients or observed as the seasoned physicians performed the more difficult procedures and treatments.

When I was certain he wasn't going to wake up and recover right away, I'd introduced a feeding tube. A quick peek under the bandages I had wrapped around his head like a turban revealed that his head had started to scab over nicely. Only a doctor would think that scabs were nice, but the fact that his body was healing itself was all that mattered.

He was going to have a wicked scar in his head that branched from his temple, where I'd been able to remove a few bullet fragments, but it didn't really affect his appearance. If anything, I'd say the scar made him look more interesting.

A two-inch patch of hair had also been shaved from his scalp where I'd had to go in deeper, drilling into his skull to relieve the pressure on his brain.

Even with two black eyes and multicolored bruises decorating his body, August was a wonderful sight to stare at. A man like him would never glance twice at someone like me.

I considered myself friendly, not quiet-natured, but not boisterous either. I was more of a slow simmer versus a boil. The kind of men who found me interesting were the perverts like Bradley or those who wanted the one-night jump offs.

On the weeks that I was released from family prison, I used an escort service to have my needs satisfied. It was a secret that I'd never tell a soul. My situation didn't leave me many options for dating. I didn't have time to cultivate a relationship nor was I motivated to put forth the effort anymore. I glanced at August.

"Before you arrived, August, Bradley was all I had to talk to or socialize with. Even though he creeped me out, anything seemed better than the loneliness. But, I was never desperate enough to go there with him, if you know what I mean."

I went on talking to August until I fell asleep next to him, holding his warm, limp hand. The act of holding on to a warm living hand was enough to provide me a certain level of happiness that I hadn't experienced in a long time.

The echoing footsteps that were growing louder by the second were what snatched me from my sleep. I was in such a lazy haze that I failed to move out of the closet fast enough. Someone was at the double metal doors and pushing into the room by the time I stepped out of the closet.

I was a kid who'd been caught with her hand in the cookie jar. I certainly felt like one. Bradley stared at the door as I eased it closed

behind me. The elongated screech it made called even more attention to it.

"Can I help you, Bradley?" I asked in a clipped tone, irritated that
he'd disturbed my time with August. It was nine o'clock at night, and
I was usually in bed at this hour or reading. Was this Bradley's usual
routine, to creep around the cellar while I slept?

"What are you doing in here at this time of night?" His glare traveled back to the closet door. "Are you hiding a man in that closet,
Regina?"

The seriousness on his face had my lips hanging open. Speechless, I stood frozen, trying to but failing to think of a quick lie.

"Ha, ha," he barked out, laughing. He pointed at my bemused
expression.

"When's your next break? This place is going to drive you crazy if
you let it. I can keep you company anytime you need it," he offered
with that grin dancing across his thin, dry lips.

I bet you can, fluttered across my mind as I fought to contain the
thoughts that my frown hardly concealed.

His tone insinuated more. I needed to tell him what I should have
months ago.

"Bradley, I don't think it's a good idea for you to be hanging
around me at all. If my family finds out, especially my cousin, Sorio,
you could end up being one of the guys on my table. Then into the
fire, I'd have to toss you."

At those words, Bradley's gaze found the incinerator before he
glared at me with a hint of apprehension on his face.

My gaze remained pinned on Bradley's as I continued to drive the
statement home. "I don't want to do that to you, Bradley because you
have been too good to me. You know how Sorio is, though. He'd make
me toss you into the flames while you were still alive just because he
can. Then, into the red plastic bags your ashes would go and then—"

He raised his hand to stop my words. "I get the point, Regina. I
was just checking on you. That's all."

He glanced at the closet door once more, before lifting his gaze to
meet mine since I hadn't moved an inch away from it.

"Well, I better go." His gaze landed on the closet door again. "See you later, Regina."

He cursed under his breath in Spanish as he left, calling me a teasing bitch and my cousin a deranged asshole. The men didn't know or had all forgotten that I spoke fluent Spanish. I never corrected them when they switched from Spanish to English when they had to talk to me about something. I never let on that I knew exactly what they were saying when they talked about me in Spanish.

"Later, Bradley," I called after his back. My statement about him ending up alive in the incinerator must have spooked him because he took another quick look back at it before pushing at each of the exit doors. If I'd known crazy talk was all it would take to get rid of Bradley, I'd have started doing it long ago.

After heaving a deep sigh, I walked over to and locked the doors, before going back into the closet to care for August.

33

AUGUST

My eyes fluttered below my lids as sparks of life pinged in random parts of my body making me twitch. The darkness circled like a hungry vulture over its prey, and I had no way of knowing what shape my body was in. At least there was movement within me this time.

Movement!

Was my sense of touch returning? Had my eyes been moving, or had I been trapped here so long, my mind made me believe I'd felt movement?

There weren't any words to describe the state I was in. I was helplessly trapped inside my own mind. Shit, maybe I was dead, and this was my hell.

The cozy voice of the stranger pierced the darkness and made my ears perk each time the sound rained over me. I clung to every word, every syllable, even when the tone faded in and out of focus—even when it had dwindled to a low murmur. The voice was my connection to the world outside of the darkness and led me to believe I was alive but physically unable to respond.

I couldn't remember anything about my life, so I didn't know if I'd been shot or hit by a car? Had someone attempted to kill me or had I failed at suicide? Was the sweet voice I'd been hearing all in my head or was someone out there watching over me?

From what I could recall, the voice belonged to a woman named Regina. According to her, I was an enemy of her family, but she didn't see me that way. She hated her family and found comfort in the fact that someone was brave enough to fight against them. She'd even admitted that one of her reasons for saving me was to spite her family.

She said she was lonely, and I seemed to be her main source of entertainment. The idea that I, someone who couldn't move or speak or remember my own name, was her entertainment made me wonder what type of situation this woman was in.

A tingle started at my toes and worked its way up my legs. If I could smile I would paste one on my face as more pangs of life started to spark back into my body. *My toes.* Were they moving? Was I wiggling them? It certainly felt like I was. Fuck, if I wasn't. When the rest of my body started to tingle, I urged my brain to move my hands, my legs, anything that would listen to my commands.

My heart may as well have been the drumbeat to a Metallica song as loudly as it banged around inside my chest, sending blood through body parts that had been immobile for an unknown amount of time. Metallica, I knew the band and knew their songs, so why was it so difficult for me to recall my own name?

Finally, my fingers moved. One of my hands was wrapped around something warm, soft, and moving. Regina had taken hold of my hand. Her warm grip was a gift I welcomed as I attempted to squeeze my fingers around hers.

The fluttering of my lids quickened, and the anticipation of seeing anything but darkness had me hysterical and full of impatience. My mouth worked back and forth, left and right. My legs and arms twitched and turned, but my stubborn fucking eyes remained closed. I sucked in a calming breath, hoping it would ease my anxiety enough for me to pour every ounce of willpower I had into opening my eyes.

When I thought I would explode with anxiousness, my eyes

blinked open and blinding light filled them. It hurt like hell, but I didn't care. I'd finally broken free of all that darkness. The calm voice soothed me as I attempted to lift my hand.

"Stay calm and give your body a chance to awaken slowly. You're okay. I'm right here."

It was hard not to listen to a voice so relaxing. After I'd forced my body to relax, pain reared its ugly head, trying to steal my joy. Sharp, poker hot pangs shot through my skull. Had Regina doused my chest in gas and set it on fire?

My leg felt like it had been put through a fucking shredder, backed out and put through again, but I didn't care. I could feel. Squinting, I started to make out dark shapes and colors as my rapidly blinking eyes focused, pulling in my surroundings.

"August, you're going to experience some pain and discomfort. I didn't want to give you heavy doses of medication when it appeared you might wake up."

My mouth moved, but my words remained stuck in my dry throat. Had I swallowed a fucking pail of hot sand? My damn Adam's apple bobbed for dear life, signaling my dismay as my eyes struggled to stay open.

"Here, I'm putting a cup of water up to your mouth. Drink slowly please."

Drink slowly? Did she have any idea that my fucking throat was one move away from cracking and flaking into a thousand pieces?

As soon as the rim of the plastic cup touched my lips, my hand came to life and shoved the cup up, sending cool water all over my mouth and chin. I gulped and gasped, not caring that I was spilling more than I was drinking.

When there was none left, I wanted to ask for more, but my damn voice and mouth weren't coordinating. However, the small amount of water that had gotten into my system seemed to rejuvenate my body even more. My focus cleared enough that I could see the blurred vision of a woman pouring me another cup of water at the foot my bed.

Her shadowy figure became clearer when she moved closer and

stood at my shoulder. The way she'd talked about being lonely and of me being her only entertainment, I'd assumed she was a homely woman with a bad acne problem.

To the contrary, Regina had golden skin that seemed to twinkle against the light. Her big, brown doe-shaped eyes shined with innocence, but there wasn't enough innocence in the world to hide the amount of hurt and pain lingering in her gaze. Her aura exuded patience and genuine sincerity.

"Here, try to sip slower this time," she instructed, her voice heavy with amusement. I think I shook my head, but my attention was taken by the refreshing water that I failed to drink at a gradual pace.

"That's enough for now, August. I don't want you to overextend yourself or over consume anything too soon. You're still in a fragile state."

"What's..." my voice inched out, my vocal cords struggling to carry my words. "Wrong..." That was the only other word I could force out before I started coughing. Regina placed a calming hand over my aching head. My fucking head weighed a thousand pounds, and it had just occurred to me that I was sitting in a lean, trying, but failing to hold my head up.

Regina assisted in easing me back. "Please lay down so I can explain your situation to you."

I calmed at her words because trying to do anything else had pain kicking me straight up and down my ass.

"You sustained a gunshot wound to the head. Judging from the injuries on your body, I believe you were tortured before you got shot. You had three cracked ribs, your right fibula was broken, and you had multiple lacerations and contusions all over your body. A few required stitching. You were nearly dead by the time you made it to me."

When I sat motionless, the pain remained, but it didn't bite as hard as it had when I sat up. *Shot?* My brain was slow to process the updates Regina had revealed. I'd been beaten and shot, but I couldn't recall any of it.

"You are in Texas. You were captured and brought here by the men who work for my cousin. My cousin was the one who likely did this to you. No one knows you're here with me. I've been hiding you from them."

Bits and pieces of the conversations she'd been having with me while I was trapped in the darkness started to make more sense now. She hated her family and wanted to keep me alive to spite them. I also recalled her wishing I'd wake up and kill someone for her.

"My name?" I croaked out, my voice struggling to crawl from my throat.

Regina's hand brushed my forehead as a sorrowful look remained etched on her face. Her touch made me aware of the fact that I had rags or bandages wrapped around my head.

"I was hoping you hadn't suffered any memory loss, but with head injuries you can never be sure. I'm afraid I don't know your name either. I've been calling you August. Your tattoos indicate that you're a part of the August Knights Motorcycle club and you were their enforcer. Does any of that sound familiar?"

Seeing her more clearly, I shook my head. My mind refused to grasp its misplaced thoughts.

"Based on some of your tattoos and the state of your body, you've lived a rough life. You survived another gunshot before this one, multiple stab wounds, and several other bones were broken previously."

My eyes panned to my exposed arms. The tattoos didn't look familiar nor did they spark any memories. One of my hands had a needle taped to it that had a tube running up to a bag of clear liquid. There were also tubes that ran under the white T-shirt I had on. The lower half of my body was draped in a pair of striped flannel pajamas. The covers were up over my knees, but my toes felt bare under the sheet and thin green wool blanket.

The constant beep had been with me so long that I'd tuned it out and only now noticed its low chirp. I was in a makeshift medical facility, a small windowless room the size of a closet. Aside from the narrow bed and the machines next to it, there was only room for the small table that held the pitcher of water and medical supplies and a brown wooden stool that Regina sat on next to my bed.

I'd attempted to count the days I'd been stuck in the darkness, but I'd only managed to get up to three. "How long?" Those words managed to escape before my throat tightened and stopped me from saying more.

"Four and a half months," Regina confirmed, obviously realizing what I was trying to ask.

No fucking way! I thought. There's no way I'd been there for four and a half months. But I couldn't voice my concerns out loud due to my inability to speak like I wanted to.

34

REGINA

My neck snapped my head up from my chest at the sound of my name being yelled.

"Regina! Where the fuck are you?"

I must have fallen asleep watching August who was as stubborn as he was strong-willed.

For a moment, I was afraid I'd have to tie him down to keep him from trying to get out of bed. Even though he couldn't remember a thing, August's instincts had kicked in. He wasn't used to being taken care of nor was he accustomed to sickness and vulnerability.

Shit!

It was my evil cousin, Sorio. The hairs on the back of my neck stood to attention. What the hell was he doing down here? He never came down here.

August's hand was still clenched in mine when I was jolted awake by Sorio's monstrous voice. I tiptoed around the small bed as I struggled not to bump into anything. The sound of the metal doors springing open and my cousin's heavy footsteps on the outside of the closet door indicated that he'd stepped into the morgue area.

I zipped out of the door, closing it behind me. I was seized by fear as I gripped the handle, not letting it go. My action led Sorio's gaze to the area of my body that hid the door handle from his view. I dropped my hands away from the door and pasted a fake smile on my face.

"Can I help you?"

He didn't answer my question. Instead, he frowned and stared me down like a detective who knew I was hiding something. I was one tremble away from freaking out. What if August coughed or stumbled while trying to get up?

"What are you doing in this dreary ass place? You've been around so many dead people that you sleep in here too?"

He didn't give me a chance to answer his questions because he was coming up with his own scenario. He usually did. It was not like he was going to listen to anything I had to say anyway, so I remained quiet.

"What are you hiding down here?"

"Nothing," I answered, my voice sounding nervous to even me.

He pointed an authoritative finger at the closet door, his brows pinching in curiosity.

"You got something in there you don't want me to see? It's eight in the morning, and you're down here in the fucking closet of the morgue? I'm only going to ask you one more time. What the fuck are you hiding, Regina?"

His agitated tone had me such a nervous wreck that I rung my hands and bit into the inside of my cheek to chase away my fright.

I couldn't let Sorio find August. Sorio was the reason he'd been tortured and shot in the first place. Now that he'd finally recovered enough to wake up, I had to do everything in my power to protect him. If Sorio found him, he was going to make me watch him kill August before he killed me.

My head dropped to my chest as my gaze landed on the floor. "It's...it's my dildo. All my sex toys, actually."

My gaze remained aimed at the floor until Sorio's voice grated across my skin.

"Why don't you do that nasty shit in your fucking room? Is it even sanitary to be doing some shit like that around this smelly-ass place? You're sick. I'm going to see about getting you moved someplace else. Frankly, I'm sick of seeing your sad fucking traitorous face anyway."

Sorio hated me because I didn't embrace the will of this family. I was also labeled the rebel because I'd run so many times.

Sorio stepped closer, and I inched back, bumping into the door before gripping the handle again. He placed an authoritative finger in my face, his mean glare backing it up. His gaze ran up and down my body, my nervous reaction making his frown deepen.

"Are you kidding me right now? You think I want to go in there and see some shit you're down here fucking yourself with? I don't want to see that shit. I got more important things to worry about than the sick shit you're down here doing. I came to let you know that we should have two bitches coming once my men round them up. I want you to bring their ashes to me instead of Luis. You understand?"

I inclined my head, glad he was more concerned about business than what I had behind the door. In the two years and seven and a half months I'd worked on the farm, there had only been three women I'd had to burn, and each time, Sorio wanted their ashes. I had no idea what he did with those women's ashes, but I was sure it wasn't something I wanted to know.

He walked off, glancing back at me with a mean scowl on his face like I was the one who had come bothering him. He shoved the doors open, sending them flying into the hallway before he exited. His heavy steps faded with each passing second, and I didn't breathe until complete silence rained over the space around me.

My cousin had set his sights on two women who he intended to kill that likely had no idea they were in the crosshairs of a serial killer. Nine times out of ten, these people weren't aware of the crime he was going to pin on them whether they'd committed it or not.

After I threw my head up to the ceiling and closed my eyes, I took in few deep, relaxing breaths of air. I didn't even mind the lingering stench of death that I was breathing in because there weren't many things I could think of that was worse than my cousin. He was the facilitator of my punishments each time I'd been captured after running. Each time was worse and had been meant to break me. And although my cousin scared the hell out of me, I wasn't broken yet.

"Fucking asshole," I said under my breath before I walked over and locked the doors to the morgue. I rarely cursed, but Sorio was a good reason to start.

When I stepped back into the closet, my patient was wide awake and attempting to sit up on his own.

"Wait. Let me help you. Take it easy."

"Where? Who?"

It was going to be a difficult task trying to explain things to August, who didn't have his memory and didn't really know who he was in relation to me. He had no idea where he was or the situation he was in either.

After ten minutes of trying to get him settled down, he'd breathed out a shaky, "Thank you," before his body shut down.

Those two words made me smile. He was developing the habit of thanking me whenever he knew he'd given me the most hell.

Now, with Sorio lurking, I was going to have to keep a close eye on August. He was the kind of man who delivered action and would find a way to figure out what was going on. Rest and calm were what his body and mind needed most, but August was not going to sit by and wait. As hard as he was going to make my job, I admired the determination in him.

35

AUGUST

I appreciated Regina more than I could express in words, but there was no goddamn way in hell I was staying here. I didn't care about what she was telling me about a traumatic brain injury. If I was strong enough to stand, I was strong enough to fight.

It was becoming obvious that she was a prisoner. She would become jumpy, whether it was the walls settling, the pipes rumbling, or any stray sound that found its way in from outside.

She'd made a valiant effort but would fail to keep me confined to this bed. She couldn't stand guard over me twenty-four hours a day. She'd stuck around for hours, waiting until I fell asleep after she'd had to practically beg me to stay still.

All I knew was her and the four walls surrounding me, and the walls had started to close in on me. Although my head felt like a band of drummers was constantly stomping around in there, it wasn't going to stop me from getting out of this bed.

When I was in the darkness, there were no constant or concrete ideas that I'd been able to latch on to that allowed me to determine time. Being in this closet was barely a step up from where I'd been.

Based on Regina's estimates, I'd been in this cellar for nearly five months. It had been nine or ten days since I'd opened my eyes, and that was nine too many for me to be lying around on my ass being babied by her.

If she thought I was going to lie quietly and not figure out how to get away, she was more out of her mind than I was out of mine. Based on the constant nagging inside my head, I didn't think I was built to roll over and play dead. I couldn't remember who the hell I was, but I was sure I could remember how to whip someone's ass. I slung my legs over the side of the bed and eased into a standing position.

My head swam, but after I adjusted to being upright, I reached up to switch off a machine I was hooked up to. I snatched the needle from the back of my hand. My gaze followed the trickle of blood that flowed from the thin vein. A tear-shaped droplet dripped to the floor before I cupped a piece of gauze over my hand.

Regina had recited a laundry list of injuries I'd suffered at the hands of who she claimed was her family. Thankfully, my wounds had healed while I was comatose, and I was able to stand and walk on my own.

After the first few steps, hot pain shot up my leg and reminded me of the trauma it had suffered. However, there wasn't enough pain in the world to stop me from figuring out how to escape or kill whoever it was keeping me down.

Aware that Regina locked the door whenever she left me, I'd been eyeballing anything I could use to pick the lock open. Two pieces of metal from the underside of the bed I slept in were going to have to do.

As I jiggled the metal inside the lock, something told me I'd done this before, but the memories wouldn't surface. A distinct click sounded, and a smile brightened my face as I gripped the metal tighter between my fingers and turned until the lock disengaged.

Removing the metal, I shoved the pieces into the pockets of the flannel pajama bottoms I had on. My feet were bare, and the button-up, short-sleeve, blue pajama top I wore didn't match the white striped bottoms, but my state of dress was the last of my worries.

I didn't know where I was going or how I was getting there, but I couldn't hide in the closet while the rest of the world went on around me. I wanted nothing more than to rip off the gauze that was wrapped around my head.

However, the way Regina had described drilling into my damn skull, the head-wrap might have been the only thing keeping my fucking brains tucked inside where they should be. The damn details she'd given about subdural and intracranial hematomas, cerebral contusions, and sensory deprivation sometimes made me feel like the doctor's monster.

When I stepped into the open space of the next room, which was considerably larger than the closet I'd been stuffed into, the scent of death assaulted my nose. A strange feeling settled over me. A big metal table with tubes running into the floor, the meat-lockers built into the wall, and machines I didn't know the names of were neatly displayed throughout the spotless but smelly room. *A fucking morgue?*

I was living in a morgue! So, the doctor had not been lying about the job her family had assigned her. She was disposing of the bodies they were stacking up, and I was supposed to have been one of those bodies. Who the hell were these people and why did they want me dead? What had I done to them?

I shuffled over to the double metal doors that swung in both directions and found that they were the only entrance and exit from the room. Thankfully, the doors were open.

I clumped out of the room and cringed against the pain that made my body jittery. Sweat dotted my face. Droplets inched down my forehead and neck as I shuffled further into the dim hallway.

A brick wall stood to the right of me and in front of me, so I turned in the only direction I could go, careful not to make too much noise. A line of light shined under the crack of the door, the only other door on the hall—Regina's living space that she'd mentioned. This meant she was probably awake and I needed to move faster. The eerie silence of this place was a living creature that tugged at that sixth sense we often ignored.

With each painful step I took, my body became heavier, but my newly-awakened mind wouldn't let go of my will to escape. When I reached the end of the hall, I had a choice: elevator or stairs.

The elevator was one of those old-fashioned ones with a metal sliding door that was nothing but an alarm system as far as I was concerned. I calculated, due to our ability to hear muffled sounds from the outside that we couldn't have been but one level underground, so why the elevator?

My body teetered a bit when a stabbing pain shot through my head, drew itself in, and exploded out. Standing in place, I closed my eyes for a few seconds until the pain dwindled. I was determined not to stop and I didn't care if I had to crawl away from this place. I sat on the steps and inched back and up, taking myself higher and higher until the top of my head thumped the tilted wooden door above me.

I gripped the metal latch and pushed, but the door barely budged. My trip down the hall must have taken most of my strength. I cracked the door open enough for daylight to enter and blind me. The heat from outside pushed at the coldness of death that had a hold on this space.

"August, are you crazy? They are going to kill you!" Regina barked in an alarmed voice.

She ran up the shaky wooden steps and took a firm hold of me as I struggled to make my way out of the door. When it became obvious to her that I was determined to either die or escape, she stopped struggling with me.

"Okay. Listen please," she begged. "It's not just your life at stake if you go out there. My family is going to kill you before they kill me for saving you. I think I know a way we can get out of this place, but it's going to take time. Please, August, come back."

My hand dropped away from the latch, but the determination on my face remained even as I drooped from exhaustion. Regina stood in a hunched position with her back to the door as she took hold of the door latch. Her gaze was on mine the entire time, scolding me without words.

"Let me show you something, August."

When she cracked the door to about twice as wide as I'd been able to, I slid up to the highest step and squinted against the brightness of the sun.

"Look to the left, August. You should see at least two guards, heavily armed with weapons, standing near a gate."

My head swiveled in the direction she had indicated and like she'd stated, there were two heavily armed guards standing there talking to éach other with automatic weapons and backup weapons strapped around their waist.

"Turn your head in the opposite direction and look up," she instructed. A warm dusty gust of wind flew into my eyes, causing me to rub them before I refocused and fixed my gaze on the area Regina had pointed out.

Although I could only see the far corner of it, I was able to figure out that it was an elevated guard tower. My gaze roved, taking in as much of my surroundings as I could. The cellar we lived in was in a separate space from the main house. The elevator opened to a small shed that stood directly to the right of the door we peeked from.

From my vantage point, the cellar sat behind the rear of the main house. A big barn sat at least two hundred or more feet away, and the tip of a smaller shack could be seen over my left shoulder. I noticed that a third guard had joined and was talking to the first two I'd seen. It appeared they were at the side of the main house, but it must have been the area where vehicles gained entrance onto the property.

The world outside, although brighter, wasn't filled with any more vibrancy than the stuffy space I'd been trapped in.

"Those are only two of the posts you can see from here. There is another building on the other side of the barn. It's the cookhouse where my cousins, Luis and Lonzo, cook batches of meth."

She stepped down and waited until I dropped down a few steps before she eased the door closed, my view dwindling as the dimness folded around me. Regina sat next to me on the steps. Our breaths fell in sync and bounced off the walls of the dim, dank cellar as we stared into the darkness.

"If you leave, they will kill you, August. Everything I told you was the truth. You and I are prisoners in this place. I don't know much about you, but I can tell even without your memory, you've never been anyone's prisoner. All I ask is that you give your body time to heal. You survived a situation that would have easily killed others. Don't waste the second chance you've been given because of male pride or impatience. Also, give me time to figure out how to get us out of here."

She shoved her arm under my shoulder and urged me to move when I didn't reply.

"Don't you think that I want to get away from here as badly as you do, August?"

I didn't answer but considered her words as I poured every ounce of my energy into clumping down the steps and dragging my legs that were as wobbly as noodles along the scratchy wooden floor. By the time we made it into the morgue, Regina carried most of my weight, and I was barely conscious. My eyes were fighting to stay in focus.

Drenched in sweat and breathing like I'd run a marathon, I tumbled into the small bed and didn't much care how I landed. Regina kept my head from striking the bed by placing her hand under my neck.

Once she had my head on the pillow, she reached down and lifted my feet to turn me into the bed.

"Thank you," I whispered and drew a sad smile from Regina. I attempted to blink back the tiredness that had overtaken me, but it was too strong, so I drifted.

36

AUGUST

Darkness had swallowed me, but unlike before, I sensed the tightness around me and the ghost lingering in my head. This time, I found flashes of who I used to be in the darkness. Death, destruction, murder, guns, faces, names, and even love lived in my ripped-apart mind.

Making sense of what flashed in my brain was difficult. I couldn't put any order to the chaos spooling through my mind. But there was one thing I was certain of. My brain was reconnecting itself to who I used to be, and the picture it painted gave me a hint of why I'd ended up in a basement right under the noses of an enemy who had tortured and almost killed me.

Since it was giving me answers, this was the first time I'd wanted to linger in the dark. Pain was the angry bastard that snapped me awake. Pain didn't ease me from my limbering state. He slung me out as my head pounded. Bombs exploded in my brain, turning it into mush. Each heartbeat seemed to expand into aching vibrations that coursed through me. My sense of balance was off as I struggled to lift my heavy head.

My eyes snapped opened to Regina staring down at me with pity on her face. "I'm aware that you're in pain, August, but the kind of injury you sustained doesn't leave me many choices as to what I can give you."

"Water," rushed harshly past my dry lips and rattled in my throat, sounding like I'd swallowed an army of frogs.

After getting water into my system, I retook the doctor's hand since she always seemed to be hanging onto my hand whenever I woke up. I'd wake to her either staring at me or asleep with her hand gripping mine.

What did I look like? Was I disfigured? She'd never looked at me with horror or surprise. It was starting to become abundantly clear that Regina was just as trapped as I was and as desperate to escape. I had to find a way to help her since she'd risked her life to save mine.

She gripped my hand, staring at me like I was something precious.

"Plan?" I asked. The word sounded normal, so I added more. "What is your plan for breaking out of this place?"

She sat for a moment contemplating what she wanted to say.

"My family...well, *my cousin* allows me a few moments of occasional freedom. However, I'm not naïve enough to think that I'm not being watched or followed. Every six months, I'm allowed a week of freedom. It's been over five months since my last reprieve, so if you can be patient enough to hang in here with me, I intend to try and sneak you out when I leave."

Stress always lingered behind her kind eyes, but when she spoke of escaping, it filled her with tension. Her warm hand tightened around mine.

"The only problem is how to get you into my car. They keep it parked in the barn."

I'd taken a long hard look at the barn where Regina was saying her car was parked. It was a good distance from the cellar, and the only pathway that would lead us to the barn was in direct line of sight of the guard tower.

As if she knew what I was thinking, she continued.

"There is also a guard who hangs out at the back of the barn. If I can figure out how to get you into the barn without either of us getting shot, we may be able to leave this place together."

"Map. If you can make me a map of where the guards are posted and where the other buildings are located, I can help."

Her smile spread wide across her face, revealing rows of gleaming straight white teeth. "I can do that. I can definitely do that," she expressed with enthusiasm.

The idea that we may have a way out eased a bit of my tension. Regina didn't know it, but as soon as I could stand without tipping over, I was going out of that door to survey what we were up against whether she thought it was a good idea or not. After seeing bits and pieces of my life, I was certain I was not the guy who laid around waiting to be saved.

"You were talking to someone the other day," I stated, capturing her gaze. I couldn't remember if it had been yesterday or the week prior that I'd heard her talking to someone, but I remembered their conversation. "You lied to keep him from coming in here to find me. It was your cousin, wasn't it? He's the one who hurts you, right?"

She attempted to hide her grief, but her eyes revealed her truth. "Yes. It was my cousin, Sorio. How do you know that he hurts me?"

"Because of the desperate lie you told about sex toys."

She cupped her forehead in the palm of her hand and peeked at me from behind her fingers.

"I'm not a good liar, but it worked. Honestly, I would've said just about anything to make him leave. He was the one who ordered his men to take you from Florida."

Based on the flashes of memory I'd gotten, I'd pieced together that I'd likely been from Florida and there was a chance I was just as dangerous as Regina's cousin.

"Sorio is also the main reason I'm stuck underground working as my family's glorified undertaker. He hates women and especially me because I refuse to embrace my family's misguided principles. He is considering having me moved to a different location, which I pray won't happen before we find a way to leave this place together."

Thoughts of her cousin had her skin crinkling around her eyes as thin creases etched her forehead. The hatred she harbored for him ran deep, so deep that I didn't think she would mind if I were to kill him.

"He's talking about killing two women. He only came down to visit me so he could rub it in my face. I've taken beatings at his hands because I refused to burn women for him. He always wants the ashes of the females, and I'm sure he only wants them for some sick and disrespectful reason."

"What about the other ashes?" I asked, curious as to why anyone would want human ashes. "Why do you bring them to your cousin? His name is Luis, right?"

Her eyes widened in surprise. "You could hear me when I was talking to you all those times, couldn't you?"

My lips twitched into a smile. When I was in the darkness, some of the conversations she'd shared stayed with me.

"Yes, some I remember. When I was out, I could hear and sometimes smell, but nothing else worked. I remember you talking about the ashes and bringing them to your cousin. Why keep the ashes of the people they kill?"

She seemed to be having a difficult time gathering her words. What the hell were they doing with people's ashes? The chirp and hiss of the machines filled in the silence as she gathered her thoughts. The thin wooden legs of the stool she was perched atop creaked as she shifted uncomfortably.

"My family deals mainly in meth," she started, her face pinched in distaste. "My cousin, Luis is my family's main chemist. Like me, he's earned a medical degree. However, he is happy to create and cook up the most lethal and addictive batches of meth to hit the market. He takes pride in it, giving his batches names like Man Slaughter, Murder One, and Homicide. The names alone have addicts waiting in line to try it."

Regina was unaware of how tightly she was squeezing my hand. Her worried expression increased in its intensity as her haunted gaze remained locked on mine.

"The key ingredient in my family's meth supply is human ash. As a doctor, I can't see—"

"Wait!" I raised my free hand to stop her before I lifted my head higher to glance into her eyes that had started to sparkle with tears.

"You're telling me that they have you down here turning their murder victims into ashes so that they can add them to their meth supply, drugs that are more than likely being distributed across this country."

She nodded her head as a tear slipped down her cheek. "My family is known as DG6, and their meth is not only being distributed across this country, but it's exported to four other countries. People have no idea what they are smoking. I don't want to be a part of this madness. Medically, adding the human element to the drug should have no relevance to the addicts high, but the drugs speak for themselves. People will do anything for it, and other chemists are out there, every day trying to duplicate my cousin's formula."

Her family was doing the unthinkable, but she was the one embarrassed.

"I don't want to disrespect the dead like this, but I'm only one woman, and my fight against my family has been useless so far."

My brain hadn't fully processed the notion that these crazy-ass people were putting human ashes in their meth supply. They had junkies smoking *people*. The shit boggled my mind, which was already out of sorts.

37

AUGUST

A week later and a somewhat put-together plan had me as positive as Regina had started to appear. Each time I closed my eyes, more of my memories returned. Every time Regina left me alone for any long period of time, I broke out of my closet and up the steps I went.

Three days ago, I'd made it about ten feet out the door before I was almost caught by a roving guard. However, I did get far enough out in the open to spot three more guarded posts.

In my dreams, I'd seen glimpses of me on this farm and the escape attempt by my friends that had gone wrong. Those flashes of memories along with my spying had helped me get a better understanding of why the doctor and I were trapped in the cellar and why it was going to be difficult to hike to her car that was supposedly parked inside the barn.

I waited until nightfall this time so that I could travel farther than I had the last time. Once I was sure Regina was in the shower or sleeping, I crept through the door, hunched low and hugging the rough brick wall opposite her door.

The door of the cellar opened to the back of the main house, which kept me hidden from the guards whose voices sounded in the background. I eased the door open and peeked, ensuring the coast was clear before I crept out into the dimmed atmosphere.

The sun had set, but a few orange sparks of day in the distance were hanging on, fighting to keep the night at bay. A few stars glistened overhead, providing a spark of energy to this bleak plot of land.

My gaze landed on the area where the guards stood at the gate as I crawled across the short expanse that would take me to the back of the house. Raised voices stopped me in my tracks as my neck swiveled in the men's direction. None came my way, nor had any guns been aimed at me, so I continued, sliding along the grassy ground on my stomach.

Once I reached the back of the house, the structure kept me from the line of sight of the noisy guards who continued to carry on their lively conversation. I rose, putting my back to the house and slid along its scratchy surface in the opposite direction of the men. Chips of paint pricked my back, flaked off the wall, and sprinkled to the ground.

My bare feet flirted with blades of grass as I peeked around the bend of the house for a full view of the tower that had two armed guards posted inside. The barn was farther than I'd initially assumed it was, and there was nothing that would keep me from the view of the guards in the tower or those on the ground.

Periodically, I'd see the men pacing in random areas, but they never lingered in one spot for long. Two were posted on the far side of the barn, likely guarding the building I couldn't see, which was the meth lab Regina had talked about.

My head darted in both directions before I reclaimed a position on the ground. My stomach raked the bristling grass as I inched my way into the dark opening. At any moment, I could have been spotted, nothing more than a human target. Approaching footsteps ahead of me sent me scrambling, rolling like an alligator to make it back to the tall frame of the house.

"Who the fuck are you?" a deep voice asked gruffly. The darkly shrouded figure peered at me, fighting the darkness to see me better as he inched closer with his weapon aimed at my head.

THE METAL STRUCK his skull and the fleshy clank sounded off loud enough to alert the other guards. Regina had sneaked up on the man, surprising him as much as she'd surprised me. She'd struck him over the head with a large iron pipe and had somehow caught him before he fell on top of me.

With her hands under the man's shoulders, she dragged him out of the opening and to the back of the house. I followed her because the doctor was certifying herself as being my guardian angel.

She propped the door to the cellar open with the same pipe she'd used as her weapon and dragged the man down the steps. The man's dangling legs thumped with every step she took down. Once I'd secured the door and caught up with them, I took the man from Regina and followed as she led the way to the morgue.

No words were exchanged between us, but I could tell she was pissed by her pinched lips, the stormy fury in her gaze, her quick, hard movements, and heavy breathing. I stood to the inside of the double doors with my forearms tucked under the limp man's shoulders.

Regina walked around us and locked the doors. From the corner of my eyes, I could see that she'd kept her hand against the doors as she breathed in her frustration. This incident could very well have messed up our plan for escape.

"We are going to have to kill him," she gruffly concluded with her head tilted to the door.

It was my fault that this man was going to die, but I wasn't the least bit sorry about it. I wished there was a way we could lure them all into this cellar so we could keep killing them. However, one missing man versus a dozen was easier to explain.

"Once they discover him missing, they are going to search this farm for him." She remained at the door, irritation almost palpable as her voice bounced off the wall. "I'm going to have to find you a better hiding place," she stated, finally turning around to face me.

She walked past me as I dropped the man on the floor and

relieved him of his knife and gun. I observed the gun in my hand, noticing it felt familiar. The weight and the smooth metal pressed into my palm as my finger caressed the trigger.

My gaze left the weapon to follow Regina's movements as she went to the wall and pushed a few buttons that ignited flames inside the small glass door. I stepped closer for a better view, realizing it was the incinerator and how she was able to produce the ashes her family used in their meth.

Next, she pulled a pair of thin plastic gloves from a box sitting on a table filled with death instruments and took her time putting them on. She walked around the autopsy table where she gripped and pushed a skinny metal table in front of her, stopping at the man she'd knocked out. Blood gushed from the hole she'd opened in the man's head, wetting his hair before sliding across his head and hitting the floor.

Regina folded the small table so that it collapsed and sat low to the floor. I assisted by lifting and rolling the man onto the table. I assumed she'd wheel the man over to the flames, but she took her time, undressing him. What did it matter if he had clothes on or not? The flames were going to turn it all into a pile of ash, right?

She stacked the clothes and his boots into a neat pile near the foot of the autopsy table and straightened the man on the smaller table, aligning him so that he was flat on his back. She went about her task, not rushing her process.

I could tell that she'd handled many bodies. She knew exactly where to grip and tug to maneuver and turn the man who probably outweighed her by a hundred pounds. Once she had the man aligned the way she wanted him, she lifted the small table as one would an ironing board until it rose to her chest level.

She wheeled the man towards the flames before placing her hands inside a pair of thick mittens. Her hands were always so soft and warm that it was hard to believe she constantly used them to handle the dead.

She went about her task as I stood in place, observing. Once she had the man and table aligned with the incinerator's entrance, she opened the small glass door.

The heat from the flames reached across the room and licked at my skin. Its bright dancing flames beckoned me closer, and I listened, taking a few steps in its direction.

This would have been my fate if she hadn't saved me. It was hard to think that my remains would've ended up being ingested into a meth addict's bloodstream. The thought of such a fate gave me a chill despite the heat of the flames that were starting to envelop me.

The doctor shoved the table closer to the flames, lifted and dropped it so that the lip of the table overlapped the edge of the fiery opening. She took a firm grip on the man's feet and pushed him, headfirst into the flames. The moment the heat stroked him, he jerked awake and fought his fiery death. His pleading screams vibrated across the room as I watched with unblinking eyes.

While keeping a wavering grip on one of the man's thrashing feet, Regina reached up and pushed a red button. A conveyer roared to life and pulled the man farther in, thrashing and yelling into the flames.

She slammed the door behind his flailing limbs and shrieking voice. I continued to stare at his wild thrashing inside the incinerator. His feet kicked against the glass door, echoing throughout the room as his screams were being swallowed by the power of the flames. His cries dwindled with every second that passed.

I expected to see tears in Regina's eyes when she turned to face me, but her defiant gaze, stiff posture, and her head, which she held high, revealed the irritation she continued to harbor towards me.

Regina's actions had dissolved any doubts I had left about where her loyalties lay. She wanted to be away from her family and she didn't care if she had to kill to make her escape.

Her gaze remained on me, more specifically, my hands, which were holding the gun and the knife that previously belonged to the now deceased guard.

"August, we are going to have to trust each other. We only have eight more days to wait, and we could ride right out of this hellhole. I can't have you trying to escape every time I turn my back."

I protested, "I wasn't trying to escape. I was trying to search for a way to get to the barn and to see if your car is even there."

She pursed her lips. "The car is there, August."

I could tell by the way she said my name that she was still upset with me. I reached up and massaged my temples, easing the headache that I'd been ignoring. Her voice drew my attention back to her.

"I went to the cookhouse yesterday, pretending I was lonely enough to chat with my cousin. On my way back, I checked the barn and had a gun aimed at my head for snooping. My car is there. And before you ask, I know it runs because the guards sometimes use it to go back and forth into town."

All I could think about was killing these people, and it was clouding my judgment. "If we do this my way, it will end in death. So, we need to figure out how I'm going to get from here to the barn without being spotted," I stated honestly.

Regina smiled at me before she cast her gaze down to the pile of clothes she'd left stacked at the foot of the autopsy table. "That's a start. Those will help you blend in and at least look like one of them."

A smile bent the corners of my lips. I was starting to like Doctor Regina and her way of thinking. She was my twisted savior.

She shrugged. "I don't know you, August, but at the same time, I do. Based on your determination, I know you're willing to die to get out of here."

She pointed her finger between us as she placed a lot of stress on the word *we*. "*We* will find a way out of this place together. Have some faith, August. We are leaving this place together, and we are going to be alive when we do it."

I knew Regina had sparks of fire in her soul to go up against a family like hers, but I'd just started to grasp how much. I pointed at what was left of the man burning in the incinerator. "They are going to see the smoke coming from that incinerator."

She shrugged, "They are, but if they ask, I'll tell them that there were some clothes that I'd forgotten to deal with from the bodies they had me burn a few days ago."

She glanced back at the incinerator.

"I'll flush the ashes once he's done, but I'm going to have to hide that gun, knife, and you, if they come searching for him. One of the guards has run off before, so they shouldn't have a reason to come searching for him down here. But we need to be prepared in case they do."

A mischievous smile spread across her face, revealing a bit more of the fire hidden below her prim and proper exterior. "It's good that we have weapons now. I don't like guns, but I get the feeling you haven't forgotten how to use them."

I TOSSED and turned as I heard myself yelling out, but the dream refused to loosen its grip on me.

"August, wake up," a comforting voice called, reaching past the chaos inside my head. The slow stroke of a soft hand grazed my bearded jaw, accompanied by a soothing tone. "You're right here with me."

Her delicate tone eased me from my crushing distress. My eyes opened to the view of Regina standing over me, her face covered in concern as her fingers traced along my forehead.

"I'm right here, August. You're okay," she said repeatedly until I settled down. Only when the last knots of tension left me, did Regina take a seat on the stool next to my bed. She seemed almost afraid to let my hand go.

"Who's Megan?" she asked with a hint of a smile on her lips.

My memories weren't easing back into my head—they were returning with a vengeance. I was reluctant to reveal the news to Regina. My life had been a hellish anarchy of blood and bodies and based on some of my memories, I don't think I minded it.

A twinge of guilt wiggled its way into my fragmented thoughts as I observed the way Regina took care of me. I owed the woman my life, so she deserved to know who she was cozying up to.

"Megan was..." *Fucking tell her!* My mind screamed. *She burned a fucking man alive because you couldn't sit still.* "I think Megan is the only woman I've ever loved."

Regina smiled at me before squeezing my hand. "I figured that much. The one constant of all the yelling you've done in your dreams is calling out for Megan. Are your memories coming back?"

"Yes," I answered honestly. "And I have to be straight with you. I'm not a nice person, Regina. I've killed and tortured people, and the worst part about it is I'm not sorry about it. I'm a fucking monster."

Her grip tightened around my hand. "August, you watched as I burned a man alive. I've lost count of the number of bodies I've turned into the key ingredient for my family's meth supply. And that first guard that went missing, he'd stumbled into this cellar drunk and tried to force himself on me. He ended up in the fire, August. You're no more of a monster than I am."

She appeared to be disappointed in herself, but I was proud of her. To deal with a group like her family, she needed the fight she had inside her.

She tilted her head slightly, her curiosity apparent. "Do you remember your name?"

I grinned at her. "You wouldn't believe me."

Her eyes widened and reflected her question as one of her brows knitted into a deep V over her forehead.

"What is it? What is it?" she questioned, shaking my hand to get the answer from me faster.

"August. My fucking real name is August."

Surprise dropped from her gaze and turned into a mixture of disbelief or disappointment or both. She likely assumed I was messing with her.

"You're serious," she said questioningly. "So, did your family name you after your club or something?"

"I think so. I still can't place everything, but I know that I don't go by August. Everyone calls me by my middle name, Aaron."

She wrinkled her nose up. "Aaron," she voiced, testing the name out. "You don't look like an Aaron. I'd like to keep calling you August. It seems to suit you better."

"That's because you don't know me, Regina. But, if you like calling me August, that's fine with me."

Curiosity oozed through her pores. Regina wanted to know it all, every sordid detail of my crazy-ass life and if she could sit through the first hour, she may be able to live in my world when we left this damn farm.

38

AUGUST

This day couldn't have gotten here faster. If I could siphon the amount of anxious energy in my body, I probably could beat out Red Bull in the energy drink market.

The guards had entered the morgue once, searching for their missing comrade. Regina had hidden me, the gun, and knife inside her bedroom. Of all the places she could have placed me. I stood inside her shower with the gun cocked and ready to blow a hole in someone's head.

At first, I thought she'd lost her mind, but the men never even crossed the threshold of her bathroom door, especially after she'd purposely sat a big box of tampons near the doorway and had singles of tampons and panty liners sitting out in the open.

Now, I sat impatiently in my closeted room, awaiting her return. The sound of her light steps registered along with the creaking of the walls surrounding me. When the door sprang open and Regina stumbled into the closet in tears, I tensed and curled my fingers into my palms. Were we going to be forced to shoot our way out of this damn cellar? I tugged her in and folded her into my arms, unsure of the reason, but hating to see her crying and upset.

"What's wrong? Who the fuck am I going to have to kill?" I asked her before she backed out of my arms laughing as tears continued to roll down her cheeks.

"After some of the things you revealed about your life, I know you would be glad to kill that asshole cousin of mine."

A laugh threatened to escape at hearing Regina curse, but her distressed state had caused me to worry. I couldn't remember the asshole's face, but the seething hatred Regina carried for her cousin, Sorio, wasn't hard to miss.

"He made me get on my knees and beg him for my leave time."

I leaned my head down to glance clearly into her eyes. "He's going to die, Regina. He's going to die in a bad way."

She shivered while gazing at me through bloodshot eyes, tiny droplets of water still clinging to her long lashes. She'd picked up on the hints of darkness blazing behind my gaze.

"I believe you," she whispered, her tone hushed like we were sharing a secret.

My declaration of her cousin's fate seemed to have lifted her somber mood. It was either that or she was starting to know me well enough to realize I meant what I'd said.

"You ready to do this," I asked her as I reached up and swiped a tear from her cheek. She nodded her head as she took in the dead guard's attire I would later dress in. The man's clothes rested at the foot of my bed as I gripped his gun, itching to put a bullet in somebody.

The bullet that had struck me in the head had put a tight grip on my fucking balls, but that shit was done, and I was starting to feel like my old self again. Regina had no idea I was crazy enough to attempt to kill every person on this farm, but I respected her enough not to risk her life to satisfy my twisted ego.

AT THREE IN THE MORNING, we crept from the cellar door, into the stilted darkness. The unmoving air around us had me breathing harder. The cry of insects and the call of animals in the distant woods sounded hollow. The stars twinkled brightly overhead, despite the gloominess that encompassed the farm.

For the first time in five and a half months, Regina and I had decided to split up. She insisted on walking me out to the edge of the house. My goal was to make it to the barn and hang out until she was released to take her leave at daybreak. The plan was a good one, but the hardest part was getting to the barn without me attempting to kill anyone or without anyone killing me in the process.

"Stay close, Regina," I whispered as we inched along the back of the house, creeping towards the bend that opened to the wide, dark space before us. The usual guards who stood at the front gate weren't at their post, but it didn't mean they weren't roving.

Turning on my heels, I faced Regina. "This is it. I'll see you later." She inclined her head once and released a shaky, "Okay." I didn't have to see her face clearly to know she was crying. I gripped her shoulders in a tight hold, making her glance up at me. "I will see you again, Regina," I said, my words firm and confident.

Dropping her shoulders, I turned and stepped out into the opening, knowing the tower guards could see me if they were watching. I hiked along the wide, dark expanse at a brisk pace, thinking maybe they weren't paying attention since I'd made it halfway across.

My feet stalled, scraping against a few pebbles that rested among the thinned grass. When I allowed myself to believe I was home free, a bright light was flipped on, shining from the elevated tower, blinding and stopping me in my sneaky tracks.

Fuck! The shadowy wall of the barn called me, but I'd been caught. I was about a hundred and fifty feet short of my destination, but it may as well have been a damn mile. I glanced back at Regina, who hadn't taken her ass back into the cellar like she was supposed to.

"Don't," I mouthed back at her, stopping her from revealing herself when she started to inch forward. The spotlight lit me up like Times Square on New Year's Eve, but I hadn't been shot yet. I turned slowly to face my destination and nonchalantly flashed a two-finger wave towards the tower like I'd observed the men do.

I continued towards the barn, knowing each step was possibly my last. The electricity of my determination powered my forward movement as I awaited the blazing impact of the bullet strike. Where would it hit this time? My chest? My back?

My shadow danced at the side of me as I gripped the gun I had shoved down the front of my pants. The sight of the barn demanded my gaze as my dangerous steps closed the distance. Eighty feet, sixty feet—only fifty feet remaining on my trek. Why hadn't they shot me yet? Was the dead man's attire I wore enough to have fooled them?

When the bright light was flipped off, the tension that had coiled in my shoulders eased, and I loosened my grip on the pistol. The shit had worked.

Now at the side of the barn, I placed my back to the wall and scanned my dark surroundings before I moved and prepared to turn around the bend, not knowing what awaited me. A quick peek around the bend revealed a clear moonlit path to the barn's big shabby wooden doors.

By the dim light of the moon, I discovered that the tall doors were cracked and not locked. Voices carried someplace in the dark. Leaning outward and away from the wall, I investigated and spotted the edge of a smaller building. The meth lab. I would have liked to engage the guards, but I couldn't. I'd be risking Regina's life, and I'd already done that enough times.

When my hands touched the barn doors that hung lopsided on their hinges, the loud creaking and whining they produced caused my head to dart back and forth. As soon as I had enough room to squeeze my way past the door, I slipped in. Once inside, I didn't move immediately as I allowed my eyes to adjust to the darkness.

My gaze skimmed my dark surroundings, searching for Regina's car. Although my mind hadn't returned a hundred percent, bits and pieces of memories of me being tortured inside this place started to filter in. My head swiveled in the direction of the stall they'd tied me in. Being inside this barn was sharpening my memory about what had happened.

The loud creaking of the doors sounded, alerting me that

someone was coming in. I tiptoed over to an old tractor in the corner and ducked behind it. One of the guards had entered the barn, and I didn't know if it was one from the tower or one from the meth lab. It didn't matter because I couldn't engage either of them. Any incident now could prevent Regina from leaving this place.

The man crept through the dark barn. His automatic weapon was aimed and pulled tight into his shoulder as he made sharp, precise turns. A flashlight was affixed to the weapon lighting his path.

"Hey, Sawyer, is that you? You don't have to hide. We thought you had taken off. The tower radioed that they thought they saw you. We spent a day searching for you."

They were assuming that I was the man who had disappeared, — clueless that Regina had burned his ass alive. The way the man searched and had his weapon at the ready, Sawyer was no longer their friend. He'd been placed on DG6's hit list.

The man left the barn, but I wasn't naïve. If Sawyer was on their hit list, the guard was headed back to report to the others. I had to find Regina's car. She'd explained to me in detail where it was parked. I stepped out from behind the tractor and headed deeper into the darkness.

Silky spider webs clung to my face, but I brushed them aside and forced my eyes to keep searching. Light quick steps took me across the dirt floor of the barn.

A large shadowy image came into focus deeper inside, near the center of the barn. It sat next to a large hay baling machine and tall stacks of what I assumed to be hay. I rushed towards the shape, which revealed a dark-color, four-door sedan.

Hoping the car wasn't locked, I lifted the door handle with ease. When the back door popped open, I climbed in and reached over the front seat to engage the automatic locks.

If the men came back, they'd likely check the car, so I searched until I found the latch that released the top of the back seat. It took swift maneuvering, but I squeezed through the tight hole that sent me into the trunk.

The air quality was stuffy inside the constricting space of the trunk, but it was tolerable given that I'd survived over four months inside my own head without the use of all my senses. Being inside the dark, stuffy trunk reminded me of that place, except this time I could feel. The hard press of the tire iron was in my back, and a prickly metal object clawed into my shoulder. My head pounded as a massive headache caused me to squeeze my eyes shut.

The sound was slight inside the trunk, but the groan of that barn door alerted me that the guard was back. The shuffle of feet scraping the hard-packed dirt of the barn floor grew louder as the steps grew closer to the car. Not so hushed chattering indicated that there were two this time. The car vibrated when the door handle was jiggled.

"Shit," one of the men cursed. "Are you sure it was Sawyer?"

"I don't know, but now, we have to stay in here until we find him or figure out that it wasn't him."

Fuck, I shouted inside my aching head. Now, I had company who wanted to hang out. If they weren't going to search the car, it meant that Regina's plan was still in play. Otherwise, I'd have to kill them and use the trunk as a body storage.

There was only one thing that eased my aches and pains when they were at their worst—thoughts of Megan. At first, it was her presence that kept me company in the darkness, but when my mind gave me the memory of her beautiful face, I considered it a gift.

When more memories of her returned, I couldn't help thinking of her fresh peachy scent. I could see myself pushing my nose into her soft curly hair, kissing her soft plush lips, or caressing her silky soft body. I could sense the truth in her words when she'd stared into my eyes and told me she loved me.

Her images eased my headache and the stress of worrying about Regina. Was that asshole cousin of hers going to let her go? Was I going to have to kill everyone on this damn farm to get us both out of here?

Personally, I preferred the idea of killing every one of these bastards, but Regina had talked me out of it, insisting I'd get myself killed. She was probably right. It wasn't that I didn't have any regard for my life. I just couldn't stomach the idea of not getting those bastards back for keeping her captive and for damn near killing me. *Think of Megan*, I reminded myself when my anger started to build.

It only seemed like moments later, but specks of light had started to sprinkle into the trunk. I'd gotten lost in my thoughts and must have dozed off. After listening for a movement, it appeared that I no longer had company.

39

REGINA

I 'd paced a hole in my bedroom floor. My nails were going through hell as I gnawed them down to the quick. After August made it to the barn, I'd been able to breathe again. The blast from guns hadn't sounded, so the guards must have mistaken him for one of their own.

Now, I had to face Sorio. I was more nervous about facing my cousin than I had been when the bright light was shined on August. Was Sorio going to give me my car keys? Was he going to go back on his word and not let me go?

The numbers on my digital clock changed from minute to minute. The seconds ticked by as I struggled with a bad case of nerves. My heart beat anxiously inside my chest as a cold sweat dampened my forehead. As soon as 8:00 a.m. flashed brightly in my face, I gripped the handle of my small carry bag and headed for the main house.

When I entered the living room, Sorio's arrogant face met me first. Our eyes connected, and it took every muscle in my body to move me forward. Had he been sitting there waiting to torture me?

Sorio's ten-year-old son, Edgar, was sitting in front of the television playing a video game as Sorio sat in the open dining area cleaning one of his guns atop the glass table.

He had seriously messed his son up. He'd taught the child to hate women, and the boy had called me so many bitches that I'd stopped acknowledging him altogether. His mother couldn't handle him, so Sorio took him from time to time and exposed him to the vicious life he led. The kid was going to need serious therapy if he ever got away from his father.

My feet scraped the hardwood floor as I inched my way towards Sorio, gripping my bag in front of me as I eyed the gun in pieces in front of him.

Standing at the end of the table opposite Sorio, I waited like a dog with an abusive master. Sadly, I was willing to beg desperately for my car keys. Sorio continued to scrub the part of the gun he'd been cleaning, but his wicked gaze tormented me the entire time.

His sinister smile broadened, spanning from ear to ear, and all I could think about was tossing him into the incinerator and watching as he clawed and screamed for me to have mercy. The dreadful thought eased my frazzled nerves.

"Sorio, I came to see if I can get my keys, so I can take my leave?" my voice cracked as I was unable to hide my fear. His evil glare shot up and down my body before he sucked his teeth at me. I stood cemented in place, frozen in fear as I screamed internally for my brain to stop me from shaking.

He pointed at the seat next to him using the metal part of the gun that had the trigger attached.

"Come here and sit next to me, Regina," he commanded.

The razor-sharp teeth of my nerves tore into me again. The idea of going anywhere near him stole the smidgen of relief I'd struggled so hard to grasp. I forced my body to move closer to him as my legs threatened to buckle under my mechanical movements.

My gaze landed on his smudged hand as he reached around the table and pushed the chair out for me. Taking the seat, I didn't scoot it closer. My grip tightened on my bag in my lap. I held it firmly against my chest as I forced my gaze up to my cousin's.

"I'm going to let you go, Regina."

A flood of relief filled me, but I suppressed my excitement since Sorio's gaze fell like shards of glass over my body.

"But," he said, making my breath catch. His lips curled, baring his teeth as his gaze filled with chill-inducing evil. He glanced down at the expensive watch on his arm. "You have your black ass back here at eight o'clock sharp next Saturday morning."

He reached around the table leg and gripped my thigh so tight that I knew I'd see his handprint there later. A tear slipped from my eye before I could stop it as I swallowed my yelp of pain.

"You know what's going to fucking happen if I have to come searching for you, right?"

More tears slipped from my eyes as my bottom lip trembled. I nodded my head in the affirmative to his question. El Diablo had nothing on my cousin because he was the true devil. The amount of evil that resided inside him didn't belong on earth.

He slipped my car keys from his pocket and slammed them down on the table in front of me. I jumped at his alarming action, so afraid that the trembles had taken over.

He raised his hand from the keys as evil bliss flashed in his gaze. A teasing smile surfaced before his snake-like tongue darted cross his lips. The sight of him made my skin crawl, and I was sure boils had popped up all over my body.

"Get the fuck away from me, Regina, before I change my mind," he barked, finally releasing my thigh.

He didn't have to tell me twice. I snatched up my keys and ran for the front door. The guards knew the deal. They knew that if my cousin had given me the keys to my car that I was free to take my leave. When I pushed the front door open, the voice of the devil snatched at my back.

"Regina!" he called in a skin-peeling tone.

My feet came to a clunky stop at the edge of the door, my body stiffened with fear. The relief I'd felt flowed out of me, spilling to the floor before burning in the devil's flames.

"Yes," I answered afraid to glance back at him.

"Don't make me look for you. I won't be as nice as I was the last time."

"I won't," I answered, knowing that if I made it off this farm with August, I was going to do whatever it would take to make sure I'd never return.

I shoved the door open and forced my legs to carry me faster. Before I took the steps down into the yard, I heard Sorio telling his son, "Now, that's how you're supposed to train a bitch."

In my haste to get to the barn, I tripped over my own feet and almost fell twice, but it didn't slow my pace. One of the guards called out in a teasing tone, "Have fun, Regina," but I didn't acknowledge the man. My mind was on one track, getting to my car, finding August, and getting the hell off this farm.

I shoved the noisy barn doors open and ran to my car. Snatching at the handle and finding the doors locked, I quickly disengaged them with one click from my key fob. I climbed into the driver's seat and slung my bag over into the empty passenger's seat.

"August," I called out, hoping he'd gotten into the car. "August," I called more loudly, turning to search the back of the car. I opened my door to get out to go and search for August, but one of the guards entered the barn and stopped me in my tracks.

"Boss man's orders. He wants me to check your car before letting you leave. So, open the doors and trunk."

Pressing the button on my key fob, I popped the door locks and the trunk. When the trunk didn't spring open, I clicked the button a few more times. The guard stood in place as I walked around my car opening doors. When I pulled at the trunk, it would not budge.

"I can't get the trunk open. I think it's stuck."

The man pursed his lips as he stepped closer to my car. I backed away from the trunk and allowed him to do his job, but all I could think about was finding August. We were so close to leaving this place.

The guard took his time peeking into every door. When he reached the trunk and couldn't open it, he glanced back at me before he tightened his grip and poured more strength into prying it open.

His plan worked, but when the trunk popped open, August jumped out, startling me and surprising the hell out of the guard.

August sent a boot to the man's chin, snapping his head up before he staggered back. The man recovered enough to go for his holstered weapon, but August had climbed fully out of the trunk. His boot came down hard, connecting with the weapon and knocking it from the guard's hand. The man attempted to go for the larger weapon that he had slung across his back, but August tackled him.

The two struggled for a moment, as loud heaves and grunts filled the barn. August quickly gained the upper hand by wrestling the man into a tight chokehold. I stood, stupefied by the scene and hoping that none of the other guards entered the barn. A gunshot at this point would not only derail our plan for escape, but Sorio would ensure that I never saw the light of day again.

The man clawed at August's arms as fear filled his wide eyes. He was struggling for release and dirt was kicked up from the heels of his feet that smacked the ground. For the briefest moment, the man's gaze met mine, as he silently pleaded for my help.

I stood there, frozen in place, not even sure if what I was seeing was real. When the man stopped fighting, and he started to go limp, August pulled the knife of the guard I had burned alive and plunged it into the man's chest. The plunging impact of the knife slicing though flesh and bone took the last of my breath away. The knife had gone into the man, ripping the khaki material of his long-sleeve top.

August had planted his knee in the man's face, over his wide mouth muffling his tortured cries. The knife had clearly nicked his heart due to the large amount of blood bubbling under his shirt and wetting it like a thick flow of dark red paint.

"What?" That was the only word I could force out through exhaustion before August shook his head, telling me to be quiet as he continued twisting the knife into the man's chest.

He held his deadly position as the man continued to shake and convulse, fighting death to stay alive.

August gestured for me to step closer.

"Why did you kill him?" I whispered, glaring at the man's arm and leg as they twitched robotically. His eyes were wide open and frozen in fear as they seemingly stared up at me.

"We leave him here, and he tells everyone what happened, and they will be right on our asses. We take him with us, and it keeps us on plan."

August yanked the knife from the man's quivering chest as a squirt of blood shot out and splattered onto the ground through the hole the knife had left in the shirt. After wiping the bloody blade on the man's pants leg, August shoved it back into the sheath on his hip.

August proceeded with disarming the man. When he handed me the man's handgun, I stood staring at the gun as if it were a disgusting object I didn't want to touch. "I don't like guns. I've never shot one."

"Take it Regina. Put it under the seat where you can reach it. You aim and squeeze the trigger. The safety is not on."

Instead of gripping the gun like I'd seen August and the guards do, I pinched it between my fingers, more afraid of it than I was afraid of the men that used them.

While the man continued to shiver, August lifted him and threw him into the trunk like a heavy bag of trash. The hard thump of the man's body signified his finality. August kicked dirt over the blood that had spilled on the ground as I struggled to comprehend what I'd witnessed.

He had given me fair warning about who he was, but it was now that I'd gotten my first glimpse of the real August. When he started to climb into the trunk with the dead man, I leaned closer, questioning him in a loud whisper.

"August, what are you doing?" My eyes darted back and forth between him and the body.

"If they check the car again, I'd rather surprise them, than them surprise me."

I simply stared as he climbed into the trunk and started to pull it down. Right before he closed it all the way, he glanced up and winked with a huge smile on his face. "Let's go, Regina, and try to act natural."

How was I supposed to act naturally with a dead body and fugitive in the trunk? Had I made a deal with a devil worse than my cousin? I carefully placed the gun on the top of my car before I ran to the barn doors and propped them open. Walking back to my car at a quick pace, I prayed, "God, please let me leave this place and never return."

The dead guard in the trunk with August had closed each of my doors as he searched my car, so I snatched the driver's side door open and hopped in. Before I closed myself inside, I realized I'd left the gun sitting on the top of the car.

My hand hovered over the gun for a moment as I was unsure of how to pick it up. I picked it up by the pistol grip and leaned into my car to place it under the seat like August suggested. Finally, I climbed in and pushed my car to a quick start. I drove towards the light shining into the barn through the large opening. Freedom was within my grasp, and I was desperate enough to do anything to get it.

When my car crossed the threshold of the barn and rolled into the full light of day, panic shot tremors through my already nervous body. All eyes were on me. The guards in the tower, the guards who stood outside the cookhouse, and even the guard who hung out behind the barn was walking towards my moving car, gawking at me.

The profiles of the front gate guards grew closer as I fought to keep my trembling foot from smashing the gas too hard. My blood pressure spiked a few notches as one started to slide the gate open to allow me to pass.

When the edge of the front of my car crept past the gate, the guard who'd opened the gate approached signaling for me to roll my window down.

"Jamie was supposed to check your car, but he never radioed that he checked it."

That's because Jamie is in hell trying to convince the devil not to eat the rest of his worthless soul.

The forced smile on my face started to fade. "He checked it already," I stated. It wasn't a complete lie.

"Pop the trunk, I need to do a check," the man said as he placed his hand on my car gripping the area between the window and inside door paneling.

I couldn't let this man check my car. August and I were so close to freedom, I could taste it. The gun under my seat popped into my mind. My grip tightened around the stirring wheel as the man stood there waiting for me to open the trunk.

"You know what, I'm sick of you all treating me like I'm some criminal mastermind. I just spent six months in a cellar, cooking dead bodies. I'm on my time now, and I refuse to let you waste it conducting worthless searches."

I shoved the man's hand off my car and slammed my foot down on the accelerator, scratching up gravel and leaving a trail of dust behind. My rearview mirror reflected the man standing there laughing.

What?

My unusual behavior must have surprised him, and instead of him coming after me, he simply stood there laughing. Maybe being mean was the only language those sorts of people understood. It didn't matter anymore because my goal now was to get as far away from this farm as possible and to lose whomever my cousin was going to have spying on me.

40

AUGUST

Regina had bigger balls than I'd given her credit for. Standing up for herself had paid off, and the guard had laughed after she'd demanded he get away from her car.

The stiff next to me wasn't stinking yet, but the remnants of his death stench had started to creep out under the heat of the sun. I waited for about an hour before I shoved him out of my way and clicked the button that allowed me to squeeze into Regina's back seat.

"Don't look back," I instructed her. "Use the rearview mirror. Someone like your cousin probably has someone following you, and I'm sure he has a tracker someplace on this car."

She didn't say anything, only glanced at me as I worked my way into the back seat before lying across it, stretching my stiff back.

"Regina, head towards El Paso. It's a long stretch, but it will get us closer to where we need to be."

Although I couldn't see her eyes, I sensed her staring into the rearview mirror.

"I thought you were from Florida? Don't you want to go back home?"

"No. No one knows I'm alive, Regina. I want to keep it that way for a little while. I have family in California and believe me; he can help us better than my family in Florida. And, he also has Megan."

"Oh," Regina said. "Are you sure your family is going to help me too? Lord knows I don't want to be, but I'm a Dominquez. How would you even introduce me?"

Reaching over the seat, I gripped her shoulder to reassure her. "You saved my life more than once, Regina. If you have any idea the kind of shit I've pulled with my family over Megan, you'd know why I know they'll help you. Trust me. I'm going to do everything in my power to keep you away from that farm, even if I have to blow it up."

"Thank you, August. I'd rather die than go back there."

"Good. That's the kind of attitude you're going to have to maintain if you plan to fight for your freedom. If you don't accept the fact that you could die fighting for your life, you're fooling yourself. As crazy as it sounds, if you're willing to die for something you want, it makes you stronger."

Her light chuckle sounded. "I get it, August."

REGINA

We'd been traveling nonstop for hours, and the body in the trunk had started to make its presence known. August never complained about being in pain, but I could tell that his head was killing him. He was a tough man. He'd been fighting through his mental demons as hard as he'd been pushing through the pain I knew he suffered.

"You ready to switch, Regina?" How did he do that? He was laid flat out on the backseat asleep as far as I knew.

"I'm a little tired," I answered, as I rolled my stiff shoulders. The sound of him rising to take in our surroundings made my gaze shoot to the rearview mirror.

"Pull over here. I'll take over," he directed.

I gladly pulled over. The shoulder of the backwoods road was not paved but grassy. I hopped out of the car, stretching my legs and arms as I walked around.

August hopped out of the back and stood outside the car, staring around for a moment before he climbed in. He edged the driver's seat back as far as it could go and didn't bother with putting on his seatbelt before we drove off.

I dug through my bag until I found my phone. When I pulled it out and turned it on, August stared at it and me.

"Let me see that," he said in a gentle tone. I handed the phone over and sat staring as he nonchalantly rolled down the window and tossed it. I hadn't been paying attention to the fact that he'd been slowing the car down. My mouth fell open, but I couldn't force my words out. August stopped the car, threw it into reverse and backed over my phone.

"August!" I finally managed, appalled by his behavior.

"Your cousin is tracking you, Regina. If you want to lose him for good, you have to get rid of everything he could use to track you with."

I inclined my head, knowing he was right. There was nothing more important than me being free of my family, especially my cousin. I used the passenger's side mirror to stare at the small pile of broken parts that was my phone until they disappeared. I'd intended to use my phone to transfer some money into my account. But, August was right, I couldn't risk my family finding me for any reason.

Later, my eyes peeled open slowly as I struggled to figure out where I was. When my focus grew sharper, August filled my view. He'd fully reclined my seat without waking me. I faced the window to wipe a little drool from my bottom lip.

"I dumped our passenger at the landfill about three hours back. I used the money he had on him for gas and some food and water for us." He tilted his head in reverse towards the bag of goods sitting in the back seat.

"Now, we are about to ditch your car into the bottom of a quarry."

What was I supposed to say? I loved my car. It was the only thing my father had given me that my cousin hadn't destroyed. However, it could also lead my cousin to me. I inclined my head towards August and allowed my gaze to sweep my surroundings.

"Where are we," I asked.

"Right outside of El Paso," he answered as he turned the car into the woods, on a rutty dirt road. After a half hour of being tossed about inside the car, we finally arrived at the edge of the quarry where the dark water below started to appear.

The flat plain we drove along led to a steep vertical drop, straight into what appeared to be a quarry surrounded by fat rocks and boulders. It had to be a fifty or sixty feet drop. There didn't appear to be any other way into the water except for the drop. It probably would take months for my car to be found, if ever. The water sat stagnant and black, making the quarry appear to be miles deep.

August drove so close to the edge that my breath hitched, thinking he would drive us over. He let down all the windows, popped the hood and trunk, and opened the sunroof. When he opened his door to get out, I grabbed my bag and our supplies and jumped out too. Twigs crackled under my feet as I backed away from Netta, my gray BMW I'd had for five years.

Surprisingly, I'd become more intrigued than worried about losing my car. August put the car in neutral before he went to the back and started to push. Netta hesitated to roll at first, but once the wheels started to turn, she went willingly, almost lurching forward. Her front end teetered over the edge for a second before she embraced her death and dived in.

August approached the bank to see how she'd landed. I didn't care to see. The loud splat she made when she hit the water caused me to flinch, but instead of sadness filling me, a sense of peace started to spread over me.

I believed August was helping me peel away the constricting binds my family had tied around me. I was slowly allowing myself to be freed from a prison I'd been forcibly placed in. I was starting to believe that August was truly going to help me in my quest for freedom.

He carried my bag on our onwards journey. It took us two hours to hike back to something that resembled a town, but I didn't mind the walk. In a way, the walk signified another step I'd taken along the path that was mapping me closer to freedom.

August pointed me to a bench in a small park near a library. I sat watching people carry on with their lives, wondering where August had gone. I saw a father tossing his son a colorful football and a couple snuggling as they watched their kids playing on the jungle gym. A teen girl with a mean scowl etched permanently on her face as she glared at her parents also caught my eye. The warm sun glowed brightly above them, filling them with the energy of life. Being held captive by your family allowed you to appreciate the simple beauty of life.

The loud honk of a horn gripped my attention, and my mouth dropped at the sight of August in an old brown Chevy pick-up truck. He waved me forward when I failed to move fast enough. After he slung the door open for me, I rushed towards the truck and climbed in.

I was scared and nervous about the path I'd chosen, but hope floated above my fears, tugging it apart piece by piece.

41

PART III

MEGAN

"Aaron?"

My legs wobbled under my weight, and I forgot how to breathe. I'd finally lost my last pinch of sanity. Aaron's death had destroyed me, and now I was seeing things. I stood, blinking, mouth agape, trying to convince my brain to unfreeze my stiff body.

Finally, I sucked in a breath and eased it past my shivering lips, my gaze locked on the image of Aaron standing in Ansel's doorway. "You're not real. You're not real," I kept repeating those words before rubbing my eyes. When he didn't disappear, I started tapping at the sides of my head, trying to bring back normal, but knowing I was losing it.

"It's me, Megan. You're not going crazy."

The image stepped into the doorway and gripped my hands, preventing me from continuing to hit myself.

"Megan, baby, it's really me. I'm not dead. I didn't die."

Although my wrists were trapped, I managed to point a finger at him. "You are dead. I saw you die. I wanted to die with you. You're gone, and now I've truly gone crazy."

"Megan!" He shook me hard, trying to convince me that it was truly him. If I allowed myself to believe what I was seeing, Ansel was likely going to have to send me to the nut house. He'd already spent months and a lot of time re-training me to be a human being again. He'd hired and kept a nurse in the house because he was afraid I'd hurt myself.

"Megan, it's me. I'm not dead. I didn't die in those woods. Touch me and see for yourself."

He released my hands, but I kept them elevated, afraid to move.

"Aaron?"

I reached out slowly, still not convinced that I hadn't gone insane.

When my hand brushed along his bearded jaw, I flinched and jerked it back, staring into his face. He stood still, allowing me the time I needed to figure this out. I inched my hands towards his face again, cupping his chin before I forced my numb legs to take a step closer.

My hands slid over his jaw line until they were at either side of his neck.

"Aaron?"

I didn't know if I was asking a question or making a statement. His skin sliding under my fingers felt real. His familiar masculine scent drifting into my nose smelled real. His handsome face filling my gaze looked real.

"If you're alive, tell me how? We left you. We...left...you, and you're not dead?"

He pulled me to his strong chest, enfolding me into his arms. Breathing him in, I melted into his warm embrace. If I was going crazy, I didn't care anymore. I'd gotten Aaron back whether it was all in my head or not. I tightened my grip on him, savoring his scent and loving the warmth he always enveloped me in.

"It's a long story of how I survived and I'm still alive."

He released me and backed away, and I followed him out of the door, not wanting him to leave me again. My hands reached out desperately as fat tears pooled in my eyes. My fingers wiggled, frantically trying to will him back into my arms.

He signaled for someone to come closer, causing me to finally take my eyes off him. A pretty lady who resembled J-Lo, only darker, walked closer with a wide smile on her face. I stared from Aaron to the lady, wondering why my twisted mind would bring another woman into my fantasy.

"Megan, this is Dr. Regina, D-d...um...Davis. She saved my life."

The lady could have been Native American, Middle Eastern, or Hispanic. Her beauty was praiseworthy. The sight of her brought back that nagging voice, telling me that I'd lost my whole mind.

She reached out, and I stared at her hand for a paused moment before I forced myself to take it. She felt as real as Aaron had felt. I felt her warmth and the grip of her hand over mine was real. I wasn't crazy, was I?

Aaron retook his position in front of me. *He isn't dead? He isn't dead? He isn't dead.* I repeated the words internally until I made myself believe them. The idea of having him back caused an overpowering amount of happiness to stream through me.

Aaron continued to stand in front of me and appeared as stunned as I was. His blue eyes softened, holding me in place and keeping me in the moment with him. I stared, not saying anything. I wasn't even blinking. I teetered as my mind fought to keep me in the right head space and time, and I almost fell into Dr. Regina.

My body wavered, and Regina caught me. "I've got you," she said, catching me with a strong grip. She slid one of her arms under my shoulders and kept it there. It hadn't dawned on me that Aaron had taken hold of my other arm until his hand slid around my waist, jarring me from my trance.

"Let's go in and have a seat," Aaron suggested as he pointed into Ansel's living room. "That way, I can tell you the story of how I'm alive and where I've been for the last six months."

Sandwiched between my seemingly resurrected boyfriend and the doctor who saved him from death, I struggled on weak legs as I was nearly carried to the couch.

My feet scraped against the shiny ceramic floor as I stared up into Aaron's face, fascinated that he was here with me. I wanted to talk. I wanted to tell him how much I'd missed him. I wanted him to know how much I loved him. I had so much to say to him, but I had developed a serious case of word jumbling. "Itz, I leez," Everything I attempted to convey sounded like a load of gibberish.

Eventually, I stopped trying to talk because talking was obviously not working for me. I relied on my other senses, and at the moment, sight was what I focused on. Aaron had a large scar that ran from his temple to midway down the left side of his head, but he was still the most handsome man I'd ever met. I breathed him in and relished his all-consuming presence.

Once Aaron and the doctor had me standing in front of the sofa, I fell back into the stiff, leathery cushions, releasing a loud sigh with my eyes fixated at Aaron. I didn't want to lose sight of him.

"Megan, where's the kitchen? I'll get you some water," the doctor asked on the other side of me. Without glancing in her direction, I pointed absently towards the kitchen, not sure I had pointed in the right direction.

My gaze was trained completely on Aaron. He'd been shot to death, yet here he stood, staring down at me, and looking like a handsome god. In loose-fitting jeans, a white T-shirt, and black boots, he had my full attention.

When he sat beside me, his warmth enveloped me, making me perk with an energy I hadn't felt in months. His hands closed around mine that were still shaking.

"The doctor said my body must have found a way to shut itself down after I was shot, to preserve my life for as long as it could. Whatever happened, it worked. By the time I was handed over to the doctor to toss in the incinerator, she'd noticed I wasn't dead and took care of me."

The story Aaron was telling me was almost unreal. He'd cheated death more times in one day than a deer crossing six lanes of rush hour traffic. I couldn't stop smiling at him, staring, and squeezing his hand, ensuring myself over and over that he was real.

I'd all but forgotten about the doctor until she returned from the kitchen. She opened and handed me the cold bottle of water, which I gulped while my gaze volleyed between her and Aaron. I didn't stop until I'd taken in more than half of the bottle. The doctor was there, standing in front of me. She took the half-finished bottle back, leaving me sitting there, dumbstruck, without anything to occupy my mind except the image of Aaron.

"Regina was a prisoner of DG6 like I was, so when we escaped, we escaped together. I wouldn't have made it off that farm without her. I wouldn't be alive if it hadn't been for her."

When I didn't respond, he reassured me. "It's me, Megan." He pulled me to his chest, folding me snuggly in his strong arms. I was starting to accept that it really was him, but I was so flooded with emotions, I couldn't decide what to do first.

I jumped up onto the couch, my crazed movements causing the doctor to lean away from me. Kneeling next to Aaron, I cupped his face. My fingers tapped across his strong shoulders and rubbed the firm lines of his muscular arms. I was like a kid who'd gotten the one gift that made all the others worthless.

"Come here," he said in that low husky voice that always did things to my body. My lips collided into his as my body followed. Next thing I knew, I was straddling him, so deep into the hot kiss that I'd forgotten the doctor until the sound of her throat clearing registered.

Aaron and I glanced at her, who had a wide smile spread across her lips. "Now, I see why he couldn't forget you, memory loss and all."

"Memory loss?" I questioned, glancing back into Aaron's unreadable gaze.

"Minor setback," he said with confidence, but I knew him well enough to know that he'd been to hell and back.

Dr. Regina stood. "Is it okay if I take a shower?" She patted the black bag she carried that I'd noticed for the first time.

"August wouldn't stop at any hotels, so I had to rough it, taking turns driving and catching naps in the four vehicles we acquired along the way. Not to mention, us driving hundreds of miles off course to throw off potential followers."

August?

It didn't matter what the doctor called him. She'd saved him. The last thing I wanted to do was leave Aaron, but the doctor was the reason he was here, so I left his warmth to accompany her to one of Ansel's spare bathrooms.

I kept glancing back at Aaron who was smiling the entire time as I led the doctor deeper into Ansel's house.

I could sense her gaze on me as I remained standing in the hall and opened the door to one of the spare bathrooms.

"I've never seen a couple like you two," she volunteered. "That man was at death's door, couldn't remember his own name, but he was calling your name in his sleep. I've seen and studied a lot, but this is the first time I've seen a couple react to each other the way you two do. It's pretty amazing."

I didn't know what the doctor saw when she'd observed Aaron and me. We were just *us*. I didn't know what to say to her, so I shrugged. "I can't explain it. We just get each other."

I gestured for her to enter. I was so anxious to get back to Aaron that my left leg started jumping.

"Towels are in that cabinet and soap choices are inside the shower on the caddy," I informed her, my leg picking up its pace, trying to tame my anxiousness to get back to the one thing that meant everything to me.

"Thanks," she said as she walked past me. I closed the door and started to take off at a run, but I didn't have to because Aaron was standing in the hallway waiting for me. I literally flew into his arms. We squeezed and hugged and kissed, enjoying each other.

"You are everything to me, Aaron—the peace I need for my mind to heal and the strength my heart needs to mend old wounds. The—"

He kissed me, stopping my words that had finally started to flow. Only when I was thoroughly kissed and breathless did Aaron ease back.

His lips sat next to my ear, "I need you to call Ansel. His men said he was at a business meeting. See if you can get him to come back, but don't tell him I'm here. I want to shock his ass."

42

ANSEL

n urgent call from Megan was never a good thing. The poor girl had finally started to function like a normal person again. "I knew I shouldn't have left her at the house alone," I fussed at myself. I'd done it before, now that she wasn't on suicide watch anymore, but I was always wary of leaving her alone. Aaron's death had sent her so far into the depths of depression that I'd had to hire a nurse to take care of her for the first three months.

I'd been so busy lately working on my master plan to take the head off DG6 that I hadn't had much time with Megan. Like Aaron, she'd somehow wiggled her way into my heart, and as much as I hated to admit it to myself, I'd been weakened by the connection I shared with her.

There wasn't anything I wouldn't do to keep her safe, just like there wasn't anything I wouldn't do to avenge my cousin. That's why after nearly six months of patience, the heads of DG6's empire were about to get chopped clean off. I, along with D, Dax, Scott, Marcus, and more of my friends who were acting as guards at my house, were going to take DG6 down.

When I drove up to my gate, Rob avoided my eyes and hurriedly waved me through. His post near the front gate was an underground station, so why was he standing out in the opening? The tension around the edges of his mouth gave way to a forced smile.

"Something wrong, Rob?"

"No, nothing. All good," he answered, but I didn't believe him.

Dude stood at his post, ramrod straight like one of those soldiers that guarded Buckingham Palace.

I drove through the gate at a leisurely pace, taking in the men's bemused expressions. I sat my gun in my lap in case they were trying to signal me somehow. What the hell could have been wrong with Megan if the men were outside and still alive at their posts?

The house wasn't on fire. Because of the men's weird expressions, a certain level of uneasiness plagued me. I was anxious to see what the hell was going on, but I intended to be careful about it.

I pulled my car into the garage, left the garage open, and walked around to the back of the house. What the fuck was going on around my fucking house? Nothing was in disarray. However, the sense that something was amiss rode my back with bucking legs, heels dug into my sides.

My best bet was to go in through the back door in case something was going down. If someone had gotten in there with Megan, they'd better have a fucking army with them because my trigger finger was itching like a motherfucker, and I damn sure had backup.

My gaze traveled to JG's and Hwang's hidden posts, although I knew the men weren't on duty. Everything appeared to be okay, so why was my fucking danger meter going haywire? I turned the knob to my back door after easing the key into the lock and turning it as quietly as I could. Slipping into my kitchen, I didn't hear anything, but the sight of a beautiful woman sitting at my table eating a plate of whatever Megan had cooked, stopped me in my tracks.

"Hello," fell from my lips as I loosened the grip on my gun, but I wasn't foolish enough to put it away.

"Hello," she greeted as her sexy lips went into a tight smile. Her gaze panned down to the gun in my hand before lifting and reconnecting with mine. Although the sight of my gun put some tension in her body, a hint of mischief lingered in her gaze and hinted that she knew a secret that I didn't know. The woman was gorgeous, smoking hot. But, who the hell was she and more importantly, where the hell was Megan?

On cue, Megan walked into the kitchen. She rushed me, throwing her arms around my neck before placing a sweet kiss on my cheek. When she backed away, she waved her hand towards the woman who ran her hands over her jean-clad legs as she stood.

"Ansel, I'd like you to meet Dr. Regina...Davis."

Doctor? I took her offered hand after I switched my gun over to my left hand, squeezing her hand between mine. Her hand was soft and warm like the way I just knew the rest of her was.

"Pleased to meet you, An...sel?"

"Ansel," I repeated, eyeballing the hell out of her. I bit into my bottom lip, unable to keep myself from admiring the full-frontal view of her. Those big, brown, gorgeous, bedroom eyes called my name. That long flowing ponytail that sat over her shoulder was waiting for me to give it a tug. That honey-hued skin that did a remarkable job of hiding her true ethnicity was aching for my caress.

She was brown enough to be African-American, but her features were exotic, so she could have also been Hispanic or Native American. She had real woman curves, nice full breasts, a slim waist and curvy hips. I couldn't see her ass, but I knew she had a nice round one, the kind I could picture myself spanking.

Keeping the doctor's hand in mine, I turned to glance at Megan. Her gaze skimmed the gun in my hand and the doctor's hand still locked in my other. I noticed the doctor hadn't bothered pulling her hand away from mine. She was either brave or unaware of just how crazy I was.

When I finally let the doctor's hand go, she backed away and retook her seat at the table. Megan needed to start explaining some shit. I'd been working on my patience since Aaron's death, but that had been in small doses.

Megan glanced up at me with a tight smile. The amount of fucking innocence the woman could dredge up should have been against the damn law.

"I'm sorry if my call stressed you out, Ansel, but there is something you have to see."

She'd sounded stressed and anxious on the phone. Now, all I wanted to know was who this doctor was and how the hell she'd gotten into my house. The guards had specific orders to shoot to kill if they didn't know who it was and if that person or persons insisted on coming in.

Megan must have read my mind because she started to explain. "Ansel, I wanted you to meet Regina because she gave us a priceless gift, one that I know you're going to be as happy to receive as I was."

"What in the hell are you talking about Megan?" I asked as my gaze bounced back and forth between Megan and Regina. I didn't know this woman. However, I could see her tied to my bed as I sexed her crazy. *Mind over impulses, Ansel,* I reminded myself, thinking of the situation at hand.

"How the fuck could this woman who I don't know give us a gift?" I asked Megan, my patience wavering.

Megan was used to my abrasive tone, so her expression didn't change.

"Megan, if your secretive little ass has more friends out there that I don't know about, I'm going to throttle you." I leveled a mean glare at Megan, knowing my ass couldn't stay mad at her for any length of time.

She raised her hand towards me in a pleading manner. "Ansel, will you put the gun away please?"

A heaving sigh left me, but I reluctantly reached under my jacket and tucked the gun into the back of my pants, ensuring it could be easily reached.

"Come in here!" Megan called over her shoulder. My gaze followed her voice towards the entrance to my kitchen. The first sight of him froze me in place. My fucking heart was about to slide clean from my chest. This couldn't be a sick and twisted joke, could it?

"Ansel," he called. His voice was one I'd never forget, one that had fed strength into me many times over.

I was staring at a fucking ghost. I couldn't move. My bad ass couldn't talk. I couldn't even think. My lips moved, but my words remained lodged in my bobbing throat. Those eyes had invaded my dreams for months. I'd stared into them as life drained from his body. That fucking face had been haunting me since the day he'd died.

He approached with a cautious stride and stopped within a few feet of me as I stood, staring at him staring at me. To say that I was speechless was a fucking understatement.

"Aaron?" I questioned, my mind not fully accepting that my cousin was standing in my kitchen right in front of me. At nearly the same height, we mirrored each other. His hair was chopped low now like mine, and he'd just started to grow his beard back. Except for a wicked scar on the top of his head, he looked like my damn cousin.

"Yes. It's me," he said, his tone low but assuring.

"I thought you were...were..." I couldn't form a complete sentence to save my fucking life.

"I was," Aaron confirmed. "At least, I thought I was dead until I woke up four and a half months later at that damn farm under Dr. Regina's care. It's a long fucking story, Ansel."

My gazed scanned him, still trying to decide if he was there. Before I could catch myself, I launched myself at him, holding him in a tight grip that he returned. I didn't know how the fuck he'd survived death, but I'd seen him die. Now, he was here, flesh and fucking blood, still among the living. The toughest motherfucker I knew.

"What the fuck is going on? How the fuck did you?" I sputtered, backing away to get a better look at him.

My neck snapped back and forth between the sexy doctor, Megan, and Aaron to make sure my ass hadn't caught Megan's crazy disease.

"How man? How the fuck did you survive that shit? We left you because we thought you were dead. I can't believe we fucking left you. D and I went back for you, but they had taken your body."

I was a sack of shit for leaving him, but Aaron must have noticed my regret because he placed a reassuring hand on my shoulder.

"As far as you knew, I was dead. You didn't do anything wrong. The doctor literally dragged my ass away from death's door. I was camped outside hell, waiting to be let in. That black-hearted mother-fucker had a tight grip on me, kept me in the dark for four and a half months before I woke up. When I first got shot, I think I even saw the white light and all the things dead folks are supposed to see."

Aaron gestured his head towards the table. "Take a seat, so I can tell you how I'm still standing."

He didn't have to tell me twice because my damn legs were threatening to give out on me.

43

ANSEL

I hung on to Aaron's words as he revealed the most extraordinary story I'd heard since he'd introduced me to Megan. The man had more lives than a fucking cat and managed to stumble upon the most amazing women.

"So, let me get this shit straight," I started as I pointed at the doctor. "You were going to burn my cousin and turn him into ash so that he could become an ingredient in your family's meth supply?"

Those words were the only ones that tore Megan's gaze away from Aaron. He hadn't fooled me by introducing the doctor as Davis. My fucking mind was twisted, but my ass had learned to think around corners.

I pointed at Regina who dropped her head at my tensed stare. "She's a fucking Dominquez and she's sitting at my table inside my house. What if this whole saving you was a setup for her to lead her people right here to my fucking doorstep? Aaron, you are the only one I told about this damn house, and you brought the enemy inside?"

Since Aaron was back, there was no reason to try to be the cool and level-headed one anymore. That was what he was for.

Without saying one word, I pulled my pistol out and placed it on the table. The loud clink of metal made Regina jump before three sets of eyes landed on my gun. My piercing gaze remained glued to the doctor's.

"Ansel, she's good. I can vouch for her. She saved my fucking life multiple times. I watched her burn a man alive to keep him from discovering me."

She burned a man alive? Damn! This information helped me dial down my tension, but not nearly enough to make me pull my blazing gaze from the doctor's.

"You know as well as I do how hard it is to get onto and off that fucking farm. She plotted against her people to get me out of there," Aaron argued, his voice demanding my attention.

My cousin's statements, however convincing they were, didn't do a damn thing to ease the suffocating amount of tension that coursed through me. His brain had been tortured by hot lead, so maybe he wasn't firing on all cylinders anymore.

"Ansel!" Aaron shouted across the table, pulling my attention away from the doctor who sat frozen in fear. Her glazed eyes stared down at the table as my crazed expression ripped her to shreds.

Was I attracted to the doctor? Fuck, yeah, I was, but I'd kill her in the blink of an eye if she was a part of the reason Aaron got shot or Megan was being hunted. My gaze turned and rose to my cousin's, creeping across the wood of the table.

"She's good, Ansel. If I weren't sure, she'd be dead already."

Those sounded like the words of my cousin and based on the certainty in his gaze, I believed him. Aaron and I sat staring at each other, coming to an understanding with only our locked gazes. If the doctor wasn't legit, he knew I wouldn't waste a second putting a fucking bullet in her head.

Aaron took a quick glance at Megan sitting next to him and then looked back at me, face alive with a mixture of concern and something unreadable.

"We need to talk," he insisted, knowing I knew the subject he intended to broach.

A devious smile crept across my lips as I sat, knowing what was coming next. He wanted to know what had gone down between Megan and me during those six months he was dead. I aimed a finger at him.

"The last thing I told you as far as Megan was concerned was that if you got yourself killed over her, all bets were off."

He didn't move. He just sat there staring at me. Aaron knew me and he knew I'd do everything in my power to make Megan mine once he was dead.

"I'll get us some refreshments," Megan offered, breaking into our stare-off. She may have been bat-shit crazy, but she was smart enough to move away from Aaron before we broached the one subject that probably had those bullet fragments embedded in his brain blazing with heat.

The doctor sat quietly assessing us, probably glad the spotlight had been taken off her. Megan walked towards the refrigerator, opened it, and started to rummage through it. With her behind the refrigerator door, mine and Aaron's gazes locked once more.

Before I revealed a damn thing to him, I wanted Aaron to suffer a bit longer for the hurt and pain he'd caused me after his death. Aaron's death was the one thing to break me. It allowed me to realize that there were a few things in the world that I gave a damn about.

His death had awakened my heart, letting me know that it hadn't been destroyed by our family and the way we'd grown up. Aaron and I had been trading women since we were in our early teens, but Megan was the first one he'd outright refused to share with me.

His posture stiffened as his words started to edge out. "I'd likely have to torture her to get the information I want, and you know that I've never put my hands on a woman, so I need you to be straight with me. It's been damn near six months, and I noticed how cozy the two of you were before I walked into this kitchen."

Something behind us fell, loud and clanging. The doctor jumped, and Aaron and I simply glanced over at the refrigerator where the noise had come from and where the open door blocked Megan from our view.

I shifted in my seat, leaning over the table a bit. From the corner of my eye, the doctor eased back, glancing at my gun that I'd never removed from the table.

"Cousin, your last words were for me to take care of her. And I warned you with my own lips what was going to happen if you fucking got yourself killed over her."

The doctor's gaze bounced nervously between the two of us as I continued to torture my cousin by taking forever to get to the point. Aaron's gaze hadn't dropped away from me and at any moment, he was going to erupt into the monster I knew he could be.

"But..."

That single word put a twinge of hope in his stressed gaze, but if I didn't get to the point in the next second, there was going to be a double homicide. Aaron had given Megan a free pass once, when she didn't tell him about her and his father. Although it had happened before they'd even met, I still didn't understand how she'd dodged that clip of bullets.

Zombie back from the dead or reanimated—it didn't matter. Aaron wasn't going to forgive her ass twice, no matter how crazy they were for each other.

"I couldn't fucking do it, Aaron. I couldn't fucking go there with her. Did I want to? Fucking right, I wanted to. But after you died, it fucking...it...it just wasn't fucking right. Besides, she probably would have slit my damn throat if I had tried anything. You think I wanted to end up stabbed eighty-something fucking times like the doctor's uncle?"

I pointed at the doctor after the statement, which sent her confused gaze roaming back and forth between me, Aaron, and the refrigerator. I shoved my thumb over my shoulder, pointing at Megan who'd finally let the refrigerator door close.

"I'm like a fucking brother to her now." My face pinched into a deep frown. "The idea of even going there with her seems incestuous." A light shiver made me twitch. "Can you believe that shit? I'm like someone's fucking brother. What the fuck is this world coming to?"

The smile on Aaron's face warmed my heart. Having him back was the single best thing that had ever happened to me.

I'D LEFT BRIEFLY and returned with Aaron's phone. I handed it to him. "As soon as you two *reunite*, we need to talk about how we're going to take down this DG6 clan once and for all."

Regina didn't even flinch when I mentioned taking down her family. Instead, a flash of intrigue shined through her gaze as she rose higher in her seat, eager for more information. Maybe she did hate her family as much as Aaron had suggested.

Aaron turned the phone over in his hands. The face had one thin diagonal crack across it. "You've had this the entire time?"

"Yep. And it's a good thing I kept it too. You remember Beverly and Laura?"

Aaron inclined his head, eyeing me with suspicion.

"Beverly called your phone, thinking you were some detective. Although she'd been in contact with Megan, she hadn't connected the link between you and her. You know how Megan loves to keep her secrets."

I stated the last part louder as I leaned my head towards Megan, who'd dropped her gaze. The woman hung on to the kind of secrets that could affect national security, and Aaron's earlier statement had been right. You'd have to damn near torture her to make her spill them.

"Long story short, DG6 had likely been watching Megan since she first approached the MC. When you went tracking her to Texas, it may have led them to her friends. Laura got snatched, and I called D and Dax up to go down there to handle business. The good thing for us is we have two very capable guys in Texas whose presence can improve our plan to rid the world of DG6 quicker and maybe even smoother than I'd imagined. But enough about that for now. I saw the way you two were staring at each other and about to burn my damn kitchen down. Don't let me hold you up. I'll get to know Dr. Regina Dominquez a little better."

Aaron frowned. "Behave, Ansel. She's not like them."

"Don't worry, cousin. I'm on my meds this week."

Aaron handed me his phone. "Call my father. Get him out here, but don't tell him why. I don't want everybody knowing I'm alive yet. I want to shock his ass too."

My gaze locked on Aaron's.

"He's been a motherfucking beast since your death. I feel sorry for the members in Florida. They've all become his soldiers, and anyone who has something to say about it gets dealt with. Shark is handling things the same way I would have. Even if you've seen any news, the media is smart enough not to release that there are members of DG6 dying like a fucking plague is being spread. Over sixty members are dead so far, and he's being smart about that shit by taking them out in different states and locations each time."

Aaron couldn't hide the flash of pride shining in his gaze, knowing that his family was waging war to avenge his death, and he wasn't even dead.

Aaron's gaze landed on his phone in my hand. "Call him. Get him out here. You know as well as I do that he could have made the decision to kill my ass for disobeying his orders and choosing Megan, but he didn't. He could've killed her too, but he didn't. You know as well as I do that he took a lot of shit because of my decisions. He could have been voted out and killed himself over the shit I pulled. He deserves to know that I'm alive."

Reluctantly, I inclined my head. I was on my Uncle Shark's shit list because he believed I'd approached avenging Aaron's death the wrong way. He didn't think I was doing anything to avenge Aaron, and for that, I had no idea what he was going to do once we met face to face.

Aaron stood, taking Megan's hand. When they turned to walk away, I called after them.

"Wait!"

Grabbing an unopened bottle of water from the counter, I handed it to him, fighting to hide my teasing smirk.

"Pace yourselves," my pointed finger bounced back and forth between them. "But, if you find that you can't, we have a doctor in the house to patch you up."

Aaron shook his head at my antics, but he took the water before leaving.

Now, I faced the hard task of calling my Uncle Shark and convincing him to come to California without telling him the true reason why. I hadn't talked to him in months, so I prepared to receive a royal cursing.

44

AARON

As soon as Megan closed the door and the lock sliding into place sounded, I pounced. My lips and hands were all over her as our heavy breathing filled the space of her room. I backed off a bit, fighting to calm myself.

For once in my life, I was going to take my time with this woman. She'd tried to take her time with me before and not only had I stopped her and rushed the moment, I'd later left her to go chasing after DG6 mercenaries.

This time, I was going to swallow a bit of my own advice and calm my raging hormones. "Let's go slower," I suggested. My voice was husky and filled with lust.

"Do you really want to go slower right now?" she asked through labored breaths.

"Fuck no," flew past my lips before they landed back on hers. I filled one hand with her plump ass and the other with one of her tits. She'd lost weight, but I was glad she hadn't let it all slip away.

The urgent flutters that only she had the ability to set off inside me had taken over my stomach and made my chest tighten, causing my heart to pound faster, louder, and harder.

She backed off this time. "God, I missed you," she whispered harshly against my lips as she assisted with dragging my T-shirt over my head.

Once the task of ridding me of my shirt was completed, I dropped it on the floor and backed her up until we were standing on the side of her bed.

With my thumbs looped in the waistband of her pants, she started to wiggle out of them. I bent to slide the pants over her feet and kissed my way up her thighs until I was face to face with the only heaven I knew. As I gripped her thighs, my lustful, heavy gaze met hers.

"You have no idea how much I missed you. But, I'm about to show you," I promised as I stood and allowed my fingers to sweep up the rest of her body.

Her tongue slid across her lips as she worked my belt loose with anxious fingers. I dismissed what she was doing. "Let me help you out of this shirt. It's in my way."

After easing her shirt over her head, her curls fell and framed her face. I stood staring before reaching out to cup her chin. "God, you're beautiful."

I leaned in and kissed her with a tender ease I never knew I could bring. Pausing for the briefest of moments, I expressed the words that only she would ever hear come from me. "I love you, Megan. Regina may have saved me medically, but it was *you* who kept me from dying."

"I love you too, Aaron. I've never loved anyone the way I love you," she said, her voice sure. Her gaze was locked on mine, staring so deep that the impact of her words hit home. Her arms slid around my neck and pulled me back to her waiting soft lips.

With my zipper down, she easily reached into my pants and cupped my steel-hard dick. I gasped into her mouth, devouring her lips. Easing her away from me was tough, but I sat her on the bed.

"Climb all the way in and lay down."

My gaze never wavered from her as I kicked off my boots and discarded my socks. I dropped my pants and boxers and climbed in next to her. My body sliding against her warmth filled me with a need

that I'd been dying to satisfy. It also filled me with a deeper apprecia-
tion for the sense of touch. Every slide of her hand over my skin,
every kiss and caress of her lips over mine, and my body sliding
against hers was a blessing I'd taken for granted before.

I nipped, sucked, and tugged at the warm flesh of her neck and
collarbone. When my hand reached the tiny metal hook at her back, I
twisted it, popping her bra apart. I removed the straps, kissing the
parts I revealed that were marked with a slight indention of where
the strap had sat.

Once the bra was removed, I tossed it over my shoulder, not
caring where it landed. I slid my hand up her sexy hip, loving the way
her supple skin seemed to melt under my fingers. I didn't stop my
play until I had a hand wrapped around one of her plump tits with its
hard chocolate tip that I couldn't wait to get my mouth on.

"Oh," escaped her lips when my mouth made first contact. Her
nipple grazed over my tongue before my lips closed around it,
pinching the tight bud with purpose. My action caused quick breaths
to escape her throat before I repeatedly plucked the tight bud with
my tongue.

Her back bowed, urging me to keep going. I took my time
pleasing each chocolate tit until she'd gotten one of her legs wrapped
around my hip. With her lower body pressed firmly against mine, she
attempted to create enough friction to get herself off by rubbing her
warm pussy against my thigh. There was no way I was going to let
that happen when I had something that was going to cool her
burning aches.

Kissing my way down her stomach, I tugged at her panties. She
hurriedly raised her bottom off the bed so I could easily relieve her of
them. Purple, she was still wearing purple panties. The scent of her
arousal was calling my name, urging me to move faster.

I balled her panties into the palm of my fist and brought them up
to my nose, taking in a deep sniff, savoring the scent that caused me
to salivate. She readily opened while I slid between her legs, placing
one over my shoulder. Her breathing kicked up a notch as her chest
rose and fell with need.

Her pussy glistened with her juices, and I intended to lick up every drop. I'd finally gotten back to the territory I'd marked as mine forever and wasn't going to let anything go to waste.

My fingers slid across her wetness, and I spread her brown lips apart before I sent my eager tongue into her soft pink folds. "Mmm," escaped, rising from my chest to throat as I lapped up her juices and alternated between sucking and licking her clit, making it poke out. Her pussy pulsed against my tongue as I licked every fold. I wasn't about to miss a single spot.

She squirmed against the tight grip I had on her thighs, but she was as good as trapped because I was going to eat her pussy until I got tired. It had been too long, and we had been through too much. If Megan knew me half as well as I thought she did, she knew this was only the beginning. As crazy as I was for her, Dr. Regina was likely going to be pulling my ass out of another coma.

"Aaron!" she screamed as she thrust her pussy against my face. Trembles radiated through her thighs and crawled over her hips, vibrating against my tight grip. I had my tongue buried so deeply in her pussy that it was touching her G-spot.

"Oh God. Oh God. Oh God. Aaron, I missed you so bad!"

"That's it, baby, tell me how bad you missed me." I couldn't help an arrogant smile.

I inserted two fingers and eased my tongue back, working her into a frenzy. When my lips clamped around her clit and I sucked, she exploded. Her body literally came apart in my hands as she shook and convulsed, screaming my name. Oh, how I'd missed that sound —her screaming my name as I made her cum. I kept sucking, decreasing the pressure as her shaking turned into light trembles.

Only when I was sure that I'd dragged every ounce of pleasure from her did I release her clit and lick her essence off my lips. I eased her leg off my shoulder and moved up to slide between her legs.

Pure satisfaction shone on her face as I moved, angling my face closer to hers and covering her body with mine. Her legs automatically spread wider to accommodate my new position. My lips met hers, giving her a taste of what I'd just had. My dick was so rigid that I was almost afraid I'd hurt her. But, if there was one thing I knew about Megan, she could take a good hard pounding.

I lifted my body, breaking our kiss as I reached between us. "I have something I want to give you. Do you want it?"

"Yes. I want it. *Please*," she begged, her nails digging into my upper arm.

The swollen head of my dick slid over her slick opening, causing us to hiss out our heated response. After we recovered from the first intense contact, I kept my gaze locked on her as I forced myself into her pussy that was so wet and tight that I had to squeeze my eyes shut as I shook involuntarily from the delicious penetration.

"Aaron!" The loud cry of my name escaped her throat when I brushed past her special spot and inched deeper into her welcoming warmth.

"Shit," I mouthed as I moved slowly, losing my strength to the weakening pleasure. I wasn't all the way in yet and I had to stop or face cumming like it was my fucking first time. Megan had no idea what her pussy did to me as she moved against me, urging me to keep going.

"Wait, baby, I need a moment." The words rushed out of my mouth in one breath. "Fuck," I growled in frustration.

"It's okay. Just let go. It's been six months. It's not like we're not going to do it again."

She had a good point, but I couldn't go out like that, so I took a moment and calmed my dick down enough for my brain to enable me to move again. This time, I eased into her with more strength, shoving my dick as deep as it would go.

Her teeth sank into my shoulder as her moans vibrated against my skin, sending a chill down my arm as her snug pussy sent more hot lust marching back in the opposite direction until my entire body was ignited.

My measured movements were killing me, but the pleasure... *Jesus,* the fucking pleasure had me about to choke on my own damn tongue.

Eventually, my mind and body stopped fighting each other, and I started thrusting faster, hitting harder, and probing deeper.

"You're fucking me so good," she whispered in my ear. "Your dick is so good." Her hot words in my ear were the kind of motivation that took you over the edge faster.

Every down stroke drove us closer to the brink as I gripped her tighter and used my thigh to spread her legs wider, placing one of mine under one of hers. Heavy grunts tore from the back of my throat as I fucked her with a relentless dominance. I forced her to take every inch of me as she clawed at my back, sucked on my neck, and bit into my shoulder to stifle her screams. We gasped, choking on our building intensity.

I was so far gone in pleasure that I didn't know how close we were until her pussy squeezed my dick so tightly that I came immediately.

MEGAN

Aaron was laid flat out on his back with a big-ass, open-mouth smile on his face as he stared at the ceiling. I was laid out beside him, my legs still spread wide after he'd rolled off me. Our heavy breathing was the only sound that filled the space. My glazed and heavy eyes, my limp and satisfied body, and the wide mindless smirk on my face, were the aftermath of the only medicine I needed.

Like a flame stroking gas, his strong hand swept along my thigh and reignited my lust. The simple act of him touching and squeezing my warm, taut flesh caused his dick to jump right back up.

My gaze was locked on his dick as I rose from my position, my teeth sinking into my bottom lip. "You're not going to let me sleep tonight, are you?" I asked him as lust hung heavily in my voice.

"No, baby, you're not about to sleep. I'm going to tear that pussy up. If there's anything left, I'm going to keep going until we're both in pieces," he declared, answering honestly.

I had a feeling we were about to have a repeat of the first time he'd fucked me. A smile laced my lips at the thought. I'd never been introduced to anything so addictive in my life. Most couples would have reunited with long drawn out conversations. Not me and Aaron. We would talk later after we were too tired to move.

When he started to rise, I stopped him with a tender hand on his hard chest. Climbing over his muscular thigh, I repositioned myself between his strong legs. He'd lost some weight, but he was still the sexiest man I'd ever laid eyes on. And his dick was still thick, long, and beautiful.

My eyes had been locked on his growing dick the entire time. It was as if it was pulling me in with an invisible beam. The moment my hands wrapped around his smooth hard length, I relaxed as I used delicate fingers to apply light strokes.

My gaze remained locked on it until my mouth slid over the swollen head that had started to leak cum. My warm mouth slipped further over his hard, peachy flesh as my slippery tongue licked over the head, making him shiver and sink into the mattress.

"Fuck, baby, your tongue feels so good on my dick," he roared. His words were rushed out before he was forced to suck in a deep breath. He attempted to sit up to see what I was doing, but fell back onto his elbows when I eased his dick deeper, slurping on it as it slid to the back of my throat.

I gagged on it, knowing but not caring that only half could fit in my mouth. My body heaved, but it didn't stop my tongue from licking the underside and sliding back up to the head. He worked his hips in response to the slick movements. "You've got me weak in the best fucking way," he revealed, licking his lips before his fingers sunk into my hair and he fisted it in a tight grip.

His dick slipped between my wet lips, eliciting a lusty pleasure that put me in a ravenous state of mind. His delicious nectar coated my tongue. I couldn't get enough.

The feel of his thick hardness sliding over my tongue and filling my mouth had my pussy clinching with anticipation as I hungrily devoured him. The sight of him, the way he smelled, and his decadent taste had intoxicated me. The way he moaned for me, the sensations he sparked within me each time we touched—Aaron was wrapped around all my senses, and I didn't want to be set free.

His eyes widened in wonder as I flooded him with pleasure,

making it build and fill him up. His muscles flexed, tightening into cords of steel and his breathing intensified to exhausted gasps.

My loud slurps and suctioning noises filled the interior of the room as the expensive mattress beneath us produced a low crinkly sound. All it took was a few more solid strokes of my hungry tongue and that last hard strike of the head of his dick slamming to the back of my throat to make it swell and explode in my mouth.

I didn't stop feasting and eased him deeper into my mouth as hot cum shot down my throat. He quaked with each hard burst, his harsh breaths sweeping through the air. I drank him all down, licking and sucking to ensure I didn't leave a drop.

He fell back into the same flat position atop the mattress, his satisfied gaze aimed at the ceiling again. Every muscle in his body seemed to be working to get oxygen into his lungs, but even as he struggled to breathe, a smile rested on his lips.

AARON

I must have dozed off for a second, but my mind wouldn't allow me to shut down. I recalled Megan getting up and going to the bathroom. She'd even taken a towel and wiped my dick off. I didn't have a clue as to how long our break was, but I was ready to be back inside her.

"Come here, baby. Let me see that beautiful ass of yours," I whispered into her ear, as I squeezed one of her cheeks and watched her eyes flutter open lazily.

I directed her to the position I wanted her in while taking the opportunity to admire her beautiful nude body. With her kneeling in front of me, I sucked on the tender skin of her neck before I placed my hand in the center of her back and nudged her forward.

Her body was a splendid piece of living art that I bent to my satisfaction and angled with precision. I tilted my head as I admired the position I'd placed her in. "This is it," I told her. "I'm about to fuck you real good, okay."

"Hurry," she called back to me as her tongue slid across her lips in anticipation. Her cheek kissed the mattress as she stared back at me, peeking around her ass, which I had perched high in the air. I had her so open and exposed there wasn't going to be shit she could do to get away from me once I started.

I leaned down and drank in her scent before I flattened my tongue and licked her pretty pussy until her legs started to tremble. When she tried to close her legs, I used my knees to inch them back open. When my dick started to ache for some of the action, I rose and aligned my body behind hers.

Her body had knotted into a hunched ball like a cat, so I placed my hand in the center of her back and pushed down hard to ensure her ass was raised just right. The head of my dick glided along her wet heat, and I tensed, knowing what was coming.

However, I was never truly prepared for what her pussy had the ability to do to me. I shoved past her folds, my thick peachy flesh sinking into her tight pink center. Holding her steady, I pushed deeper and deeper, my eyes slamming shut at the extreme levels of pleasure that swallowed me whole.

The sound of her harsh breathing mingled with mine as I eased back and plunged forward with a hard thrust that tore a loud groan from me, a ragged moan from her, and flesh slapping echoes from the impact of our bodies colliding.

I repeated the forceful pounding, unable to stop myself from going in deep. With me gripping each of her plump cheeks, the visual of my dick being swallowed by her tight pussy was killing my concentration. I plunged into her wet heat, the head of my dick throbbing when it hit home.

Thrust after glorious thrust, my dick beat against her walls, causing me to bite into my lower lip and hiss in oxygen. I plunged into her with a crazed passion, chasing the pleasure that surged into me and snatched at my core before encircling my entire body. She'd reached out for a pillow that she held in a death grip and screamed into.

The blood vessels in my dick were about to blow the hell up one by one if I didn't simmer down and if Megan didn't stop backing her pussy up on my dick so vigorously. But, I didn't have to stop and neither did she. As soon as her pussy started to convulse, my dick exploded into pieces and killed us. We suffocated on the pleasure, letting it carry us away.

45

ANSEL

As I stared across the table at Dr. Regina Dominquez, I was surprised to see her gaze meet mine with confidence. She had a little bit of fire in her that I hadn't seen before. She was being sized up, and she knew it.

"If you're afraid because I wanted to kill you earlier, you don't have to be anymore. I wanted to kill Megan too when I first met her."

A smile teased those lush sexy lips. "It's understandable. I share the last name and have blood ties to a bunch of heathens."

"Why don't we go into the den, so we can sit more comfortably?" I suggested as I stood and waited for her to walk by me.

Damn! Just as I'd imagined, her ass was so fucking nice and thick. I could already see my fingers sinking into those plump cheeks, my dick lying on top of it as I prepared to invade the valley below it.

Once we were seated on the couch, separated by the four feet of space she'd put between us, I started the conversation. It was only a matter of time before that space she'd created would disappear, so I remained patient.

"So, Doc, you want me to believe you're going to sit by and watch us kill your family?"

She shook her head in the negative. Not what I'd expected, but I waited for the rest of her words. "No, I'm not going to sit by. I'm going to *help* you kill my family."

The statement sent a spark of lust to my dick, making it harder as a sneaky smile crept across my lips. "You hate them that much?"

"I was their prisoner. My blood tie to them was nothing more than the reason they needed to turn me into one of their work mules."

"Why don't you tell me how you became your family's *work mule*, as you put it? Tell me the parts of the story my cousin didn't tell me. I want to know how the daughter of the infamous Emilio Dominquez became the family's caged bird."

Surprise flashed in her gaze when I called her father's name.

"My father never wanted me anywhere near this life. After my mother was killed when I was seven, he put even more effort into shielding me from them. He sent me to the best boarding schools and visited me when he was able to. He'd never lied about what he was and what my family did, which made me understand why he'd chosen to keep me from them."

That's why she's so prim and proper. The knowledge made me want to fuck every proper mannerism she had clean out of her. Her voice pulled me away from my impure thoughts.

"When I graduated from medical school, it was the best day of my life. Thankfully, my father was still alive to see it. He was later killed in a drug sting operation. Well, at least that's what my family told me at his funeral. After his death, they left me alone for the most part, occasionally checking in on me from time to time. I was prepared to go on with my life without getting involved with them."

Here was the part. The turning point in her life that sent her into a family she clearly didn't want.

"My family left me alone long enough for me to become a practicing doctor and after nearly eight months into my residency, they showed up and blew up my life. They told me they needed me to work for the family. I refused, but soon found that there was no such thing as refusing my family, especially if my father wasn't there to protect me."

Her story had awakened my curiosity. "So, you were a practicing physician opposed to one of those people who bought the degree and labeled themselves a doctor?"

She nodded her head, struggling with the emotions that had started to flood her. "All I'd ever wanted to be was a doctor so I could help people. And my father had ensured that my dreams become a reality. But, my family didn't care about what I wanted or what my father had wanted for me."

She shook her head, the memories apparently stirring hard inside her.

"Since I hadn't had any real contact with them, I had to learn my lessons about my family the hard way. I refused their request for me to leave New York and move to Texas to work for them. I'd been told about my cousin, Sorio, but I'd never met him. I met him face to face for the first time when I woke up to him sitting on the side of my bed inside my New York apartment with a gun aimed at my head."

She glanced up, snapping herself from what must have been a vicious memory.

"Let's just say my cousin didn't give me the option to say no again. I put in my notice and left New York for Texas a week later. That was three years ago."

She shifted in her seat. The hatred she harbored for her family had started to become crystal clear now. She probably wanted them dead as badly as I did. Although I didn't voice my compliment, I was impressed with Regina. She had saved my dying cousin with limited resources while facing the stress of being imprisoned by her own family.

"I managed to escape them three times, but they tracked me every time. Each time they dragged me back it gave me a glimpse as to how vicious my family truly was. After three escape attempts in less than a three-month period, they finally put me in the one place they knew I couldn't escape from unless they allowed it—the farm. Like an animal that no longer valued escaping, I stopped trying to run even when I was released on my breaks. It's not that I didn't want to run, but I knew if I didn't have a good enough plan that would keep me from their grips, they would eventually kill me. When I found out who your cousin truly was and some of the things he'd done, I believed he was the chance I'd been waiting for."

Studying her tense posture, I eyed her suspiciously. "If your father were alive, would you have rebelled against your family? What if he'd asked you to work for the family? How do you know that he wasn't grooming you to be exactly what your family wanted you to be in the first place?"

She shrugged. "I honestly can't say how I would have turned out. I whole-heartedly believe my father's intent was to keep me away from them. Sometimes, I believe they killed him. Yes, he did some dirty deeds for the family. He murdered people, blew up buildings, and tortured people. Some of his stories are legendary, but he never let me see that side of him. I know it may sound sick, but I loved my father even though I knew he was a monster."

You have no idea, sweet doctor. You're surrounded by monsters, I thought as one of my brows lifted.

"If he was alive, I honestly can't say what may have happened, but I can only deal with where this life has led me. The opportunity to exact revenge on my family is in my grasp, and I want to take it even if it means my death."

I was beginning to like this woman more and more by the minute.

46

REGINA

What was up with these unusually attractive men who claimed they were bikers? They claimed to be members of an MC, but it didn't take but a minute with each of them to find that they were so much more than they pretended to be.

Ansel, with his charming good looks that failed to hide that bad boy peeking out, was downright sinful. For goodness sake, the man was dressed in a tailor-made suit, and his house was something out of a magazine.

I was attracted to Aaron for sure. What woman in her right mind wouldn't be? Ansel, on the other hand, had my panties drenched each time his eyes stalked my body. And the worst part was I knew he would kill me if he had a reason to.

He stood and started removing his suit jacket and tie. I gave a valiant effort, but I failed because my gaze was locked on his every move. He took his time with the task with his eyes on me the entire time, watching me watch him. Neither of us said a word until he was done and had slung his jacket and tie over the back of the nearby chair.

He made some of the space I'd put between us disappear when he retook his seat. When he peered at me with those damn intense green eyes, I forgot my own name. Nothing about a man should be pretty, but Ansel had pretty eyes; the kind you admired while trying not to get caught staring into them. They were the kind that radiated a magnetism that entranced you.

His olive skin tone against his dark hair and stubbly face added a depth to his sexiness. And his body... Good Lord in heaven! He could make a woman have an orgasm by just taking off his clothes. I denied my eyes the pleasure of looking at him by diverting my gaze as often as I was able to.

He wanted to do things to me. I could sense it...*naughty things*. After being caged up in the cellar at my family's farm with dead bodies for company and a man whose heart belonged to another woman, there wasn't much I could do to control my attraction and reaction to Ansel.

A loud thud drew my attention away from him as the floorboards creaked above us. What the heck were Megan and Aaron doing up there? This house was easily a multi-million-dollar property, so it was well put together. If the couple was causing things to creak, they were enjoying one wild reunion. A telling smile crept onto my lips although I attempted to hide it.

"I can certainly see why Aaron didn't want me. That's for sure. He looks at Megan like she's the only woman in the world."

Ansel shook his head. "Tell me about it. When I first met her, I wanted to fuck her so badly, but he wouldn't let me."

"What do you mean he wouldn't let you?"

"Doc, in our world, sharing a woman isn't an uncommon occurrence."

My lips fell apart. "You're kidding," I exclaimed, appalled.

"No, I'm not kidding. But, from the start, I could see how serious my cousin was about Megan, so I didn't push the issue with her as hard as I knew I could have. After watching her lose her mind over his death for months, I just couldn't go there with her."

"So, you've never found anyone that you didn't want to share? Don't you want someone that only *you* can have all to yourself? Someone that's willing to be only yours?"

The last thing I wanted was to hear was him say no, but he did, and I couldn't figure out why I cared. My gaze fell from his as I took in his fit body. Under his long-sleeve, button-up shirt, tight muscles moved rhythmically in his chest and arm areas. My hungry gaze caught his muscular thigh flexing under his pants, and I quickly returned my gaze to his while rubbing the back of my neck.

"Haven't found anyone like that yet," he said, reminding me of the conversation we'd started. "I've never felt the need to look for anyone. Besides, I don't do relationships. I fuck on a whim when I'm intrigued to do so, and I have subs that I call when I get a taste for them."

My brows arched high on my forehead. "Did you say subs as in BDSM?" I whispered as if I was afraid to say it out loud. I'd heard so many negative things about people who embraced that life that I was almost afraid to know any of the details.

"Trust me, Doctor. Don't knock it until you've tried it."

I shrugged. "I'm not knocking it. I just don't know anything about it, and the few things I do know would lead me to believe that all you do is get off on torturing each other."

"You're right, Doctor. You don't know shit."

He almost sounded as if I'd offended him, so I decided to change the subject. "So, what's your big plan for taking down my family?"

He ignored my question. "You said my cousin didn't want you, but it doesn't mean you two didn't fuck. Did you fuck my cousin, Doctor?"

My lips fell apart as my mouth went dry. Ansel was direct, so direct in fact that he'd rendered me speechless. His penetrating, green gaze bore into me, waiting for my answer.

"First of all, that is none of your business. But if you must know, the answer is *no*. I didn't have sex with August. I took care of the man for months, so I saw every part of him, but there was never a spark between us. Was I attracted to him? Of course, I was, but I could tell almost immediately that he didn't want me romantically. I consider myself a bit of a realist, so I accepted what was clearly in front of me. But, just because he didn't want me in that way doesn't mean I don't care about him."

Rambling and talking about sex with Ansel, caused me to shift uncomfortably in my seat. I hadn't intended to tell Ansel all that I had, but he seemed to have a way of getting things from a person no matter what they may have wanted.

He hadn't changed his expression. His face remained unreadable as he took in my words. He also seemed to be reading my body language. Although I was uncomfortable under his gaze, I found the confidence to continue.

"Once I was around him long enough, I discovered his heart belonged to someone else. It was an eye-opening experience to watch him struggle to remember his own name, yet he'd called Megan's name countless times in his dreams. It was powerful magic at play. The idea of his mind building a bridge over a connection that the brain had lost was a miracle. Once we arrived here and after the way he reacted to Megan, it made me understand him even more."

The information I had just shared raised Ansel's eyebrows. However, a conniving smile spread across his sexy lips, which were perfectly moist although he hadn't licked them.

Why did he have to be so damn hot? He knew it too. He was the kind of man who breathed confidence and sex appeal and didn't give a damn about breaking a woman's heart once he was done with her. Based on the way he dressed and the large, expensive fortress of a house he lived in, I'd say he was also smart and calculating.

His home reminded me of the kind of houses my family owned from the millions they made in drug money. This was the kind of house I'd grown up in. It had a manicured lawn, authentic classic paintings hanging on the walls, and expensive Italian furniture that had likely been imported directly from its manufacturer.

However, Ansel had taken things a step further than fine furnishings and a professionally decorated home. When August and I first arrived and were met by armed guards, it made me wonder if August's family wasn't worse than mine.

My gaze raked over Ansel's chest before it fell to the big bulge at the crotch of his pants. I directed my gaze in another direction, my cheeks burning with embarrassment.

Had he noticed what I'd been gawking at? Did he know what I was thinking? I shook off the distraction.

"Just like that," he said before he snapped his fingers. "You accepted that he didn't want you and stopped trying to tempt him?"

I laughed. "Who said I tried to tempt him? Besides, I didn't think he'd be interested in me anyway because of our ethnic differences." *Shoot!* My eyes slammed shut. I wasn't supposed to let that part slip out.

Shaking his head with a wide grin, Ansel didn't hide his roving gaze as it scanned my body, making my nipples harden. He was playing me like a fiddle, making me spill my guts even though I hadn't intended to. I was telling him things that I'd never even told August.

"Memory or no memory, Doc, with a body like yours, my cousin had to have been out of his fucking mind not to at least touch you. I refuse to believe that bastard wasn't tempted."

Ansel's head tilted like he was working an idea around in his brain.

"But, he and Megan..."

I could see a flood of memories flashing across Ansel's expression as he contemplated his cousin and Megan.

"There is no coming between that. But, back to you, Doctor. Most women would have tried everything in their power to get a man to bend to her will, especially if you were the only thing keeping him alive."

I shrugged. "Well, I'm not most women."

"You sure the hell aren't," he stated matter-of-factly as his gaze fell to my lips.

His words were as stuck in my head as his eyes were stuck on my lips, distracting me until I forced myself to start talking again.

"I've been my family's prisoner for three years. All sorts of plans started hatching in my head about how August may be able to help me escape them. He became the hope I'd so desperately prayed for just as much as I was hope for him."

Ansel had no idea what his presence was doing to me. I could hardly think straight. The husky tone of his voice was laced with sin and seduction. He knew it and he wanted me to know he knew it. Yes, I'd been attracted to August, but it was a fleeting attraction that died the moment I realized he was in love with someone else. Ansel, on the other hand, set my mind on fire and my sex-deprived body had been thrown into a state of lust and confusion.

A series of knocks sounded that seemed to make the house vibrate. It was hard to sit with this seductive man knowing that August was upstairs screwing the hell out of Megan. I reached for the water I'd brought from the kitchen and took a quick swallow. A heaving breath left me as I pretended not to notice Ansel's flirting gaze on me. I kept my sight on the coffee table and folded my arms over my chest to hide the fact that my damn nipples were hard.

"Can I ask you a personal question, Ansel?" I asked, finally glancing in his direction.

That sneaky smile on his face let me know what he was thinking, and his gaze traveled straight to my hard nipples when I accidentally dropped my arms.

"Yep. Ask me whatever you want, Doc."

"The whole time I was with August, it had never occurred to me that Megan was an African-American woman. Forgive me for assuming, but I thought biker clubs like yours didn't believe in that sort of thing. Do you all date outside your race?"

He pasted an are-you-kidding-me frown on his face before his gaze dropped and roved leisurely over me. I'd picked up on the signs that said he was attracted to me, but I wasn't an aficionado when it came to men.

I'd been so engrossed with school and becoming a doctor that I'd neglected men. It wasn't that I didn't have desires. I had them like any other woman. I'd just learned to suppress them and accepted that I was severely lacking in the area. My smart brain warned me that it was better that I remain standoffish, especially where Ansel was concerned.

He straightened his posture, his unwavering gaze making me

squirm. "Sweet Doctor, it's a wonder you haven't cum already. I've been fucking you with my eyes from the moment I saw you."

His voice was thick and course, sending prickles all over me as my heart hammered inside my chest. His explicit words had impacted my body and damn near made me cum. I drew back with a sharp, quick gasp. I was stuck between excitement and shock, but Ansel had no problem continuing.

"Was that your way of asking if I'd date a woman like you?"

I struggled to remember what I'd asked him. We'd gone too deep into this conversation for me to lie now. I recovered quicker than I thought I would. "Yes," I answered. "I guess I was asking, but not for myself. I was just curious." I dropped my gaze, realizing I sounded like an idiot.

"It's okay if you were asking for yourself. As a matter of fact, I was hoping you were asking for yourself."

His direct statements made one of my brows lift, and I decided to be honest with him. Besides, what did I have to lose? I was on the run from my own family.

"I'm what the world considers brown, not white or black. I'm not light enough for some men, but I'm not dark enough for others. And as far as my body is concerned, I am definitely not skinny enough for most."

Ansel didn't offer a response, but the way his gaze assaulted my body revealed more than his words ever could. He made no attempt to hide that he liked what he saw.

He waved me closer with one finger. "Will you slide closer, Doc?"

What the heck had I gone and started? I was afraid of what this man would do to me, especially after he'd admitted that he was into BDSM and multiple women—if that's what he'd meant by subs. I slid closer, despite my reservations. My voice sneaked from my mouth, my nervousness apparent.

"I don't know anything about what someone like you likes. I'm not interested in being tortured or being someone's love slave for that matter."

"Who said anything about you being a slave? That comes later, much later, Doc."

I damn near swallowed my tongue at Ansel's words. "So, you actually make women your slave?" I asked, my voice a faint whisper.

If there was one thing I was learning quickly about this man, he was going to be honest.

"Fucking right, I make them my slaves," he confirmed with no hint of remorse in his tone. He grinned at my alarmed expression as he eased closer.

"You can let the shock slide right off your beautiful face, Doc. I don't mean the kind of slave you're talking about. I want a woman to be a slave to my commands and our desires and to my fucking dick."

I cleared my throat, surprised that I was turned on by his sharp words.

"Come a little bit closer, Doc. There is something I want to show you."

How much closer could I get? If I kept going, I would end up on his lap. The white leather of the couch creaked as I slid closer. My gaze was merged with his and the way it roamed my body. It had been a long time since a man had paid me that much attention. I didn't cease my movement until my knee bumped his muscular leg.

Keeping me locked in his gaze, Ansel reached for my hand. He lifted it and placed it on the thick bulge between his thighs I'd noticed earlier. I attempted with little effort to pull away, but he squeezed my hand in a tight grip.

"My dick's been hard since the moment I laid eyes on you, Dr. Regina."

My gaze flashed up at his after I dragged it away from where my hand was sitting. There was a confusing mixture of shock, excitement, and speechlessness flowing through me.

"Dr. Regina," he repeated with a devilish smirk. He'd made my name sound glamorous and dirty all at the same time. I trembled with a burning lust I'd never experienced before as my hand flexed against his hardness.

"I've been dying to introduce you to someone I think you're going to like."

His hand slid up my forearm, causing goose bumps to prickle on my skin and my heart to shift into overdrive.

I jumped when Ansel's phone rang, the sound zapping me from the trance he'd put me in. I removed my hand from what felt like a snake in his pants.

He lifted the buzzing phone to his ear, but his gaze remained on me. "Yeah," he answered, his tone clipped. The voice on the other end was loud enough that I heard the muffled words. Ansel's face fell into a deep frown that caused him to stand. His voice rang with agitation as he walked away from me.

I sucked in a deep breath, just realizing he'd stopped me from breathing.

47

MEGAN

huffling around Ansel's large stainless steel and black marble kitchen, I hummed and cooked up a storm. I felt bad about leaving the doctor alone with Ansel, especially after I'd caught him staring at her like she was a scoop of ice cream that he couldn't wait to devour.

A good hearty breakfast might make up for leaving them alone for nearly a full day.

The first person to make an appearance was Dr. Regina. She peeked into the kitchen before coming all the way in.

"Good morning," I greeted her, trying to gage her mood.

"Good morning," she returned good-heartedly.

As soon as she sat down, I turned and faced her. "I'm sorry for leaving you alone with Ansel yesterday. He didn't try to drag you down to that dungeon of his, did he?"

"*Dungeon?*"

Thank God he hadn't tortured the poor woman. My question left her forehead pinched with concern and her gaze lingering on me.

"Never mind." I waved my question away. If she didn't know about Ansel's playroom, she might not have been in danger of becoming his next victim.

"What would you like for breakfast? I made biscuits and gravy, grits, scrambled eggs, bacon, toast, ham, and potatoes. I also made coffee if you drink it."

Regina gazed at me as she thought over the food choices. The thick bubbling of grits in the pot behind me sounded as the aroma of bacon made me inhale a little bit deeper.

"It all sounds so good, but may I have biscuits and gravy and bacon please?"

"I love a woman who's not afraid to eat," Ansel's voice rumbled as he entered the kitchen and took a seat next to the doctor.

"Did you sleep well, Doc?" The hint of amusement in Ansel's voice wasn't lost on me.

"I slept fine. Thank you for letting me stay," Regina answered.

They thought I was crazy. Well, maybe I was, but it didn't mean I didn't see certain things. Ansel was interested in Regina, and I didn't know if it was a good or bad thing. He always complained about looking for a replacement submissive after he'd broken one.

I presumed that lifestyle wasn't for the weak-minded or faint at heart even if I didn't understand it. I also noticed that Aaron cared for Regina the same way Ansel cared for me now. I didn't believe Aaron was going to let Ansel turn the good doctor into some play thing that he'd break or throw away when he grew tired of her.

"What about you, Megan? How did you sleep?" Ansel asked. "Never mind. Don't even answer because I know you didn't sleep."

There was no comeback to Ansel's statement because I hadn't slept. I think I'd passed out instead. Aaron had put a fucking on me that I'd never forget. My pussy was so sore that I couldn't stand at certain angles and making sudden movements was out of the question. My damn body ached so good that all I could do was smile when a twinge of pain surfaced.

As soon as I placed Regina and Ansel's plates in front of them, the doorbell rang.

Ansel mouthed the word "shit," before his head dropped to his chest. Seeing him shake his head in dismay as he took a piece of bacon from his plate and walked out of the kitchen wasn't a good sign. Having someone at his door wasn't a good sign either. I'd been in the house for nearly six months, and this was only the second time the doorbell had ever rung.

Regina glanced at me, her curious gaze asking the question on my mind. I fixed myself a plate and sat, but a familiar roaring tone stopped me from taking my first bite. It was a voice I never thought I'd hear again.

Ansel re-entered the kitchen with Shark behind him yelling and cursing. "I'm fucking here now, so you need to tell me why the fuck..." His devilish words and hard, quick steps stopped when his gaze landed on me.

His stare became riddled with anger and rage before his mouth dropped open. His hot gaze shot to Ansel's like a heat-seeking missile.

"You mean to tell me this bitch has been here with you the entire time? I told you to kill her. She's the fucking reason my son is dead."

Shark stalked around the table, coming for me as my fist clenched tighter around the fork in my hand. The storm clouds that gathered in Shark told me that if he got his hands on me, nothing was going to stop him from killing me.

ANSEL

Could a reunion be any more twisted than a Knox reunion? As I hung on to my angry uncle, he spat every curse word he knew at Megan. If he really wanted to kill her like his angry words insinuated, he would have broken out of my grip no matter how tightly I held on to him.

My amused gaze fell on the doctor who sat, staring at the scene in obvious shock. She looked about ready to get up and start running.

"Doc," I called to her over my uncle's angry words as I kept a tight grip around his shoulders, pinning his arms down. He barked his words out like one of those old dogs who sought to bite people for the hell of it.

The doctor hesitantly took her gaze away from Shark to glance at me. When she did, I introduced her.

"Doc, this is my Uncle Shark, Aaron's father. He slept with Megan too, but it was before she'd met Aaron. Aaron forgave her for it, but Shark hates her for getting Aaron to claim her and for getting himself killed."

The doctor was in obvious distress over what I was telling her, taking in words that she probably thought I'd made up.

"Unc here..." I tilted my head towards the back of my uncle's head as I allowed him to vent his frustrations at Megan. "...had ordered

Aaron to kill Megan. Of course, Aaron didn't do it. After Aaron was killed, Unc ordered me to kill Megan too, and I didn't do it either. So, now he's mad at the world and wants to kill us all."

"You're fucking right I'm mad at the motherfucking world," Shark shouted, bucking against my tight hold. "Aaron was all I had left, and *she's* the reason why he's gone," Shark spat his words, yapping at my face like a snapping turtle.

"I'm not gone, dad," said a strong voice from the doorway.

Shark went stalk still in my arms, frozen so stiff that the only sound in the kitchen was his heavy breathing.

After I released him from my tight grip, he gradually turned as if seeing too much, too fast might trigger his undoing. Like me, he stood staring at his son, eyes locked.

"Aaron?" he questioned, his face scrunched in a mixture of pain and confusion.

"I'm alive, Dad. It's best that only a select few know it, which is why I asked Ansel to get you out here."

"Aaron?" he repeated, as his head shook seemingly, involuntarily while he attempted to wrap his mind around what he saw.

I'd never seen my uncle tear up before, so it was a true testament to how much he truly loved his son. He ran to Aaron and gripped him in a tight bear hug, lifting him off his feet.

If there was one thing that could pull my uncle back from the edges of the darkened path he'd taken, it was Aaron. Not because it was necessarily the wrong path, but because Aaron was usually the one who carried out most of the MC's dark deeds.

I clamped my hands above my head as I watched the father-son reunion. Even Megan smiled after almost being mauled by the vicious old dog that had threatened to attack her. The sexy doctor didn't appear to know whether she should be smiling or running from the dysfunction that was my family.

Shark cupped Aaron's chin before slapping his hand against it a couple of times. He shook his head in disbelief. His smile spread so widely that I could see it from his side view as he stared into his son's face.

"Pop, will you ease up on trying to kill Megan? It's not her fault that any of this happened. You know me. If I get it in my head to carry out a mission, no matter how deadly, I'm not going to back down from it."

Smiling wide, Shark inclined his head once and pulled Aaron into another tight bear hug.

My gaze landed on Megan. "To be on the safe side, keep your distance from the old man. Who knows what kind of worms has gotten loose in his brains."

"I can hear you, asshole!" Shark said without turning to glance back at me. "I suggest you keep your fucking distance too, you goddamn hard-headed son of a bitch."

I clamped my lips shut and struggled to stifle a grin.

"Are you hungry?" Aaron asked his father. "Why don't you have a seat, so I can tell you how I escaped death?"

Aaron waved a hand towards Dr. Regina. "Dad, this is Dr. Regina Davis."

Megan's gaze met mine, likely wondering the same thing I was. How was Shark going to take the news when he found out that Regina was a Dominquez?

Shark reach out his hand, taking Regina's as he allowed his gaze to roam her body. "Nice to meet you, Doctor? They sure are making pretty doctors these days."

"Unc, last time I checked you were a racist. In case you haven't noticed, she's not white," I pointed out, not liking the way his gaze lingered on Regina.

Every eye in the room landed on me. Regina dropped her gaze and snatched her hand from my uncle's, not doing a good job of hiding her alarm. My comment didn't appear to have fazed my uncle. He reached and tapped the back of Regina's hand a few times and threw his thumb over his shoulder, pointing at me. "Do you have any idea what that asshole does to women? If he comes your way, you're better off locking yourself in a cage with a fucking wild lion. You'll need a doctor by the time he's done with you."

"Doc, don't believe any of that mess," I reassured her when her face contorted in horror.

Megan placed a plate of food in front of Aaron and took the long way around the table to avoid passing by Shark. When she fixed his plate, I reached for it.

"Let me take that, sweetie. I don't want those old teeth breaking your skin because you might catch something that can't be cured."

Just because Aaron was back, it didn't mean I wasn't still protective of Megan. Besides, my uncle was an old, uncompromising bastard. However, everyone at the table, including him, laughed at my remark about Megan catching something. It seemed to ease a little of the tension that had been swarming around the room.

Shark couldn't stop glancing at his son. Megan couldn't stop staring at Aaron either. The good doctor and I, on the other hand, were eye-fucking each other every chance we got. Based on the way I was fucking her in my head, it was a wonder she wasn't pregnant already.

Aaron started the story of how he'd ended up in the doctor's morgue, barely clinging to life. I sat and listened to the incredible story intently for the second time. Except for the occasional question from my uncle and the clink of silverware, no one said a word as Aaron retold the incredible story and referred to Dr. Regina for her point of view.

AARON

Dialing D's number was familiar even after all this time. Ansel had used my phone to contact him from time to time, so he was likely expecting to hear Ansel's voice. I placed the phone on speaker as my father, Ansel, Regina, and Megan listened. I didn't miss the mean eye rolls my father was sending Megan's way, but with me back in the picture, hopefully, it would quell his desire to kill her.

"Hey, man, what's up? Y'all good in Cali?" D's voice came across loud and clear over the phone.

"Derrick Wesley Michaels," I said into the phone with a smooth tone. I was one of the only people who knew D's middle name.

"Who the fuck is this? Knox? Look, I don't have time for no motherfucking jokes. Who is this?"

"It's me D, *Aaron*."

The line went silent. Had he hung up?

"Prove it, motherfucker," he said. "Yemen, operation, how many, and why?"

"Black Death, five, nerve gas. We were stuck in that fucking place for four months."

"Knox! What the fuck, man? How the fuck are you talking to me right now?"

"It's a long-ass story, D. Death had me by the fucking balls, but that dark evil bastard wasn't ready for me yet."

"No fucking shit!" I could hear the shock and excitement in his voice.

"D, Ansel's been filling me in on the plan y'all have been working on to take out the leaders of DG6. I'm not at full strength, but I'll be damned if I sit around while you all deal with these poisonous serpents."

"Man, I can't believe this shit. Wait until I tell Dax that your nine-lives-having ass is still alive. Motherfucker got more lives than a *Mortal Kombat* character."

D's comment made everyone chuckle in the background.

"Aaron, after we thought you'd died, we fully intended to go ape-shit and kill as many DG6 members as we could, but Ansel stopped us. He got us to calm the fuck down and go at this how you would have. So, we slowed our roll and now, we're in line to put DG6 out of commission. With the top gone, the rest of those fucking leeches are going to feed off and devour each other until there's nothing but pieces and parts left."

Hearing D talking about the plan to bring down a common enemy sent a different type of excitement through me. DG6 was going down, and I was going to bear witness to its downfall.

48

ANSEL

Operation Take Six or OTS was what I had named the plan I'd created to take down DG6. Although I hadn't fully revealed the plan to Aaron yet, he hadn't hesitated to put a call in for more big guns—the fucking suicide squad, if I'd ever seen one.

Galvin and Luke had arrived and were from his old military squad since I'd had to send D and Dax to Texas for Operation WTF, Watch the Friends. WTF was a side operation that consisted of them watching Megan's friends who'd apparently also become a target of DG6. D and Dax had also picked up targets to take out under OTS since they were capable and in the area. Galvin and Luke would come in handy if DG6 decided to make a chess move on our operation.

Galvin was one of the men in the woods in Texas fighting along with us when we'd lost Aaron, so he knew the back story. I had never met Luke, but as soon as Aaron introduced us, I learned that Luke and Galvin ran a *security* firm in Georgia, so he was as up on criminal knowledge as the rest of us.

Galvin reminded me of me. He liked to joke around, but when it came to business, he turned about as cold as an iceberg. Luke was the big and silent type. The damn man had to be seven-feet tall and at least three hundred pounds, not the type you'd want to go hand to hand with. Shit, I wasn't sure bullets could penetrate his snow-white skin. With his crystal blue eyes, he reminded me of a big-ass *Game of Thrones*, White Walker.

Max, Finn, and Lucky were members of Aaron's gun-running team. Max was butch and sexy, a fucking walking contradiction. She was a six-foot lesbian with a pretty face and nice body that she hid under loose-fitting clothes. With her short blonde hair and baggy clothes, it was easy to forget she was a woman until her delicate voice sounded. The shit was confusing even to me. But, Max had worked with Aaron for years. Her skills in electronics and explosives were impressive, and I'd used her expertise on a few side operations.

Each of the team members Aaron and I had brought into the plan possessed a special skill set that would come in handy when dealing with a group as dangerous as DG6.

My own suicide squad consisted of Dude, Rob, JG, and Hwang. Like Marcus and Scott, they'd been a part of my ranger team when I was in the military. JG and Hwang had come after I'd sent Scott and Marcus to track their OTS targets in Mexico.

The group stood inside my study, surrounding a large 3-D model of my house and its grounds. I'd built the house over three years ago and had started installing weaponized updates immediately. I was like one of those battle-scorned crazies, preparing for an apocalypse or a war that may never come.

The house was built on spacious acres of land in the foothills of California, my just-in-case-shit-went-bad escape hatch of sorts. I'd purposely chosen land that was semi-surrounded by large hills. Who knew it would play a pivotal role in my plan to take down DG6?

The nearest neighbors were a few hills away, about a half mile, but I'd deliberately been an asshole to them when they'd stopped by to be neighborly and introduced themselves. That had been over two years ago. I'd given them such a bad first impression that they probably wouldn't pour piss on me if I were a walking flame. They had no idea my asshole ways were for their own protection.

"So, what is this master plan of yours, Ansel?" Shark asked with a hint of agitation in his voice.

"Since you asked, Unc, let me tell you. We went at DG6 twice, and each time we failed. First, we allowed them to get away with Aaron. Then, we went onto their turf in Texas with a quick rescue plan that ended up getting Aaron killed. That tough bastard beat death, but the reality is we lost in a life-changing way."

Admirable gazes and smiles landed on Aaron. I was certain that everyone at the table would have died for him a hundred times over because they knew he'd do the same for them. I placed my index finger at my chest.

"I take full responsibility for each of those failures and I hate fucking failing. My quick temper and hyped-up ego has to take a back seat this time. I had to figure how to go at this thing in a way that would put DG6 at a disadvantage."

Intrigued gazes were locked on me as everyone hung on to my every word. Aside from a few heavy breaths, silence reigned over the space.

"Since going after DG6 hasn't worked, I figured I'd make them come to us."

"How the hell are you going to make them come to us? What do you have that would make them want to come to us?" Shark asked, his menacing blue eyes locked on me and spewing heat.

Aaron's squinting gaze landed on me, but he didn't comment.

The conniving smile that danced across my lips was filled with venom. Aaron knew, without knowing the full plan, that I'd come up with a plan that was going to produce multiple deaths.

"I took their fucking guns," I stated and paused, letting the statement hang in the air.

"I started taking DG6's guns a few weeks after we left that farm in Texas without Aaron. Then, I started taking the guns of everyone who could re-supply them with guns."

Aaron immediately caught on, shaking his head in my direction with a wide grin. Eventually, other gazes started to spark with realization.

"I didn't just hit them here in Cali. I took it to those bastards nationwide. Aaron, I had your girl, Max, blow up one of their warehouses in Arizona. Scott, Marcus, and I took them for just about every damn thing that spat bullets in Texas. DG6 needs guns so badly right now that they're willing to deal with the devil. So, you can call me Lucifer Knox."

The pride on the faces of the men made me puff up my chest that was already poked out, but Aaron's praise meant the world to me.

"The guns I didn't burn or destroy, I traded them to the MC's supplier for the guns that DG6 is planning to buy from me. About three weeks ago, I set up a small transaction with Fernando and Alonso, two of DG6's top three here in Cali. I wanted to confirm my legitimacy and establish some type of rapport with them."

A prideful smile crossed Shark's lips as he side eyed me.

"That's right, Unc. I haven't been sitting around with my thumb up my ass. While you were killing off the minnows and keeping them distracted, I was trying to figure out how to take out the fucking shark. No pun, Unc."

Aaron's fist bumped mine. "Man, this is brilliant. I can't believe you all did all this shit because you thought I was dead."

"Fucking right!" I said. "They must fucking die," my uncle declared sternly.

"We're not chasing them anymore. We are going to lure them to our neck of the woods this time," I said, glad to see that they liked the plan so far.

I pointed at the model I'd built. Aaron was the perfect person to plan this sort of thing and had already started to point out where he thought everyone should be located based on their strengths. My gaze locked on Aaron, ensuring he didn't miss the best update I'd received since I'd started planning.

"I received a call yesterday, informing me that Sorio Dominquez would like to meet me. He's going to be here, which means you're going to have to stay out of sight, cousin."

Aaron inclined his head. He didn't care one bit about having to stay out of sight of Sorio as long as he was dealt with. After hearing the news that the evil bastard would be here, the smile on Aaron's face made my evil grin look like a silly smirk. I could see hell's flames dancing around Sorio inside my cousin's mind.

AARON

My cousin was a fucking genius, plain and simple. Except for a few minor kinks that had to be worked out, he'd come up with a master plan. The fact that he had four key members of DG6 in line to buy guns from him was remarkable. He'd hobbled their asses, taking their main source of power and weakening them so they'd be willing to make deals that they normally wouldn't.

They didn't know my cousin the way that I did. I'd seen him lure helpless victims in with charm and grace before he flipped the script and ripped them to bloody pieces.

I took my time observing each man surrounding the table. They had gone against an enemy who outnumbered our MC and friends by the hundreds to avenge my death. My heart swelled with gratitude and motivated me to do everything in my power to help them get rid of DG6 once and for fucking all.

Working on the plans for Operation Take Six and reconnecting with my old squad from the military as well as my gun-running team was the kind of therapy I'd needed. Time with Megan and her magic seemed to have cured me of the headaches I'd been suffering from my gunshot. Regina was adjusting, and seeing her smile was a far cry from the sadness she'd endured when we were stuck in that cellar.

Ansel had set up his study like a damn gallery. Another long table sat against the wall and consisted of an arsenal of weapons.

Clack! Clack!

The sound of Max shifting the level of a pump-action shotgun broke the silence of us drooling over the display of weapons that had taken our attention. Although we'd discussed the mission repeatedly, we continued to hammer home the details.

D and Dax were with Laura and Beverly in Texas, running side operation WTF. They were also planning the executions of their Texas targets for Operation OTS.

Our crew here in California were set to take out Tomas, an original DG6 member, his two sons, Fernando and Alonso, and now Sorio. Marcus and Scott were in Mexico, tracking down the final two that made up the core power for DG6.

We all had our targets in our sights, but if we didn't stick to plan and take out the identified targets, the entire operation could blow up in our faces.

Later that evening, I lay in the calmest peace I'd ever experienced. Megan was stretched out on top of me, butt-ass naked and sound asleep. Smiling, I bent my neck to kiss the top of her curls.

Our team was a week away from Operation Take Six. The pride I felt towards my cousin was immeasurable. Ansel had summoned patience and planned a mission that could very well take down one of the most formidable gangs in our country's history.

49

ANSEL

A week under the same roof with Grumpy Cat had me ready to lock his ass up in my playroom with five hookers. An amused smile teased my lips when my uncle's gaze shot up to the ceiling in frustration. Although their voices didn't carry through the thick walls of my house, the sounds of bumping and knocking made their way to our ears.

"Would you still want to kill her if she had chosen you over him, Unc?" I knew my uncle was not going to answer me, but I'd always been the most annoying motherfucker in the family who talked about the things no one else wanted spoken of again. "Frankly, I think she would have killed you." I snickered, continuing to taunt him. "Your heart can't take that much action."

"Ansel, shut the fuck up. I'm trying to watch this game while praying the fucking ceiling won't come crashing down on top of us."

The doctor eyed my uncle and me. She sat between us, but my spacious couch left about a foot too much space between me and her. The confusion on her beautiful face was apparent. She leaned in my direction and kept her voice low. "Am I the only one who thinks that this is...is...*weird*?"

"Dr. Regina, there is so much I have to teach you. Like I

mentioned before, it's not uncommon for MC members, especially ours, to share women. Aaron, my Uncle, and I have slept with..." After I leaned forward, my gaze landed on my uncle who pretended to be ignoring me.

"How many of the same women, Unc?"

Shark waved his hand through the air, brushing away my question with a grunt. He knew he'd enjoyed that shit. My nonchalant behavior on the subject seemed to baffle Regina even more.

"But, it's just..." she uttered, searching for the right words.

My hand cupped her thigh. I'd been dying to put my hands on her again, and she'd been lucky I had decided to exercise control where she was concerned. Everything about her was natural and pure, sexy and alluring. I wanted nothing more than to drag her sexy ass down to my playroom and fuck her into submission. It was difficult to keep my distance from Regina, but my sexual discipline was something I took pride in.

I tapped my hand against her thick thigh, loving the way my hand bounced against her jean-covered flesh. I liked that solid sound it made. "I know, Doc. We take some getting used to."

She inclined her head although I sensed that our fucked-up ways of doing things bothered her. The poor woman didn't know the half of it. She was clueless, and if things would work out the way I wanted them to, I couldn't wait to introduce her to my world.

"Excuse me," I announced as I stood and headed towards my bar. After fixing myself a drink, which was something I didn't do often, I slid the door open and stepped outside. I stopped at the edge of my pool.

There were more stressing concerns for me to worry about, and Regina's distracting presence was shattering my otherwise unshakable willpower. Damn it, I wanted to be good, but Regina was making it hard. Clueless, she had no idea the kind of urges she had surging through me.

By the time I made it back into the living room, my uncle had slid his ass closer to Regina. For someone who claimed to be a racist, he sure as shit didn't shy away from women of color. I'd never seen this side of him, but he'd let the cat out of the bag the moment he'd allowed Megan to live with our MC and work as their maid. I think a sister had blown his mind in a way that he'd never recovered from.

However, he still had a charm about him that I hoped to have by the time I reached his age. He was at least a hundred and fifty years old, but he had the ability to cast spells over younger women. So, I was keeping a close eye on him where the doctor was concerned.

The game he'd been so interested in on the television earlier clearly wasn't as interesting as he found Regina. As a matter of fact, the volume on the television had been turned down low. Now, it was nothing more than a hum in the background. Back in the day, I wouldn't have given a second thought to sharing the doctor with my uncle but seeing him viewing her with such desire in his eyes had me feeling possessive.

I plopped my ass down in the tight space between them, wiggling my body to make room to separate them. My uncle moved over with a frustrated huff as my hand automatically went to Regina's thigh. I think I'd officially marked my territory and the doctor didn't appear to mind one bit.

50

AARON

A nsel slammed his phone down on the 3-D model, breaking off a chunk of the model's clay roof.

"Mother fuck!" he shouted, his voice drawing gazes from around the room. The heavy silence filled the space as tension tightened our postures. We had all gathered like we'd been doing daily, going over the plan. We were constantly studying different scenarios and formulating reaction strategies for events that may or may not happen.

Rage, anger, confusion, and an emotion I couldn't describe flashed over his face.

"Those motherfuckers are coming right now, a fucking day early. This is their way of showing me they don't trust me. This is their fucking way of foiling any plan we might have to destroy them. The sons of fucking bitches!"

Attempting to calm him, I placed a firm hand on Ansel's shoulder. "We know this plan like the back of our hands. If they want to get this started today, we're ready."

Eager voices around the room agreed. The devious smirk that inched onto Ansel's face revealed the full story of the firestorm rolling through his twisted mind. He'd been itching for months to kill somebody...hell, *anybody*. And today he was about to get his wish. I didn't believe that bullshit about him playing it cool while making plans to take down DG6. Ansel had dropped some bodies in the six months that I'd been away. I was sure of it.

My watch flashed 3:17 p.m. Before I could ask the question on my mind, Ansel answered it. "They are sending an advanced party, which will be here by 4 to check out the house for bugs and to ensure I'm not setting them up."

"The fuckers don't trust a soul," Galvin stated.

"They don't, but neither do we. So, let's get ready. Let's make DG6 disappear," I declared with firm conviction.

"Either they die or we die," Shark, Ansel, and I declared in unison, our gazes spilling over with hate and evil intentions. More expletives about dying pieces of shit followed as the room became filled with enough hostile intent to choke on.

LIKE A SCENE out of an old western movie, a tumbleweed blew over the flat portion of the hilly plains we were located in. Except for the plush vegetation of the interior yard, the grass grew in patches and was more beige than green along the hills. The only visible trees were the few that Ansel had bought and transplanted in his yard. The landscape was a vast portrait of rolling hills, some stories high, as far as the eye could see.

Clear plastic goggles kept dust out of my eyes as tiny particles swept against my face and peppered my exposed skin. Ansel had considered everything. I stood inside a foxhole that blended into the grassy ground a few hundred feet from the house at the bend of his fence in the front yard.

My location was the furthest from the front entrance of the house, but it gave me the best view of the front grounds, the hills outside the property, and a distant view of the street that dead ended at Ansel's entrance.

There were four foxholes inside the gated property. Dude, Rob,

Max, Hwang, and I manned those areas. At my suggestion, we'd dug three additional foxholes outside the gates in the nearby hills. My father, Galvin, and Finn manned those areas. We had JG and Lucky on the roof.

Ansel had planned for an all-out war. Each of the small underground foxholes contained enough reserve ammunition and weapons to support the war to come. I knew from experience that DG6 employed soldiers willing to fight their battles, so our efforts weren't unfounded.

Fernando and Alonso Dominquez traveled with at least a four-man detail watching their backs. The family believed in backup, and if they were bringing an original member to Ansel's front door, they were likely bringing a fucking army. Now that Sorio had decided to join the party, the army had grown.

From my vantage point, a small doorway that slid up and down allowed me to see above ground. Dust flew into the air in the distance. The subtle tremble in the ground registered as the roar of an engine traveled along the air and landed in my ears. At least two vehicles indicated that DG6's advanced recon team had arrived.

Although unseen, I knew it was Rob and Max who were manning the front gate bunker. Two black Hummers sat at the tall iron gates waiting to be allowed entrance. The thick iron bars of the front gate entrance were wide enough to allow me to see what was happening outside the gate.

The metal screeched, filling the air with its whine as the gate slid open at a lingering pace. The bunker Rob and Max manned was double the size of the others and served as a small command and control center.

The gate slid closed, the heavy metal left its screeching cries in the air, signaling the start of OTS. I turned my gaze to the circular driveway as the Hummers parked side by side in front of the large bulletproof glass door at the front of Ansel's large two-story home.

Four heavily armed men exited each vehicle. The first four climbed the steps and entered Ansel's house after he opened the door. The remaining four divided into teams of two and went in opposite directions to inspect the outside of the house.

Ansel's plan was to lure the flies into his web and destroy them. It was a great plan, and although we hadn't counted on them arriving a day early, I believed we were ready. We had to assume that DG6 had access to just as much technology as we did, so we'd put in an emergency call to D to work on scrambling any spy devices they may have attempted to sneak in overhead.

Once the initial inspection was completed, two of the guards who'd entered Ansel's house exited and took a firm stance at the front door. Two reappeared from the back of the house and positioned themselves in Ansel's front yard. They hadn't discovered any of our foxholes nor had they bothered to check outside the property.

An hour after the advance team had arrived, the sight of dust alerted us that the main party was on the way. This time, four SUV's were granted access. With four men in each vehicle, we were looking at twenty-four hostiles so far. They parked the vehicles on Ansel's grass, ensuring the two vehicles that contained *the four* DG6's leaders were sandwiched between the outside vehicles.

Four guards exited each outside vehicle and fanned around them with their weapons at the ready before one talked into a device on his wrist—his call to alert the others that it was safe for Tomas, Fernando, Alonso, and Sorio to exit the vehicles.

My body tensed up, every muscle threatened to snap when I saw his face. My mind, back in one piece, zoomed in on him like facial recognition software identifying a criminal. The cracking sound my bones made, echoed off the dirt walls surrounding me, and the blood in my veins had been replaced with liquid fire.

It was the face of the motherfucker who'd tortured me, the same motherfucker who'd sent men to track, hunt, and kill Megan. The motherfucker had also put his fucking hands on Regina. I prayed my face would be the last one he saw before the fires of hell opened and swallowed him.

The arrogant prick walked up to Ansel's door with his cousins and uncle. He was the only one of the four who was on full alert as two guards led them and two followed. I could tell at a distance that the Hummers they'd exited were armored. Four of DG6's top men were walking into my cousin's house, and if we had anything to say about it, they weren't going to be walking back out.

When the mic went live in my ear, I started talking. "Luke, what does it look like out there?" Luke was on roving patrol on foot. He'd gone about setting up distinct hiding spots along the path of the only street that led to Ansel's house.

"They have a Hummer hanging back. Four inside," he confirmed. His voice was scratchy in my ear, but understandable.

"Keep eyes on," I suggested.

"Tracking," Luke replied.

"Shark, what does it look like out there?"

"How the fuck do you think it looks? I'm on a fucking hill inside a hole in the ground."

The hint of laughter in my father's tone made me smile. He was an asshole, but I loved his grumpy, old ass.

I went down the line checking the men's status and ensuring our mics worked as I kept a keen eye on the targets entering Ansel's house.

51

ANSEL

Two DG6 guards staked out my living room after they had conducted their bug scan, and two stepped outside the front door. No words were exchanged between us as we awaited the main party. I sat on my couch and flipped through the channels of my television.

Thanks to D, I was actually using the remote to re-arm our listening devices so I could communicate with the rest of the team. D had fixed it so that all devices could be turned off and rendered undetectable in the event DG6 decided to conduct a scan. They had, and we'd taken the extra precaution to be prepared for them.

With a few clicks of my remote, we were back up and running and able to hear each other.

My device was on the lowest setting, but I could hear Aaron making a round of mic checks. The sound of the front gate sliding open alerted me that the main party had arrived.

My job was to escort the members of DG6 into the designated spots in my study while they inspected a sample of the guns they were prepared to purchase. If I succeeded in getting them to the right locations, our team could take their asses out with the flick of their trigger fingers.

Aaron was outside, but he hadn't placed himself in one of the locations that would allow him to take out the one I knew he wanted to kill most—Sorio. Aaron and I would have preferred to kill these assholes slowly with our bare hands, but there were times when you had to sacrifice self-gratification to complete the mission. Also, with the amount of armed guards DG6 had brought, we had to stick to the plan.

The first two guards, who had led the men, entered my living room and fanned out like soldiers. They strategically placed themselves at my windows and interior doorways, so they could protect the four bastards who'd followed them into my house.

It was time for me to put my acting skills to work. With a smile pasted on my face, I walked towards the four with my hand out, attempting to shake Tomas' hand, since he was a well-respected original. The metallic click of weapons as they were drawn and aimed at me alerted me to throw my hands up in surrender. Little did they know, I'd had so many guns clicked at me, the sound did nothing but amp me up.

"I was attempting to shake the hands of one of my idols," I explained, keeping my gaze on Tomas. Saying those words had damn near killed me. All I truly wanted to do was rack bullet after bullet and watch them fly into that asshole's face until his head melted into pieces.

A smile crept across Tomas' prune-like lips before he waved a disarming hand at the men and reached out his wrinkled hand towards me. The skin covering his face was cracked and leathery, and his pores were so wide that it appeared they'd been surgically enhanced. Gray and black hair dotted his head, and he was no more than 5'5". It was hard to keep a straight face when all I wanted to do was laugh before I brutally committed murder.

"Mr. Blake, it's so nice to meet you. I've heard wonderful things about you."

Antonio Blake was one of several aliases I'd had my friend at the FBI create on my behalf. I was sure DG6 had thoroughly researched me, so I'd left them a shadowy past that they would appreciate.

The identity I didn't want them to find was the real me and my association with the August Knights. I'd quickly grown to trust D as much as Aaron had, and he was the only one I wanted handling the task of hiding my true identity: Tyler Ansel Knox.

I took the older man's hand as the sack of shit, Sorio, eyeballed me, sizing me up before letting his gaze travel around my house. Fernando and Alonso were the two who I'd dealt with previously, so they were the most relaxed. I was smiling and shaking asshole's hand, but I was also taking in our four targets. Were their lives so important, that although armed, they still felt the need for extra protection?

I waved my hand towards my study where I'd removed the mock model of my house. Only a table of weapons remained for them to view.

As I led them towards my study, two guards moved into position, first and last, placing the four DG6 members between them. Once inside the room, the guards again took up positions at the windows and exits.

Fernando, Alonso, Tomas, and Sorio approached the table and started to inspect the weapons. Their tension seemed to ease when the cold steel of the weapons was gripped in their eager hands.

"I'll deliver the shipment myself as a show of not only my gratitude for your business but also as assurance that I'll do what is necessary to earn your trust."

Tomas and Fernando nodded. Sorio studied the gun in his hand with an unreadable expression on his face.

Alonso was the first to speak. "Thank you for seeing us. We weren't sure you were going to be able to accommodate a request a day early for such a large order."

"I'm a businessman. My goal is to provide what my client wants, whenever they want it."

Fernando took a step closer and handed me a briefcase. "As soon as we receive the shipment and our people inspect it, the other eighty percent will be transferred."

Easing a smile onto my face, I inclined my head when Fernando stepped back to the table. They'd handed me a million in cash like it was nothing. All I needed now was them standing in place at the table. The area surrounding the table was a key location, a kill zone, our snipers needed that would allow them to light those bastards up.

"Hey, don't I know you?" one of the guards standing at the entrance said, pointing at me. His words drew Sorio and Alonso away from the weapons to focus on me. I ignored the man's question, but he continued to scrutinize me. Attempting to release the knot of tension that had gathered in my neck, I tilted my head to the side. *Stop looking at me, motherfucker.*

The guard lifted a crooked finger and pointed it at me again, before reaching down and drawing his weapon. I kept my cool, but shit was flowing downhill fast, all because asshole face thought he recognized me.

Tension saturated the room. Every man's chest bobbed as gazes locked on me and more weapons emerged and pointed in my direction.

"You were in the woods in Texas. You were one of the people who attacked us when you came to rescue your buddy."

Of all the motherfuckers that Sorio had chosen for his detail, he'd pick the one man who'd remembered me from a dimly-lit stretch of woods. My fucking cover was blown, and I had eight guns pointed at my head.

My gaze darted around at the mean faces glaring at me, studying their body language. The fact that I made no attempt to correct the guard made them even angrier. I scanned the room, weighing my options. My ass was toast unless I knew how to stop eight guns from making my head look like a big glob of overcooked oatmeal.

I viewed things in slow motion, my eyes catching every nuance of their body language. My breathing had slowed, but my heart was pumping like the pistons in a revved-up Bugatti. The moment Sorio's finger slid around his trigger, I yelled my ass off. "I've been made! Phase two! Phase two!" The last sound to cross my ears was a series of loud pops before my body dropped.

52

AARON

The vision of one of the DG6 guards at the window taking a direct hit to the head before his body disappeared from my view was a welcomed sight.

The DG6 guards outside sprang into action, gathering near the Hummers. One made a foolish attempt to climb into one of the Hummers, but one of our snipers painted the side of the black SUV with splatters of chunky dark red dots.

Two attempted to re-enter the house. When they couldn't get in the traditional way, they started shooting the door and discovered that they weren't going to shoot their way through the bulletproof glass.

It didn't take long for our snipers to light their asses up. One's brains went flying into the door he'd tried to get into. His body fell and tumbled sideways over the side of the steps in a dramatic fashion. The other dove for cover behind the thick bushes that lined the house.

After I climbed out of my foxhole, I dove right back in when a barrage of bullets pelted the ground and pinged against the camouflaged metal of the door. If those assholes thought they were keeping me in this damn hole, they were sadly mistaken.

Bending at the knees, I slung my rifle across my back before I snapped the cover off the large pipe that would take me into the crawl space under Ansel's house.

The suffocating tightness inside the pitch-black pipe caused me to struggle for every breath as the weapon on my back clinked, hitting the top of the thick metal. The burning ache in my kneecaps and elbows as they dug into the dirty underbelly of the metal shot waves of pain straight to my brain.

Although I knew it was seconds, the closed-in confines had me thinking it was hours that I'd been crawling. The dark, suffocating tightness had my lungs burning as every breath echoed around me and moved over my exhausted body like shivering fingers. I seriously doubted I was breathing air. It was more like a mixture of dust and carbon dioxide.

The darkness was so thick that I didn't know I'd made it to the end of the pipe until my head thumped into the rounded metal door. My anxious fingers reached through the darkness as my nails scraped metal, searching for the latch.

Finally, my fingers locked around the latch and sprang it free. Fresh air flooded my lungs and almost immediately renewed my strength. Each of our foxholes contained pipes that led to a different location under Ansel's house. Although confined, I was able to stand in the tight space leading to a secret entrance into the house. I punched in a combination that would open another small door into Ansel's study, the area where the bullets had started flying first.

I waited, listening for signs of movement before opening the door. Had Ansel been able to avoid the barrage of bullets that had been sprayed? I inched the door open, knowing it would lead to the inside of the small closet in Ansel's study.

My head turned robotically at the sound of muffled gunshots. I pushed through the opening, being careful to remain quiet. The sound of the repeated clapping of weapons met me as soon as I stood. Bullet holes were what filled my view after I tipped over to the closet door and inched it open.

Where was Ansel and where the hell was *the four*? The condition of the study would have you believe the Taliban had been invited to this party. The bodies of the two DG6 guards who'd been posted at the window lay crumpled in bloody heaps. There was no sign of Ansel. Had he survived this shit? Maybe they had taken him as a hostage.

A quick glance from the cracked window showed two more dead DG6 guards stretched out on the lawn. The front gate was closed, and all the Hummers were in the same place. My main goal now was to find my cousin and kill any asshole I came across.

Following the sound of gunfire, I peeked into the wide open space of the living room. Two guards shot from the window, as Tomas stood there waiting for them to fight his battle. They were going to try to get Tomas to one of those armored vehicles. If they succeeded, it would be hell to get him out of one of those Hummers unless we had a tank.

Like a bat out of hell, I sprinted into the line of fire and fired off a shot that sent Tomas' brains splattering against the wall behind him. Using the momentum I'd built, I tucked my body, dived, and rolled behind Ansel's thick leather couch. Bullets pelted the couch from two directions, sending chucks of wood, pieces of leather, and fibers raining over me. The angry shouts of the men blended with the unapologetic blast from their weapons. The couch would only protect me so long before I was forced to create an exit strategy.

53

ANSEL

I was thankful that Aaron had strategically placed Galvin, Finn, and my grumpy-ass uncle out in the hills that partially surrounded my house. They were three of the best snipers we had on our team. They were in locations that sat at a distance and high enough on the hills that it allowed them to fire into the study as well as various other parts of the house and grounds.

Someone out there had put a bullet in Sorio, who'd been aiming for my fucking head. He hadn't waited to hear me attempt to explain what was going on after the guard recognized me. The bullet had struck Sorio in the shoulder, sending his gun in one direction and his body in the other. Right before Sorio released the first shot, I yelled for backup, hit the small clicker I'd sewn into the inside of my shirt and braced myself for the short free-fall into the bed below in my playroom.

The assholes up there were probably wondering where I'd gone. The muffled sound of gunfire caused me to scramble to get back into the fight. I reached blindly under the bed and pulled out an AR-15. I slapped in a magazine and grabbed two extras. Before I exited the room, my gaze swept over the shelves of sex toys that hid the door to the safe room where we'd stashed Megan and Regina.

I prayed that Megan would keep her little ass put. She had a way of stumbling into the craziest types of situations, and this one was certified the craziest as we were engaged in an active war with known cartel members.

Easing from the room, I shut the door quietly behind me and tiptoed up the stairs that would lead into my kitchen. Gunfire erupted, splintering the wood of the door as it slipped from my hand and creaked noisily open. I tucked my body behind the doorframe, listening for a chance to engage. The heavy thump of footsteps softened, the person retreating into their hiding place.

Motherfucker better hide. I ran from the doorway, dashed over the short expanse, and dived between the area of the stove and sink in my kitchen. The momentum of my movement was still in play, but it didn't stop me from preparing my weapon to shoot.

My gaze locked on a flash of black scampering away like a wild rabbit. The targets couldn't get out of my house unless they went through a window, in which case they'd end up dead. So, they were still inside, hiding.

The hard taps of gunfire came from my living room, so I ran in that direction. A quick glimpse at the situation revealed a blood-spattered wall and two guards who hadn't spotted me because they were busy aiming at my couch, letting off round after round.

I checked my rear before stepping into the doorway and letting the gun spray bullets over their bodies as I gifted them a one-way ticket straight to hell. Their bodies had barely dropped when none other than Aaron emerged from behind the couch.

"Thanks, man. How the fuck did you get out of that study?"

"You're welcome. Trapdoor," I answered as I took in Tomas splayed out on the floor with a hole pierced through the center of his forehead. *And then there were three.*

Aaron shook his head and made a circular motion with his hand before angling his head towards areas we needed to search. We split the living area in half, sweeping and peeking into the dining room, den, and halls.

As I walked towards Aaron to meet at the stairs, his frozen gaze over my shoulder sent a chill inching up my back, alerting me that death lurked behind me. Before I'd fully turned to shoot the asshole behind me, Aaron's knife swished past me, landing in Fernando's gun arm. His weapon fell to the floor with a loud thud. I raised my weapon, preparing to blow the man's brains out, but Aaron stopped me.

"I got him," he said, his voice as cold as an Arctic glacier. I shrugged and stepped aside to allow Aaron to pass. Who was I to get in the way of a man and a fresh kill?

Fernando must have known death was approaching him. His eyes widened to twice their normal size, and he was either too afraid or too stunned to run. Aaron calmly placed his hand over the man's mouth as he snatched the knife from his limp arm. Fernando attempted to fight, but it was too late.

A deep frown creased my face when Aaron sent the knife plunging into the man's belly. Fernando's muffled, throat-scratching groans filled up the living room.

Next thing I knew, the ripping sound of the knife sliding through the man's flesh and abdominal muscles sounded. Aaron pressed his forearm forcefully over the man's face, muzzling his anguished cries as he used his strength and body weight to keep the man in place. Fernando's quivering body thumped against the wall as his bladder released right before a bundle of his internal organs spilled onto the floor with a noisy splat.

The man stopped fighting Aaron with his good hand and clawed at his protruding organs, attempting to put them back inside his body. I choked back the vile odor that assaulted my nasal passages. My fucking cousin was a damn lunatic who disemboweled people like a twisted butcher. Aaron could say what he wanted, but those damn bullet fragments in his brain had made him meaner.

He stepped away from the man, letting him slide to the floor as his internal organs dangled from his belly. His bloody intestines continued to slither out like a bunch of wild red snakes. A hissing sound escaped the man, some punctured organ releasing air.

My enlarged eyes tightened, lids thinning as I took in the gruesome sight. The fact that Aaron had released someone's internal organs and hadn't gotten a drop on his clothes or boots froze me in place.

"Really?" I asked him.

He shrugged and glanced up the stairs like he hadn't just done some horror-movie type shit.

We climbed the stairs as sporadic gunfire reminded us of the fight outside. As soon as we crested the stairs, I cut a right and Aaron went left. Everything appeared to be normal until bullets started flying, coming from Megan's room at the far end of the hall.

A bullet missed my face by an inch, but the next came hissing through the air at an inescapable speed and caught me in my shoulder. The force of the impact twisted me in a full circle before I was able to straighten myself out and take cover inside Regina's room.

Closing my eyes for a second, I sucked in a breath and swallowed the pain. I peeled my shirt back and glanced at my wound. Blood seeped from the hole, thick and dark, as my left arm blazed in searing pain. The pain captured my arm, rendering it useless, and the blood continued to flow. I ripped off a piece of the bed sheet, stuffing it inside my shirt to help staunch the bleeding. I'd not worn a Kevlar vest, to keep my cover with our four targets.

Our team was dangerous enough to fight in hell, but the radio silence was a matter that concerned me. The thud of gunfire had never ceased outside, but the silence let me know that I'd lost communication with our men.

As soon as my arm started to twitch back to life, letting me know that I hadn't permanently lost the use of it, I inched the door open and prepared to trade shots with the bastard who'd shot me. I slapped a new magazine in my weapon and aimed it down the hall, preparing to turn Megan's room into a sheet of target paper.

I carried and fired the weapon with my one good arm, letting off burst after burst that shook my body with intense force. Each blast also kept the shooter hiding and allowed me to step out into the hall and closer to the target.

After only three steps closer, my target stumbled out into the hall after he'd thrown out his weapon. "I give up," he shouted. *Dumb fuck!*

Unfortunately, it was one of the guards and not one of our targets. He'd been shot in his torso region as he clamped his hand around his wound. The crisp white shirt he wore under his black jacket had been painted red. His weak legs wobbled under his weight, and he let his body slide down the wall into a sitting position.

The ache in my shoulder reminded me that this was the asshole that had shot me. I took a knee in front of the man. "You should have kept shooting," I told him, shaking my head. The man's eyes filled with fear when his gaze locked on mine, just realizing that he'd surrendered for nothing.

"Let me help you," I offered. A sinister smirk bent my lips as I planted my knees on the man's thighs to keep him in place. My good hand rushed forward and clamped tight around the man's neck.

His fist pounded against my locked arm. His fingers clawed, raked, and scratched uselessly at my arm that was dead locked around his throat. He jerked mercilessly as his feet thumped against the floor and he bucked under me.

Both his hands were wrapped around my arm, but I didn't feel them. His horror-filled gaze was locked on mine. My eyes were nothing more than black orbs of pure death. My mind had descended into that dark place I embraced whenever I killed someone.

I felt none of the emotions I should have; no remorse, regret, or sorrow for taking another life. Instead, the thrill of seeing this asshole die filled my psyche. I enjoyed seeing the man's life seep from him, fading with each breath I failed to let him take.

Peering at his ghost-white reflection, I squeezed tighter. Red branches of blood vessels sprouted in his bulging eyes as they frantically darted left and right in a desperate search for help. His tongue fell limp past his lips as his eyes started to flutter. He stopped fighting the inevitable. He stopped fighting me. He'd accepted the great fires of hell as his forever.

54

AARON

There was only a large entertainment room off the hall. Being careful not to stand directly in front of the door, I stood off to the side, before I turned with a quick hard kick, slamming my foot below the knob.

The door went flying inward, and I expected bullets to come flying at me, but none came. The room was clean as far as I could tell. Where were the rest of the assholes we needed to kill?

I crept over to the window to survey the scene below since we'd lost radio contact again. The muzzle flashes from our snipers in the hills flashed like hidden gems. I couldn't see any of our crew on the ground, but they had the DG6 guards pinned down, stuck on this compound with us. The sound of gunfire on Ansel's wing prompted me to scramble for the exit.

By the time I arrived, Ansel was marching in my direction with his hand clutching his hunched shoulder, and his gritted teeth were bared. A large patch of blood was visible on his shirt. I hustled closer to check out his wound.

After checking his shoulder, I slapped the rag he'd been using to stem the blood flow back into place when I noticed that the bleeding had stopped. "It's going to hurt like a motherfucker, but you'll live. Can you still shoot?"

"Tell me some shit I don't already know, asshole. And yeah, I can shoot."

Laughing, I shook my head at him and proceeded back towards the stairs. At the top of the stairs, a loud, angry squeal sounded in my ear followed by an elongated stream of scratching.

Our mics had been on the fritz since the shooting had started, but the connection had now been restored to our communications devices. I tapped my finger against my ear a few times. There was so much commotion going on outside that I couldn't understand what anyone was saying because they were stepping on each other's transmissions. I picked out what I could understand.

"Shark, say again you're last. Over," I spoke in an elevated tone, hoping he could hear me.

"A heli...pter! Don't..."

Ansel and I glanced at each other with wide eyes before we took off running. "Did he just say a fucking helicopter is coming?"

"I don't know, but it's going to be hard to hide that shit if there is one coming. We didn't plan for a fucking helicopter. It could be the media or DG6's backup."

The last thing we needed was the media getting a hold of all the shit that was going down in these hills. If DG6's backup was a fucking helicopter, we were in deep shit.

We traveled through the garage that had a door that led outside. Ansel punched in a code to get us out of the door. The first image that filled my view was of two of our team members firing at one of the Hummers. Two of DG6's guards were in the front, and Alonso was in the back, ducking as the driver attempted to ram the vehicle through the thick barricade that Rob had raised. Somehow the guards had managed to get him out of my house. If the vehicle broke through the barricade, they were going to try to ram the front gate. I was happy to see more of DG6's guards laid out dead on the lawn.

Another of DG6's guards appeared from the corner of my eye, running towards the gate nearest him. I raised my gun, aiming to take him out, but Ansel stopped me. "Let him go," he said in an uncaring manner. "Max, you copy, over."

"Copy," Max replied.

"Activate the gate," Ansel said.

"Tracking," Max replied with a hint of excitement in her voice. However, Max and Ansel's exchange didn't explain why no one bothered to light the running guard's ass up. He was about to attempt to go over the gate. And where was this helicopter that my father was yelling about?

"You're letting him go?" I asked Ansel as I dropped my weapon and eyed him suspiciously before putting my gaze back on the fleeting man. "What the..."

As soon as the man's hands reached out and gripped the thick bars of the gate, he started dancing and his hands automatically clutched the bars tighter. The high voltages of electricity radiating through him emitted fleshy pops. Although most of our people and snipers weren't visible, I knew they were out there watching the scene just as I was.

The wind carried the stench of frying flesh that assaulted my nostrils and taste buds and forced me to scrunch my face up as I choked down a gag. When Ansel said that DG6 was coming into his place and not getting out, he wasn't kidding. He hadn't revealed all the tricks he had up his sneaky sleeve.

Now, we had to find a way to get the guards and Alonso out of the Hummer. The powerful thrust of the tires scratching against the cement driveway sounded as the driver attempted to force the vehicle through the barricade. A thin sheen of white smoke billowed out from under the hot rubber.

The sound of the helicopter drew my attention away from the Hummer. Why wasn't our team lighting that damn thing up?

When Ansel and I raised our weapons to take aim at the helicopter, I heard "Don't fire! Don't fire! The Hummer! Pop smoke! Pop Smoke!"

It was Galvin calling for us to pop smoke, alerting us to mark the Hummer with smoke so the helicopter would know exactly where to aim. It meant the helicopter was a friendly force and not DG6's backup.

A knowing smile spread across my face, catching on to Galvin's call. The smile on Ansel's face indicated that he'd understood the call as well. My father's broken call earlier was likely trying to warn us not to take out the helicopter. The bird made a pass over us, the roar of the engine demanding attention as the swish of its rotors swept dust in our faces.

"Rob, Dude, Hwang, do you have any smoke?" Ansel asked.

"No,"

"November Golf,"

"No go," they replied.

Since Dude and Hwang had exited their foxholes to assist in fighting, they didn't have access to their munitions. I'd taken inventory of everything inside my foxhole and knew exactly where the smoke was.

"I need to get back to my foxhole!" I yelled. "Shark! Finn! Galvin!"

"We got you. Go," my father barked in a scratchy voice.

A wild, mindless rush shot through my veins, and I zipped into the opening, unsure of how many of DG6's guards remained on the loose. I ran past the Hummer, the driver nearly killing the engine in an attempt to get away. He hadn't accepted the fact that they were clearly surrounded by death.

Our team's bullets couldn't penetrate the armored vehicle, so for now, Alonso and the two guards were at an advantage and could possibly escape if they found a way to ram the front gate open. The whereabouts of that sack of shit, Sorio, crossed my mind as I ran towards my foxhole.

A bullet pounded the ground at my feet, spitting up dirt. It reminded me that DG6 was still in the fight and aiming to kill us. I ran in a zigzag pattern, unsure of where DG6 was and having faith in our snipers to keep a bullet out of my ass.

Once I made it to within a few feet of my foxhole, I slid into the small opening and made a wobbly landing on my feet, which sent my back slamming into the tight space of the dirt wall. I rummaged through the wooden box containing the ammo and grabbed two smoke grenades. After I'd attached them to my waistband, I scrambled through the hole just as fast as I'd slid in.

I was unsure, due to how fast I was moving, but it appeared Lucky was in one of the upstairs windows, slitting the throat of a guard that was trying to escape.

With the team keeping a bullet out of me, I sprinted back towards the roaring vehicle that had broken through the barricade and was backing up so it could ram the front gate. Our team riddled the Hummer with bullets, attempting to stop it from getting away. The black dot in the sky in my peripheral grew larger. The helicopter was about to make another pass.

Stalking the Hummer, I jetted forward, edging close to the vehicle that was revved up and ready to pounce the front gate. The Hummer roared forward and struck the gate with maximum force. The impact of crunching metal sent vibrations through me. Our team, aware of what I was trying to do, stopped firing at the vehicle and prepared to lay down cover fire for me.

The impact of the vehicle against the charged metal gate stalled its momentum. I inched closer, being careful not to draw the attention of the occupants. It was too bad the tires were stopping the assholes inside from being electrocuted.

"Max, cut the power!" Ansel shouted.

Parts of the front gate were dented and broken apart, but not enough to allow the vehicle to get through. The pop of electricity in the fence stopped. I ran towards the vehicle that was gearing to back up. I pulled the pen on one of the smoke grenades labeled green and tossed it onto the windshield. It slid down between the windshield and hood, which was the perfect spot that would keep the grenade in place on the vehicle.

I ran at full stride, searching for the nearest foxhole to drop into as green smoke spewed into the air in a large colorful cloud. The roar of the helicopter grew closer as I pushed my body to move me further away from the marked vehicle.

Rob must have seen me running in his direction because he'd

cracked open the camouflaged door to the foxhole nearest the gate. I dived into the open door, scrambling for cover and nearly toppled Max as she sidestepped out of my way in the nick of time.

An explosion erupted, vibrating my eardrums inside my skull as the ground shook around us angrily. Rob's hands covered his ears. When the ground stopped shaking, he pointed at a set of monitors mounted on the wall. This foxhole was also a little surveillance center.

Plumes of green smoke and fire filled the monitors. The helicopter had done its job by taking out the Hummer before they had broken through the fence. One more impact from the vehicle probably would have set them free.

However, the smoke and fire of the Hummer were going to draw attention we didn't need. I climbed out of the hole, preparing to hunt down the last of the four targets, when I was met with the sound of the helicopter making its approach again.

"Incoming!" a chorus of voices yelled in my ear as soon as I stood up.

The mics were phasing in and out, so I'd missed something. I dropped to the ground and searched for a clue as to what was happening. The heat from the burning Hummer and the black and green smoke clouded my vision.

Why the hell were they yelling incoming?

When it smashed into me, so breathtakingly cold, I could do nothing but lie there and let the impact of its crushing blow pound me. The helicopter had dropped what had to have been a ton of water onto the burning vehicle.

I hadn't a clue as to who'd ordered us a fucking helicopter, but they may have saved us from becoming a national news headline. I could hear the helicopter making another approach, only this time it was behind me, the powerful wind sweeping up grass and dirt as I struggled to watch it land on the front lawn near where my foxhole was located.

As the whirl of the rotors slowed and the engine's roar turned into a wheezing hum, a man exited the helicopter with his weapon drawn.

He looked familiar, really fucking familiar. All I could do as he stood over me, shaking his head, was laugh.

"Aaron, get the fuck up. You look like a wet baby calf bathing on the lawn out here."

He reached his hand down to help me up. I gripped his forearm with a wide grin on my face as he assisted in yanking me to my feet.

"Nathan, man, what the fuck?"

He shrugged, grinning but keeping a steady aim on his weapon.

"Galvin called yesterday and asked me to be on standby. He said y'all might need a little assistance with some not-so-friendly visitors you were trying to get rid of. I run a touring company that conducts helicopter tours out here in Cali. It's some real boring shit. So, when Galvin called, talking about real action, I was all in."

Nathan wasn't a member of my old military squad, but he was a fellow black-ops soldier. He had the amazing ability to fly a helicopter through hellfire and gun smoke and not get a scratch on it. We had nicknamed him TC like the character from the TV show Magnum PI. He'd picked us up and flown us from some of the most hostile hot zones we'd ever encountered.

55

AARON

After I introduced Nathan to Ansel, thanked him, and informed him he was about to get a big-ass bonus for his help, we fanned out in search of the last of the guards and Sorio, our final target.

"Aaron, can you hear me? Over," Shark asked.

"Yes, tracking, go for me, over," I called back to him.

"Aaron, take your weapon, aim at the front driver's side tire of the Hummer to your left and shoot it."

I didn't question my father's instructions. I aimed and shot at the tire. Immediately, one of DG6's guards rolled away from the tire. His dark attire and the angle of his body had kept him concealed. He was still under the vehicle, but he made a costly move as I watched his head explode. Chunks of his skull and blood flew into the air as he twitched under the vehicle. When his damaged head finally dropped, blood poured from it like a spigot had been turned on.

"Thank you, son," my father said, causing my grin to spread wide.

"You're welcome."

I didn't think anyone but the old heads in the MC knew that my father could do wicked things with a sniper rifle or any gun for that matter. He'd taught me everything I knew about guns. When I'd suggested he be one of our snipers, Ansel had glared at me like I was crazy, not knowing what I knew.

It took me an hour to finally find a few droplets of blood that would possibly lead me to the last of the four main targets. One of four of Ansel's cars parked in the large garage was where my search had ended. With my weapon aimed and at the ready, I used the toe of my boot to hit the latch on the white Maserati, springing the trunk open. A wide grin spread across my lips.

Laying on his side inside the trunk, Sorio raised his hands. Recognition flashed in his gaze as a touch of defiance lingered under the fear that covered his face. He understood that I'd show him no mercy.

With Sorio in my crosshairs, I felt like I'd won the grand prize. The cowardly bastard was hiding in the one place we'd failed to check. He must have been too busy running and hiding to arm himself. I'd expected more of a fight from him.

Footsteps alerted that someone was approaching. Ansel walked up and stood next to me. A conniving grin spread wide across his face when he discovered who I was aiming at.

"Any last words, motherfucker?" Ansel asked. The hint of satisfaction in his voice was easily noticed.

Sorio shook his head nonstop. Was this his sorry ass attempt at asking us not to kill him? His hands remained raised and his wide eyes roved back and forth between Ansel and me.

"Never thought these would be the last two faces you'd see, did you?" I asked taunting him.

"Oh, and *Regina* is downstairs. She saved me after you tortured me and after one of your men shot me in the head."

At this news, Sorio's lips parted and he fought a frown.

"She's smarter than you. She is better than you in every way. I was at the farm for nearly six months right under your nose. You tried to break her, but you failed. She broke you."

A sinister smile bent my lips as death filled the dark places in my mind. I leaned in closer to the asshole who'd started this war. "I'm going to ask Regina to do one last burn, and I'll make sure your ashes make their way into the lowest grade meth on the market."

His eyes grew wide as his breaths kicked up an extra notch and a shiver became visible in his body. I didn't know if he was upset that Regina was here or that I wanted her to burn his body and feed his ashes to meth addicts. A single tear slithered down his quivering cheek.

The rumble of gunfire had ceased outside. My ear was free of noise and static. The inside of the garage was filled with a tomblike silence that blended perfectly for the occasion.

The tip of my finger slipped over the trigger, and a sense of peace fell over me, knowing that a piece of shit was going to hell where he belonged. Knowing that he could no longer hurt Regina or give orders for men to hunt Megan.

I could envision Sorio's brains splattered all over the trunk. The tension in my trigger finger tightened and it flexed against the hard metal. However, at the last possible moment, something stopped me from pulling the trigger.

Putting a bullet in Sorio was too easy. Fuck following the protocol we'd set for this mission. Sorio needed to suffer. He needed to get what he had coming to him. I wanted to make him pay for all the years he'd gotten away with murder, abuse and any number of evil deeds.

Holstering my pistol, I unslung the rifle from my back. I was preparing to use the butt of the heavy weapon to beat that mother-fucker senseless.

I turned the rifle backwards in my hand, gripping it by the barrel. Sorio's fear-frozen eyes were on me the entire time. He'd wedged his body as far back into the trunk as he could get it, but there was nothing he could have done to save himself. His whimpers sounded over the frozen silence that filled the garage.

The first blow connected with the side of his head, sending it slamming against the interior of the trunk. The loud wallop surprised him. He cried out in pain, his voice casting louder due to him being inside the trunk.

The hurt must have been shockingly intense because Sorio's legs started to kick against the interior of the trunk. His thrashing appeared to have been involuntary. He lifted his head slowly, using his arm as protection from the next blow. His eyes were so wide, they appeared all white as he peeped over his raised arm.

Ansel released an elongated whistle, no doubt preparing to enjoy the show. Sorio waved his shaky hand at me, gesturing for me to stop as my grip tightened around the rifle. "Please, don't do this," he cried out. The hole I'd put in his broken jaw made his voice sound as if he were talking without moving his lips.

The asshole begged shamelessly for his life. He was man enough to put his hands on a woman, but not man enough to face his death. When I was in that barn, he'd beaten me to the point that he'd had to take a break before he instructed his men to take over. Not once had I cried. Not once had I begged.

Seeing Sorio beg and cry amped up my rage. Had he taken pity on Megan after what his father had done to her? Nope. That motherfucker had been hunting her, so he could kill her. Had he taken pity on Regina? Nope. That motherfucker had beaten her and confined her to an underground prison where he forced her to cremate bodies.

Sorio clutched his bloody face and groaned in agony as blood seeped out of the hole I'd opened. A second blow was aimed at his head, but he ducked out of the way and it caught him in the neck. He coughed, gagged and attempted to plead for me to stop. "P-p-please," he gurgled.

I think he was attempting to talk, but not one fuck was going to be given where he was concerned. I was too far gone. All I wanted was to beat this motherfucker until the devil himself tapped me on the shoulder and informed that he was ready to take him to hell.

Gripping and twisting his shirt collar in my fist, I yanked Sorio from the trunk. He hit the shiny cement floor of Ansel's garage with a series of rumbling thuds as he attempted to fight.

The asshole had the nerve to shout. "Please. I'll pay you!"

Ansel stood with has arms folded over his chest, shaking his head. He didn't have an ounce of remorse for what he was witnessing if the wicked smile on his face was any indication.

I twisted the grip I had on Sorio's shirt until his head was aimed up at me. His distressed gaze met mine. "After what you did, you offer me money? That's a fucking insult."

The frown on my face deepened, as a mixture of rage and anger consumed me. My hand released his shirt and he crumpled to the floor. I stood over Sorio staring down at him. His hand was raised as a weak barrier of protection. I raised the gun high, preparing to strike him again. I waited until his gaze connected with the raised gun. I wanted him to see it coming. I wanted him to anticipate the pain that would follow the blow.

I glanced at his head, leading him to believe I'd go for his head again. Instead, I repeatedly swung the weapon into his body with relentless force, making him fold into a ball as he struggled for air. Once I had him attempting to protect his body, I aimed for that fucker's head again.

Ansel hopped back when a bloody tooth popped into the air and flew past his leg. Sorio's attempt to block one of the blows resulted in the rifle connecting with his hand. His fingers crunched under the force of the strike. Three fingers on his left hand were bent backwards, dangling in an unnatural position.

My uncaged anger sought retribution for what was done to Megan and Regina. Sorio's wide mouth, contorted face, and pleading eyes, hinted at his vocal anguish, but I couldn't hear anything. Rage fueled my mind and snuffed out the sound. However, the vibration of his shouts pulsed around me like the base from a speaker.

The next strike connected with his jaw, knocking the bottom half of the right side apart from the top half. Strings of skin and tissue, stretched like gum between his broken apart jaw. Blood spilled from his damaged mouth as saliva and snot stretched down to his heaving chest.

"Jesus!" I think I heard Ansel say.

Sorio's mouth was left contorted, one side hanging and ripped apart from his swollen and bloody face. His quivering body, gaping mouth and haunted gaze brought life to his pain.

When he lost his strength to agony, he stopped trying to protect himself as he took the punishment I dished out. Blow after blow rained down on him, until the gun became slippery in my hands. It began to sound as if I were chopping wood as the blows ripped his body apart.

"Aaron!" Ansel yelled, before he placed a hand on my shoulder. "Aaron that motherfucker's dead!"

Ansel's words didn't stop me. I'd beaten Sorio to death and still wasn't done. I continued to pound on him until he was nothing but a crumpled pile of bloody flesh at my feet.

Yelling and shaking me, Ansel tried to snap me out of my murderous haze.

"Aaron, the motherfucker's dead! Snap the fuck out of it!"

I couldn't help myself, I hit that dead bastard one more time for good measure before I stood staring down at the mess I'd made. Winded, my breaths heaved out as I sucked in deep gulps of air. My body had finally started to feel the impact of my actions.

Sorio's blood had been slug high enough to paint the ceiling of the garage and was splatted over the back of Ansel's white car. Some had even reached the garage door to my rear and small red spots dotted the front of my clothes. My gun was soaked and dripping, and my hands appeared as if I'd dipped them into a bowl of blood.

"And then there was none," Ansel commented, while staring down at what was left of Sorio. White bone fragments peeked from the mangled mess of bloody clothes and ripped apart flesh. I couldn't tell if I was seeing the white tips of his spine or his ribs peeking through the bloody disaster.

"Do you realize that you've killed three out of the four targets?" Ansel asked.

I shook my head absently at Ansel's question not realizing I'd placed murderous hands on more than one Dominquez.

56

AARON

"Get out here!" Shark screamed.

My gaze met Ansel's before he keyed in the code that raised the garage door from the inside. As soon as we cleared the edge of the garage and were able to see a full view of the front yard, we saw a black Hummer that sat outside the gate, appearing to be trying to get in.

"Shark, Finn, Galvin, can any of you see who the hell that is?"

"It's Luke," Finn informed us. "Let him in."

One side of the gate was so damaged that the loud grating of metal against concrete sounded as it slid open wide enough for Luke to drive through. We listened to the grating sound again as Rob attempted to close the damaged gate.

We'd lost contact with Luke after the first mic check, so he'd been out there on his own. Luke stopped the vehicle near Ansel and me as we walked closer. He gave a rare smile and leaned his head towards the back seat.

My gaze landed on a stack of dead bodies piled in the back seat. It was the backup team DG6 had on standby. Grinning, I shook my head at Luke. He'd been alone, but he most certainly wasn't the one in danger.

My father, Finn, and Galvin remained at their post to be our watching eyes until we were sure the authorities hadn't been alerted to what had taken place at Ansel's house. They were also waiting to see if any of the DG6's guards had gotten a call out to anyone else that might show up.

Luke put a call into his and Galvin's company. They were flying out a special five-man cleanup crew. He claimed the crew could have Ansel's house as good as new within twenty-four hours, including body disposal.

We gathered in the living room for an impromptu debriefing of sorts as my father, Finn, and Galvin listened in. Ansel had made reservations and had plans to put everyone up at The Four Seasons for a week, all expenses paid.

He'd divided up the million he'd gotten as the partial payout from DG6, so each man, including our men in Texas and Mexico, would walk away with about sixty grand. Ansel also wanted the men to stick around in case any DG6 stragglers decided to show up. Aside from Ansel being shot in the shoulder, which he seemed to have forgotten about, no one else was seriously injured.

Knowing I was agitating his injured shoulder, I slapped Ansel's back and watched him wince.

"Let's go and get our women," I stated, waiting for him to correct me on my comment. He never did.

Even though she appeared to be clueless, I hadn't missed the way Ansel's eyes followed Regina's every move. Did Regina know that she was a claimed woman? Ansel's way of life wasn't for the faint of heart, and I wasn't talking about his criminal side either. Sorio had put Regina through enough hell, so Ansel and I were going to have a man-to-man talk about Regina.

I followed him into that sin den he tortured women in. Glancing around the area, I took in instruments and devices that I didn't know how to operate and didn't have the slightest idea of what they did.

Ansel slid the wall of sex toys aside and keyed in the code to a vaulted metal door before he walked into the safe room to greet the women. I could see Megan's small arm go around his waist. When he reached out for Regina too, my grin widened.

Although I couldn't see her face, Megan's shaky tone found my ears, "Aaron?"

"I'm right here, Megan!" I called out to her.

Her head darted around Ansel's body before she ran and leaped into my arms, gripping me like we'd been apart for months. Her lips covered mine before she sprinkled kisses all over my dirty face. She didn't care that I was dirty, smelly, and grimy from one of the craziest operations I'd ever participated in.

THE FOLLOWING DAY, more good news poured in as D and Dax reported success in eliminating their targets. Marcus and Scott had succeeded in taking out theirs as well. As promised, the cleaning team from Galvin and Luke's *security* firm had Ansel's house as fresh and as good as new.

You'd have never have known that we'd killed twenty guards, four key members of DG6, and the four additional guards who Luke had killed and driven in. We'd also blown up a Hummer with a helicopter and put out the fire to keep our hostile activities from being noticed. Regina had removed the bullet from Ansel's shoulder, and he was pretending to be in pain so she'd take care of him.

Although it was only a day later, the media hadn't released any news about DG6 or the fact that key members of their leadership had gone missing. It likely meant the small fish were already nipping at each other, preparing to commit criminal genocide.

It was also likely that the media was bound by high-ranking law officials to stay clear of reporting what was happening with DG6. If it were reported that the heads of DG6 had gone missing, it would unearth other vicious vultures that'd be ready to make a major move, not only in the meth industry but also to claim the top spot in the crime-boss category.

No one would know the truth—that a small group of dangerous and determined men had organized a plan and were powerful enough to destroy an organization as infamous as DG6.

EPILOGUE

People in hell must be drinking cold sweating glasses of water with fat ice cubes—this was the thought roving through my brain as I glanced back at the ordained minister. Since I had as good as accepted it the first two weeks I'd spent with her, and Ansel had insisted she'd already earned the title, I figured I'd go ahead and make things official. I'd asked Megan to marry me.

Yep, that's right. A motherfucker like me was about to get married. Megan had said yes to the three words I'd blurted: "Let's get married." Once we'd finished our celebratory fuck, I called Ansel and updated him on our plans.

At his insistence, of course, Regina had turned down my offer to stay with Megan and me and agreed to stay with Ansel instead. She claimed it was until she got back on her feet. He claimed it was to protect her from any of her family that were brave enough to come looking for her. They had agreed to stand as our witnesses at our wedding ceremony.

After Megan said yes, I was prepared to march down to the justice of the peace, but she wanted to wait until D and Dax flew her friends from Texas into town. We'd decided to stay in California for a while since I'd discovered that my cousin had four other houses spread across the state. Also, my soon-to-be wife had millions tucked away, so we could have gone anywhere we wanted.

A few days after we'd decided to tie the knot, I sat patiently in one of those hard, white plastic chairs in the justice of the peace's office, and I observed as Megan reunited with her friends. The sight of them together made me glad I'd waited.

The two of us becoming a legal couple probably meant something different to Megan than it meant to me. To her, it was holy matrimony, love, and happiness in sickness and in health. For me, I liked the idea of having her until death do us part. A legal marriage also gave me the right to kill a motherfucker if they touched my wife. As far as I was concerned, I was getting a license to kill.

Ansel, Dax, D and I sat and watched the women hugging and laughing. The best thing about seeing them together was knowing that we'd eradicated the DG6 problem that had been preventing them from openly seeing each other.

Laura, the smallest thing in the group, stepped away from the women and approached me with her arms folded over her chest.

Dax seemed to tense before he said, "Oh shit," under his breath and winced as he rubbed his sore side. He'd sustained a non-life-threatening gunshot wound during his portion of Operation Take Six.

Laura parked her tiny feet inches from mine and stood waiting until my gaze locked with hers. She stared down her nose at me like I couldn't just stand up and fling her little ass. One of her small fingers was aimed at me as she gave me the evil eye.

"If Megan ever tells me you hit her or that you've done some vile shit to her, I'm coming for your ass, Mr. Biker."

Laura's gaze filled with the kind of viciousness that I understood well.

"Yes, ma'am," I replied.

I knew one when I saw one, had realized it the moment I'd first met her in Texas. Laura was a killer. Dax had also filled me in on how well she'd handled herself on their portion of Operation Take Six.

Her gaze traveled down the line, ripping the rest of the men apart before she stepped away to join her friends who had pulled Regina into their circle.

We sat there, watching the women huddled in a circle like they were over there making a fucking play book. Occasionally, I'd see Megan shaking her head, agreeing to something one of them had said.

"So, what do you think they're talking about?" D asked in an amused tone.

Ansel's gaze roamed the group before he replied, "Man, with that group, those damn women are probably over there either trying to figure out how to cut your balls off, so Megan can tie them around her neck. Or they may be plotting on how they could get us to take down another fucking cartel, which they've likely started shit with. There isn't anything about any of those women that's innocent, so don't let those sweet faces fool you. Think about it," Ansel said, getting into professor mode. He'd been studying those women like his life depended on it.

Ansel pointed. "That one, the one who looks like she could make a room full of priests start jacking off."

D's smile grew wide. "That's Beverly."

"After you told me about her skills with a blade, and now that I see her, she screams *danger, danger, danger.*"

Ansel pointed at Regina. "Don't get me started on the sexy doctor, who from what Aaron tells me has a penchant for burning men alive."

D and Dax straightened in their seats, staring at Ansel and me, probably thinking we were making this shit up.

"And the littlest one, who just waltzed her barely one-hundred-pound ass over here and directly threatened a man who could devour her whole—"

"Laura," Dax said, and I couldn't tell if it was irritation or admiration in his voice.

"Laura," Ansel continued. "She'll slit your fucking throat and drink your blood."

A smile crept across Ansel's face when he glanced at Megan. "And innocent-face Megan, who harbored enough secrets to start a fucking nationwide war and is the reason that we are all sitting in a fucking justice of the peace's office about to witness a marriage that could very well slam the gates of hell shut."

As soon as I started laughing, the rest of the men joined in. Ansel was talking shit, but he wasn't immune. Regina was going to have him so twisted up that he was going to need a fucking crew of sailors to untangle his ass. The good doctor was prim and proper but dealing with her family for the last three years had hardened her.

Finally, the women broke up their cackling, so we could get on with this. Once we were ready, the justice of the peace rep called us all into a ceremony room. It was a small, nicely put-together wedding chapel with flowers and a row of seats for guests. The women had their phones out, snapping photos.

I wore my usual jeans and T-shirt and Megan had taken the time to straighten her usual curls, applied light makeup, and wore a pale purple strapless dress that gave her a glamorous quality that I appreciated. Seeing her looking so beautiful had me feeling like the luckiest motherfucker on the planet.

We approached and stood in front of the justice. The idea of what was about to happen socked me in the jaw and a moment of doubt hit me until I reminded myself of all that Megan and I had gone through.

MEGAN

I was a nervous, hot mess. I couldn't believe Aaron and I were about to get married. Having my friends here with me was a blessing. Because of Aaron and the men sitting behind us, I didn't have to hide or run anymore.

The minister talked, but I couldn't hear a thing he was saying until he'd directed Aaron and me to face each other and say our vows.

"I take her as my wife," Aaron stated in a firm tone that dared anyone listening to protest. When he didn't say any more, the minister lifted his brows and faced me.

"That's a damn shame," someone grumbled in the background.

"Umh, umh, uhm," someone else said under their breath.

"I take him too," I declared before the minister glanced back and forth between us.

What the hell was I supposed to say? Instead of keeping my thoughts to myself, I shrugged and started saying what I was thinking.

"You and I have been to hell and back more than once, but we're still standing together. There are no words that I can say that will describe what you mean to me. All I can do is to try to show you. I love you."

The smile on Aaron's face meant everything.

After we joined hands and repeated the words that were meant to bind us forever, the justice asked about rings. The idea of rings hadn't crossed my mind. I wasn't even sure if Aaron would wear one. When it came to traditional, Aaron and I were not it...not even close.

When the minister prepared to conclude the ceremony, without the exchange of rings, Ansel stood and walked towards us.

"I have the rings."

"You do?" Aaron and I asked in unison, staring a hole in Ansel.

Ansel leaned into Aaron, but I could hear him speak. "Your ass is not getting off this easy. Here," he huffed, shoving a small black box into Aaron's hand.

"Now, put a fucking ring on it, you fucking Neanderthal."

Ansel's unapologetic gaze shot up to the justice.

"Pardon my language, sir, but this bastard needs parental guidance sometimes. He hasn't been fully domesticated as you can tell by that mangy-ass beard of his."

Ansel walked off, leaving the poor justice standing and looking just as shocked as Aaron and I were.

Aaron opened the small black box that Ansel had shoved into his hand. He slid a beautiful, floral halo ring with sparkling purple diamonds on my finger. The thin white gold band fit my finger perfectly. I admired the ring before mouthing a big cheesy, "Thank you," to Ansel who simply inclined his head.

When Aaron's turn came, I removed a simple white gold band and slid it onto his finger before the justice announced, "You may kiss your bride."

Aaron leaned down, and I went up on my toes. Our lips melted together and what seemed like a short moment to me must have been a long moment for our friends as a few throats cleared.

The justice gestured his hand towards our friends.

"Ladies and gentlemen, I present to you, Mr. and Mrs. August Aaron Knox V."

*** END OF TWISTED SECRETS ***

AUTHOR'S THANK YOU

My sincere thank you for reading this book. If you enjoyed it, please pass it along to friends or anyone you think would enjoy it. Please leave a review letting me and others know what you thought of the book.

CONNECT ON SOCIAL MEDIA

Subscribe to my monthly Newsletter for exclusive updates and much more. Join my Facebook Readers' Group, where you can live-chat about my books or any of your favorite books, enjoy contests, raffles, and giveaways. You can also follow me on Twitter, BookBub, or Goodreads.

Links:

Newsletter: https://mailchi.mp/c5ed185fd868/httpsmailchimp

Facebook Readers' Group: https://www.facebook.com/groups/380642765697205/

Twitter: https://twitter.com/AuthorKetaK

BookBub: https://www.bookbub.com/authors/keta-kendric

Goodreads: https://www.goodreads.com/user/show/7338764I-keta-kendric

OTHER TITLES BY KETA KENDRIC

CPSIA information can be obtained
at www.ICGtesting.com
Printed in the USA
LVHW082035150822
725931LV00003BA/531

9 781986 033206